HAVENWOOD FALLS
VOLUME FOUR

A HAVENWOOD FALLS COLLECTION

AMY HALE   AMY MILES   KALLIE ROSS

ABOUT THIS BOOK

Welcome to Havenwood Falls, home to sexy men, strong women, and neighbors who bite. Discover supernatural mystery, thrills, and romance in a place where everyone has a deep, dark, and often deadly secret. This collection features three novellas in this multi-author shared world series.

Flames Among the Frost by Amy Hale

Trouble has a way of finding Jetta Mills, and she quickly learns that the best place for a frost dragon shifter is back within the warded borders of home—Havenwood Falls. When Conrad Monroe is hired to find a thief, the trail leads him to the Colorado mountains and Jetta. He doesn't know what he's getting into with her, and she has no idea that Conrad has quite a few secrets of his own.

From the Embers by Amy Miles

Driven to avenge her momma's brutal murder, Ember Ramsey infiltrates a world of bloodthirsty monsters, but as a flame-wielding fighter, she might be the deadliest of them all. When she comes face to face with the black-eyed demon who haunts her nightmares, Ember trails the killer to a quaint mountain town. Never before has she been so close to her goal, but her control is weakening. Soon the fires will spread, and Ember's no longer sure she can hold back the power she possesses. Or that she wants to—even if it means burning Havenwood Falls to the ground.

Defying Gravity by Kallie Ross

Wolf-shifter Tate Kasun is expected to safeguard the ancient magic of Havenwood Falls, but when Alex Newton crashes into his arms, he begins to question everything. After years of trying to prove the supernatural world doesn't exist, Alex discovers that the ancient ring she wears holds powers that make her a threat to the Court of the Sun and the Moon, and puts her in imminent danger from those who want the power for themselves.

HAVENWOOD FALLS BOOKS

Forget You Not by Kristie Cook

Old Wounds by Susan Burdorf

Fate, Love & Loyalty by E.J. Fechenda

The Winged & the Wicked by T.V. Hahn & Kristie Cook

Alpha's Queen by Lila Felix

Ink & Fire by R.K. Ryals

Lose You Not by Kristie Cook

Tragic Ink by Heather Hildenbrand

Nowhere to Hide by Belinda Boring

Flames Among the Frost by Amy Hale

Rock Me Gently by Susan Burdorf

From the Embers by Amy Miles

Defying Gravity by Kallie Ross

Break Me Not by Kristie Cook

How the Dead Lie by Stacey Rourke

The Lurkers Within by Danielle Bannister

The Collector: Awakening by Kristie Cook, R.K. Ryals, Belinda Boring & Nadirah Foxx

Addicted to You by Belinda Boring

Affliction Mine by C.J. Pinard

The Ward & the Wanderers by T.V. Hahn

Toil & Trouble by Melissa Wright

Of Salt and Stars by Seven Jane

Redefined by Morgan Wylie

Betrayal Among the Frost by Amy Hale

Forever Loyal by E.J. Fechenda

Fate's Demand by Emily Cyr

The Wu & the Wand by T.V. Hahn

A Demon's Redemption by JD Nelson

Also try the YA line, Havenwood Falls High; the historical paranormal line, Legends of Havenwood Falls; the darker, sexier side of town, Havenwood Falls Sin & Silk; and the local supernatural college, Sun & Moon Academy.

Stay up to date at www.HavenwoodFalls.com

FLAMES AMONG THE FROST

AMY HALE

A Havenwood Falls New Adult Novella

HAVENWOOD FALLS

FLAMES AMONG THE FROST

AMY HALE

BOOKS BY AMY HALE

For Sarai, and our mutual love of salad shooters.

CHAPTER 1

JETTA

I'd be lying if I said I'd never imagined myself in jail. I'd always been a hot mess with a talent for getting in way over my head. I'd never considered myself a bad person, but I was certainly no angel either. I always ran with the wrong crowd, said the wrong things, dressed the wrong way, and generally pissed off my father by merely existing. Lawrence Mills had been making my life miserable for years, although if you'd asked him, I'm sure he'd have told you the same about me. Despite my love for the rest of my family, I had to escape him. Which, in a roundabout way, was why my ass was going numb as I sat on a cold concrete bench in a six-by-eight cell.

"Damn," I muttered as I adjusted my position. "Hey assholes," I yelled, "are cushions against your religion or something? I can't feel my legs anymore."

I didn't expect an answer. It'd been six hours since I'd been arrested, and outside of my being booked, no one had spoken a word to me. My roommate, Frankie Hopkins, told me she'd be here to bail me out, but I'd yet to see her.

I stood and stretched, hoping to bring some of the feeling back into my limbs. The bland, gray cell was chilly, but actually the perfect temperature for someone like me—a frost dragon shifter. We generally preferred the cold to the heat. I guess when your roots traced back to

Iceland, loving the frigid temperatures made sense. It still pissed me off, though. The jackwads didn't even offer me a damn blanket. I think they hoped I would freeze. If so, the joke was on them.

The large metal door at the end of the hall opened, and I listened as footsteps approached. A uniformed officer and Frankie appeared on the other side of the bars. Her tall slender frame, shoulder-length red curls, and blue eyes were a welcome sight after hours of staring at the same cinderblock walls.

"About time," I growled, as the officer unlocked the door. His name tag read Barnes.

"You're free to go, Ms. Mills." Officer Barnes's expression appeared as if those words were painful to push past his lips.

I looked at Frankie, and she smiled. I shoved past them both and stalked down the hall to collect my personal items. The lady behind the window slid a paper bag toward me, and I inspected the contents. I grabbed the pen attached to the clipboard and signed to verify everything was there. Frankie held my jacket open, and I pushed my arms through before stuffing the bag into my pocket.

"May I go now?" I asked with more than a little disgust in my voice.

She nodded. Without another word, I walked to the main doors, Frankie on my heels. I pushed one door open, turned to face the officers standing in the lobby, and flipped them off. "Thanks for nothing."

Frankie rolled her eyes as she shut the door behind us. "Is it really the best strategy to piss off the cops who just arrested you?"

"Are you kidding me?" I glared at her. "Was I supposed to thank them for falsely arresting me, handling me like a piece of meat, and then ignoring me for hours?"

"Of course not," replied Frankie, "but being a bitch isn't going to help anything."

"But . . . I'm so good at it. It'd be a shame to waste my talents."

Frankie put one perfectly manicured hand on her hip. "And it wasn't exactly a false arrest. You did break into that safe, right?"

I didn't know how to explain what had happened. Partially

admitting to the altered version of events would make more sense to her than the truth ever would.

"The item I was after belongs to me. I didn't want any of his other shit." I grimaced as I searched for her car in the now dark parking lot. "Thanks for bailing me out."

"Oh . . ." Frankie's voice was hesitant. "I didn't actually bail you out."

My eyebrows rose. "So, how'd you spring me?"

"It was Brandt. I talked him into dropping the charges." She looked nervous.

I felt my temperature rise. I shook my head as I found the nearest wall and leaned against it. As my eyes closed, I saw large claws, scales, and reptilian irises flash in my mind.

"Damn it, no!" I shouted in frustration.

Frankie placed a hand on my arm. "I'm sorry, Jetta, but I couldn't come up with the cash. I didn't know what else to do! I promise it'll work out. Brandt said he'd forgive everything that has happened. That's better than a bail bond, court, and a record, right?"

Frankie didn't understand that, while I was really pissed at her for working out a deal with Brandt on my behalf, the "no" was not about her negotiations. I was commanding my inner dragon to stay back. Being a shifter could be amazing at times, but this was not the time or place to let the beast come out to play. Anytime I felt threatened or upset, she tried to push through and take over. I couldn't allow that. Not again. I wasn't back home in Havenwood Falls anymore, where stuff like that was somewhat normal. This was Atlanta, and supernatural creatures of any kind were still considered part of myth and legend. My kind wasn't welcome in the human world.

I opened my eyes and released a heavy sigh. "So, what did you promise him?"

I quickly walked to her car, not waiting to see if she was following.

Frankie's heels clicked as she ran to catch up. "Not much. Just that you'd give him a chance."

"Oh hell, Frankie," I shouted.

"C'mon, just one dinner. Let him attempt to wine and dine you one more time. Enjoy an expensive meal, then brush him off and move on." She spoke as if her plan was simple, but she didn't know Brandt like I did. She didn't know I'd already been down that road.

"No one walks away from Brandt Sawyer if he feels he's owed something. It's why I'm in this mess to begin with." I frowned. "And now you're in the middle of it, too." I pushed my hands through my hair, still caught off guard by the length since having extensions put in. "Damn it!" I banged my fist on top of her car.

She unlocked the car, and we both climbed inside. "Stop being so dramatic. You act like you're dealing with a mobster or something."

I looked at her and wondered how she could live in such a big city all her life and still be so sheltered. "He pretty much is. He'll use our friendship against me."

"Oh shush." She started the car. "He's an arrogant, rich club owner, and your boss, but I highly doubt he's fitting anyone with cement shoes in his spare time." She rolled her eyes as she pulled out of the parking lot. "I know I haven't known you for long, but your paranoia has gotten really bad lately."

I shook my head. "It's not paranoia. The man is insane. He—" I cut myself off before I let my secrets slip. Frankie didn't need to know all the dirty details about my evening with Brandt. Or the reason it all went to hell. "Let's go home. I'm tired."

She nodded and steered us toward our apartment. We drove the rest of the way in silence, but once inside, I made a beeline for my whiskey stash. I opened the bottle, poured a healthy amount in a tumbler, and downed it in one swallow.

"It's gonna be one of those nights, huh," Frankie stated in a flat voice. She wasn't a fan of my drinking, but I'd made it clear from the beginning that I had vices and those vices would move in with me. Another perk of being a dragon—or con depending how you looked at it—it took a lot of alcohol to get us shit-faced. Thankfully I had a well-stocked bar.

"Yep," I muttered. "It's absolutely gonna be one of those nights." I poured another glass and threw it back, letting the comforting burn slide down my throat. "Do we have mac and cheese? I'm starving. Getting arrested makes a girl hungry."

Frankie jerked her thumb in the direction of the kitchen. "Cabinet."

I nodded and strolled the few short steps it took to travel from our living area to the kitchen, the whiskey bottle my constant companion.

THE ALARM CLOCK screamed in my ears. I rolled over and glared at the blue glowing digits. Seven a.m. wasn't terribly early, but it felt that way when you'd consumed all the alcohol in the house. I slammed my fist down on top, knocking the clock to the floor.

"Shiiiiiiit," I moaned loudly as I rolled over. My mouth felt like I'd swallowed a distillery. All I wanted to do was go back to sleep, but I really needed to run errands before rehearsals that afternoon. *Rehearsals! Work!* I bolted upright in bed as my mind reeled with the events of the previous night. Brandt. Our fight. The safe. Jail.

I couldn't stay here, not now. I slid from the bed and pulled my suitcase out from underneath. Tossing it on the bed, I unzipped it and made a beeline for the dresser. Without care or organization, I dumped the contents of my drawers into the suitcase, followed by my clothes in the closet. I had to sit on the lid to zip it shut, but after no small amount of effort, I managed to force it closed.

"I need to get dressed," I muttered as I realized I'd just packed everything. Out of the corner of my eye, I saw the clothes I'd worn the previous evening. Frowning, I looked them over. They were wrinkled, but even worse was the blood on the right sleeve and back of my shirt. I wasn't sure if all that blood was mine. Some of it may have belonged to Brandt. Both of us were injured the night before. Anger seethed beneath the surface. I had to take care of this problem before it became impossible to correct.

I pulled my bloody blouse on over the T-shirt I'd slept in and slid my legs into my jeans. I crammed my feet into my boots, not caring that I was without socks. I took a few minutes to pack the rest of my personal items scattered around the apartment, and then I hauled it all out into the living area near the door.

My eyes scanned the small two-bedroom apartment I'd been calling home for over a month. The dingy yellow paint, the kitchenette, the tattered secondhand furniture. I'd miss it all.

"What the hell are you doing?" Frankie whined as she stepped out of her room. She was rubbing her eyes and yawning, her red curls a wild mess around her head.

"I'm going home." I grabbed my jacket from the back of the sofa and put it on.

"What?" The shock of my announcement woke her up fully.

"I tried this. It didn't work. It's time to go back to Havenwood Falls."

She stepped forward and put a hand on my arm. "Are you sure? You hated it there."

I nodded. "Now, I hate it here more."

Frankie frowned, and I realized what I'd said sounded harsh. I pulled her in for a hug. "It's not you, sweetie. I love you. It's this city. I'm better off in a small community. And I can't be in the same area as Brandt. It's not safe."

Puzzled, Frankie sighed. "Okay then. I think you're overreacting, but do what you gotta do."

I slipped her a wad of cash. "This should cover my part of the rent for the next six months. That'll give you time to find a suitable roommate, and you won't have to accept the first weirdo that answers your ad."

She grinned. "You mean like I did with you?"

"Exactly." I smiled. "Don't let another freak cross that threshold. You were lucky with me. The next one might not be so great. Be picky."

She pulled me in for another hug. "I'm gonna miss you, roomie. You're weird, but I like that."

"I'll miss you too," I said softly. "I need to load this stuff in the Jeep, and then I'm out of here. Do not engage with Brandt or any of his goons, okay? Once I'm gone, he'll likely leave you alone."

She nodded. "Will do."

It took three trips to haul all my belongings to the Jeep. Once my stuff was packed away, I said a final goodbye to Frankie and pointed my vehicle in the direction of Sawyer's Bar. I'd been away from home for roughly 41 days. I'd tried to assimilate, but the time had come to accept defeat. I had one final stop to make before I put Atlanta in my rearview mirror.

CHAPTER 2

CONRAD

Smoke filled my nostrils as I walked into the dimly lit club. I allowed my eyes to adjust and then exhaled a slow, steadying breath. I'd always been sensitive to smells, but places like this violently assailed my senses. Sawyer's Bar was a sickening mixture of alcohol, sweat, tobacco, drugs, and bodily fluids. Thankfully I had developed a strong constitution over the years.

"Mr. Monroe?" A petite blonde with large blue eyes and a heart-shaped face appeared before my eyes.

"Yes, that's me," I stated.

"Mr. Sawyer is waiting for you in the back room. If you'll follow me, I'll take you to him." She flashed a nervous smile.

I nodded and waited for her to lead the way. The building was sparsely occupied. We passed between a long bar and a row of high-top tables before we reached a large stage. Instruments were placed at key points to surround a single barstool and microphone. At this time of the day, most people were still working or picking up kids from school. But here, people were slowly filtering in to drink their sorrows away. The musicians wouldn't start their evening shift for a few hours yet, so the only sounds were a faint playlist humming from the overhead speakers.

I followed the young woman through a door to the left of the stage, and we entered a hallway that was slightly darker than the main part of the club.

I willed my senses to stay alert, and I instinctively felt for the gun snugly stashed in the holster under my jacket. Assuring myself my weapon sat within reach, I made my way to the end of the hall and a set of double doors. The young woman knocked twice.

"Come in," a raspy male voice answered.

She turned the knob and pushed the doors open, motioning for me to enter. "Mr. Monroe is here."

"Please, have a seat. I'm Brandt Sawyer." The man behind the desk looked to be roughly my age. Maybe a year or two older than my thirty years. His short blond hair was combed to one side, and he had a scratch that trailed from his left cheek to the corner of his mouth. It appeared to be healing, but the mark still had that angry red hue that indicated it had been a recent injury. His smile was friendly, but something in his dark brown eyes set me on edge. I wasn't generally a trusting person, and I tended to keep most people at arm's length. This guy absolutely belonged in the "keep at arm's length" category. He reeked of bad decisions and arrogance.

I occupied the chair directly across from Brandt's desk and crossed my arms.

"How can I help you?" I asked. I'd never seen the point in making small talk.

Brandt's smile grew, his perfectly straight teeth gleaming back at me like some damn toothpaste commercial. "Direct. I like it."

He reached for a pack of cigarettes, pulled one out for himself, and then offered me one. I shook my head, giving his teeth a second glance. He must over-whiten to compensate for the tobacco stains. He lit the cigarette, and I steeled myself for the aroma that would permeate my nose.

"I have a bit of a predicament, and I'm told you are the man that can help me." He put the cigarette to his lips as he studied my face.

"I've been known to help people. It's part of my job. It does depend on what kind of predicament you are in, though."

"Of course," he stated. "So, I'll jump right to it. A disgruntled employee has stolen something very valuable from my safe. I want you to bring it, and her, back to me."

I sighed. "I'm not that kind of help."

I stood to leave.

"Wait, you need to hear the whole story."

I stepped away from my chair.

"I'll pay you a lot of money. And I do mean a lot."

His offer stopped me in my tracks. I hated working for guys like him. His type always thought money could solve everything—could get them whatever they wanted. It frustrated me, that in this case, he was probably right. I needed the money. Badly.

I sat back down. "You have five minutes to make your case."

He wasted no time. "A woman named Jetta Mills worked for me here at the club. She's been my main act for the past month. Very talented musician. A few days ago, I caught her breaking into my safe, and she attacked me."

My eyes flew to the scratch on his face.

He pointed to a large fire safe nestled in the corner of his office.

"I have friends at the police station, so I had her arrested, hoping to just scare some sense into her. No official charges were filed." He stood and turned to face a tall cabinet behind him, opening one of the doors. "I haven't seen her since." He turned back to face me, a folder in his hands. "When I came to the office the following morning, I once again found my safe open, and this time, important items were missing."

I shrugged. "So why not call the police again?"

He handed the folder to me. "Because they won't be effective. Not in this case. She's not your typical thief. I need quick results. The items she stole are time sensitive. Law enforcement's hands are tied by procedure."

I opened the folder and glanced at the contents. He had very little information to go on: an address in the city that was likely no longer valid; a description of the stolen contents, which were a metal lockbox containing some cash, jewelry, a sealed envelope, and a cell phone; and a photograph of the young woman he called a thief. She was a beauty, although something about her style seemed a little exaggerated. Her hair was long and dark, her eyes an icy blue, and she had a diamond stud in her nose. A ring decorated her eyebrow, and she had various other piercings in her ears.

"Is this all you have?" I placed the folder on his desk.

"Yes, at the moment." He sighed. "Her roommate claims to have told me all she can, although I suspect she's hiding something."

"So, you've already checked for her at that address?" I inquired.

"We did. Frankie, her roommate, said she'd packed her stuff and left town shortly after waking up the morning after her arrest." Frustration laced his features as he spoke. "Frankie knows very little about Jetta's past, but she did mention a hometown in Colorado. Something that ended in falls. She couldn't remember the exact name, but Jetta told her she was going home. My boys have been looking all over, but have found nothing that helps. I knew the time had come to hire a professional."

I mulled this information over a bit before speaking. "So, you want me to find her and return your items."

Brandt nodded. "And bring her back to account for her crimes."

"Did she skip bail?" I asked this knowing there wasn't any bail to skip if he hadn't pressed charges.

"No, but that doesn't mean she shouldn't be held accountable." I could sense his anger at the young woman.

"I'm mainly a bail enforcement agent. If she hasn't skipped bail, I can't legally detain her. You'd need the authorities for that. As you said, there are procedures." I stood once more, eager to get out into the fresh air.

"The friend that recommended you said you have ways of working outside the law to achieve the desired results. It's why I called you instead of the police." He snuffed his cigarette out with agitated movements, the well-used ashtray already full.

I didn't reply. I had been working hard to put my illegal activities behind me and make money by legitimate means. Renewing those pursuits didn't interest me.

"Like I said, I can pay you well." He opened a desk drawer and pulled out several stacks of cash wrapped neatly in rubber bands. "Fifty thousand. Twenty-five of it now, and the other half when you deliver my stolen items and Miss Mills."

I closed my eyes. I did not want to work for this man, but fifty thousand was hard to turn down. It would take care of my debts and leave me a little seed money to work with, so I could start over elsewhere. I needed out of Atlanta. My brain screamed at me. *Take it. One last quick and dirty job. Just this last one. Pay off your debts, and then you are done forever.*

"That's a lot of money. Are the items stolen really worth it?"

He pressed his lips into a thin line. "The contents of that box are priceless. It's worth any amount to retrieve them as soon as possible." He paused as he gave me a hard stare. "As well as Ms. Mills. It's important she returns to make things right. But that's not your concern. Just bring them back to me."

I reached for the folder. "Fine. I'll start first thing in the morning."

I hated myself. I hated that I could be bought.

Brandt smiled. "Fantastic." He placed the stacks of cash in a paper bag and sat them in front of me. "I want you to check in with me all along the way. Keep me apprised of your progress." He handed me a card. "This has my cell number. I can be reached here at any time."

I nodded and tucked the card into the folder.

He handed me the paper sack. "I'm looking forward to hearing from you soon."

I nodded again and left the room. My mind was already at work, putting together what little info I had and determining the best place to start my search.

Once outside, I inhaled a huge breath of air and blew it out slowly. I wouldn't exactly describe it as fresh, but breathing out there was ten times easier than inside of Sawyer's Bar.

I strolled to my motorcycle as I secured the folder and cash under my zipped jacket. The engine fired to life, and I smiled at the familiar and comforting rumble. I enjoyed the brisk twenty-minute drive to my small apartment, all the way wondering why this young lady had stolen from Brandt Sawyer. He was a rich, spoiled brat who had connections. Dangerous connections. She obviously hadn't known who she was messing with.

Once inside my living room, I powered on my laptop and did a search for Colorado towns with "falls" in the name. I found several, but I had no idea which would be correct, so I made a list of them all. I intended to speak to her roommate Frankie first thing in the morning. I also did a search on Jetta's name. I found zero results, which puzzled me. Almost everyone had some kind of online presence these days. She was a young entertainer. Surely, she had, at the least, a Facebook page or website. But my searches all came up empty, save for a couple of elderly women who were most definitely not my target. I leaned back on the sofa and closed my eyes, working to shut out all the noise of the city. I focused on the image in my mind of the woman I was now hired to find. Her smiling face was the last thing I remembered before falling asleep.

I KNOCKED on the door of apartment 28B and stuffed my hands in my pockets. I could hear faint movements before a deadbolt clicked and the door cracked open. One blue eye stared back at me over a gold chain that stretched from the frame to the door.

"Yeah? What do you want?" The woman was obviously cautious. Smart.

"I'm looking for Jetta. Is she home?" I flashed her my friendliest smile, hoping it would put her at ease.

"She moved." She looked ready to slam the door in my face.

"Oh no. Well, that's unfortunate." I did my best to mimic disappointment. "I'm Conrad. I'm an old friend of Jetta's. I was hoping to surprise her, but . . ." I let my voice trail off and shrugged. "This was the address she gave me a couple of weeks ago."

"Well, she's not here anymore." The tone of her voice held suspicion.

"Are you Frankie?" I asked.

She nodded.

"Jetta told me you two shared the place." I knew I'd have to play this carefully.

Frankie nodded again. "We did. Past tense. She went back home."

"Back to Colorado?"

Frankie's brows furrowed. "Yeah."

I scratched my chin. "She grew up in that town . . . oh shoot. What was the name?" I pretended to think and pulled random names out of the air. With any luck Frankie would help fill in the blank. "Woodward Falls?" She didn't move a muscle. "No, that's not right. I was sure it was something like that. Cedar Falls? Rocky Falls?"

Frankie sighed. "Havenwood. Havenwood Falls. Can I go now? My breakfast is getting cold."

I nodded, and before I could push the word *thanks* past my lips, she'd slammed the door and locked it.

I smiled as I pulled out my phone and did a search for Havenwood Falls. I was surprised to see that name as the first result. It wasn't on my list. *Why didn't I see it when I searched yesterday?* I clicked the link and found myself temporarily pulled in by the gorgeous scenery. The home page was full of photos of a quaint little town boxed in on all sides by mountains and dense forest. A glance at the community calendar showed a busy schedule, jam packed with events all year round.

I shoved my phone back into my pocket and made a mental list of what I'd need to pack. Colorado in April was a bit colder than Georgia. I'd need to prep accordingly.

CHAPTER 3

JETTA

I pulled into the parking lot of Whisper Falls Inn and shut off the engine. I was exhausted. I'd driven it straight through, with only minimal stops, in fear that Brandt would follow me. I'd longed to stop at hotels for a few nights and see all the corny sights along the way. Who knew when I'd be able to leave Havenwood Falls again? After my experience in Atlanta, maybe never. I'd realized just how risky it could be for a supernatural being living outside the magic bubble of our town. Havenwood Falls was founded specifically to keep various non-human species safe. We did have human residents. Most of them had no idea that they lived among a variety of creatures they would normally consider monsters, but that was by design as well. My hometown was never dull.

The downside was that there were memory wards in place. Wards I had to convince a witch friend of mine to help me bypass, so I could come back home, should I wish to. I also asked her to concoct a spell that made my moves untraceable. I didn't want to be tracked, should I have decided the relocation would be permanent. Without the powerful ring given to me by my magically talented friend Ani Rukska, I would have succumbed to the amnesia spell that protected Havenwood Falls. It's kind of genius actually. Visitors who leave our little town forgot all about us once they passed twenty-five miles outside of the city limits. Their time here became more like a vague recollection or dream to them. For residents, the situation was a bit different. We couldn't be gone for more than a moon cycle. We only had twenty-eight days, or we lost all memories of home.

I left to break away from the constricting influence of my father. And I wanted to try something on my own. To take a huge leap and see where I landed. Sadly, I landed in the office of Brandt Sawyer. A step I sorely regretted. I hated coming back home with my tail tucked between my legs, but I knew I had made the right move. I was safe here. Brandt couldn't find me or Havenwood Falls. I could finally relax.

I glanced over at the metal lockbox sitting on the passenger floorboard. The contents of that box had to be well hidden. No one could ever find what I had pilfered from Brandt's safe. I closed my eyes and leaned my head against the steering wheel.

A familiar voice sounded next to me with "Long day?" and caused me to jump, a yelp escaping my lips as I turned to see Madame Luiza Petran sitting in the passenger seat.

"Damn it, Madame Luiza, you scared the hell out of me," I chastised.

"Good afternoon, dear. It's nice to see you, too." Her eyes twinkled as she spoke. "Are you gonna sit out here in the cold all day? We have some fresh coffee in the lobby, if you'd care for a cup."

"That would be wonderful. Thank you."

She smiled and then disappeared.

"Fuckin' ghosts," I muttered. Madame Luiza was a vampire who had run the large three-story Victorian manor for a while after her brother- and sister-in-law died. She'd passed away, too, and her ghost now haunted the place. I'd always liked her, but sometimes I thought she enjoyed surprising people a little too much. She was damn good at it.

I draped a blanket over the lockbox and slid out of my Jeep.

Once I reached the entrance, I steeled myself for the many questions I expected would be hurled at me, and then walked inside. I was welcomed by the familiar sight of polished oak flooring, beautiful stained-glass windows, and intricately designed rugs. The large manor had a comforting mix of Victorian era design and modern conveniences. Electric fixtures were now hanging in areas where old wall sconces had once existed. The heavy wood doors to the dining area hung from shiny new hinges, yet somehow still managed to creak as they moved, giving the house an ambiance that was often prevalent in older homes. Unexpected emotions rose from my chest and caught in my throat. I never would have believed I could miss Havenwood Falls so much. And this lovely inn was merely a small part of the town I called home. If only my father were a different man, I might have been perfectly content in this canyon.

"Jetta!"

I looked up to see Sindi Scott smirking at me.

"Where'd you take off to? Everyone's been looking for you." She raised one perfectly sculpted eyebrow. I hated how perfect her eyebrows were. My eyebrows looked like drug-crazed caterpillars compared to hers.

I shrugged. "I needed a vacation."

Sindi crossed her arms. "Liar."

I bit back a smile. Sindi was one of my favorite people since she'd moved to Havenwood Falls the year before. She was a sultry, redheaded goth vampire. She didn't bullshit, and I loved that about her.

"I checked out your old stomping grounds. Atlanta's a crazy place. But you're free to believe whatever you want. It won't change my answer to anyone who asks." I held up my credit card. "Do you have any rooms available?"

"We do. But why aren't you staying at home? Your father would be happy to see you." She took my card and began the registration process.

"My father is never happy to see me. Besides, I'd prefer not to see him just yet." My words were tight, and I hoped my tone didn't seem snippy. The mention of my father always made me pissy.

She shook her head. "You are so predictable, Mills."

I shrugged. "It's not a secret that Dad and I don't get along."

She handed me the room key and my credit card. "Let us know if you need anything."

I nodded and swiftly went back out to grab my things before anyone else had a chance to corner me.

～

I TOOK A LONG, luxurious nap. By this point, I had no doubt that several people had spotted my Jeep and word had spread. Jetta Mills was back in town. The way I'd left, I'm sure there were those who expected to never see me again. Hell, I didn't know what I'd do once I passed the city limits. I just knew I had to leave. I was tired of fighting with my father over . . . well, everything. He hated my style, my attitude, my language, my music. Anything uniquely a part of me, he disliked with an intensity I could only describe as utter disgust. Of course, knowing this, I did all I could to exaggerate those characteristics. I'd acquired more tattoos, more piercings, and acted out more than ever. We engaged in a constant battle of wills, that old man and I. I was determined to win.

I showered and put on a fresh change of clothes before I looked myself over in the mirror. My black jeans were skin tight and ripped in several places. The gray shirt I wore had a wide neck and hung loose enough to expose all of my collar bone and part of my shoulders. My black boots shone, with the silver buckles on the sides catching the light when I moved. I loved those boots. The four-inch spiked heels alone could be considered deadly weapons.

I put my favorite silver hoop earrings in and smiled. Since removing the extensions and washing out the temporary dark color, I now had my natural silver hair back—an unusual color I'd had since I was a teen. I felt like myself again. The extensions were a fun experiment, but I missed my pixie cut, and the time had come for another trim. I was also happy to no longer need makeup to cover the tattoo on my neck. I'd worn long sleeves everywhere while in Atlanta, so my partial tattoo sleeves were hidden, but the dragon on my neck was unique, and I hadn't been comfortable letting anyone outside of

Havenwood Falls see it. I wasn't sure why. Maybe some sort of instinctual protective mechanism took over—I didn't know, other than my gut told me to hide it, so I did. Frankie was the only person who had seen the beast that hugged my neck.

If I was being honest, I think a part of me knew that leaving home was risky enough that I should take some precautions. I'd almost changed my name as well, but decided that was taking it too far, considering our little box canyon was all but impossible to find if you weren't drawn to it by the town's magic.

I placed my usual rings on my fingers, except for the one Ani had given me. I no longer needed the protections it granted. I had to destroy the abomination before anyone learned of its existence and we both got into trouble. For the time being, the lockbox would keep my secrets.

I grabbed the box from the nightstand and sat it in my lap before I punched in the four-digit code I'd stolen from Brandt's desk. The soft click of the lock indicated the door was open. I raised the lid and froze. I allowed myself a moment to push down the bile that rose in my throat, then I tossed the ring inside and slammed the lid shut.

At that moment, a knock sounded at the door, and I pushed the box under the bed with haste. I moved to the door and unlocked the bolt, then opened it. My father stood on the other side, his tall, bony frame and piercing green eyes filling my vision. I looked at his bushy white hair and matching eyebrows and silently wondered if it'd take a hedge trimmer to get those suckers under control. His appearance was frailer than I'd ever seen him.

"Oh, it's you," I said.

"Yes, it's me." He pushed past me without invitation. I watched as his shrewd and critical gaze roamed the small room. His sour face made it obvious he didn't approve of the lodgings I'd chosen, even though the décor was beautifully done. Dark wood trim and floors mixed with lovely antique furniture and eggshell colored paint, and pastel lampshades, drapes, and linens accented the room, lightening up the heavy feel created from the darker furnishings. If my father hated this, he'd have died on the spot over my apartment in Atlanta. But his disgust was no surprise. He was a snob of the highest caliber. Nothing was ever good enough for Lawrence Mills.

I shut the door and leaned against it. I knew what was coming, and I braced myself.

"Where have you been, young lady?" His voice was stern, barely restrained anger at the surface.

"Not here," I replied as I crossed my arms.

"Don't be an idiot. If you'd been here, I wouldn't be asking the question."

I raised my eyebrows at him. "I think the idiot is the one asking the stupid question."

He growled, and the low rumble was a warning sign that he was about to lose his temper. While I'd love to see the always composed and proper Lawrence Mills shift due to anger, it wasn't fair to the other guests or the employees at the inn. Dad could make a mess when his temper flared.

"Chill, before you hurt yourself. I'll tell you." I motioned to the bed. "Have a seat."

He continued to frown, but he did as I directed.

"I took a road trip. I needed a change of scenery. I landed in Atlanta and got a job for a bit, then decided I was done with the big city life, and I came home. The end." I put my thumbs in the pockets of my jeans and rocked on my heels. "So, now that we're caught up, you can leave, and I can continue with my plans for the evening."

"Did you ever stop to think I might have been worried, Jetta?" His voice was low, but still held that hard edge I'd become accustomed to when he spoke to or about me.

"Not really. You have plenty here to keep you occupied. Especially now that Tristan and his family are back." I shifted my stance, eager to get out of the room.

"It's nice to have your brother back, although things with him certainly haven't gone as planned." He looked at me with those eyes that once held all the love in the world for his little princess. That love had been gone a long time.

"Well . . ." I drawled. "Maybe if you stopped trying to run

everyone's life, you'd be less disappointed when they didn't march to your drum." I smiled sweetly, knowing my words and expression would irritate the hell out of him.

"Bah." He scowled and stood, relying on his cane more than usual. "I can't talk to you when you're like this." He hobbled toward the door, and I stepped out of his way.

"I'm always like this." I opened the door for him.

His hard gaze met mine. "I know." Then he walked out without a single glance back.

Well, that went well.

I grabbed my keys and locked up my room. My stomach rumbled, reminding me that I needed to eat. While I was out and about, I had a bartender to see.

CHAPTER 4

CONRAD

I pulled my truck into a little gas station just outside of Grand Junction and plucked a map of Colorado from the center console. I suspected the GPS was taking me in circles, and the sunlight was fading fast. I'd traced the route the GPS had been using and groaned. Yep, circles. I knew Havenwood Falls had to be somewhere close, but the GPS coordinates were screwed up, and the map didn't show it even existed. The GPS said my destination was nearby, yet no matter what direction I drove, I ended up back near Grand Junction. It felt like I was in the Twilight Zone.

The high-pitched squeal of brakes caught my attention, and I looked up to see a shuttle bus at the other end of the parking lot. The advertising on the side said, "Vacation in Havenwood Falls!"

"Hot damn." I tossed the map into the passenger seat and hopped out of the truck. I jogged over to the shuttle just in time to catch the driver as he disembarked.

"Hi," I said. "Are you going to Havenwood Falls?"

The driver smiled, the laugh lines around his eyes deepening. "I sure am. It's about time you got here. We'll be heading out in about twenty minutes. You need a ride?"

I shook my head. "What?" He must have had me mistaken for

someone else. "No, I have my vehicle. I'm just having a hard time finding the town."

He glanced behind me at my old truck. "That thing got four-wheel drive?"

"No," I stated.

His expression changed from friendly to concern. "Well, it might make it out there. Sometimes it's a little rough." He scratched his head a moment, then adjusted his cap. "You're welcome to follow me, if you like."

"Thank you. I appreciate that very much."

He nodded and looked at his watch. "We leave on the hour, so be ready to go."

"No problem."

I walked back to my truck and put the map away. The folder on Jetta Mills sat on the passenger seat, the corner of her photo poking out of the edge. I pulled the photo out and studied her face. Her beauty struck me again. Not a Miss America kind of beauty, but more like the sweet girl next door who had indulged in her bad girl tendencies. She didn't look innocent by any stretch of the word, but there was a softness in her face that spoke of the hopeful girl she once had been. Her ice-blue eyes were the kind a man could lose himself in, if he weren't careful.

I shook the thought from my head. It wouldn't do for me to lust after the target. I had to keep a clear head, especially if getting her back to Atlanta meant using illegal means.

"Shit!" I slammed my palm into the steering wheel. I hated that I was in this situation. No doubt, this would have to be the last time I took a sketchy job, no matter how much I was offered.

I wanted to take one more look at the Havenwood Falls website while I waited, so I searched it on my phone, but could no longer find it. No matter what I put in the search bar, there were zero results. I was starting to wonder if someone was playing some kind of elaborate prank with the place.

The bus pulled out of the parking lot, and I hurried to catch up. I stayed close behind it as we made the somewhat treacherous drive up, down, and around the mountains. When I saw the "Welcome to Havenwood Falls" sign a couple of hours later, I breathed a sigh of relief. It did exist. I wasn't losing my mind. Step one down, many more to go.

The shuttle stopped at the town square. The quaint little area included walkways, a large fountain in the center, and a gazebo on one corner. I rolled down my window and signaled to an elderly gentleman getting off the bus.

"Excuse me. Can you recommend a hotel?"

His eyes squinted at me as he stepped closer. "Unless you're staying at the ski lodge, the only other place is Whisper Falls Inn." He pointed straight ahead. "It's on that corner."

"Thanks."

He nodded and continued on his way. I drove the short distance to the inn and put the truck in park. My wrist began to burn. I removed the brown leather cuff I'd always worn over a tattoo on my right wrist. I'd collected a lot of tattoos over the years, but I must have been really drunk when I agreed to that one. I didn't remember doing it. I couldn't complain about the quality. The tattoo was a Celtic triskele, roughly two inches in circumference. The three arms, made entirely of flames, swirled forward to meet the next. The artist did a great job with clean lines and subtle shading. For a colorless tattoo, the details were immaculate and well done. A triskele symbolized a balance between your inner consciousness and your outer self, but I had no idea why I chose one made of flames. Normally I would have loved a tattoo like that, but something about this one bothered me. I'd started wearing a cuff over it several years ago, and that had become habit. Every once in a great while, it would burn, similar to the sensation of a tattoo needle as it marked my skin—just as it did in that moment. I rubbed the spot with the thumb of my left hand and scanned the area outside my truck. The wind was picking up, and what few people were out and about scurried to enter the businesses that were still open. I put the cuff back on my wrist and ignored the stinging. It'd been a long day, and all I wanted was a warm bed and some uninterrupted sleep.

I woke up the next morning surprised to realize I'd overslept. I was generally an early riser, but the drive straight through from Georgia to Colorado must have wiped me out. I glanced at the bedside clock that said eight fifteen a.m. I sat on the edge of the bed and stretched. A shower sounded like heaven, so that was my first objective of the day. I allowed myself to soak under the hot water for just a few minutes before washing up and toweling off. I slipped on a long sleeve T-shirt with the AC/DC logo on the front, then pulled my jeans up over my hips. After slipping socks on my feet, I donned my boots. They were brown leather with a thick heel and steel toe. Perfect in my line of work, especially if head-busting was necessary. Bail jumpers didn't often go peacefully. I glanced in the mirror and gave my hair a quick swipe with my fingers, gathering it into a ponytail at the nape of my neck. My black hair was thick, and while I liked it long, I'd been keeping it no longer than my shoulders for the last couple of years; I preferred ease over length.

I took a moment to run my fingers through my neatly trimmed beard as well. I was thankful it mostly hid a one-inch scar that ran down the right side of my lower lip. Another injury I didn't quite remember.

"You gotta quit drinking," I said as I glanced at myself one last time before walking to the door. I swiped my keys and wallet off the side table, stuffing them into my pocket, then grabbed my cuff and put it on my wrist, wondering once again why the crazy tattoo burned at weird times.

I had just made it down the stairs when I felt a firm pinch on my ass.

"Whoa." I turned around. My mouth opened, but nothing came out. Behind me was the sweetest looking woman. Her gray hair shone, and she wore a purple gown. She smiled at me as if all she'd done was wish me a good morning. I snapped my jaw shut, turned back around and hurried out the door. I was sure I hadn't imagined that pinch, but I couldn't fathom the older woman doing it either. Just before the door shut behind me, I heard the girl behind the registration desk say "Madame Luiza!" as if to scold her.

I shook my head and grinned as I grabbed my jacket from my truck and slipped it on. *Time to do some digging into the life of Jetta Mills.*

~

I'D SPENT all day wandering Havenwood Falls. On the surface, it certainly appeared to be a nice little town, although all towns had their undesirable components. The people seemed friendly enough. I knew I couldn't just blurt out that I was looking for Jetta. If word made it back to her, and in a small town like this, it always did, she might bolt, and I'd have to start my search all over again. My best strategy was to blend in as a tourist, get to know the people for a few days, and keep my eyes and ears open at all times. Someone would eventually say something, or I'd see her. Finding her was inevitable. She was a beautiful woman, so it wouldn't be hard to fake interest in her and hopefully gain a little of her trust.

I'd heard someone mention that the Mills family had a large house in the fancy part of town up the hill, so that was information I stored away for later. I'd also heard that Simple Treasures Pawn Shop was owned by her family, so that was my next stop.

I opened the door and stepped inside. The store was brighter than I'd expected, with two-tone walls of gray and white, separated by a black chair rail. The wood floor had been polished until it shined. The overhead lighting appeared to be LED, and it gave off more of a nice jewelry store vibe than that of a place where people hocked stuff out of desperation. One side of the room had a long glass case with everything from jewelry to collectibles. The other side contained shelves of all sizes. Delicate dishes shared a shelf with vases, small statues, and those geode rock things that seemed to be so popular. Another section of the room, near the back, had instruments neatly lined up, as if waiting for a concert to start.

"Hi, are you looking for something in particular?" a young female voice said from behind me. I turned to see a teen girl with white-streaked dark hair and blue eyes. Her smile was friendly, so I returned her greeting.

"I'm new in town and just looking around." My words were clipped, and I had to remind myself, for the hundredth time, to be more outgoing. Being my usual reclusive and suspicious self wasn't going to win me any favors. Old habits die hard. I stuck my hands in my jacket pockets and glanced around the room some more, looking for anything that might interest me. I needed a reason to hang around for a bit without seeming creepy.

"Are you here on vacation?" she asked.

"Yeah. Although if I like it enough, I might consider staying." I spoke slowly this time, making sure I didn't rush my sentences. I walked toward the jewelry case and glanced inside. "Do you like living here?"

She moved behind the case and nodded. "Oh yeah. It's an awesome place to call home." She studied me for a moment, then stuck out her hand. "I'm Zoey."

I shook her hand. "It's nice to meet you, Zoey. I'm Conrad."

I prayed I didn't sound gruff. I was told my demeanor could scare small children. If I sounded like a jerk, she didn't seem to notice. She continued to smile at me.

I kept my eyes focused on the contents in the case. Her cheerful attitude was making me uncomfortable. I never had been good with kids, even when I was a kid.

My eyes roamed a row of thick rings, and I bent down for a closer look.

"Aren't those cool?" said Zoey. "My grandpa has a lot of items flown in from all over the world. Some of those rings are really old."

My eyes snapped to one ring in particular, and a lump caught in my throat. The silver ring was flat on top with an insignia embossed into the metal. An image that matched my weird wrist tattoo exactly. *What the hell?*

I pointed to the ring. "Can I see that one?"

"Oh, I really love that one. I tried to buy it once, but my dad said it wasn't meant for me." She huffed out a frustrated breath. "He's so picky about what I wear." She turned and pulled a set of keys from a drawer. After unlocking the case and sliding the door back, she pulled the ring out and laid it on a blue velvet pad, placing it in front of me.

I leaned down and inspected the ring, but didn't dare touch it. I wasn't a superstitious person, but I believed, for at least a few moments, that if I touched it, something bad would happen.

"Yeah, that's cool," I mumbled.

"Wanna try it on?" Zoey's enthusiasm for making a sale had me biting back a true smile.

"No, thanks. I just wanted to see it up close." I glanced at her. "Do you know the origins of the ring? Or what the symbols mean?" I was oddly desperate for an answer that would clear up my confusion.

"Not really. My dad and Grandpa are the ones that deal with most of that."

"Zoey? Honey, who are you talking to?" A man who appeared to be in his mid-forties stepped from a room in the back of the store. "Oh, so sorry. Didn't realize we had a customer. Has Zoey taken care of you?" He smiled at the teen.

"Yes, thank you. She's been very helpful." I couldn't keep from stealing another glance at the ring still sitting on the counter.

"Ah, I see you're interested in a very unique ring." He smiled as he walked toward us.

"I've never seen one like it. Zoey thought you might know its history." I put my hands in my jacket once more, resisting the temptation to pick up the ring.

"Oddly enough, I don't. It's a Celtic triskele, which in and of itself isn't unusual, but the flamed arms aren't anything I've seen before." He picked the object up. "Admittedly, I haven't had a lot of time to investigate it, so I've likely just not stumbled across the right information yet." He held the ring out to me. "Is it your size?"

I backed up, unable to avoid the ludicrous reaction. "I don't think so." I glanced at my watch. "I need to run, but it was nice to meet you both."

The man smiled. "Please come in anytime. You've met Zoey, but I didn't introduce myself. I'm her father, Tristan Mills."

I nodded. "I'm Conrad Monroe. Thanks again for the hospitality." I flashed them one last nervous smile and slipped out of the store, my heart racing in my chest.

"What the hell was that?" I whispered.

CHAPTER 5

JETTA

"Simon, c'mon man. You owe me," I grumbled, adding a little female whine in for good measure.

He raised an eyebrow at me. I'd considered flirting, but I'd learned a long time ago that strategy didn't work with Simon. He only had eyes for his boss Odette Alverson, the owner of Fallview Tavern & Grille. The fact that he was a dragon shifter and she was a siren didn't seem to deter him in the least.

"Seriously, I need a job. I don't want to live off my father or his money. I need to get back to making my own way before I run out of savings." My elbow was on the black marble bar, and I placed my chin in my hand and tilted my head. "Please?" I begged.

He nodded. "Fine. I'll tell Odette you're the new entertainment. I think she was getting tired of the old act anyway. You can work the off nights for now, and we can phase the other group out in time."

"Thank you!" I leaned across the bar and hugged him.

Simon blushed. "We're even now, though. No more bringing up how you helped me settle here and all that noise."

I nodded. "You got it." I flashed him a wide smile. "You love me. You know you want me around."

He shook his head. "I don't know. You didn't even tell me you were leaving town. I had to find out from your very angry father, when he came looking for you. He was sure I was holding out on him. And then you didn't bother to let me know once you were in town again?" He shook his head. "Not a lot to love about that."

"I didn't say anything so you could plead innocent when Dad came around, as I knew he eventually would. And I did come to see you last night, but you weren't here."

Simon sighed. "You're one of my closest friends. But I need you here like I need a third eye." He crossed his arms and gave me a stern look. "No troublemaking."

I nodded in agreement.

He narrowed his eyes at me. "You agreed to that way too easy."

I shrugged. "Maybe Atlanta changed me. Maybe I'm not the rabble rouser you once knew."

He snorted. "No one will ever buy that. Try to sell me something else."

"Fine. I need the work, so if I have to be on my best behavior, I'm willing to at least attempt it." I fidgeted with the silver skull ring on my index finger.

He nodded. "That I believe." He poured a beer and slid it across to me. "Be here at eight sharp. It'll be nice to hear some decent music again."

I took a sip. "Only decent? I must be losing my touch."

Simon sighed. "You do plan to leave soon, right? I have work to do." He sounded annoyed, but he winked at me.

"As soon as I finish this beer." I tilted it back and chugged it quickly.

He shook his head at me. "Ya know, normal girls don't guzzle booze."

I slapped some money on the counter. "I'm not normal."

He let out a full chuckle then. "Damn straight."

I slid off the barstool and gave him a wave as I strolled to the door. "See you tonight."

I stepped out into the bright sunlight and allowed my eyes a moment to adjust. I had a few hours before my first set at the bar. It'd

AMY HALE

been forever since I willingly let my dragon out. I needed to visit the falls.

~

I CAREFULLY TREADED the natural stone steps that led to one side of Smalls Falls. My favorite spot was some distance from the falls near Fallview Tavern & Grille, but this particular waterfall had special meaning to me and my family. Just behind the rush of cool water that spilled over the cliff, there was a small, very dark cave. At least, to the non-dragon eye, that's how it appeared. In truth, a large cavern that led deep back into the mountainside hid behind the falls. This was the Mills family cave, and my father had had it warded over a century ago so that our private retreat would stay a secret. We felt comfortable shifting into our dragon form in this cave. The large space had been especially great for learning, and I had recently taken my sixteen-year-old niece, Zoey, to the cave to practice shifting. It was scary for her, but she took to it quickly, and I'd been so proud of her.

I pushed my hand through the inky darkness and let out a contented breath as I walked the rest of the way inside. Home. This cave had always felt like home, no matter what else was going on in my life. I pulled a lighter from my pocket and lit the candles that lined the walls of the first room.

For a moment I stood there, basking in the sounds of rushing water while I inhaled the earthy scent that surrounded me. Then I heard soft sobs coming from the larger room.

I cautiously made my way to the next entrance and noticed a single candle sitting on the dirt floor, next to my niece.

"Zoey?" I whispered.

Her head snapped up, and she wiped a tear from her eye. "Aunt Jetta?"

I stepped forward. "It's me, sweetie. What's wrong?"

She stood and ran into my arms, wrapping hers around my torso in a big hug. "I'm so glad you're here! I missed you!"

"I missed you, too." I tilted her face to look at mine and noticed

38

the dirt-streaked smudges on her cheeks. Tears had cleared small trails from her eyelashes to her chin. "Why are you crying?"

Zoey stepped back and inhaled a deep breath. "I had a fight with Jordan."

I frowned. "What happened?"

"It was stupid, and it was my fault. I got jealous over something petty." She sniffled. "And now I may have ruined our relationship."

I pulled her back to me for a hug, and I stroked her hair. "I'm sure you didn't. You just need to talk it out. Remember what I told you? Relationships only work when there is communication."

She nodded. Then, as an afterthought, she said, "Where have you been? I came here hoping I'd find you, even though I knew you'd left town."

Guilt landed like a rock in my stomach. I should have been there for her. At the least, I should have kept in touch with my brother. Tristan was one of the few people not intimidated by my father. "I'm sorry, sweetie. I should have checked in. I just needed to some downtime for a bit. Clear my head."

She sniffed again. "I understand."

"I'm sorry I haven't been here for you." I released her and stepped back. "It'll all be okay, though. I bet Jordan is feeling just as bad as you are about the argument."

"You think? I mean, he shouldn't. It was my fault." Her lovely blue eyes were so full of hope, it almost broke my heart. She was such a sweet young woman. So much the opposite of me.

"Maybe, but I doubt he enjoyed fighting, regardless of the cause. Call him when you get home. Apologize if needed. Talk it out."

"Thanks, Aunt Jetta. I feel a little better."

"Good. Now, you know what would make us both feel better?" I gave her a sly grin.

She looked up at me, and a slow smile replaced her frown. "Flying?"

I held up my hand for a high five, and she met mine with enthusiasm.

"First one to the top of the cliff is a bloodsucker!" I yelled, as I ran to the back of the cave while pulling my shirt over my head.

"Hey now, my best friend is a bloodsucker," Zoey said in mock offense.

"Sorry, not the vamp family I had in mind." I'd instantly envisioned the Roca brothers and their many escapades.

I kicked off my boots and peeled off my jeans, folding them neatly to place beside my shirt.

Zoey stood next to me, undressing as well. "Hey, we need to make ourselves Velcro clothes or something. I'm so tired of having to undress. Wouldn't it be cool to just shift, and our clothes fall away?" She smirked.

"So, like the Hulk without the tearing?" I asked.

"Yeah! Like that."

I chuckled. "Sure, we should work on that. For now, we'll have to be content with undressing so we aren't running around naked afterward."

I stepped back, assuring I had plenty of room and had left Zoey her needed space as well. Then I closed my eyes and summoned my dragon. I saw a quick mental picture of my shifted self—white scales with a bluish tint that matched my eyes; large jaws containing smooth and serrated teeth; claws, wings, and a tail at least half the length of my forty-foot-long body. My head crowned with a regal row of horns that started from the back side of my jaw and wrapped around behind my head, meeting the other side in a mirror image. Next, the stretching and popping began. The pain of my limbs elongating and bulking up was always there, but I'd become so used to it that I hardly took notice anymore. I opened my eyes as my vision clouded temporarily, then cleared to an almost telescopic vantage.

I looked down to see my beautiful niece as she began her own transformation. She made a few uncomfortable sounds, but the general act of shifting didn't appear to cause her a lot of trauma. It had always brought me relief to know young dragons didn't have the excruciating pain that older dragons experienced. I'd been told a gene evolved over time so that we wouldn't fear shifting. I'd always equated it to procreation. If the actual act were extremely painful, no one would do it, and the species would die off. I'd believed shifting was the same way. If the process was terrible, our younger generation may purposely choose to avoid shifting. Over time, the dragon gene could die off as we evolved once more. But that was just my theory. It wasn't like we had the world's greatest minds trying to figure it out.

When her shifting was complete, I lowered my head to hers and gave her a nuzzle with my snout. Some of my favorite times with Zoey had been in our dragon forms. She was a great kid, but she had a little wild spirit in her too, and that side I resonated with very well. She could be that side of herself when she let her dragon take over.

I pushed my enormous head through the falls, immediately triggering my camouflage so that I blended in with my surroundings. The frigid water felt fantastic on my neck, so I allowed it to run over me a moment before a hard nudge from behind alerted me to Zoey shoving at my tail with her head.

"Okay, I'm going." I laughed as our telepathic communication took over.

I stepped out, clearing the way for her, and she followed immediately. We both gave our wings a good stretch, then I glanced at her, noting the faint outline of her camouflage and the light puff of frost escaping her nostrils. Without her camouflage, she was a carbon copy of myself, only instead of twenty feet high, she was closer to fifteen. She also had the most mesmerizing iridescent scales. At times, I'd been a little jealous of her coloring.

I smiled, as much as a giant reptile can, and said, "Race you to the top!"

I hit the bank running, pushing my way through the dense forest. Unable to fully spread my wings, I tucked them in close and lumbered up the mountainside toward our favorite cliff. I could hear Zoey directly behind me. She'd gained some speed since our last outing and appeared to have no trouble keeping up.

Just as we'd reached the clearing that led to the edge, she zoomed past me in a blur.

"Holy hell," I muttered.

Once I reached her side at the precipice, I huffed out an annoyed breath. "So, where'd you learn that speed, kiddo?"

"You're not the only dragon who can teach me stuff, ya know," she teased.

"I'm getting old," I complained.

"Nah, it's just hard to compete with my awesomeness."

I chuckled. "So true." I leaned my head forward and looked down. "Shall we?"

"Let's," Zoey said with excitement. She obviously loved the freedom of flying as much as I did.

We both leapt off the edge, letting our wings work as gliders and slow our descent, then we tilted ourselves toward the sun, and with a powerful push from our wings, we were both rising among the clouds.

We spent a few minutes just enjoying the wind rushing past us. The cool, crisp air was invigorating. No matter my troubles, flying had always given me a respite. It allowed me a moment to breathe. That moment was about to be interrupted by Zoey's incessant matchmaking.

"Hey, Aunt Jetta," she sang in a high-pitched voice as she zoomed by me. "I met this cute guy at the shop today. He'd be perfect for you."

CHAPTER 6

CONRAD

I rolled my eyes as my phone buzzed for what felt like the billionth time. I pulled it from my pocket and slid the bar on the screen to answer it.

"Conrad," I stated.

"I've been trying to reach you." Brandt's annoyed tone assailed my ears.

"And?" I didn't appreciate being badgered, even if this was the guy paying me.

"And you haven't given me an update! It's been three days since you left Atlanta. What progress have you made?"

My eyes narrowed at accusations in his tone. "First, I don't care how much you are paying me. Talk to me with that attitude again and I'll break your face. With your own fist." I gave him a very brief moment to let that sink in. "Second, when I have news worth sharing, I'll let you know." I hung up on him.

Within seconds the phone buzzed again, and I turned it off. To be honest, the cell service here was shit anyway, and I fully planned to use that annoyance to my advantage. His impatience could have sabotaged my plans to bring her back peacefully.

I pushed my phone back into my pocket as I walked through the door of Fallview Tavern & Grille. The place was packed, and the only open seats were a few spots at the end of the bar, farthest from the stage. I settled in and flagged down the bartender.

"What can I get ya?" He eyed me curiously.

"I'd love a beer." I pulled cash out of my pocket.

"Sure." He took a few steps backward and placed an empty mug under the bar gun. A push of a button dispensed my favorite beverage. He slid it to me and took the bills I'd placed on the bar.

I took a swig and sighed. That was some damn good beer. I looked up to see the bartender staring at me.

"Can I help you?" I did my best to keep the irritation out of my voice. It wouldn't do to start a fight on my first real night out. The plan was to make friends, not alienate them.

He smirked. "I'm Simon Turner." When I didn't reply, he continued. "How long have you been in Havenwood Falls?"

"A couple of days," I countered. "My name's Conrad."

He nodded. "Well, welcome to our little canyon, Conrad." He busied himself with an empty glass. "Have we met before?"

I froze. "No, not that I can remember."

"Yeah, probably not. You just seem familiar."

The strum of a guitar caught my attention, and I shifted my eyes to the stage. A petite young woman with short silver hair sat on a stool, acoustic guitar in her hands. My distance from the stage made it a little difficult to see her clearly, but I could see the glint of piercings. When she turned her head, there was a large dark marking on her neck. I could only assume she had some kind of tattoo. I smiled. I liked her already. Then she began to sing, and my heart seemed to follow the rhythm along with her.

> You look, but you don't see me
> My soul vacant and stark
> Darkness the only friend
> I can trust with my heart.
>
> If I could show you clearly,
> The true me far beneath,

Would you run? Could you embrace me
As reality bared its teeth?

Until then I'm transparent,
The illusion kept intact.
One day you'll see what no one can
And I'll finally be more than that . . .
Transparent.

Her voice was beautiful, with an edge to it that made me think she could easily slip between soft ballads and heavy metal. It suddenly occurred to me that she could be my target. But this woman's appearance was very different from the photo I had in my truck. I caught Simon's attention.

"Who's that?" I nodded my head in the direction of the stage.

"Ah, that's Jetta Mills." He shook his head. "If you're looking to take that one on, you'd better buy life insurance. She could eat you alive."

I chuckled and tried to hide the adrenaline rush of knowing my target was within reach. "Sounds like my kind of woman."

I took another drink of my beer.

"I can introduce you, if you'd like." Simon glanced her way. "She's a good friend. My only condition is that you don't blame me for anything that happens after that introduction."

"Sure, I can live with that." I was overly eager to meet this unusual young woman.

I sat at the bar for the next couple of hours, listening to Jetta perform and getting to know Simon, in between his various duties at the tavern. He was a likable guy, and if the situation were different, I could see us being friends.

As Jetta thanked the audience and slipped the guitar over her head, Simon leaned across the bar. "She'll come over for a few drinks before she heads back home. Her favorite drink is whiskey."

I nodded. "Gotcha. What brand?"

Simon's eyebrows rose in unison. "All of them."

"Damn," I whispered.

"Exactly." He put a shot of whiskey before me. "Enjoy."

Jetta made her way through the patrons seated in the bar, taking the time to say hello to each one, with the exception of one guy who appeared to have grabbed her inappropriately. I didn't see the full exchange, but I did witness the right hook she rewarded him with. He went down like a sack of potatoes.

Simon came around the bar and walked to where the guy slumped on the floor. "Damn it, Jetta. It's your first night. Did you have to punch a customer?"

She put her hands on her perfect little hips. "I sure as hell did. Next time he wants to get to second base, he should make sure he's on the right field."

She stomped toward the bar, and I turned my attention back to my drink. Taking her back to Atlanta would suck. Not because I didn't like her, but because I did. I couldn't say I'd met many women like her. Truth be told, I'm not sure I'd ever met any women like her.

She approached the bar, climbed up on a stool two seats from mine, then leaned over the bar and grabbed a glass. She picked up the bottle of whiskey Simon had just used to pour my drink, glanced at the glass in her hand, then promptly returned the glass to its previous spot. She put the bottle to her lips, and for a moment, some very erotic images came to mind.

I held up my shot toward her and said, "Cheers."

She nodded and took another swig from the bottle.

"That guy step out of line?" I nodded my head in the direction of the unconscious man Simon was dragging to the door.

She glanced over, then rolled her eyes. Eyes that were every bit the soft blue of the photo Brandt had given me. "He's used to it. He tries to feel up everyone when he's drunk. I'm just one of the few who refuses to put up with it."

I smiled. "Well done."

She turned to face me. "Really? Most men are intimidated by a strong woman."

"Nah, I like it. It's rare."

She looked me over, and then one side of her lips quirked upward. "Obviously."

Simon took his usual place behind the bar and poured a soda. "I see you two have already met."

I shook my head. "Not officially."

"Jetta, meet Conrad. Conrad, Jetta. There, now it's official." Simon took a sip of his drink and watched Jetta closely.

She nodded an acknowledgment and held up her bottle. "To new friends."

I held up my shot, which Simon had so thoughtfully refilled with a different bottle, since Jetta had commandeered the other one. "To new friends."

Simon held up his own. "To you two getting the hell out of my bar soon so I can close down."

CHAPTER 7

JETTA

*S*imon shooed Conrad and me out of the bar rather hastily. Something was up with him. I'd known him long enough to sense when he was hiding something. In the past, he used to love my company while he closed things up. He obviously liked Conrad. Why did he kick us out like he'd rather chew glass than look at us? I'd get to the bottom of it eventually. I always did.

As for Conrad, well, he was an enigma in tight jeans and a leather jacket. And had some seriously sexy brown eyes. I'd always been a sucker for the biker look, and he wore it very well. He could have easily fit in with S.I.N., our local motorcycle club. His dark hair was pulled back in a ponytail at the nape of his neck. His neatly trimmed beard blended seamlessly with his sideburns and had tiny flecks of auburn infused here and there. His mustache matched perfectly as well.

He caught me staring, and I smiled. I didn't care. He was hot, and I had perfect vision. Nothing wrong with enjoying the view. As long as he was only in town for a short while, I saw no harm in hanging out with the sexy tourist. I gave up on long-term relationships ages ago, so occasional flings were more my style. Of course, that would be after I made sure he wasn't some kind of nut job. I was fortunate that I didn't have to be quite as paranoid as most single women my age. I could simply shift and eat him if he turned out to be a psycho jackass. At that thought, another psycho jackass came to mind. The one I ran from back in Atlanta. I should have eaten him.

"Hey, are you okay?" Conrad asked.

"Yeah, I'm fine." I shook the image from my mind.

"You looked a little sick for a moment." His concern was obvious in his voice.

"Yeah, I'm good. Just dealing with some memories. Must have been triggered by the groping back there."

He frowned. "Did someone hurt you?"

I chuckled. "No, not really." *Not in a way you'd ever believe.* "But thanks for asking."

I wrapped my arms around my torso, and an involuntary shiver ran up my spine. I wasn't cold, even though my jacket wasn't lined. But the memories of what I had encountered were troubling. I felt Conrad's jacket wrap around my shoulders in a gentlemanly gesture.

"Thanks, but you'll get cold if you don't wear yours." I shrugged it back off and handed it to him.

"I'm actually comfortable at the moment." He draped the jacket over his arm as if it proved his point.

I couldn't tell if he was lying or not. As we walked to our vehicles, I watched for any signs that he was cold, but saw nothing that gave him away. I reached my Jeep and unlocked it.

"It was nice to meet you, Conrad. Maybe we'll see each other again soon."

He nodded, and I saw his gaze land on my neck.

"I know you're dying to ask." I pulled the collar of my jacket aside, so he could get a better look. "It's a dragon."

He leaned in closer, and I could feel his breath on my cheek, warming the spot in front of my ear. The movement was innocent, yet felt extremely intimate. I had to command myself to stay still. I battled between wanting to step back and longing to lean into him.

He pulled back just enough to look into my eyes. "It's amazing. Did it take long?"

I shrugged. "Not terribly."

He had no idea how amazing it really was. Supernatural residents and visitors had to register with the Court of the Sun and the Moon. We were each tagged with a magic tattoo that helped them keep track of anyone who broke the carefully constructed rules that made our town a true haven for us. Mine was designed by a friend and tattooed and magically infused by Addie, one of the official tattooists for the Court.

He stepped back to his former spot, which wasn't quite an arm's length away. Conrad reached for the inside of his right wrist and rubbed it absentmindedly, which wouldn't have been overly weird except he wore a large leather cuff over it. He was rubbing the cuff, and I wasn't sure he even realized he was doing it.

"So . . ." I attempted to divert the conversation to him. "Do you have any tattoos?"

He nodded. "I do. Quite a few actually." He pulled up one sleeve of his shirt, only to reveal another sleeve of the tattooed variety.

I gasped. "Holy shit, that's amazing."

I moved in for a closer look. Vines with thorns threaded their way around and through an intricate graveyard scene, complete with bones, tombstones, and heavy fog. In the distance a lone motorcycle sat near a large monument shaped like a cross. I reached for his arm and turned it to see the backside. In that moment, I felt him stiffen. I looked up into his eyes and noticed an intensity I'd never seen in anyone before. Heat seared my fingers where they touched his flesh. It wasn't your average attraction kind of warmth, but almost as if his veins were filled with hot magma. I couldn't let go. I didn't want to.

"Jetta," he whispered.

I straightened up slowly, still gripping his arm. That arm snaked around my waist and pulled me closer as my palms rested on his chest. My brain screamed at me to step back, that this was way too fast, despite my attraction to him. But my damn body wouldn't cooperate with my head. I melted into him, the extreme heat now flowing over every part of my body that touched his. It should have been uncomfortable, but I only wanted more.

He bent his head to mine, and our lips touched softly. It wasn't wild or passionate, as I'd expected a kiss from someone like him to be. Instead, the gesture was tender, filled with an emotion I wasn't sure either of us understood. When he pulled back, he looked just as confused as I felt.

"That was . . . nice." I struggled to find the correct words.

His eyes roamed my face for a brief moment, then he made a deep growling sound in the back of his throat and said, "I'm not even remotely nice."

His lips crashed down on mine, and the kiss I'd originally been expecting took over. His grip tightened as his tongue slipped between my lips. I opened for him, letting him explore and tease. I held fistfuls of his shirt as I tried to somehow pull him even closer than we already were. His large hands ran over my back as he pressed himself into me. This had to be what heaven felt like. Desire coursed through me, and I sank into the feeling just before logic forced its way through my lust-induced haze. I did not know this man. This was way too fast, even for me.

I pushed him away. "I'm sorry. I can't do this."

I turned and opened the door to my Jeep.

Conrad leaned his forearms on the top of my door. "Jetta, I apologize. I didn't mean to cross any lines." I looked up and his expression of contrition was genuine.

I shook my head as I took my place behind the steering wheel. "You didn't. I'm just not ready for something like this."

"Something like what?" he asked. "It was just a kiss."

"I don't know, Conrad. I just . . ." He was right, and I was probably overreacting, but I could have sworn there was something else happening while we kissed. I had no idea what that could have possibly been, and it made no sense. I couldn't think. Any words that came to mind were inadequate to describe the terror that pulled at my chest when I realized how lost I'd been while kissing him. It wasn't a danger kind of fear, but more of a warning signal. There was something happening on a spiritual level that I didn't understand.

I couldn't allow myself to lose control. Ever. Anyone that could fracture the carefully cultivated mastery of my emotions was someone to stay away from.

He had the potential to destroy me.

"I'm sorry. I need to go." I shut the door, jerking it out from underneath him. The gears protested as I slammed the Jeep in reverse and backed out of the parking spot. I refused to allow myself to even a peek in the rearview mirror.

I WOKE up in an unusually grumpy mood. I'd never been a morning person, but today I felt like terrorizing the village, so to speak. I needed to rein that in if I didn't want an incident on my hands. The Court had been lenient with me on past transgressions, thanks to my father, but I was running out of get-out-of-jail-free passes. Eventually they'd boot me out of town, and as much as I hated my father, I truly did love Havenwood Falls. My time away had only driven that point home all the more.

Lots of strong coffee was in order, so I grabbed a table at Coffee Haven and ordered the largest cup of coffee they sold. I was halfway through it when Zoey and her boyfriend Jordan walked through the door, hand in hand.

"Aunt Jetta!" Zoey skipped to my table, with Jordan in tow and trying to keep up.

"Hey, guys. Have a seat." I motioned to the chairs opposite mine.

"We can't stay. We just came to grab coffee before school." She looked at Jordan and smiled. "And since we saw you, we wanted to come say thank you."

"For what?" I asked, taking another sip of my coffee.

"For reminding us that we can make it through anything as long as we talk to each other honestly," replied Jordan.

"Ah, well . . . normally I'd not be the person to take relationship advice from, but I learned that tidbit from your parents." I directed my gaze at Zoey. "They're pretty smart when they aren't being stuffy."

She laughed. "Yeah, I guess you're right."

Jordan glanced at his watch. "We'd better grab our coffee and get going, or we'll be late for first period."

Zoey bent down for a hug and then waved goodbye as they made their way to the counter, still holding hands.

"Ah, young love. Isn't it sweet?" said a voice from behind me. I recognized that voice, and it set my teeth on edge.

"Hello, Bradly. What caused you to crawl out from under your rock?"

He stepped around my table and took a seat across from me. "You're so cheerful. I'm amazed the mayor hasn't named you citizen of the year."

"I'm amazed you haven't been named douche-nozzle of the year," I shot back.

"Tsk, tsk. Such language." His sardonic smile revealed a row of crooked, yellowed teeth.

I had a few choice words for him, but we were in public, so instead of sharing them, I said, "What do you want, Bradly?"

"Do I have to want something?"

"You always want something." I glared at him. "Spit it out."

"I heard you were in possession of something special. Something that might be of great interest to the right buyer."

My mind flashed to the lockbox under my bed at the inn. "I have no idea what you're talking about." I kept my face passive as I continued to sip my coffee.

"Oh, but I think you do." He winked at me. I generally loved the fae population, but Bradly was the rare exception. He was a dishonest and disreputable member of the Unseelie fae. I was amazed he had the gall to show his face in public after some of the stunts he'd pulled.

"Do you have something in your eye?" I asked when he winked a second time.

"What? No." He looked confused at my questioning. He wasn't exactly the sharpest crayon in the box.

"Would you like me to put something there?" I held up my spoon and pointed it at his face.

He shrank back. "Why are you always such a bitch?"

"Now who's using language?" I placed the spoon on the table, glanced around to assure we weren't drawing attention, and then leaned forward, looking him directly in his beady little black eyes. I felt my pupils constrict, and I knew they had changed to their reptilian form. "Don't ever try to pull me into your illicit activities again. I don't work for you or any of the Unseelie. You tricked me once, shame on you. Try to trick me twice . . ." I leaned back and stirred my coffee, letting my pupils regain their human shape. "Well, let's just say I've heard fae are a delicacy in some circles. I'd be happy to introduce you to those particular connoisseurs."

"You dare threaten the Unseelie?" he sputtered.

"No, I'm threatening you. Stay away from me. Stay away from my family. Stay away from my friends. If you don't, I'll be sure you disappear forever." I stood up and tossed my napkin on the table. "Goodbye, Bradly." I left him sitting there as I worked on calming my nerves.

I made the short walk from Coffee Haven to Simple Treasures Pawn Shop. Tristan was working, and I needed a distraction, and possibly some brotherly advice. I didn't foresee that distraction showing up in the form of Conrad. I walked into the shop only to run directly into him, my face colliding with his chest. His hand lurched out to steady me so I wouldn't fall. That same intense heat started at his fingers and traveled up my arm.

"Sorry," I blurted out quickly and stepped away.

He hooked his thumbs in his jean pockets.

"No need to apologize." He tilted his head slightly, and his gaze landed on my lips. I knew from the way he looked at me that he was thinking about that kiss, and to be honest, so was I.

I stepped aside. "It's good to see you again."

I hoped he'd take the hint and finish walking out the door. He didn't.

"Yeah, you too. Hey, since you're here, maybe you can help me with something." He smiled, and my heart jumped in my chest.

"Okay." Maybe if I kept it short and sweet, we could get this over with faster. I hated that he could reduce me to emotional tatters when just minutes ago I'd been handing out death threats with nerves of steel.

"I was in here shortly after I arrived in town and have been considering this ring." He led me over to the glass display counter and pointed to a silver ring with a Celtic emblem on it.

I squatted down for a better look.

"And?" I asked, with a bit more impatience than I'd intended.

"What do you think? Do you know anything about the symbolism?" He crouched down next to me.

I closed my eyes a moment and tried to focus on anything other than his cologne, which was spicy and a little smoky. That scent assaulted my senses in ways I did not want to experience.

"Not really. It looks Celtic. That's about all I can tell you." I stood and stepped back from the counter.

He followed me up and put his hands in his pockets. "Yeah, that's about all anyone seems to know."

"Jetta! So glad you finally came by to see me." My brother Tristan emerged from the back room with a large book in his hand. He glanced between us. "I see you've met Conrad."

I nodded. "Yeah, he was at my set last night."

Tristan smiled. "She's very talented. And neglectful." He turned to face me directly. "Bianca is furious with you for skipping town without keeping in touch. She's insisting you join us for dinner tonight."

I cringed. "So sorry. I owe you all some explanations. What time? Six?"

Tristan nodded. "Hey, Conrad, you should join us as well. We could finish discussing some of those historical ruins we'd been talking about. I think I found more in this book."

I felt my eyes bulge out of their sockets. If it were physically possible for them to jump from my head, I think they would have bounced all over the room. Why the hell was Tristan inviting this stranger to his home?

Conrad glanced at me, then back at Tristan. "I'm not sure—"

Tristan interrupted. "I insist."

He didn't even glance my way. He just kept smiling at Conrad like he was some kind of visiting dignitary. *Idiot brother.*

"I'd be honored," Conrad answered, as his gaze quickly flickered from Tristan's face to mine once more.

"Yeah, that'd be great," I muttered with exactly zero enthusiasm.

CHAPTER 8

CONRAD

$\mathcal{I}$ sat on my bed at the inn and stared at the photo of Jetta. She'd changed her appearance quite a bit from her time in Georgia, but there was no mistaking I was looking at the same woman. I hadn't yet figured out how I was getting her back to Atlanta, but I hoped tonight's dinner would move me closer to an answer. Jetta was quite a woman. Strong, independent, rebellious. She appeared to know what she wanted and how she planned to achieve it. And damn it all— the more I was with her, the more I wanted her for myself.

This was a new experience for me. But in truth, all I could do was enjoy her company, learn everything I could, and hope this entire situation would have a peaceful resolution for everyone involved. I still needed to figure out where she'd hidden the lockbox she'd taken, but that might be something I'd have to deal with once I'd revealed my purpose here. I still held on to hope that I could convince her to trust me. I'd only known her a short time, but she'd already made that plan hard to execute.

I turned on my phone to check messages, and the screen informed me I had missed ten calls from Brandt. I groaned. "Son of a bitch. Give me time, asshole."

I pushed the button to call him back and half hoped it wouldn't go through. It did.

"Monroe! Why the hell haven't you been taking my calls?" yelled Brandt's voice.

"I'm in a canyon. Reception sucks and only works on rare occasion." I knew he heard the exhaustion in my voice. I was tired. Of him.

"Do you have any updates for me?" His voice was calmer now.

"I do." I hesitated. I wasn't ready to divulge everything, so decided to be vague. "I think I've found her. If I can verify it's her, I'll take the next step," I lied.

Her identity was not in question, but I still held my reservations on how much to involve him. Knowing Brandt's type, he'd send his goons down to help and screw it all up. I needed to keep him in the dark until I was almost there.

"Well . . . that's something anyway." He huffed and sounded like a spoiled teen.

"This kind of thing takes a little time, but I will deliver. Just hang on until I can be sure I've got everything you need taken care of." I hoped my reassurances would get him off my back for a while.

"I'd appreciate frequent updates," he said, adding, "when you have cell service."

"When I can." I hung up.

The more I talked to him, the less I liked him. And that was saying a lot, considering I didn't like him to begin with.

I buttoned up my blue dress shirt, leaving my sleeves rolled halfway up my forearms. I didn't own slacks, but I'd felt certain the Mills family weren't that formal, so my best pair of jeans would be fine. Once ready, I hurried to my truck, surprised at how anxious I was for the evening to start. I could have pretended it wasn't because I was seeing Jetta again, but that would only have been lying to myself. I was very attracted to her, and while it wasn't wise, I was enjoying this self-torture more than I should have.

I studied the small map Tristan had drawn for me. Havenwood Falls was a cozy little town, easily traveled from one side to the other in minutes. Finding Tristan's home was easy, and I'd arrived with time to spare. Tristan lived in a nice house. Better than anything I can ever remember calling home. The ranch-style brick layout looked spacious, even from the outside. I stepped out of my truck and turned to see Jetta pulling in behind me. She wasted no time getting out of her Jeep and confronting me.

"Why are you here?" Her voice held every bit of the suspicion her words did.

"Dinner," I said, as I held up a bottle of wine I'd picked up for Tristan's wife Bianca. "Everyone I asked said Stone Falls was the place to buy a good bottle of Pinot. Were they right?"

She took a step closer, her eyes boring into mine. "Don't try to change the subject. What are you up to?"

I put one hand on my hip.

"My, if we aren't a little paranoid," I said defensively. She was getting too close to finding me out, and I couldn't allow that yet. I pushed down the urge to blurt the truth out and be done with it.

"I . . ." She balled up her fists. "I have good reason to be." She grabbed my shirt collar and pulled me to her, nose to nose. "If you have even the smallest hint of nefarious intentions toward my family, I will end you." She shoved me away and stomped into the house.

"Well," I muttered to myself. "This should be fun."

TRISTAN POURED a second glass of wine and offered some to Jetta.

"No, thanks. I've had two glasses already," she said.

She'd been quiet all evening, and that obviously wasn't her normal modus operandi when in a family setting. Zoey had chatted excitedly off and on throughout the meal, the subjects ranging from school to the latest fashion trends. I listened attentively and smiled in what I assumed were all the right places. She was a sweet kid, and her enthusiasm for subjects she loved was infectious. She helped fill the awkward silences anytime the conversation included Jetta, whose replies were short and indifferent.

Bianca stood, gathering dishes. "Jetta, would you help me in the kitchen?"

Jetta nodded and stood, picking up her dishes and scooping up Zoey's as she passed.

Tristan motioned for me to join him on the sofa. The living room, dining room, and kitchen were all connected in one large open floor plan. I glanced toward the back of the room, where Jetta, Zoey, and Bianca had gathered around the sink.

"Shouldn't we help with the cleanup?" I'd always hated the idea that the kitchen was "women's work."

"Normally, I'd say yes, but that request to Jetta was code for 'let's talk in private.' No way I'm interrupting that." Tristan chuckled. "I value my life too much."

I understood. "You have an amazing family, Tristan. You're a lucky man."

I meant every word. I'd never had a family, even as a child. He was blessed with something I hoped he didn't take for granted.

"I am indeed. Those three women in there are the center of my world." He opened the book he'd brought from the pawn shop. "I found something interesting."

I sat next to him, both of us now facing the fireplace on the opposite end of the room, our backs to the kitchen. Tristan placed the book in my lap, opened to a specific page. A Celtic triskele rested above the description of its meaning. Below that were several paragraphs explaining variations of the symbols that had been found over the years.

"I ran across something vague, but it might explain that ring you were talking about. It also may have a connection to the ruins in the Andes mountain range that we'd discussed."

"Those are connected?" I couldn't believe my ears. The subject of the ruins had only come up because I'd noticed a painting in the pawn shop, and it reminded me of a favorite book I'd had as a child. I couldn't even remember the name of it. I just recalled being fascinated with the chapters on volcanoes, ruins, and mountains in South America. Odd how that book was one of the few memories I had of my childhood. "What a weird coincidence."

Tristan smiled. "I don't think it's a coincidence at all."

"You don't believe in coincidences?" I asked.

He shook his head. "Not in Havenwood Falls."

My eyebrows drew together in confusion.

"Hey, guys," Bianca interrupted. "How about we start a fire?"

"Sounds good. I'll grab some wood from the bin." Tristan moved to stand, but I stopped him.

"Please, allow me. It's the least I can do for such an amazing meal."

Bianca smiled. "That'd be very kind of you."

Tristan pointed to the back door that led from the kitchen. "There's a small shed just outside that door. You'll find plenty of firewood in there."

"Great, I'll be right back." I was happy for the excuse to get some fresh air. My head was spinning from the odd bit of information Tristan had given me. How did my tattoo and South American ruins connect?

I shut the kitchen door behind me and inhaled sharply. Havenwood Falls had clean, crisp air, and I greatly appreciated that. Even the air in the bars was less stale and putrid. I allowed myself another deep breath, and then I walked to the shed. The door was unlatched and slightly ajar. With caution, I slowly opened it. Then the smell of whiskey hit me, mixed with a floral scent that I instantly recognized as Jetta's.

I leaned against the door jamb and crossed my arms. "Do you always sneak drinks in the woodshed?"

She jumped. "Damn you. You scared the hell out of me."

"Maybe you shouldn't be skulking in your brother's backyard."

"I'm not . . ." She put her thumb to her temple and rubbed it. "I needed a break."

"So your idea of a break is hiding in the dark, drinking whiskey, surrounded by dead trees. Lovely. I now know what to get you for Christmas."

"You're an asshole." She threw back the last of her drink and sat the cup on a small pile of wood near the door.

I entered, blocking her only exit. "You know what I think?"

She shook her head. "I don't care what you think."

I ignored her. "I think you're out here because you're avoiding me."

She huffed. "Don't flatter yourself."

"I'm just stating facts." I continued to smile at her. She was so fun to rile up.

"You are in my way. Move." She put her hands out to physically move me, then thought better of it. "Please."

I couldn't help it. I had to push her buttons. "So, you're not scared of me at all."

"Not a bit," she countered.

"Then move me." I stood my ground.

"What? That's stupid. Just step back and let me by." She glared at me.

Instead of stepping back, I stepped closer to her.

"Wrong way, moron." She reached out and pushed me back one step.

I felt her tense up as her hands lingered on my chest. In the next moment, I had her back against the wall, my arms on either side of her shoulders.

"Why are you fighting this?" I whispered.

She looked up at me, and her hands slowly lowered to her sides. "I'm not fighting anything."

Her eyes were focused on my chin.

"Can you look me in the eye and tell me you don't feel anything between us?" I stared down at her.

She raised her eyes to mine and took in a shaky breath. "No."

Her hands slid up my chest, and she hooked them behind my neck. I stepped closer, and she pulled me down to her.

When my lips met hers, a rush of electricity pulsed through me. My blood heated, and my skin became over-sensitized. Every touch made me crazier than the one before. I wanted to be closer to her. I needed to be a part of her in every way.

I slid my hands to her ass and squeezed. She pulled herself up, wrapping her legs around my waist. I pressed her into the wall and ground against her. I was consumed by my need for her.

She reached a hand between us and slid it down my stomach.

Once she reached my waistband, I felt her pop the button of my jeans. I groaned into her mouth as I felt the jerky movements of her fingers working my zipper.

"Aunt Jetta? Are you out here?" Zoey's voice drifted through the doorway.

Jetta gasped and pushed me away. "Oh no." She hissed. "Zip your pants up. Hurry." She worked to straighten her clothes.

I turned my back to the door and quickly buttoned my jeans.

"Damn it," I muttered.

"Uh, yeah. I'm in here." Jetta glanced at me quickly to be sure I was decent.

The door swung open wide, and Zoey stood on the other side.

"Hey, sweetie," Jetta said. "We're just, uh . . ."

"Getting wood for the fire." I turned to Jetta. "Do you think one armload is enough? Or should we both grab a load?"

"Our fireplace is big, but it isn't that big," laughed Zoey.

"Good point, short stuff. Two loads would be overkill." Jetta pulled her into a quick hug. "Let's let Conrad handle that, and we'll go find the cake your mom made."

I grabbed a stack of wood and followed them into the house.

CHAPTER 9

JETTA

I kept my distance from Conrad the rest of the evening. We'd almost made a huge mistake. Despite my attraction, I didn't trust him. He'd shown up out of nowhere and within days had integrated himself into our lives. I didn't know why Simon and Tristan seemed to like him so much, but I refused to let my guard down. I'd never claimed to be a romantic. And while I could understand lust easily enough, when Conrad kissed me, it felt like he'd been expecting so much more than I was willing to give. More than I was *able* to give.

He was human. And even if I were to decide I wanted a soul mate, I didn't think it would ever work. I adored the humans in my life. My sister-in-law was a blessing from above. Jordan made Zoey extremely happy. But I didn't think I had what it took to spend my life with another person, dragon or otherwise. Not to mention that my instincts told me something wasn't quite on the level where Conrad was concerned. But my instincts hadn't always been correct. Could I have been so wrong about Conrad? Was I denying myself his touch simply because I'd had a few bad experiences?

I excused myself early and went back to the inn. Visions of my encounter with Conrad played on repeat in my head. I didn't want to think about him. I needed to rid myself of this odd obsession, so a friendship with him would be possible and a relationship wouldn't be tempting. At least then I wouldn't be on high alert every time I saw him. But I was worrying for nothing, right? He was only here for a short time.

I approached my room and noticed my door was slightly cracked. I knew I'd locked up behind me. Panic ripped through my chest as I entered the room and found it had been ransacked.

I went straight to the bed and flipped up the mattress. It landed with a thud against the opposite wall. The lockbox was gone.

"Damn it all to hell!" I shouted.

I slammed the door shut behind me as I stomped down the stairs and into the lobby. Sindi had just hung up the phone as I reached the check-in desk.

"Have you seen that little squid-faced pile of shit in here tonight?" I asked.

Sindi's brow raised. "You'll have to be more specific. I know a few who fit that description."

"Bradly Russo." I put my hands on my hips and tapped my foot with impatience. I needed to find him fast.

"Oh, that little squid-faced pile of shit. Yeah, he was here not twenty minutes ago." She pointed to the door. "He left, heading toward the square."

"Thanks." I ran out the door and looked around. A few people milled about the square, but the hour was late enough that most of the normal nighttime crowds had thinned out.

"Looking for someone?" Conrad's voice was amused.

"You have a talent for knowing the worst possible time to talk to me," I muttered. "Why aren't you still at my brother's?" I continued to scan the area, hoping to catch a glimpse of Bradly.

He shrugged. "I was worried about you. We didn't get to talk after making out, and I wanted to be sure you were okay."

I rolled my eyes. "Why do men assume that women are so fragile that they can't handle their emotions after sex?"

"I never said that. I said I wanted to be sure you were okay. You seemed pretty mad at me." He grimaced. "And we didn't have sex, although I'm still up for it, if you are."

"I don't really have time for this right now." I ran across the street to the square, trying to determine which way Bradly might have gone.

Conrad's heavy steps were right behind me. "What are you looking for?"

I ran my hands through my hair in frustration. "Someone stole something from me. I know who did it, and I need to find him. Now."

Conrad's face changed from amusement to concern. "What did he take?"

"A lockbox," I said. "It had some family heirlooms in it. I can't lose them."

He nodded. "How can I help?"

I frowned. The last thing I wanted was to owe Conrad, but we could cover more ground quicker if we split up. "You take the south side of the square and then the west. I'll take the east side and move to the north. We'll meet on the corner. Ask people if they've seen Bradly Russo, and if so, which way he went. They'll know who you mean."

He nodded. "One problem."

"What?" I sighed.

"I don't know who he is. I might walk right past him." Conrad had a point.

"You can't miss him. Dark hair, beady eyes, short and plump. He looks like a pale Oompa Loompa."

"Wow, that's quite a description," he said.

"It's mostly accurate," I replied.

"Okay then, see you at the corner."

Conrad followed Main Street as I made my way up Eleventh. I peeked my head between buildings and in doorways, hoping someone had seen him, or that I would spot him. Nothing. Once I reached City Hall, I ran into an elderly man I'd seen a time or two at Coffee Haven. I couldn't remember his name, but he'd always been friendly.

"Hi." I approached him. "Would you happen to have seen a friend of mine? He's short, dark hair and eyes, kinda round—"

The man nodded. "Yeah, I just saw a guy like that running up Eighth Street with a box in his hands."

"Thank you!" I shouted as I sprinted toward Eighth. Conrad must have seen me running because he followed me. I ran almost three blocks before realizing I was near Havenwood Heights.

"Fuck!" I kicked a tree and shouted again. "Son of a bitch."

Conrad jogged up behind me, only slightly out of breath. "Did you see him?"

"No. I was told he went this way." I looked around and then remembered that Bradly used to have a small shack out in the wooded area that stood between the back of Sun and Moon Academy and Alverson Road. "I think I know where he is."

I jogged back the way we'd come, pacing myself a little better than the first time. I needed to reach my Jeep and find his place before he figured out a way to open the lockbox.

Conrad kept up, and when we reached my Jeep, he climbed in the passenger seat.

"Really, you don't need to help," I said.

"I want to. I promise not to put my hands on you."

I glanced at him with skepticism.

He grinned. "Or my lips. Or any other part of my body."

I felt a smirk coming on. It wouldn't help my cause if he realized he could make me laugh. I cleared my throat and started the car. "Fine."

I backed out and hauled ass across Main until I hit Fourth, then drove north until Fourth became Alverson Road. As we neared the edge of town, Conrad spoke up.

"So, what's in this box that's so important?" he asked.

"I told you, family stuff." I pulled into a small cutout near some trees and cut the engine.

"What kind of family stuff?" He was annoyingly curious.

"A salad shooter," I said and hopped out of the car.

"A what?" His voice held disbelief.

"Haven't you ever seen a salad shooter?" I asked. "They're hard to find, and this one is special." I knew he heard the sarcasm in my voice.

"What, was this one passed down from Thomas Edison?" He crossed his arms as he approached me.

"Exactly. He invented them." I was no longer paying attention to

AMY HALE

him. I was mentally plotting out the land and trying to remember exactly where that little weasel's hideout was.

I glanced at Conrad, who now stood at the edge of the tree line, looking into the dark expanse of the forest. I needed to shift. Making good time was critical. I also had a better chance of spotting the shack from the air.

"Hey, Conrad, would you mind looking in the back of my Jeep for some flashlights? I'm pretty sure I have some in there somewhere. We don't want to head out into that copse of trees without them."

He nodded and jogged to the door. Once he'd crawled in back, I took off at a run. I didn't have time to undress, and for a brief moment, Zoey's idea of Velcro clothes came to mind. Maybe she was on to something there. I allowed myself to shift as I ran, my clothes tearing from my body and falling to the forest floor. Being naked later would suck, but I'd worry about that when the time came.

I remembered there was a small clearing up ahead, so I pushed my way through and then stretched my wings. With a few powerful flaps, I was high in the air. Activating my camouflage, I started circling the area, diving here and there to move in for a closer look as I expanded my radius. For a few minutes, all I saw were trees. My vision wasn't as sharp at night, so I was having to move slower than I liked to.

Then I saw and smelled a small trail of smoke coming from what appeared to be leaves and branches. It had to be Bradly. I made a light landing and slowly pushed my way to the spot where his shack was hidden. He'd covered the roof to match the forest floor, and if it hadn't been for the fireplace, I probably would have missed it.

I shifted back to my human form and crept to the door. I listened but could only hear light humming. It sounded as if he were alone. That would sure make it easier.

I glanced down at my naked body. "Well, Bradly, get ready for a thrill. It might be the last thing you ever see," I whispered.

I pulled the door open slightly, trying to be as quiet as possible. The candles and glow of the small fireplace gave off a dim light. Bradly had his back to the door and was bent over a small table. His humming was off-key as he fidgeted with whatever was in front of

68

him. I could only assume he was working on my lockbox, or rather, Brandt's lockbox.

One glance around the room revealed that he spent a lot of time there. Rickety wood walls were lined with shelves containing pots, pans, canned goods, and dishes. A small mattress was nestled in one corner of the room, blankets thrown haphazardly on top. Dirt covered every inch of the floor, and I couldn't tell if it was truly a dirt floor, or if he was just a disgusting pig. My money was on pig. The beat-up wooden table he worked at sat in the middle of the room.

All dragons had a special gift, and mine was stealth. It helped me in both my human and dragon forms. A light step allowed me to sneak in and out of my father's house many times as a teen. My ninja-like gifts had made me popular with the seedy crowd, such as Bradly and his ilk, when I'd been dumb enough to lend my services. Since fae possessed keen senses, I relied heavily on that gift now as I snuck inside the shack.

I tiptoed behind Bradly until I was only a couple of feet away.

His head popped up, and he stopped singing. He sniffed the air, his body appearing stiff and on alert.

"Hey, asswipe, that doesn't belong to you."

He gasped and turned around, the lockbox clutched firmly in his hands. Then he looked at me and dropped it on the ground. I let him take in an eyeful. It wouldn't matter what he saw once I'd fed him to one of my friends—or ate him myself. That thought almost made me gag. Friends it was.

"Uh . . . how'd you . . ." He gawked, staring at my womanly body parts. Parts he'd probably only ever seen in pictures. "You're naked."

"Yep, and you're dead." I stepped forward, and he lunged for the box, landing on top of it. I grabbed him and held him up in the air, the box dangling from his fingers.

"Let go, and I might have mercy on you."

He gasped and twisted, trying to wrench free. "No, I need the ring!"

"What?" I asked.

"You wouldn't let me finish telling you. I need the ring! I want out of this town. I can't be followed." He grunted as I dropped him.

"That's all you wanted?" I asked, still not sure I believed him. "How do you know there is a ring?"

He rubbed his lower back and stood up. "Because Ani told me about it. She said she gave you a ring, so you could leave town without a trace."

I glowered at him. "Ani should really keep her mouth shut. If the Court finds out about her shenanigans, they'll string her up by her toes."

Bradly nodded, then resumed staring at my naked torso.

"Do you have a blanket or something I can cover up with?"

He shook his head.

"Fine, give me the damn box."

He handed it to me, and I turned from his view. I punched in the code and heard the lid click open. When I turned back around, I found he'd been staring at my ass.

I held the ring out to him. "Here, take it." I snapped the box shut. "But if you ever tell anyone where it came from, I will deny it. It'll be your and Ani's word against mine. I'm not the town saint, but they'll all believe me before they believe you, got it?"

He nodded.

"Great, now I don't ever want to see your grubby little face again."

I turned—to see Conrad standing in the doorway. His jaw hung open, and his eyes shifted from me to Bradly, then to me again.

"Oh, dear goddess," I groaned. This just became way worse.

He held my shredded clothes in his hands. "What the hell happened?" He glanced at Bradly. "Are you having sex with this troll? Is this why you keep shutting me out?"

"Hey now, there's no need to be nasty." Bradly bristled.

The very idea. I started laughing. I know I should have been embarrassed and angry, but goddess help me, I started laughing.

Conrad looked at me like I was a lunatic, which made me laugh even more. Behind me, Bradly released a nervous laugh, and Conrad shot him a look that could have turned him to stone.

Bradly stopped his laughter abruptly and said, "I need to get out of town. Now. Please leave."

"My, we are in a hurry," I drawled. "What did you do this time?"

"Nothing. Go away." His face pinched together in frustration.

I shrugged as I turned and walked toward Conrad. The lockbox was in my hand as my other reached for the clothes he held. Once I'd stepped outside the door, I sat the box on a stump and examined what remained of my jeans and sweater.

Conrad stood behind me, and I could feel his eyes on me. The urge to laugh faded, and now I was acutely aware of his nearness. Of the fact that I was naked in front of the man I so desperately wanted but should never touch.

His warm hand brushed the back of my neck, and I froze, unsure of his next move. I felt his breath for a brief moment, then his lips touched the spot where my spine and shoulders met. His warmth spread through me, and I closed my eyes. Then his jacket was placed around me.

"Zip it up," he ordered.

I turned to face him, my emotions in turmoil as I followed his command. He handed me the lockbox, then looked down at my bare legs and feet. "I'm not gonna ask right now, but I will eventually."

Then without another word he picked me up and carried me out of the forest.

CHAPTER 10

CONRAD

I needed a stiff drink and a very cold shower. I had no idea what the hell I'd stumbled upon in the forest, but it would take a hell of a lot of booze to erase it from my mind. No, scratch that. I'd go to my grave with the vision of Jetta's gorgeous body engraved in my brain. It wasn't fair for a woman to be that alluring. The need for her was already suffocating me, and seeing her naked only intensified that desire to claim her.

"This is not going as planned," I muttered under my breath as I drove us back to the inn.

"What was that?" Jetta asked from the passenger side of the Jeep. Her long, shapely legs were tucked under her as she leaned against the door.

"Nothing. I'm just tired." I glanced at her. "It's been a weird day."

She nodded. "You're telling me."

I found a parking spot and turned off the ignition. "Why are you staying here, instead of at your house?"

It frustrated me to know we'd been staying at the same inn since arriving in town and I'd missed it. I must have been losing my touch.

She stretched for a moment, and I caught a glimpse of her thighs. "My dad and I hate each other. I can't stay there anymore."

I nodded in understanding. "You don't have your own place?"

"Not at the moment. I refuse to buy anything with Daddy's money. When I buy a house, I want it to be something I've earned." She opened the door and stepped out, taking the lockbox with her.

I exited as well and walked around to her side of the Jeep. "Do you think you're decent enough to walk into the lobby?"

She looked down at the jacket that hit just below the top of her thighs. "Close enough."

I motioned for her to lead the way. "Age before beauty."

She snorted. "You have no idea."

We stepped into the blissfully empty lobby. She hurried up the stairs, and I was only a few steps behind her, trying not to look but enjoying the view as the hem of the jacket rose and fell with each step.

We reached her room, and I gauged its distance from mine. There were only seven rooms on the second floor, and I was at the end of the hall, so the walk to my door would take less than a few seconds. I gave myself a mental shake. No matter what I saw or what we'd done so far, she was still closing me off. Not just sexually, but even personal discussions were off limits. I needed to remove the intimacy idea from my mind. Besides, that's not what I came here to do. Not exactly anyway.

"Well, good night, Jetta," I said softly, before pulling out the key to my own room.

She put her hand on my arm and stepped closer. "Thank you, Conrad. You went above and beyond tonight. I appreciate it." She tilted up on her toes and gently pressed her lips to mine.

I studied her face as she pulled back, and she gave me a genuine smile. Something stabbed at my heart.

"Anytime." I walked to my end of the hall, and just as I unlocked my door, I turned to see her watching me from her own doorway. I smiled at her. "By the way, that dream-catcher tattoo on your hip is pretty hot."

Her mouth popped open, then shut just as quickly. I chuckled as I closed my own door.

∾

MY DREAMS WERE FILLED with images of Jetta. Naked. Not that I hadn't imagined her that way before, but the truth was so much better than my imagination. I'd spent the morning trying to think of anything but her, which was difficult since she was the reason I was there. I now knew she had the box, but getting it from her could be tricky. If I could convince her to give it back, maybe Brandt would be content enough to let her punishment slide. But last night proved Jetta was willing to do whatever it took to keep the items she'd stolen. There wasn't anything about completing this job that was going to be easy.

I parked my truck down the street and watched her Jeep. Once she left, I could break into her room and grab the box. Then I'd try to negotiate with Brandt. With any luck, she'd be left out of it completely. Brandt would recover his belongings, and Jetta would never know what happened. I was being selfish, but I didn't want her to ever learn the truth of my visit to Havenwood Falls. I'd like to leave her on good terms. I wasn't sure why that really mattered to me, but it did. If Brandt couldn't accept that outcome, well . . . I'd received my twenty-five thousand. I'd just have to make that work. I wasn't going to force her to do anything she didn't want to do, including going back to Atlanta.

By noon, I was about to give up on the idea that she might leave her room. Just as I'd started to work out a new plan, I saw her exit the inn, with the box under her arm. *Shit.*

She pulled away in her Jeep, and I did my best to follow at a discreet distance. Once we left the residential areas behind, I became suspicious.

She pulled up to a small trail and parked at the entrance. I hung back so she wouldn't notice me. I watched as she stepped out of the Jeep with the box and started up the trail. I pulled over enough that I wouldn't be in the road, then I parked and jogged to the footpath she'd just entered.

Jetta hiked her way up the pathway, stopping occasionally to adjust her hold on the box. Then she veered off the well-used trail and tromped through the dense trees. I struggled to stay quiet now that I had branches and leaves underfoot instead of a dirt road. I moved slowly, keeping her in sight as much as possible without getting too close.

After about fifteen minutes, she'd arrived at a beautiful little lake with a small waterfall at one edge. I held my breath as I witnessed her walk the treacherous looking stone steps to the edge of the falls. She adjusted the box once more, then stepped forward and disappeared into a dark cavern.

I frowned. She didn't just disappear into the darkness. It's more like she was swallowed by it.

I took cautious steps as I neared the stairs. Once there, I realized they were actually wide and sturdy. I moved slowly, giving myself a moment to pause before advancing to the next step. As I moved closer, the stone surface became shiny from the mist coming off the waterfall. At the last step, I looked around for a good hiding place, should I need it. I saw a narrow indention behind some foliage and decided that would have to do in a pinch.

The mouth of the cave was incredibly dark. More so than seemed possible. I stepped around the corner and into the darkness. From the outside, the cave seemed small, but once I passed what could only be properly described as a veil of endless midnight, the space grew substantially. It was impossible, yet there was more light in the back of the cave than there was at the entrance.

I listened for Jetta but heard nothing. I stayed close to the outer wall as I took my time inching toward the back. I neared another small doorway and froze. I could hear someone moving around. I slowly poked my head around the door and caught a glimpse of a shimmering dirt wall before everything went black.

My head throbbed as if someone were using it as a bass drum. The sunshine above temporarily blinded me. I reached for my forehead and winced at the large knot above my left eyebrow. Once my vision cleared and the world stopped spinning around me, I managed to pull myself up into a sitting position. I'd been laid out flat on the bank next to the partially frozen waterfall. Jetta sat on a log at the edge of the tree line, watching me.

"Why are you following me?" Her expression was pure anger.

"It's a long story," I said.

She crossed her arms. "I have time."

I needed to think of something quick. "I was worried about that creepy troll guy getting to you."

She raised one eyebrow. "I don't think so."

"You don't?" I had no idea where to take my lie from there.

"No." She stood and then crouched down in front of me. Her eyes searched mine. "How did you get into my cave?"

"Uh . . ." I was the one hit on the head, so why was she asking the stupid question? "I walked in."

"How?" she asked again.

I looked down at my legs, wondering if I'd somehow overlooked an inability to use them that I didn't know about.

"With my legs," I replied slowly.

She stood and paced. "That's not what I mean."

"I have no idea what you're asking me, then." I tried to stand, but I was still a bit wobbly on my feet and needed a nearby tree to steady me. "What the hell did you hit me with?"

"A shovel," she said absentmindedly, then turned and looked me in the eyes again, as if she were trying to drive a point home. "Only very specific people can enter that cave. Very specific." She stared at me as if she were waiting for something. "Are you going to tell me your secret? It's not like I don't already know."

I felt my throat close. She knows I'm after the box? After her? "Listen, it wasn't my intention to deceive you. I was going to tell you the whole truth once I figured things out."

"Why does everyone say that *after* they are caught lying?" She still watched me closely.

"I couldn't tell you, yet." I didn't know how to explain my feelings and all that had happened over the last three days. Had it really only been three days? It felt like I'd known her forever.

She let out a harsh laugh. "This is Havenwood Falls, Conrad. People like us, we don't have to hide from each other. It's safe here."

"People like us?" I asked. Now I was really lost.

"Oh, you stubborn man." She kicked a fallen branch. "What clan did you originate from?"

"Clan?" I asked again.

"Are you a parrot? Why do you keep repeating my questions?"

"Because they aren't making any damn sense," I shot back, pain in my head stirring up my irritation.

"This." She pointed to the tattoo on her neck.

"Your dragon tattoo," I said.

She nodded.

I shrugged, still clueless.

"Only dragons can enter that cave!" she shouted as she pointed in the direction of the falls.

"Dragons? What is that, some kind of club?" I stretched my back, feeling every spot that had been stabbed by rocks and twigs as I lay on the forest floor.

She stepped closer and took my hand. The friction that existed between us flared to life. "I'm one too, Conrad. It's okay."

I was really getting tired of this odd conversation. "One what?"

"A dragon, just like you."

CHAPTER 11

JETTA

*D*amn, this man was thick. Didn't he realize he was surrounded by the supernatural? Didn't he realize he was safe here? It all made sense. Why he clicked with Simon and Tristan instantly. Why he and I had such chemistry. He wasn't a frost dragon, but he was a dragon shifter of some kind. There's no way he could have walked into my cave otherwise. The warding only allowed dragons to enter.

I looked up at his handsome and somewhat battered face. *Oops.* I probably shouldn't have beaned him with the shovel. I'd just finished digging a hole for the lockbox when he'd surprised me. Already in my hand, it made a convenient weapon, so that's how he ended up unconscious on the ground moments later.

I'd made sure I hadn't killed him, then I quickly buried the box. After assuring my secrets were well out of reach of anyone who might want them, I dragged him outside and waited for him to come around. Thankfully, it hadn't taken too long.

I motioned to his head. "I should probably take you to Zoey. She can help with that nasty bump."

"Your teenage niece?" He rubbed the area lightly, and I could see it hurt, even if he was trying to pretend it didn't. "Did she graduate from medical school as a prodigy or something?"

I laughed. "No, it's her tears. That's her gift."

I assumed he knew about dragons having special gifts. Zoey's happened to be that her tears could heal. Her gifts were amazing, but also dangerous. Only other dragons were allowed to know of her ability, as there were many supernaturals that would seek to harvest her for such a powerful endowment.

"Her tears," he repeated. He stepped closer to me, finally having regained his balance. "Are you on drugs or something? I know pot is legal here. How much have you had?"

"I don't smoke pot." I'd tried it once, but, just like alcohol, it didn't do much for dragons unless consumed in large quantities.

"Well, you're on something, because nothing you've said since I woke up is logical."

I frowned. Did I hit him too hard? I gasped. What if I'd damaged his brain and now he couldn't remember everything? *Shit.*

"Never mind. Let's get you home and have a doctor look at that head." I needed to talk to Tristan and find out what to do from there. I had to be sure I hadn't damaged him permanently.

I put my arm around him, and he leaned into me slightly. "Are you gonna be okay to walk?"

He nodded. "I think so."

He wobbled a moment.

"I'll help you, just in case."

He muttered something under his breath, but I didn't catch it. I chose to ignore him and focus on getting him back to the trail where there were fewer obstacles to trip over. It took longer than it normally should, but thankfully it was still early afternoon and we had no reason to rush. This part of the mountain wasn't always the safest place to be at night, even for dragons.

I helped him settle in to the passenger seat, then I held out my hand. "Keys."

"What? Why?" he asked.

"So I can move your truck over here where it's not near the road. It'll get sideswiped if we don't move it."

He shook his head. "Nah, it's okay. Just leave it."

I frowned. "It'll only take a couple of minutes. Give me the damn keys."

"Just take me to the doctor. The truck is fine."

I narrowed my eyes at him. "Why don't you want me in your truck?"

He sighed. "I just want to get my head looked at, okay?"

Guilt forced me to give up. He was suffering because of my actions, although to be fair, he shouldn't have been stalking me.

I sat in the driver's seat and turned the engine over. Trees flew by as we sped back into town. I didn't know the first thing about amnesia, but I figured the sooner he received care, the better.

"What do you think, Tristan?" I asked. I'd been pacing in the living room, my hands sore from wringing them as I walked.

"I think it's an odd situation," he stated.

"Odd how?"

"He doesn't recall his childhood at all, except a few things here and there. He says he was orphaned and doesn't have any living family. But I believe you're right, Jetta. He's a dragon shifter. I'm just not sure he remembers it."

"Oh no. I didn't mean to hit him that hard."

"I'm not convinced it was you," Tristan replied. "He'd told me about being orphaned the first day I met him. We'd discussed some ruins in Peru that he'd been infatuated with as a child, which led to us talking about childhood in general. He hadn't fully opened up, but he had told me his family was all gone."

I glanced at the spare bedroom Conrad was currently resting in.

Tristan motioned for me to follow him, and he pulled a book from one of his shelves. The same book he and Conrad had been poring over the night before. "That symbol Conrad was so interested in is here."

I recognized the triskele. It matched the ring in the pawn shop, with the exception that this one was comprised of jagged black lines.

"It turns out some clans added their own personal touches to these to represent their family line. I've seen a lot of varieties. The fire represents lava dragons."

I took a moment to roll the info around in my head. "So, Conrad is a lava dragon?"

Tristan shrugged. "That's my guess."

"But he doesn't remember it," I stated.

"Again, just my guess."

"Wow. This is heavy." I wasn't sure how to process it all. "Wait, how can he not know? Wouldn't he have shifted a few times?"

"Yeah," Tristan said, "there is that." He glanced at me, and his brows drew together. "What if he has something on him that prevents him from shifting?" He nodded at my neck. "We have magic infused tattoos. Maybe he has something similar?"

That made sense. He did have a lot of tattoos. It could be any one of them. Or maybe a piece of jewelry.

"It just seems so crazy that he wouldn't have a clue. When I mentioned dragons, he looked at me like I'd lost my mind."

"As far as he's concerned, dragons are just fantasy creatures in books and movies." Tristan ran a hand through his hair.

"So, what do we do?" I wasn't good with delicate situations. And while I wouldn't label Conrad as delicate, this whole secret dragon thing would have to be handled carefully.

"I think for now we go on as if we know only as much as he does. Play it by ear until we see the need to change that strategy."

The door to the guest room opened, and Conrad walked out. The knot on his head had started to turn a sickly yellowish-green. *Why wasn't he starting to heal already?* Most shifters healed faster than humans. This situation confused me.

"Hey, how are you feeling?" I asked.

"I'll survive." He took a swig from the water bottle in his hand.

"Good." I couldn't seem to find anything else to say, so I kept my mouth shut.

"Would you like me to drop you off at your truck?" Tristan asked.

"That'd be perfect. Thank you." Conrad looked down at his shirt, as if he were assuring himself it was properly buttoned up.

"I could take you, if you want." I didn't understand why I felt so guilty. I wasn't totally to blame. Besides, we might never have learned about his dragon gene had he not wandered into the cave.

"I'll go with Tristan, but thank you." His tone was hard, and I could tell he was upset with me. I probably deserved it . . . a little. But I refused to waste too much time feeling remorse. We were both at fault.

Tristan followed Conrad out the door. Before closing it behind him, he turned to me and smiled. "It'll all work out fine. You'll see."

I hoped he was right. My life always seemed to be unnecessarily complicated.

CHAPTER 12

CONRAD

S ilence hung in the air during the trip from Tristan's home to the spot where I'd parked my truck. I'd refused to see a doctor, and Tristan had expressed his concern over that. He was a nice guy and genuinely cared about people. It's one of the reasons he was so easy to like. I couldn't say I'd ever clicked with a friend as quickly as I did with him, which was a nice change from my usual routine of isolation. I worked alone, and I lived alone. All my adult life, I'd only known a solitary existence. My earliest memories were of growing up in foster care, moving from one family to the next, but never settling anywhere. I'd always assumed that I was destined to be a rambler.

We pulled up behind my truck, and I dug my keys out of my pocket. "Thanks, Tristan. I appreciate the ride, the injury care . . ." I gestured to my head. "All of it."

"You're welcome." He smiled.

I opened the car door and climbed out of the seat.

"Hey, Conrad." Tristan leaned across the seat and looked up at me. "Don't be too upset with Jetta. She's been through a lot over the years. She may seem like a lunatic at times, but I promise she has her reasons for the things she does."

I nodded. "I'll keep that in mind."

I shut the door, and he waved as he pulled onto the roadway. I stood by my driver door until he was out of sight, then put my keys back in my pocket. I knew the box was in that cave, and I still had a job to do.

It only took me about twenty minutes to find the spot where the trail veered from the direction of the cave. The sun was starting to set, and the only flashlight I had was on my phone, so I needed to make this quick.

I retraced my previous steps and entered the cave with less trepidation than before. I turned on the flashlight app from my phone and immediately went to the room Jetta had been in before she'd knocked me out. My head still throbbed where she'd hit me, but the ibuprofen I'd taken was helping.

After stepping into the larger room, I took a moment to appreciate the sheer magnitude of the cavern. The space was enormous, and you'd never know from the outside that something so massive lay behind the small waterfall.

As I moved the light around the room, it glinted off a wall on the opposite side, and I moved closer to inspect it. The sides of the cavern were embedded with a smattering of rocks. There appeared to be crystals of some sort, but I had no idea what they were. That wasn't my area of expertise.

I shined my light toward the floor, looking for any signs of the box. Nothing. I supposed she could have taken it back to her car while I was out cold, but I doubted it. I didn't remember seeing it as she drove me back to town. My gut told me she'd left it in the cave.

She'd said she hit me with a shovel, so there was a good possibility she'd been digging. I started searching for areas in the dirt that had been freshly excavated. Sure enough, there was a spot toward the back of the room that had been dug up and repacked.

I located the offending shovel and put it to work. In minutes, I had the lockbox in my possession.

"You've caused a lot of trouble," I said as I inspected the metal box. The digital keypad and display were covered in dirt from where she'd buried it so haphazardly. It puzzled me that she hadn't put it in something to protect it. Unprotected electronics encased in the earth would eventually ruin the circuits.

I wiped it clean with my sleeve and looked it over one last time before repacking the dirt and putting the shovel back where I'd found it. With any luck, she'd never know I took it. At least, not until I was long gone, and this fiasco was behind me.

The thought of leaving Havenwood Falls was a tad bittersweet. I had things to attend to back in Atlanta, before I could move on with my life, but the little canyon was starting to grow on me in the short time I'd been there.

I tucked the box under my jacket and left the cave. Time to call Brandt and make a deal.

~

CELL SERVICE once again proved to be a challenge. I'd decided to just send him a text message, knowing it'd go through when my phone eventually caught a signal. I was ready for a hot shower and a warm bed. My mind flashed to Jetta. A certain willing woman would have been welcome as well, but the reality was that no matter how much I wanted her, avoiding that complication was for the best. I'd already made things difficult by becoming too invested in her. It's why I wanted to amend the deal we'd made to bring her back. She was happy here. Brandt would have his box back. All's well that ends well. I'd be fine taking less payment if it meant he'd leave her alone.

I stashed the box inside my duffel bag and shuffled to the bathroom to start the shower. I let it run while I brushed my teeth, then stepped beneath the hot water and sighed. The feeling was heaven on my sore muscles.

Once I'd washed, the exhaustion from the day hit me hard. I couldn't wait to fall into that bed. I wrapped the towel low around my hips and left the bathroom.

"Well, that's a new look. I hadn't pegged you as a skirt kinda man." Jetta's voice startled me.

"Holy shit," I barked. "How'd you get in here?" I quickly shifted my glance to my duffel bag, assuring it had been undisturbed.

"The door was unlocked." She reclined on the bed, her legs crossed in front of her. "I did knock. When you didn't answer, I got worried."

I gave her a knowing smirk. "You were worried about me? That's sweet."

Jetta released a sigh. "Don't make it weird. You could have a concussion. I just wanted to check on you."

"Uh huh," I said, letting her know I didn't believe that was the only reason she was there. "So, you being here, on my bed, while I'm in nothing but a towel. That's you checking on my wellbeing and has absolutely nothing to do with you wanting me."

She frowned. "Why do you have such a dirty mind?" she grumbled.

I stepped closer to her. "Why do you constantly elicit dirty thoughts?"

"So, you're blaming me for your perversions now?" She scooted off the bed and stood in front of me.

"I'm blaming your dream-catcher tattoo."

She grinned. "It is pretty spectacular."

I stepped closer, no longer caring why I shouldn't touch her. "So are you."

Jetta said nothing, but I could feel her shiver from where I stood. Every time I tried to deny that there was something unusual between us, something else would happen that proved me wrong. I could feel her around me. She gave off an energy that drew me in like a magnet. The more time I spent with her, the stronger it grew. I was now at a place where I could no longer resist. I wanted her. Needed her. To hell with Brandt and his money. To hell with my promise to avoid complications. This woman was complicated as hell, and I wanted to be lost in that forever.

"Jetta," I whispered, and her eyes locked with mine. "I want you."

Her lips parted, and she inhaled a deep breath. "I want you, too."

I pulled her to me and kissed her, funneling all my pent-up need into that one action. Breaking my lips from hers, I trailed kisses down her neck. My blood heated as I ran my hands over her body, savoring each curve. She put her arms around my neck and pulled at my hair. I picked her up and carried her to the bed, carefully laying her down before covering her body with mine.

Her lips explored my collarbone as I blindly worked the buttons on her shirt. I pulled back, so I could see what I was doing, and she closed her eyes, tilting her head back. She was so damn beautiful. She was everything I never knew I wanted in a woman. Smart, independent, sexy. And I was about to make her mine.

My body screamed for me to hurry up, but my mind suggested I be sure she understood the ramifications of what we were about to do. This was more than just sex. The feeling that she was made just for me became an incessant pounding in my head. *Mine. Mine. Mine.*

I realized then that if we took this step, I could never walk away. And I needed to be sure we were on the same page.

"Jetta," I whispered near her ear as I kissed up her jawline. "We should talk."

"No," she moaned. "We can talk after." I felt her hand slide between us, her fingers pulling at my towel that had somehow managed to stay on during our tumble to the bed.

"Baby, I'm serious. Before this goes any further, we need to talk expectations." I kissed her lips just as she found my hard length and squeezed. Anything I'd wanted to say fled my brain.

"Conrad." She raised her head up and lightly bit my earlobe. "Shut up and make me scream your name."

Loud banging on the door broke us out of our desire-fueled frenzy.

"What the hell?" I muttered. "Go away!"

The banging started again, but this time even more insistent.

"This had better be important," I said, "or someone is dead."

I grabbed my jeans and slipped them on, glancing at Jetta as she quickly buttoned her shirt. When I opened the door, a creepy elderly man with a cane stood on the other side.

"Can I help you?" I said in an annoyed tone. I mean, he did just interrupt what was sure to be some of the hottest foreplay I'd ever had.

"Where is my daughter?" The old man's voice came across as an animalistic growl, and for a moment, I was taken aback.

"Oh, hell no." Jetta's voice was full of fury as she leapt off the bed and joined me at the door. "What do you want?"

"What I want," said the old man, "is for you to stop destroying the family name." He stepped across the threshold and then around us as he moved to sit in the only chair in the room.

Jetta put her hands on her hips. "Conrad, this is my father, Lawrence Mills."

I nodded. "Nice to meet you, sir."

His green eyes met mine, and his bushy eyebrows rose above them as if to say, "Is it really?"

He turned his gaze back to his daughter. "You've been back less than a week and are already in a mess of trouble."

Jetta paled. "I don't know what you're talking about."

He leveled a hard stare at her. "You were seen yesterday morning with Bradly Russo."

She pushed out a breath that resembled relief. "It was nothing. He asked for my help. I said no. We went our separate ways."

"He's dead, Jetta. Rusty Higgins found Bradly's body while patrolling the woods. He'd been torn to shreds."

She gasped. "That's horrible."

Lawrence's expression was grim. "You were the last person seen with him. And you were asking about him last night. He's now dead. And Sheriff Kasun found an unusual ring among his belongings." His eyes narrowed at her. "You wouldn't know anything about a warded ring, would you?"

She put her hands on her hips. "Not a damn thing. Now, you listen to me, you old codger. I did not kill Bradly. He'd told me he was leaving town in a hurry. My guess is he crossed the wrong person one too many times and it finally caught up with him." She pointed a finger at him. "As for the Court, you tell them I don't know shit about any ring and they are barking up the wrong tree."

I watched this odd exchange with interest. Warded ring? The Court? Damn, the people in this town were strange.

"When did he die?" I asked.

Lawrence turned his irritated gaze on me. "They believe late last night."

I nodded. "It couldn't have possibly been Jetta. We were having dinner at Tristan's, then spent the rest of the evening together."

Jetta's eyes quickly shifted to mine in surprise, and I thought I saw a glint of gratitude.

"And I'm supposed to take your word for it?"

The old man had a point. I was a stranger in town, so I wasn't exactly a solid character witness.

"Daddy, do you really think so little of me that you believe I'd kill someone?" Her question obviously held more than what was visible on the surface. There was a hint of pain in her voice.

"Of course not," he snapped. "But that ring is another matter altogether."

She shook her head. "Again, I have no idea what you're talking about."

Lawrence stood and looked me up and down, then spoke to Jetta. "Don't get pregnant. You'd make a lousy mother."

Her mouth went slack, and my muscles became rigid as my fists balled at my sides. What kind of asshole father says something so cold to his daughter?

I felt Jetta's hand on my back. "Let it go. It's not worth the trouble."

Lawrence walked out the door without so much as a goodbye.

CHAPTER 13

JETTA

I should have been used to my father's insults by now, but his words still stung. Conrad's demeanor proved he had never witnessed such contempt for one's offspring before, although in truth, I wasn't biologically Lawrence's daughter.

"Are you okay?" Conrad rubbed his hands up and down my arms in a soothing manner.

"Yeah, I'm used to it." I moved to sit on the bed.

Conrad followed. "So, what's his problem?"

I shrugged. "Me."

"Seriously?"

I nodded. "More or less."

"What a dick." Conrad spat out the words in anger. I was moved that he felt the need to defend me.

I sighed. "My dad and I haven't gotten along in years. He doesn't like my hair, my music, my tattoos. He really hates my piercings." I laughed. "He says I look like a pin cushion." I ran a hand over my face. "But I think it really stems from the fact that I'm adopted. I'm not his actual flesh and blood, so despite taking me in, he doesn't feel I can accurately represent the family."

Conrad frowned as he sat next to me. "That's not fair. It's not your fault."

"No," I said. "It's not. But when I was a teen, I decided I wanted to know who my biological parents were, and he went ballistic. He felt I was ungrateful to be in the prestigious Mills family. My search took me nowhere, but in the process, I spent some time discovering who I really was inside. It led to my pursuit of music and my individuality. Dad really hated that. He feels a woman should be ruled by her father, and then later by her husband. I refused to live under his thumb or by his rules. We've been at odds ever since. I've kinda made it my life's goal to remind him at every turn that he doesn't own me or run my life."

Conrad smiled. "And he hates that."

"So much." I laughed.

"I don't know my parents either." Conrad absentmindedly rubbed his wrist. The same spot where his cuff usually was.

My interest was piqued. Maybe he'd tell me something that would lead to understanding his background and why he'd forgotten it.

"Really? Tell me about it." I leaned against his shoulder, hoping the intimacy would help him relax.

Conrad put an arm around me. "Not much to tell really. I bounced around from foster home to foster home for as long as I could remember. I never seemed to find the right fit. Once I was old enough to be on my own, I started traveling around the country, doing odd jobs."

I reached for his hand and laced my fingers through his. That's when I saw it. The tattoo on the inside of his right wrist.

"Conrad. Your tattoo matches the ring at my brother's shop." The surprise was evident in my voice.

He pulled his hand back. "Yeah. It's weird."

I reached for his hand once more and placed it in my lap, palm up. I traced the lines of the triskele with my fingertips. "When did you get this?"

He shook his head. "I don't remember."

I frowned. "None of this makes sense."

He let out a self-deprecating laugh. "Well, I have made some stupid decisions while I was drunk."

"No," I said. "I mean the ring. The tattoo. Your lack of memories."

He frowned. "Yeah, the ring and tattoo are weird, but I'm not missing memories. My life just hasn't been that memorable."

I shook my head. "There's more to all this. I just haven't figured it out yet."

He turned my face to his. "It's not important."

He kissed me gently, and I felt the tension from the confrontation with my father melt away.

"Listen, about earlier." I ran my fingers over his beard. "I'd love to pick up where we left off, but after hearing about Bradly, I think I'd better go. I need to be sure they aren't trying to pin this on me."

He nodded. "I understand."

"I promise I'll be back." I kissed him again.

"It's late anyway. I should get some sleep. We have tomorrow, right?" he asked.

"We do," I said. "And the next day, and the day after that."

I WENT to my room and made a few phone calls to be sure the Bradly thing had been properly dealt with. All was clear there, as everyone else had come to the same conclusion I did—his past had finally caught up with him. I went to bed knowing that wasn't going to chase me around the rest of my life. The only thing that kept me from a truly good night of rest was this dragon situation with Conrad. There was a connection with his tattoo and the ring. There had to be. If there was anything I'd learned over the years, it's that you needed ties to your past. To align the origins of your existence with who you are now. Somehow, that symbol meant answers for Conrad.

The following morning, I walked into my brother's pawn shop with one purpose in mind. The ring.

"Tristan, I think that ring belongs to Conrad." I crouched down and studied it through the glass case.

"I think it does, too." He was scribbling something on a notepad.

"We need to give it to him," I said.

"I'm fine with that." Tristan crossed his arms. "What are you thinking?"

"I don't know. It's just this gut feeling that he's supposed to be wearing that ring. It's like a family heirloom or something."

I couldn't shake the thought that this was why he was meant to come to Havenwood Falls. This explained why he was able to stumble across our little town.

"Since when did you become so sentimental?" Tristan teased.

I shrugged. "It's not sentiment. It's magic. Or fate. I don't know. You've always told me what's meant to be will be, right?"

He nodded. "I still believe that."

"This ring might just convince me that you're correct."

Tristan handed me the ring, and I examined it closely. The smooth metal was cold to the touch. The embossing was flawless.

"You should be the one to give it to him." Tristan handed me a ring box to keep it in.

Butterflies danced in my stomach at the thought of what his could mean for Conrad. What would happen when he finally put the ring on? Nothing? Everything? A part of me would be terribly disappointed if I were wrong. Maybe I was a *little* sentimental.

"Thanks." I placed the ring in the box and closed the lid.

"Be careful, Jetta. If that is the key to restoring his memories, there is no telling how he'll react."

"Good point. I don't know how it will affect him, but I do know this—Conrad would never hurt me." His integrity and protective nature were two things about Conrad I felt sure of.

CHAPTER 14

CONRAD

I woke up to the buzzing of my phone. The pain in my head had thankfully diminished to a dull ache. I rolled over and looked at the caller ID.

"Hello," I said, my voice still gruff from sleep.

"Well, you're still alive." Brandt's snarky tone came through loud and clear.

"I am. If you don't lose the snark, I won't be able to say the same for you." I was tired. Sore. And had no patience for his asshole behavior.

"Do you always threaten your employers?" He'd gone from sarcastic to pissed.

"Only the ones that treat me like shit." I sat up.

"I've treated you rather well, Conrad, and yet at every turn, you blow me off. I want an update, and it had better be good."

"Fine," I said. "I retrieved your box last night."

"Excellent. It's about time." I could almost hear his conniving grin. "And Jetta?"

"That's a little more complicated," I said. "I have your belongings. It might just be best to let her go."

"No." Brandt's resolve was firm.

"She's not gonna come willingly." I needed to make him see reason.

"Then force her."

"I can't kidnap her." I couldn't believe he was suggesting such a thing.

"Okay, then blackmail her. Remind her that we have the box, and if she knows what's good for her, she'll come back to me quietly."

"What's good for her?" I asked. "What does that mean?" Anger rose in my chest at the very thought of him threatening her.

"That's none of your business. She'll know what it means, and that's all that matters." He hung up without another word.

From the moment I walked into Brandt's office, I'd known he was slime, but there was a lot more to this story than he was telling me. I had to find out what information he'd omitted from his account of that night.

Just as I'd pulled on my jeans, a knock sounded at my door. Shirtless and barefoot, I opened the door to find Jetta on the other side.

I admired the view. "Well, you are a sight for sore eyes."

"Am I?" She looked at my bare chest. "I'd have to say the same about you."

I chuckled and opened the door wider. "Please, come in."

"Actually, I'd like to take you somewhere." She was tapping her fingers on her thighs nervously.

"Okay. Give me a minute to finish getting dressed." I left the door open and grabbed a shirt from the closet. Jetta stood in the doorway and watched me, her eyes following every movement I made. I could feel her gaze even when my back was turned. All she did was stand there, and she was turning me on.

"Okay." I motioned. "After you."

I shut the door behind me and followed her down the steps and out to her Jeep. Once inside, we drove out of town, and I realized she was taking the same road we'd been on the day before.

"Where are we going?" My curiosity was piqued.

"I'm taking you back to my cave." She quickly glanced at me, I assumed to gauge my reaction.

"Okay. Why?" I reached up and felt the slightly smaller knot on my forehead. "It's not like I have good memories there."

She pursed her lips together, and for a moment, I thought she wasn't going to answer. "I hope to change that today. I want to give you good memories."

"Well . . ." I shifted in my seat, so I could face her more. "I like where this is going." I envisioned a blanket on the ground, the waterfall behind us, and Jetta naked underneath me.

"Umm, probably not the direction you're thinking." Her expression was serious.

"Damn. Can we change that? Because the map I was following was pretty hot."

She chuckled. "Maybe afterward."

"After what?" I asked. Now I was really curious.

"You'll see." She gave me a wink.

Before long, we'd reached the trail she'd used to climb to the falls. We walked in silence. Several times I'd wanted to say something, but each time I opened my mouth, I found myself at a loss for conversation. Sometimes silence was a good thing.

We reached the falls, and she led me to the mouth of the cave. "Do you remember my telling you that only special people could enter the cave?"

I nodded, also remembering that I'd entered it again last night and that I now had her box. It dawned on me then that she might be bringing me there to show me the contents of the box. My throat constricted, knowing she'd freak when she learned her hiding place had been discovered.

"I know you thought I was crazy, but I want to show you what I was talking about." She took my hand and led me through the curtain of darkness into the first large room.

My eyes darted around, silently praying she didn't want to enter the larger room, where she'd buried the box.

She lit the wall sconces, and the cave became considerably brighter.

We stood in the middle of the room, and Jetta held up my right hand. Her fingers trailed over the leather cuff.

"May I?" she asked.

I nodded, unsure what the purpose of removing it was.

She unsnapped it and put it in the pocket of her jacket, then she pulled out a ring box.

"Are you proposing to me?" I teased. "Because if so, let me warn you. I'm old-fashioned. I'm all about empowering women, but when it comes to marriage, a man still likes to do things the traditional way now and then."

She rolled her eyes. "Not even close, lover boy."

She opened the ring box and held it out to me. Inside was the ring that matched my tattoo.

I took a step back. "What is this?"

"It's yours, Conrad. Tristan and I firmly believe this is supposed to belong to you." She pushed the ring toward me.

"No." I couldn't. Something about that ring didn't sit right with me. I'd felt sure I'd regret having anything to do with it.

"Conrad," she said softly. "Please, just trust me on this. This ring will be life-changing."

"That's what I'm afraid of," I muttered.

"You're afraid?" She ran a hand down my chest. "My big, bad biker hunk is afraid?"

I swallowed hard. "Yes," I admitted. "And how did you know I'm a biker?"

"It's written all over you." She still had her hand on my chest. I loved feeling her touch me. It calmed and excited me all at once.

"So, I'm a hunk? And I'm yours?" I couldn't resist pointing out her change of heart. Obviously, she'd changed her mind sometime last night while in my room, but this was the first time she'd verbally admitted we might be something more than friends.

"Maybe," she teased. "But before we can explore that, you need to conquer this." She pulled the ring from the box. "Please, Conrad. Trust me."

I stared at the ring for a minute more before nodding my head. She took my right hand and looked into my eyes.

"No matter what happens, remember I am right here beside you. I won't leave."

That sounded ominous. "Okay."

She inspected the ring and then my fingers. She must have determined that the ring would fit best on my ring finger because that's the one she chose and slid it over my knuckles. Then she clasped my hand closed and stepped back.

My hand burned where the ring touched my skin. It traveled to my other fingers, then my palm, then to my wrist. I watched in shock as an odd orange glow followed the fiery path of my black tattoo, as if bringing it to life. The burning I felt on occasion became more like an inferno.

I closed my eyes, and images began to flash through my mind. My mother, her soft brown eyes and round face, appeared before me.

She kissed my forehead and sighed. "I hate to do this, son. But I've been left no choice. I'm dying, and the world can't ever know about you. The only way to protect you is if you forget who you are."

I felt tears run down my cheeks, but I was too lost in the memories to bother wiping them away.

My mother took me to a strange woman's house. The woman said some weird words I didn't understand, and I fell into a trance of sorts. The woman then tattooed my wrist with the triskele.

She handed my mother a small box. "If your situation ever changes, this ring will bring it all back. But for now . . ." She looked at me. "By tomorrow he'll remember nothing of his past. He will be unable to shift into his dragon form. When he comes of age, that tattoo will become visible and will allow him to seek the truth, should he desire it."

My mother hugged me and sobbed. "My sweet Conrad. Please forgive me. I have to let you go so that I may save you."

I sucked in a deep breath. Images of fire and molten rock ran through my mind. The ruins I'd been so obsessed with as a child had been a castle once, a part of our family heritage for centuries, before time and humanity had destroyed it all.

The most terrifying vision of all hit me with such force that it brought me to my knees. My dragon. The beast was fierce and angry. Two long twisted horns jutted from its enormous head. Black scales covered every inch of its body, except the leathery red wings that extended from the shoulder blades and the crest of fire that ran from the top of its head down to the bottom of its neck. The beard matched the crest, tendrils dripping like magma from its chin. Eyes the size of tractor tires stared back at me, the slanted pupils restricting and contracting as if trying to focus. The yellow irises glowed like embers.

I closed my mind to the horrendous beast, not wanting to believe what I was seeing. Then I was racked with a pain unlike anything I'd ever experienced. Bones cracked. Muscles stretched. Skin tore. When I opened my eyes again, I was standing in the cave, my head almost brushing the top of the cavern ceiling. Jetta stood before me, a small human figure with a large smile on her face. *Holy shit! How is this possible? And why isn't Jetta running for her life?*

I bent my head, and she walked toward me. I let out an involuntary snort, and flames shot from my nostrils.

Jetta jumped back. "Whoa, big fella. We're gonna have to get that under control. We can't have you roasting the villagers. Or me."

She stepped closer again, approaching from the right side of my face. Her hand reached out to stroke my scales, and despite our obvious differences, I still felt that spark of desire she'd always sent through me.

My mind reeled. How did I forget I was a lava dragon? Obviously, my mother was hiding me in plain sight, but how was it possible to lose the memories of something so significant? This was a lot to take in, and I knew I'd need time to adjust to finding myself after almost two decades of being lost.

Jetta brought my attention back to her. "Conrad, I'm a frost dragon. This cave is warded so that only dragons can enter."

Jetta's a dragon, too? I felt sure I was losing my mind. A range of emotions rushed through me: loss, anger, confusion, relief. I hated the events that led me to this place in my life, yet I was happy to find my way back to the truth. Elated that I was no longer alone in a world in which I'd felt I'd never belonged.

She quickly removed her clothes. The human side of me was thrilled for the show, but I had no idea what she was doing.

She stepped back and closed her eyes. I watched in fascination as she transformed before me. Beautiful white scales replaced milky porcelain skin. Her silver hair morphed into a crown of horns that surrounded her head and neck. She was only a few feet shorter than I was once she'd fully shifted. She was gorgeous as a human, and gorgeous as a dragon. Her eyes were the same icy blue as in her human form, and I couldn't help but stare into them as I allowed the implication of this transformation to wash over me.

We were both dragons. On opposite ends of the spectrum, but dragons just the same. Our dragon genes recognized each other, long before we did. We were drawn to each other so desperately because we were meant to be each other's mates. She was mine, and I was hers. Now that I'd found where I belonged, and who I belonged to, I was never letting go.

CHAPTER 15

JETTA

*H*e was beautiful. I'd never met a lava dragon, but I'd read about them. Conrad was damn amazing. Simon, on the other hand, was a fire dragon. The distinction was small, but a distinction nonetheless. Lava dragons appeared to be made of the very molten rock they were named after, where fire dragons were more like those you usually read about in fairy tales.

After a few moments of silence and a quick nuzzle of his neck, Conrad used his telepathic communication.

"I need to change back. This is too much, too fast."

"Absolutely," I said. "Just envision your human self, and it'll happen."

He looked down and noticed his clothes were shredded. "Ah, so now that makes sense."

I nodded.

"I might have a problem. I don't have clothes."

I thought about it a moment. "I think I have the solution."

We shifted to humans and ran back to the Jeep as quickly as possible.

Lucky for him, I always carried a change of clothes with me. They were pink sweat pants and a t-shirt, and they looked totally ridiculous on him, but he was thankful to have anything to cover his adorably naked ass. The sweats were snug on his hips, the elastic ankles only reaching mid-calf. He slipped the V-neck tee over his head and worked it down his torso. His muscles stretched the fabric to the point that when he bent over, it ripped up the side.

"Fuck it." He ripped it the rest of the way off and tossed it in the back seat.

"That was pretty hot," I said as I drove us back into town.

He grinned. "You think that's sexy? Wait until we get back to the room, and I rip off these sweats." He turned his eyes to me. "And then it's your turn."

I grinned. "I'm looking forward to that."

"So, tell me about the cave."

"It's been warded so only dragons can enter. My father purchased the cave before the settlement became a town. He knew we'd need someplace we could shift and be ourselves."

Conrad scratched his beard. "Settlement? How old is your dad?"

I smiled. "He's pushing two hundred."

Conrad choked. "He looks pretty good for his age." He paused. "Wait, how old are you?"

"It's rude to ask a woman her age. Lucky for you I don't care. I'm one hundred and two, but everyone thinks I'm twenty-eight."

He coughed. "Well then . . . let's change the subject."

I laughed. "Not into older women?"

He grinned. "Not usually, but I'm totally into you."

"What about you? How old?" It dawned on me he might not be the younger of the two of us.

"My memories are still a little fuzzy, but I believe I'm the age I look, so thirty." He frowned. "I'm gonna have to do some research to be sure."

He looked a little distressed over that lack of knowledge, so I obliged his earlier request and changed the subject. "Did you know our cave has diamonds?"

He shook his head. "Really?"

"Yep, it's where we get some of the family fortune. I'd wager it was another reason my greedy father bought it up before someone else had a chance. He doesn't do anything half-assed. He researches the hell out of every deal he makes." As an aside I threw in, "We don't own the falls, just the cave."

"So, you're loaded and beautiful. I'm a lucky guy." He winked and skimmed his fingers along the back of my neck, sending shivers down my spine.

"You are. And I haven't even had a chance to show you my talents in bed."

He closed his eyes and groaned. "You're killing me, woman."

We pulled up in front of the inn, and I glanced up at the window of my room. "How quickly do you think we can get up there?"

He shrugged. "Not quick enough. I don't want to wait another minute."

We walked into the inn, hand in hand. Conrad was on the receiving end of some odd stares, but we didn't care. We were too lost in each other.

I was amazed at how my life had changed in just a few short days. Weeks ago I was fighting to escape the worst relationship of my life. Now here I stood, next to the man I felt sure was my soul mate. I'd never considered myself the kind of girl who would settle down. But the truth hit me square in the face. The right person can change everything. Not that I was gonna turn into Betty Crocker anytime soon, but for once, I could envision a lifetime spent with someone by my side. Someone who would love, protect, and comfort me. Someone who wouldn't try to change me or fit me into a mold of his choosing. He wanted me just as I was. He was perfect as he was, too. And he was mine. There was no doubt. We'd connected on a level that only dragons could understand. We'd become linked in a way that was deep, meaningful, and beyond the limits of the natural world.

Now that his dragon had emerged, he'd have to register with the Court, but that should be an easy task.

I was truly happy, even with all the other shit life threw at me. I had someone who would stand by my side as I jumped those hurdles that before I'd always had to face alone.

My room was closest to the stairs, but Conrad needed clothes that fit him. I pushed him forward as we treaded the short hallway that led to his door. Conrad swung it open. My blood froze in my veins, and my stomach soured. Brandt Sawyer sat on the overstuffed chair in Conrad's room. The lockbox I'd buried on his lap.

"Hello, sweetheart. I've missed you." Brandt's smile was wide, but the sentiment didn't reach his eyes. He was furious with me.

"How in the hell?" I wanted to run, but my legs wouldn't cooperate. My feet were rooted in place.

I sensed Conrad tense up next to me. I'd have to explain why this strange man was here, sitting on his bed, using terms of endearment toward me. How did he find me? How did he know I'd be with Conrad?

Brandt held up the box, and I felt the bile rise in my throat. "Thanks for your help, Conrad. I couldn't have located this without you."

The words didn't register immediately, but my hand went slack in Conrad's grip.

"Why are you here?" Conrad demanded between clenched teeth.

Brandt stood. "Well, you know what they say. If you want something done right, you have to do it yourself." He handed the box to a large man standing to his left. I assumed the bodyguard-looking buffoon was one of his goons from the bar. "You were taking far too long, Conrad. I didn't pay you to play house."

His stare went straight to our clasped hands.

I stepped back. "Conrad? What is he talking about?"

I was going to be sick. I couldn't believe what I was hearing. I didn't *want* to believe it.

"Jetta, let me explain." Pain filled his expression.

"You son of a bitch." My hurt and anger bubbled to the surface. I couldn't believe I'd let my guard down again. I'd *trusted* him.

"Aw, how touching. You really must have had her going, Conrad. She doesn't usually become so emotional over the men she screws."

Brandt's barb hit its mark. Conrad lunged at Brandt, but the oversized bodyguard beside him stopped him from reaching the smug-faced prick now standing by the bed. I could tell Conrad was fighting for control of his emotions. With his dragon and memories back, he needed a tight rein to avoid an incident.

Brandt motioned for me to come closer. "Let's explain to Conrad how important it is that you, and he, cooperate with me."

I stepped in the room and shut the door behind me. Brandt wasn't going to tell Conrad anything he didn't already know, but if he left town with the contents of that box . . . none of our kind would be safe.

"Have a seat, Conrad. I have a few things you should see." Brandt unlocked the box and pulled out a large manila envelope. Inside was a sandwich-sized zip-lock bag containing bloody white scales. I cringed as I remembered the events that led up to him cutting those scales off my tail. Conrad hadn't moved, so Brandt nodded to the larger man. "Chance, would you mind?"

Chance pushed Conrad to sit on the bed.

"Do you know what these are, Conrad?" Brandt shook the bag in front of Conrad's face. "No, of course you don't. How could you?" He pulled a cell phone from the box next. "I could tell you, but you'd never believe me. So how about I show you?"

Brandt moved to sit next to Conrad and lowered the phone into Conrad's field of vision. I didn't need to see the video he was about to display. I'd lived it.

"Brace yourself." Brandt tapped play. I saw the change in lighting flash across Conrad's face as the audio took me back to that night.

I'd gone to dinner with Brandt after a couple of weeks of him badgering me for a date. After dinner, we'd gone back to the club to discuss a new set. I'd wanted to change my act up a bit to keep it fresh for the regular patrons. Brandt wasn't interested in work. I'd grown angry and stormed out the back door. He'd chased me outside and pushed me against a wall. I pushed back but couldn't shove him off me. In a panic, I'd shifted. That's where the video began.

Conrad frowned as he watched the visual evidence of my dragon's existence. Brandt's voice was loud and clear over the phone's speaker.

"What the hell are you?" he shrieked as his shaky hands worked the camera.

My responding growl was clear and predatory.

"Well, whatever you are, Jetta Mills, I've now got proof." You could hear the click of Brandt's switchblade. He lunged for me and missed. I'd done my best to escape, praying no one had seen me yet and I could shift back to my human form. As I turned my back on Brandt, he swiped at my tail and removed a few scales in the process. Instinct kicked in, and I jerked my tail back and forth, causing Brandt to slice the skin on his own cheek.

I moved behind a neighboring building that was thankfully abandoned and shifted to my human self. My back was bloody where he'd taken the scales. Brandt had captured the whole thing on his phone.

Brandt stopped the video. "I'm sure now you can see why I not only wanted the lockbox back, but also Jetta." He shook his head, clearly enjoying his victory. "You had no idea you were being duped by a monster."

He put the phone back into the box and placed the scales on top of it. "Jetta, love, why don't you tell Conrad the rest."

I cleared my throat. "It's not hard to guess what a douchebag like you would do with that kind of evidence."

Conrad refused to look at me. Damn him. This was his fault. Fury renewed within me, and I decided he deserved to hear every excruciating detail. He needed to know who'd he'd aligned himself with. He needed to understand what his betrayal could cost me, and what it had just cost him.

I crossed my arms in front of me. "Brandt found me hiding behind a bush, bare-ass naked and bleeding. He had my scales in a handkerchief and the cell phone in his hand. I knew he had me. He forced me back into the club through the rear door, then allowed me to grab a change of clothes from the small area I called my dressing room." I took a deep breath. "We were both bleeding."

I fought back my own rage as I recalled his actions. "He downloaded the additional video from the security feed to his phone, which shows the entire indent, including my shifting from human to dragon. He then locked the evidence up in that box and put it in the safe. Then he told me I would not only continue to be his main act, but that he owned me, body and soul, or he'd show the world what I really was. I argued with him, and he called the police, claiming I'd broken into his safe and attacked him."

Brandt shrugged. "I thought a few hours in lockup would cool your jets. I knew they wouldn't believe a word you'd said. Hell, half the cops in that jurisdiction are on my payroll." He chuckled. "I could have kept you in there indefinitely, had I chosen to do so. You needed to see the kind of power I can wield, Jetta. I'm a king."

I glared at him.

"And then you decided to break into my safe for real and go on the run." He nodded at Conrad. "That's where you stepped in, Mr. Monroe." Brandt looked at me. "He's been keeping me apprised of his progress, for the most part. Then after a text from him wanting to renegotiate, I'd realized he'd fallen for you and wasn't going to cooperate with the rest of the plan. Finding this shithole town was a pain in the ass. We did some digging into the subject of dragons and found an individual with his own connections here. He lives right here in Havenwood Falls and travels out of town regularly for . . . business. He was willing to sell us the information we needed to find you both. We flew into Grand Junction, then met our new friend at a rest stop. With the right monetary motivation, he happily led us right into town. You can't outsmart me, sweetheart." His lecherous smile was vile and made me want to puke.

I knew the kind of person Brandt was describing. We had an underground element, such as Bradly, that would sell out their own grandmother if it brought them a profit. A handful who snuck in and out of town on short trips to do business, keeping their activities hidden as much as possible. Some dirt bag accepting money for a guide into town didn't surprise me much, but if caught, they'd face banishment—or worse. I did find it remarkable that Brandt was successful. A stranger in town, who wasn't welcomed by the town itself, was a rarity.

Once again, Brandt proved to be the lowest form of life in existence. Still, Conrad's deceit was more painful than anything Brandt had done to me. Brandt had cut my skin and tried to steal my dignity, but Conrad had shattered my heart.

CHAPTER 16

CONRAD

I was seriously pissed. Not only had Brandt played me, but he'd assaulted Jetta. And now he might have ruined my relationship with the only woman I'd likely ever love. My mate. My new reason to exist.

I couldn't bring myself to look at her. I deserved her hatred and scorn. Yes, I'd been fooled, but I should have followed my gut. I should have told her everything. Especially after I'd realized that Jetta wasn't the hardened criminal he'd made her out to be. But the truth was, I didn't care what she was, because I loved her and would have excused anything in her past.

"Jetta, I think he has us by the short and curlies," I said, giving her a look I hoped she'd recognize as a signal to play along.

"Don't talk to me," she growled.

"We need to tell him everything." *We need to get them out of town. Come on, Jetta. Get with the program.*

Brandt's eyes narrowed. "What are you leaving out, Jetta?"

She shook her head.

"She has a shitload of diamonds."

Jetta stared daggers at me. "Shut up, Benedict Arnold."

"Brandt, if we give you the diamonds, will you let Jetta go?" I prayed he'd take the bait.

"I'll consider it." I knew he was lying, but I'd take whatever we could get.

She continued to glare at me. "Fine. Whatever."

Brandt walked over to her and put his arm around her. He kissed her temple, and I wanted to rip his lips and hands off for even daring to touch her.

"Good girl," Brandt murmured in her ear. "Now, Conrad, you need to get dressed. You look like an idiot."

I grabbed a change of clothes and dressed quickly, not caring that there were three other people in the room.

Chance picked up the box and waited for me to finish putting on my shoes. I followed Jetta and Brandt out the door, with Chance taking up the rear. I knew how this would play out in Brandt's mind. We'd show him the diamonds, and Brandt would take what he could from the cave. Then he and Chance would leave with Jetta, the evidence, and the gems. My body would never be found again, and Brandt would take back what was left of the twenty-five thousand he'd already paid me.

We stepped outside, and Brandt led us to a black Humvee.

"Well, that's not obnoxious or conspicuous," I remarked.

Chance gave me a hard shove.

I turned and stared into his eyes. "If you value your hands, you'll keep them to yourself."

I sat in the front with the big fella, while Brandt sat in back with Jetta. I gave them directions to the trail, then we spent the rest of the drive listening to Brandt's incessant jabbering about how smart and powerful he was. Every now and then, I glanced back at Jetta and saw her staring out the window. She refused to acknowledge me. I hoped that someday I could make her understand that my intentions were pure, even if my results were less than desirable.

We reached the trail and resumed the same formation as before: Jetta next to Brandt, me in the middle, and Chance bringing up the rear.

Chance pulled out a gun and pointed it at my side. "If either of you try to run, Conrad dies."

I wasn't sure Jetta would care at that point, but I hoped she did. She nodded but didn't say a word. When we reached the waterfall, I addressed Brandt. "The cave is behind the waterfall, but it's a little hard to reach. The entrance is that opening just to the right."

Brandt motioned to Chance. "Give me the gun and go check it out."

Chance handed over the weapon and cautiously made his way down the steps. I glanced at Jetta, but her expression gave nothing away. Brandt thought he had the upper hand, but he was about to learn that the only thing more dangerous than one dragon was two.

I took a step back and kicked off my shoes. Brandt's eyebrows drew together. "What the hell are you doing?"

I shrugged as I pulled my shirt over my head. "I know you plan to kill me." I unbuttoned my jeans.

Jetta's eyes flashed with understanding. She'd finally caught on to what I was doing. She pulled off her shirt as well, and Brandt's eyes went wide.

"What is wrong with you two? Are you hoping to freeze to death?"

Jetta stopped short of pulling down her jeans. "Do you want me to stop stripping?"

There was an alluring hint of wickedness to her voice, and I knew Brandt would be distracted by it.

He shook his head. "I will never complain about you getting naked in front of me."

"Then shut up." She continued taking off her clothes until she was in nothing but her underwear.

"Boss," yelled Chance. "There's nothing in here. Just a small, dark cave."

Brandt chuckled. "Nice distraction, but you've wasted your time."

"Not really," replied Jetta. "We got you out here, so I'd say we hit our objective."

She stepped back and began to shift. Brandt panicked and grabbed my arm, shoving the gun in my back.

"Now you listen to me, Jetta. Conrad dies if you don't change back." His voice was loud and authoritative, but fear laced his words.

AMY HALE

Chance hurried up the steps, almost slipping a time or two. He reached our side and looked up at Jetta's dragon in awe.

"You overestimate her feelings for me." I shook my head. "She doesn't give a shit what you do to me."

Brandt responded by pushing the gun to my head. Jetta bent her head low, her focus on the gun. She snorted, and Chase jumped.

"Calm down, Brandt. I know how we can resolve this." I braced myself for impact.

Brandt's gaze turned on me, and that's when Jetta's tail came down hard behind us. It knocked us all off balance, but it gave me just enough space to jump away. I didn't waste a moment, shifting into a version of myself I'd long suppressed.

Brandt and Chase stepped away from me, their eyes widening in horror. While Jetta was beautiful, almost magical looking, I looked like something straight out of hell. I widened my stance and lowered my head, a rumble building in the back of my throat. When I opened my mouth, fire shot out like a flamethrower, and the two men threw themselves to the ground. They covered their heads in a futile attempt to protect themselves.

Brandt located some of his backbone and looked up at me, sheer terror still in his features. He held up his hands in a gesture of surrender as he cautiously stood.

"Let's talk about this." He tried to keep his tough guy persona, but he was visibly trembling, and his voice cracked as he spoke. Chase was frozen by fear, not moving an inch. Brandt kicked him, prodding him to move.

Jetta moved to stand beside me, and our telepathic communication took over. "We could drown them. The water in the falls is poisonous to humans."

"That might work," I said.

"But . . . I really don't want to get my hands dirty, so I have a better idea."

"I'm up for whatever you have planned." I shot another stream of fire above the men, just in case they had any ideas about running. "Jetta, I'm sorry about everything."

112

"Not now, Conrad. We'll talk later." She stood to her full height. "For now, follow my lead."

At that moment, Chase and Brandt made a beeline for the trees, almost stumbling as they leapt over small branches and rocks.

"Slight change of plans," Jetta said. "Catch them."

Jetta turned on her camouflage and instinct helped me follow suit. We took off in opposite directions, intending to cut them off before they ran very far.

Jetta lumbered alongside Chase as he ran. His terrified gaze darted around him. He could barely hear her, and he couldn't see her at all, but he had to know she was there. He pushed himself against a tree and looked as if he was trying to calm his breathing.

I was a few yards in the opposite direction. Once Chase was cornered, I gave my full attention to capturing Brandt as he ran directly in front of me. I focused on him and lowered my head, snorting out a stream of fire. Brandt screamed, then turned and shot at me. The first bullet missed by a mile, but the second grazed my cheek, leaving a trail of blood running down my jaw.

"Conrad!" screamed Jetta. She sounded terrified. I shot another stream of fire toward Brandt, and he hit the dirt, his hands attempting to protect his head as he curled into a fetal position.

"I'm okay. It's just a scratch," I said. "Get Chase."

She reached out her front claws and grabbed a screaming Chase. She tucked him in close to her body, effectively hiding them both in her camouflage. I did the same with Brandt, both men screaming like little girls at a horror movie.

I laughed as we rose into the air. Jetta was graceful, where my flying skills were in need of some practice.

"What's so funny?" she asked as we soared over the tops of trees and outcroppings.

"Listen to them. They sound like one of my foster moms when she saw a mouse."

Jetta laughed, too. "They really do." She paused and pointed one of her back claws toward the large falls not far from Fallview Tavern & Grille. "These two are gonna *love* the Alverson sisters."

"Who are they?" I asked.

"Sirens," Jetta replied.

"Damn, those exist?" I was in awe of this revelation.

"You have a lot to learn about Havenwood Falls." She paused. "All those monsters you were told about during your childhood? They're all real."

"Holy shit," I muttered.

"Exactly."

We slowed our descent and landed at the top of the falls. The men were silent now, and I wondered if they'd died of heart attacks during our short trip. Jetta placed her front paws on the ground and opened them slowly. Chase was white as a sheet, but still alive. He carefully stood up, then tried to run. He'd only made it a few steps when Jetta's large claw hooked the back of his shirt and pinned him to the ground.

I opened my paws as well but made sure not to let Brandt escape.

"What are we waiting for?" I asked.

"Simon," she said. "He can't hear us, but he knows we're here. He can sense it."

That was news to me.

Brandt mustered the courage to speak up. "Please, let us go. We'll never bother you again. Just let us go."

Jetta snorted in disbelief, frost escaping her nostrils as she made herself visible once more. I followed her lead, waiting to see what would happen next.

As she'd predicted, in less than five minutes a large, dark brown dragon landed behind us. Simon's voice boomed in my head. "What kind of trouble have you brought me now, woman?"

Astonishment banged around in my skull like a pinball machine. That explained why Simon thought he knew me. He was a dragon, too. I really needed a stiff drink.

"Looking good, Conrad. I knew you'd be an impressive specimen."

"Thanks. You're rather intimidating yourself."

Simon nodded his head in thanks. "Now, why are you here with two crying men under your paws?"

"A gift for the Alverson family."

Simon nodded. "They will be most appreciative." He paused. "No one will miss them?"

Jetta chuckled. "Not anyone that matters. In fact, you'll be doing the world a favor."

Simon nodded and stepped forward. We released Brandt and Chance as Simon scooped them both up into his grip. The men screamed loudly once again.

Before flying to the bottom of the falls, Simon chuckled. "These two should have never come to Havenwood Falls."

CHAPTER 17

CONRAD

I watched Simon land at the bottom of the falls and then disappear into some trees. Jetta camouflaged herself again, then walked to the edge of the falls and jumped, falling just a few feet before rising into the air like a giant kite. I followed her, trying to catch up. Using my wings still felt a bit awkward, not that I'd admit that to her.

"What will happen to them?" I asked.

"Do you really care? They were horrible humans. The world is better off without them." Her tone was flat.

"I agree. I'm just morbidly curious."

She slowed down a bit, and we glided side by side through the clouds. "The Alversons will keep them in a holding cell until the council has a chance to decide their fate. If I had a say, I'd let the sisters feed on them."

"Shit, that's gotta be a hell of way to go." It would take me a while to adjust to all this new information. Once my dragon returned, so did some of the stories my mother had told me. Most of them were dragon-related, but every now and then her stories had included a witch or a goblin. I'd always thought she was embellishing to make it interesting. I'll be damned if she wasn't telling the truth about all of it.

Jetta nodded. "In my opinion, men like Brandt need to be dealt with permanently. But that's not for me to decide. I'll testify against them, if the Court asks." She picked up speed again.

The view below us was stunning. Snow-covered caps jutted above waves of evergreens and pines. But nothing was more striking than Jetta flying over the peaks and valleys of the canyon. It wasn't just visual, although I could make out her outline easily despite her invisibility to the human eye. I could tell her spirit felt truly free up there. She was happy, for the most part.

We landed back at her cave, and she shifted back to her human form quickly. She jerked her clothing on in hasty motions as I shifted and moved to do the same.

I'd pulled my shoes on when she picked up the lockbox, removed the scales, and then hurled the rest into the pool of water at the base of the falls. Everything inside rained down in pieces before settling somewhere beneath the surface.

"Is it over? Will you be safe now?" I asked, truly worried she may have to face this again in the future.

"Yes, it's over." She held up the scales. "I'll keep these in the cave for now. Dragon scales are too valuable to leave lying around. They should be safe there, assuming some deceitful asshole dragon doesn't dig them back up and bring them out again."

"Jetta, you have every right to be angry with me. I should have told you the truth in the beginning. But I swear to you, I really believed you'd just taken random valuables from him. I didn't know the contents of the box until he showed them to me at the inn."

She hung her head, and her voice was soft. "I trusted you, Conrad."

"I know. As you said, I was a deceitful asshole. I'm sorry that I broke that trust." My heart ached, knowing I'd hurt her so deeply. "If it helps, once I'd gotten to know you, I'd decided I was only returning the box to Brandt, even if I had to forfeit the rest of my fee." I stepped toward her. "I'd realized shortly after I met you that regardless of what you'd taken, you weren't the criminal he said you were. I couldn't allow him to hurt you. If I'd only known the real story . . ." My voice trailed off in regret. "I'm so sorry, Jetta."

She shrugged. "Yes, you are a deceitful asshole, but if you'd known the real story, you never would have come to Havenwood Falls," she said. "I'd never have met you, and you may have never found yourself again."

I nodded. "True." I looked into her eyes. "But if it would have saved you all of this pain, I would do it all differently. I'd have stayed away forever if it would have protected you. I know it's hard to believe, after all I've done, but I love you. I think I have from the minute I saw you."

She took a moment to compose herself. "It's not how I would have preferred to have met you, but I believe you were supposed to be here. It's what was meant to be."

I looked at the tattoo on my wrist, the flames of it now a vivid red instead of the dull black it'd been before putting on the ring.

"Maybe you're right." I closed the distance between us until we were face to face. "No matter what happens from here on out, I owe you a debt of gratitude. You saved me. Before learning the truth, I was drifting from job to job, restless and unhappy. Never allowing myself any kind of meaningful relationships. Solitude was easier. I wanted to avoid the risk of being hurt. But now I feel I belong somewhere." I shook my head. "I wish Mama would have known about this place. We could have come here. She wouldn't have died alone or had to worry about who'd care for me later."

Jetta placed her hand on my cheek. "I wish she would have, too, but that ring got here somehow. We may never know the whole story, but someone expected you to find your way here one day and discover your truth. I'm glad I was able to help you with that." She kissed me gently.

My heart swelled at the love I still saw in her eyes. She didn't completely hate me.

As if she'd read my mind, she said, "Now, that doesn't mean I'm not gonna put you through hell to make you prove yourself. Payback is a bitch, Monroe. You have a lot of work ahead of you."

I nodded. "Yes, ma'am. I'll do my best."

Then I kissed her thoroughly.

~

WE SPENT the next couple of weeks making arrangements for me to stay in Havenwood Falls as a full-time resident. I went back to Atlanta and paid off my debts, thanks to a donation from Jetta's diamond collection and what was left of the money I'd gotten from Brandt. Then I hauled my motorcycle and what few belongings I owned back to Havenwood Falls. I rented a little house near the Havenstone development and began my search for a job. Jetta moved in with me.

I registered with the Court, and after hearing my story, they allowed Addie to make minor modifications to my current family tattoo. Besides infusing it with the town's magic, she also added something meaningful to me, per my request. I couldn't wait to show Jetta, so as soon as her set was done at Fallview Tavern & Grille, I rushed to carry her off the stage.

"What are you doing?" she hissed. "Put me down. Everyone is looking at us."

"Good," I said, "let them." I kissed her just to be sure there was plenty of fodder for the town gossips. I whispered in her ear, "I have something special to show you."

She chuckled. "Oh, I bet you do."

I shook my head. "And you say I'm the dirty-minded one."

She clutched at my neck as I hurried outside with her in my arms. I sat her down in front of my truck and rolled up my sleeve. I no longer wore the cuff.

She gasped. "Is that a snowflake?"

"Yes. I asked Addie to put it in the center of the triskele."

"But why?" Her beautiful eyes searched mine.

"For you, of course. You are the center of my universe. My happiness—my very life— revolves around your happiness." I bent down on one knee and took her hand. "Jetta Mills, will you make me the happiest deceitful asshole on earth and become my wife?"

She grinned at my use of her new nickname for me.

I kissed her fingers. "I don't have a ring yet, but I was hoping this could be our new family crest."

She traced the lines of the snowflake. "It's beautiful, Conrad." Her eyes met mine, and her usual mischievousness replaced the emotion I'd seen moments earlier. "You know, if I say no, you are totally screwed. You'll be stuck explaining that weird-ass tattoo for the rest of your life."

I shrugged. "It's a risk I was willing to take. I'll just tell people I was drunk."

She closed her eyes and pulled me to my feet. "Damn it."

"What?" I froze, wondering if she truly was going to say no. I felt my heart beat so hard I thought it would knock a hole in my chest.

"My dad is gonna be so happy that I'm marrying a dragon."

I picked her up and swung her around. "It'll be okay. We'll find other ways to make him miserable."

"We?" she asked.

"Oh yeah. We are in this together. I go where you go. I piss off who you piss off. It's a package deal."

Her smile turned devious as she took my hand in hers. "I can't wait to see what kind of trouble we'll get into."

～

ABOUT THE AUTHOR

Since childhood, bestselling and award-winning author Amy Hale has been creating exceptional stories that summon a whirlwind of emotions and inspiration unto the reader. She loves creating characters and worlds from nothing but her imagination and a few glasses of wine. Her love of the written word has not only resulted in her writing some of her readers' favorite adventures, but has also manifested itself in the form of book hoarding. She's convinced it's not a sickness.

She debuted her first fiction novel in 2015 after retiring from thirteen years of nonfiction writing for various online entities. For the last couple of decades, she's also carried the titles of Laundry Goddess, Chef, Butt Wiper, Soother of Temper Tantrums, and in more recent years, Moderator of Sarcastic Eyerolls and Sass. She resides in Illinois with her husband, as well as two grown children who claim they are never moving out. Regardless, they are the center of her universe, although her cat believes otherwise.

If she had any spare time, she'd love music, photography, watching Mystery Science Theater 3000 with her family, and long rides on the back of her husband's motorcycle.

Learn more at authoramyhale.com

ACKNOWLEDGMENTS

I always worry I will sound redundant while writing this page, but I firmly believe the words Thank You can never be said enough.

I give thanks to God and all he provides. My faith in Him has helped me through some pretty rough storms in recent years.

John, my husband, is the most amazing man I've ever known. He gives so much of himself and asks very little in return. He is the reason I keep trying. He's my support, my cheerleader, my shoulder to cry on. The things I've achieved so far are because he's given me the boost to climb higher. I love you more than words could ever say.

Thanks to Matt, Rachel, and Wes for understanding how crazy things get when I am on a deadline. You kids are the best.

Thanks to Kristie Cook for once again entrusting me with a small part of her amazing project that is Havenwood Falls. Jetta and Conrad were really fun to write and I'm looking forward to more of their story in the future.

Many thanks to Kristen Yard for allowing me the generous use of the Alverson sisters, Simon, and Fallview Tavern & Grille. I also want to thank Kristie Cook for allowing me to add Whisper Falls Inn, Madame Luiza Petran, and Sindi Scott to my story.

Thanks to Kristie Cook and Liz Ferry for your superb editing skills. You ladies make my writing shine in ways I could never achieve on my own.

Thanks to Regina Wamba for once again creating the perfect cover. I'm ever in awe of your talent!

Thanks to my beta readers, Danielle, Ashley, Jenell, and Amber, for your input while I worked through this story.

Much love and gratitude to our growing Havenwood Falls family! I'm honored to work with some the most talented people I've ever met. You guys and gals keep me excited about this project and your support has meant the world to me.

To my readers, Thank You will never be enough. Your trust in my words, the use of my imagination, to entertain you is a feeling I can't describe. I hope I give back a fraction of the joy your readership gives me.

FROM THE EMBERS

AMY MILES

~ A Havenwood Falls New Adult Novella ~

HAVENWOOD FALLS

FROM THE EMBERS

AMY MILES

ALSO BY AMY MILES

THE AROTAS SERIES
Forbidden ~ Reckoning ~ Redemption ~ Evermore

THE IMMORTAL ROSE TRILOGY
Desolate ~ Savage

THE RISING TRILOGY
Defiance Rising ~ Relinquish ~ Vengeance

THE WITHERED SERIES
Wither ~ Resurrect ~ Affliction

THE TRICKSTER TRILOGY
Trickster ~ The Ruby Eye ~ The Last Trick

Zombie High Chronicles #1

Jasper

STAND ALONES
Obsidian Flames ~ Nailed It ~ Blogged That ~ In Your Embrace

WRITING AS EVERLY DALTON
The Brit Affair ~ The Last Call

To all of the dreamers out there still waiting for their moment to shine.

Now is your moment. Shine on!

CHAPTER 1

Smart people knew to duck when the world took a swing at them. I guess I hadn't learned that lesson yet. Taking a hit was something I knew how to do. Knowing when to stop before my luck ran out—well, that was another story.

A cheer rose from the crowd. My hair blocked the view of the approaching wall, but I sure felt it. With a groan, I collapsed into the gutter. The murky water tasted of rotting trash, and I didn't want to think of what else. I spit to the side before I rolled to my back.

That one hurt.

"You sure you're up for another round, Ember?" Two glowing orb-like eyes stared down at me. They looked far too small compared to the eggplant-sized nose they flanked. "You're lookin' a bit rough after Fluffy took that last chunk out of you."

The troll wasn't wrong.

A single tear rolled down my cheek, and I caught it with my fingertip. It shimmered there like a summer sunset against the night. The instant I touched it to the gouge in my right side, sweet relief rushed in. Having healing powers sure came in handy.

"Whoever named that seven-foot-tall bastard of a skinwalker Fluffy deserves to have their head kicked in," I said.

I'd been fighting against scum like him for six years, but he was my first skinwalker. The stories were few and far between. Some relayed tales of creatures that could assume the skin of a man instead of a beast. Staring up at Fluffy's three heads, I wished I'd taken on one of them instead.

Fuzzbert laughed. "That's my girl."

The hand that yanked me to my feet was the size of a large serving platter, dotted with tufts of hair. It was a tight squeeze to escape around his belly. The friction of his wet poncho trapped me. I wiggled free and leaned against the wall to catch my breath.

There were dozens of wounds in need of healing, but they would have to wait. Fluffy paced, watching me. Saliva dripped in thick strings from his gaping jaws. Blood matted the soaked fur near one of his right eyes and his hind leg. It was hard to tell which of his three heads was the dominant one. They were all glaring at me with blackened hatred through the rain.

Fluffy made the hound of Hades look like a puppy. Not exactly fair in hand-to-hand combat, but most street-fighting clubs didn't have rules. At least not rules that went in favor of anyone but the man in charge. Or rather the troll in charge, in this case.

Like most in the crowd, Fuzzbert waited for me to call the fight. Like heck was I tapping out. A lot of money was riding on this.

But I wasn't here for the money.

"Ember?" Fuzzbert stepped toward me. He cast a wary glance at the sky. Trolls didn't like lightning.

I held up my hand. "I need a minute to breathe."

That last hit was the hardest I'd ever taken. Fluffy must have been on steroids. Or a drug that was less than legal.

I'd fared well enough against two of his heads, but that third one literally bit me in the backside. It was a shame they confiscated my dagger at the start of the fight. I'd love to stake one of his heads to the wall.

"Time's up, Ember." The crowd pressed in closer to hear Fuzzbert. They were a rainbow of colors, each with ponchos of various sizes.

Folks in Denver sure took their fight clubs seriously. "Are you tapping out?"

Wiping a mixture of blood and rain from my brow, I grinned and thumped Fuzzbert on his warty nose.

"If you were half as smart as you are ugly, you'd already know the answer to that."

Fuzzbert's breath wheezed around the gap in his lips. Crooked teeth, as long as my fingers, jutted from his gums.

"Speak for yourself." His laugh sounded like an old lady who'd smoked for three lifetimes.

"Aw, come on, Fuzz. You know it's not nice to make a girl cry," I said.

I wasn't as ugly as a troll, but I wasn't a beauty queen either, thanks to a run-in I had a few years ago with fire. Turns out healing tears did squat on that.

Fluffy's hackles rose at the first rumble of thunder in the distance. He squared off with me. A sharp bark sent the crowd back to clear the area.

"That mutt has got a hair up his backside tonight." Fuzzbert might look menacing to most, but I knew his sweet spot. He loved money. It didn't matter how he got it.

I palmed him the last bit of cash I had to my name. "I need some information. He's going to give it up, one way or another."

The troll shook his head. "It's your funeral."

"You'd better be careful, Fuzz." I tied my hair back into a semblance of a bun. "Someone might think you've gone soft on a human."

He snorted and stomped away. If I wasn't paying so well, he'd probably eat me for that comment.

"Hurry up. Place your bets." Fuzzbert cast a scowl at the clouds. "I haven't got all night."

I leaned against the wall, trying to appear unconcerned as Fluffy paced. There wasn't much room in the back alley for the two of us, let alone the crowd that had gathered. Fluffy had a fat butt, which slowed him down. His love of cupcakes and the forty years he had on me didn't help him much. The thinner air up here in Denver wasn't exactly treating me well, either.

"I'm going to gnaw your bones into splinters." Fluffy's words came out in a raspy snarl.

If it weren't for Fuzz warning me ahead of time that Fluffy was a skinwalker, I'd have been shocked the first time he spoke.

"I always wondered if your kind eats humans." I pretended to shudder. "That's cannibalism, you know?"

He clawed the ground.

"Tell me who you work for, Fluffy, and I may let you walk away from this fight."

His growl vibrated in my chest. "I work for no man."

"Man? Nah, I'm looking for a demon with black soulless eyes, a fancy suit, and a thing for stealing young girls."

The golden glow of his eyes dimmed. "That describes quite a few of my friends."

"Yes, but you're the lapdog for only one of them," I said.

The upper lip of his middle head curled back to reveal a set of wicked canines. I had no intention of tangling with those again.

"Suit yourself." I pushed off the wall to saunter toward him.

He watched the sway of my hips in the tight leather pants I wore. The metal clasps of my biker boots jingled with each step. The shredded remains of my black tank hung from my chest. A new layer of skin had begun to form over his telltale claw marks.

Fluffy sniffed the air when I stopped less than five feet from him. His sneeze coated me with slime.

"Gross." I wiped my face clean.

"I knew it. I suspected earlier that you weren't human." All three heads dipped low to glare at me. "I'm allergic to only one creature: birds."

I met his condemning gaze. "Do I look like a bird to you?"

"You're a shifter."

I laughed. "If I were, don't you think I would've shifted by now?"

He rolled his eyes to look back at Fuzzbert. "You may not be a shifter, but you aren't human, either."

I'd always known I was different. Healing wasn't the only ability I possessed. I also had a way with fire.

"What's it to you?" I crossed my arms and jutted out one hip.

His laugh made the hair on the back of my neck rise. "Foolish girl. A skinwalker's bite leaves more than a scar."

"You son of a—" My arms fell to my sides. "You bit me, knowing I'd turn into your kind?"

It was sickening, barbaric even. It was also annoyingly brilliant. Not that I would tell him that.

"You chose me as your opponent, remember?" His heads fell in line with each other so his statement sounded in stereo. "The risk was yours to take."

"Bastard," I muttered under my breath. I took hold of his center head. His fur crawled with bugs where I buried my hands to reach the skin. "Give me a name."

Heat flooded into my palms. It started with a familiar tingle but rapidly built to a blistering heat. Steam rose from his wet pelt. The wolf's laugh cut off, and his screams began.

The teeth of his left head sank deep into my arm. Blood flowed around the wounds. His hindquarters slammed into the alley wall. Mortar gave way in chunks, coating his back.

"What's going on over there?"

Fuzzbert's heavy footsteps headed our way.

"Give me his name." I tightened my grip, and the scent of burning fur filled my nose. Pain flared in my shoulder when Fluffy's third head attacked. His teeth ripped at muscle and scored bone. The pain made my vision darken, but I held on.

"Let him go," Fuzzbert demanded.

"Stay out of this, Fuzz. I don't want to hurt you."

"Hurt me?" The troll rocked to a stop. "Have you lost your ever-loving mind, girl? I could grind you into dust in seconds."

I released one hand holding Fluffy and pointed it at Fuzz. Fire erupted in the palm of my hand. A swirling ball of vibrant orange hovered there. In the very center of the flames was a blue so bright, it forced Fuzzbert to look away.

"What are you?" the troll asked from behind the shield of his hand.

That I didn't know. I'd spent years looking for the answer. So far, all I had were questions.

"Get her off me," Fluffy whimpered.

Where I'd gripped Fluffy, the imprint of my palm was beginning to heal. I needed to remain in constant contact with him.

Fuzzbert inched forward. With each step he took, the flames rose higher from my hand. "I don't want any trouble, Fuzz."

"You've got a fine way of showing that."

I broke eye contact with Fluffy to look at the troll. "This man knows who killed my momma. I'm not leaving until he gives me a name."

"Bugger." Fuzzbert rubbed the back of his head, forgetting that he wore a poncho.

"Don't just stand there. Do something!" Fluffy moaned.

Digging my nails into Fluffy's neck drew out a terrible howl. The heat cauterized on contact. His eyes rolled back. The scent of his burnt hair was thick in the air.

Murmurs rippled through the crowd. Several pressed against the protective barrier hiding us from the humans. The mages on Fuzzbert's payroll had to work harder to keep us hidden.

No amount of warding could shield Fluffy's frenzy. His thrashing sent tremors through the concrete. Screeching yelps of pain echoed out of the alley. The doorman standing in front of the small condo building across the street peered into the dark. He couldn't see us. Not yet, at least.

"This is getting out of hand," the troll said, surveying his paying crowd. He was losing them. "Tell her what she wants to know, then bite her head off."

The wolf's eyes glistened with tears. "He'll kill me for saying!"

Fuzzbert gave him a withering glare. "If you finish her off, no one will know but you and me. My silence comes at a very fair price."

That was loyalty for you. It started and ended with the highest bidder.

The stench of fear and urine rose from Fluffy. I wondered if the enchantment could hide that smell, too.

"You'll let me live?" He yipped as flames curled the ends of his fur, spreading out from my hands.

I'd heard my fair share of the tales of his exploits in the human world. He was filth, undeserving of life. But he still had his uses.

I nodded, not trusting myself to say the words in case I changed my mind later. Fluffy sniffed and raised one head, turning it in the direction of the crowd.

"They won't help you," I said and followed his gaze. The vampires in attendance might pay a good price for Fluffy's blood if I decided to fry him.

I wonder if he would taste like a human or an animal to them.

I knew very little about the Navajo legends of such creatures. Only that they were once human—witches who turned only after killing someone close to them. Or at least, that was one rumor floating around. This particular legend was very sensitive to the Native American tribes. So, during my travels, I steered far away from it, out of respect.

There were a couple of shifters in the group that might attack if I did kill him. Even though a skinwalker wasn't the same species, they might stick together. I'd seen pack mentality cross species lines before.

"Quiet!" Fuzzbert shouted to the nervous crowd. Whatever he was trying to hear, I was sure his elephant ears would pick it up. "I hear it, too."

It took another minute for me to hear the sirens.

"Who called the pigs?" A tiny faerie of some sort, sitting on the shoulder of a man at the front, fluttered her wings with agitation.

"Maybe they aren't coming our way." A small goblin beside the faerie wrung his hands. He wore a little suit coat. The glint of a golden pocket watch caught my eye. Fuzzbert was too panicked to notice this tempting treasure.

Another flare from my hand sent Fluffy into spasms hard enough to crack the brick wall. The metal scaffolding fixed to the front of the building collapsed to the street. A great puff of dust burst across the entrance to the alleyway. Pieces of the historic landmark crumbled. The doorman dove for the phone, ensuring that the police would be coming.

That was exactly the advantage I needed.

CHAPTER 2

"*This* is not a drill. Get to your assigned escape routes." Fuzzbert fisted handfuls of cash into the front of his pants. Several bills floated in the puddle at his feet. "And no refunds!"

Chaos erupted. The instant Fluffy's extra head released its grip on my shoulder, I knew he was going to make a run for it.

"Not so fast, furball." I tossed a flame at his third head to redirect his momentum. "I still need that name."

"You're insane. Those cops will be on us in minutes," he said. "We gotta get out of here."

Wings, paws, and claws beat against the bottleneck at the end of the alley. Fuzzbert should have known better than to pick a location with only one exit—a fact he was now grumbling about as he launched a panther shifter out of his way. He bowled through the crowd and charged across the street. Even with his glamour enchantment in place, he was one butt-ugly woman.

"You're not scared, are you?" I wedged myself around Fluffy so I could grab his tail, but it swung out of reach.

He didn't have to answer me. The scent of his fear was rancid in my nose, burning my eyes.

"I can't be here." His black fur trembled as I gripped his neck. If he shook me free now, he'd have a chance to regain his strength.

"What's the big deal? Can't you just shift?" I'd heard rumors that Fluffy didn't perform well under pressure. "Is someone having performance anxiety?"

His snarl sent my hair into a whirlwind of tangles. I blew it away to level him with a glare.

"I reckon you might find a way to shift by the time the cops show." I raked scorching nails across his side. He screamed. "Give me a name, or I'll show them my bite marks. They put mutts down for stuff like that."

In hindsight, poking a cornered skinwalker wasn't the smartest idea. But then again, it wasn't exactly out of character, either.

Fluffy turned on me faster than I anticipated. Two sets of teeth pierced flesh, one in my left thigh and the other around my neck. If I'd been human, I'd have bled out. But my body's natural healing powers kicked in.

"Are you kidding me?" I spat blood onto the ground. "That was a cheap shot, even for you."

Searing heat exploded from my palms, setting Fluffy's entire flank alight. His shriek echoed in my ears as he scraped his side—and me right along with it—along the wall. The brick tore at my skin.

Fluffy bounced and twirled as I sent flames flying in unpredictable directions. Disoriented and in pain, he trampled over a nymph. A second one scurried out of his way. The goblin took a hard hit from Fluffy's tail and slammed into the wall. His pocket watch rolled into the street as the creature crumpled and fell still.

A well-aimed flame sent Fluffy's hind leg collapsing to the ground. Planting my boot in the crook of his leg, I hoisted myself onto his back. He bucked like a wild stallion.

"End this," I screamed, tossing another flame at the head of the alley to block his escape.

Fluffy was beyond reasoning with now. Pain and fear made his hackles rise around me. His heads came up, biting and tearing. There was no way to defend myself and hold on at the same time. Squeezing my knees into his sides, I tossed flames at each of his heads.

But that third head did me in again. Razor sharp teeth buried into my thigh. With his mighty tug, I hurtled over the heads of the fleeing creatures and into the street. I landed hard, earning road rash in more places than I cared to count. I rolled several times, then slammed into a Rolls Royce. The driver's side door buckled under the impact.

"Son of a—" I pushed to my feet.

The glamour surrounding the alley faded as the last mage fled. Fluffy was in mid-shift. One of his heads was already gone. The second disappeared into a gaping hole of fur. Bones shattered and then mended as he shrank in size.

"That's disgusting." I held my stomach, sure that if I stuck around to listen to the full transformation, I'd be ill. I'd seen shifters before, but their transitions were more fluid. This was nauseating.

The instant irises began to replace the blacks of his eyes, I knew the cops wouldn't arrive in time to capture him. If that happened, I would lose any advantage I'd fought and bled to gain.

"Oh, no you don't!" I swayed on my feet. Everything hurt now. Blood soaked my clothes. My head felt like I'd had a few too many sips of a spiked witch's brew.

"Fluffy!" My scream made the skinwalker whirl around.

He was not much larger than a Great Dane now. I ran straight at him, flames swirling around my hands. It didn't matter that I was visible. The streets were empty of all but the supernatural. Even the doorman had abandoned his post.

Fluffy raced to the back of the alley. With no way to escape, he turned and bared his teeth.

"You might have stood a chance if you'd stayed full size," I said. My flames lit the space, revealing him pacing in the corner.

"Leave it alone, girl. I'm warning you. You don't know what you're getting yourself mixed up in." His voice had lost much of its gruff tone. With each second that passed, he began to sound more human.

"I don't have a choice." I stalked toward him. "Your boss killed my momma. Tried to steal me. I'm only alive to seek justice."

"Justice?" He snorted. "Men like him don't pay for their crimes. They just go on inflicting new pain."

My hands flexed at my sides, but I didn't attack. "You sound like you can relate."

The wolf's body quivered, and it lowered its head. A moan rippled through the alley. "Not everyone has a choice in who they serve."

That made me stop. "You're a victim too, aren't you?"

Sadness filled the animal's eyes when he looked up at me. "If he wanted you as bad as you say, then run. Get as far from here as you can. He always finds his prey. Always."

I blinked. "So I was right. He is in Denver."

Fluffy's irises lightened to a dingy brown. The whites of his eyes began to return.

"Tell me his name." I rushed forward, desperate to hear those two little words. A name was a small thing. But the price that confession would cost the skinwalker might be higher than I'd imagined.

"I can't." His head swayed back and forth. Another moan escaped his elongated throat but it was not brought on by his shifting. "There's so much more you don't understand—"

"Nakai!"

I turned at the shout. A solitary man stood next to the dented door of the Rolls Royce. The streetlamp highlighted the salt-and-pepper tones of his hair. Deep lines surrounded eyes as black as the night around us. A fine suit clothed his muscular frame.

I knew his face. It had aged, but not enough for me to forget the man who killed my momma.

"Have you been fighting in the streets again like a common mutt?" The man brushed his hand over the dented door. "You'll be paying for this damage in full, I assure you that. Now leave the girl and come along. We have work to do."

"No." This time, Fluffy spoke as a man instead of the beast.

"No?" The killer's eyes narrowed. He swept his gaze in my direction. I instinctively moved toward him.

"Run, girl!"

I glanced back over my shoulder to see the skinwalker in his human form for the first time. He was Nakai now, a Native American man of stunning beauty, apart from the hollowness in his eyes.

He stood without a stitch of clothing on. Burnt flesh spread along his chest and side. Long black hair fell across his shoulders, the ends still smoking. Three full-length pelts lined his back, one head draped on each shoulder and the third over his own head. Now I understood how he was able to transform into a three-headed wolf.

In human form, I doubted he would survive long from his injuries. Death might be preferable now that his boss had discovered him.

My momma's killer stopped short at the skin walker's shout. When his gaze swept between us, recognition lit his eyes. "You!"

Before I could sprint toward the man, he raised his hand. I spied the briefest glow of light before a bullet spiraled toward me. A blinding light exploded out of me before my mind could process that I'd been shot at. Nakai's scream cut off. A two-story wall of flames scorched everything in its path and burst from the alley.

Glass panes from the second-floor windows melted and dripped from above. The mortar burst apart, forming huge holes in the wall. Pieces of the building stung as they split open my cheek and buried in my arms. Streetlamps became twisted metal lumps, plunging the alley into darkness. Smoke rose from the smoldering heap of the Rolls Royce. The face of the condo building was black with soot.

There was no sign of my momma's killer. In the blink of an eye, he'd vanished.

I never felt the bullet that tore through my arm. Never felt the flames die out as I collapsed.

My head lolled to the side. It took immense effort to breathe as I stared at a pile of dust where Nakai had stood. A set of teeth with two large canines perched on top. The tip of a bullet stuck out from the center of the dust.

But it was not the bullet that killed Fluffy. It was me.

"He wasn't shooting at me," I whispered, reaching for the bullet.

Nakai had known something. Information I wasn't supposed to get my hands on.

The first glow of the police lights flickered against the brick wall as the dust began to settle. The sirens sounded muffled and distorted. A face hovered over mine, and I swam in and out of consciousness.

One thought kept me lucid. I'd seen my momma's killer.

He was long gone by now, lost to me again. But he had been here. This was the closest I'd ever come to finding him. I would hunt him again.

The police swarmed around me where I lay in the epicenter of devastation. The police report would likely say the commotion had been caused by a gas explosion. Tales of strange aftershocks from Fluffy's earlier prancing would be written off as a gas bubble on the move. There would be little that could explain away his cries of pain, but I knew humans well enough. They would convince themselves it was only their imagination.

I would be the only living witness to the events, and I wasn't going to say anything.

Closing my eyes, I tried to focus my healing energies on several places at once. Having the cops interrogate me about bite marks would delay things. It was better to make it look like I'd been in the explosion. Wrong place. Wrong time.

As healing energy ran along my nerve endings, I opened my eyes. I blinked several times, sure that I was hallucinating. Seared into the brick above Fluffy's remains was the blackened shape of a large bird. Exactly where my shadow would have been.

The shape of a firebird.

CHAPTER 3

*M*y head hurt when I woke. Not from my injuries, mind you. I had developed a high pain threshold years ago. What wounds still lingered would heal soon enough. This headache was from the stupid drugs the doctors pumped through my IV They always made me feel hung over.

"You messed yourself up pretty bad this time." The voice was calm and came from the chair seated next to my bed.

"Hey, Susan," I said.

No matter where I found myself in the country, somehow she was always there when I woke up in a hospital. I'd lost count of how many wards I'd visited since she took me in two years back. Or how many airline miles she'd racked up on my account.

Fostering a troubled kid a year before she aged out of the system took a huge heart. Susan Wick had the biggest one I'd ever known. Apart from my momma, of course. Once I turned eighteen, I should've been out on my own. Susan insisted I stick around till I got my footing and all that. She loved me, but also knew admitting that would be awkward for me.

So I used her as a home base of sorts, coming and going as I pleased while I hunted. I didn't have anywhere else to call home. She was the only family I had.

Susan placed her hand on mine, and I closed my eyes. I hated disappointing her.

"I'm sorry," I whispered. And I was.

I wasn't sorry that I'd run away. Or that I'd hitchhiked my way to Denver. Or even that I'd damaged half a city block. I was sorry that I made her worry again.

"Did you find him?" she asked.

I opened my eyes to stare at the ceiling. In the off-white texture, I could picture every detail about him, right down to the dark circles under his eyes. Susan knew I was hunting my momma's killer. Past that, there was only so much truth a human could take.

"I saw him," I said. "He was standing at the end of the alley."

She sighed and leaned back. The plastic chair creaked under her weight. "I suppose I'm not surprised. You're the most stubborn little lady I know."

Stubborn was putting it nicely. Though we never spoke about it, she knew there was something off about me. She'd seen plenty of scrapes and bruises heal overnight while I lived with her. A lesser woman might've worried about an impromptu visit from social services, but not Susan. She had faith.

Not just in God. But in me.

I wished that I could tell her that I wasn't involved in that alley mess. That it had been an unfortunate accident, but I couldn't lie to her. So I said nothing at all.

"What are you going to do now?" she said.

Tension lingered in my healing muscles as I blew out a long breath. I'd need another day before the pain faded. A day more to return to my normal self.

"I can't give up now, Sue." I needed her to understand that.

"I know, darlin'." She squeezed my fingers, ignoring the bindings that held my wrists to the bedrail. One look at my extensive police record would explain the straps. Lifting my head, I spotted the officer standing by my door with his hand on his holster.

"Looks like I have company again." I laughed.

Susan smiled. "You seem to collect admirers wherever you go."

It was a sad smile. One that filled me with guilt so acidic, I wondered if it would burn right through my chest. I deserved that, for what I'd put her through.

"You gonna stop me?" I rolled my head to look at my foster mom for the first time.

There were patches of gray at her temples that hadn't been there before I arrived at her home. Her pale skin looked paper thin in the dim glow of the light behind my bed. She seemed far older than her fifty-seven years. Jetlag didn't do that. Being in my life did.

"Let's call it an early birthday gift." She laced her fingers through mine. "You're a fine young woman, Ember. I'd love nothing more than for you to come home with me, but I know you too well. This is where you need to be."

My heart swelled with love. Susan didn't need to know the gory details of my past to understand how important this was. Every terrible situation I'd found myself in was because of that black-eyed bastard. I'd done plenty of things I wasn't proud of to find him, but apart from hurting her, I could justify them.

I'd spent my teen years convincing myself that there was some purpose to all of this. I needed to believe my momma didn't die for nothing. The older I got, the more I realized there was a reason. It just wasn't one I was sure I could live with.

That man came for me.

I was different. A freak. No matter how many creatures I came across, none were like me. I was the unicorn of the supernatural world.

That man knew something about me. Enough to hunt me down. While my momma lay burning on the floor of my childhood home, he'd stepped over her and reached for me.

"You've blamed yourself for your momma's death for far too long, child," Susan whispered. "It's time to let that burden go."

"I will," I said. "I need to know why."

"What if he doesn't give you the answers you're looking for?"

"He will," I said.

"You seem so sure of that."

I could no longer look her in the eye. "It's best you not know."

"Yes." She sighed. "I suppose you're right."

"I will come home someday."

Susan smiled. "I know you will. When you're ready. You gotta find your peace first, Ember. It's there waitin' on you. You'll find it when the time is right."

We sat in silence for several minutes, listening to the rain pattering the window behind her. Judging by the dim lighting in the rooms across from me, it was nighttime.

"What day is it?" I asked.

"It's after midnight, so I guess it's Friday now. You've been asleep for three full days." Susan glanced at the nurses' station, visible through the sliding glass door to my room. "The doctors couldn't figure you out. Your wounds were healing, but your brain didn't want to work quite right. I told them when I arrived to give you a little time. I knew you'd come around when you were ready."

The memory of the scorched bird on the alley wall and Fluffy's pile of dust flashed before my eyes. My breathing hitched, but I said nothing. That's not something I could share.

"I'm assuming now that you're awake, you've got your brain all sorted out."

I nodded, though I wasn't sure that was entirely true until those pain pills wore off.

"Well, good. That's very good." She patted my hand again. "Your brothers and sisters send their love, of course."

We both knew that was a lie. Back home, I had three brothers and four sisters of various ages who lived with me. All were foster care rejects that Susan took in. No matter how many candles they had on their birthday cakes, they were smart enough to avoid me.

While living in the small town of Eufaula, Alabama, I'd had my fair share of unkind words spoken about me. Freak. Hooligan. Pyro. Most of them started by my own foster kin. I'll admit they were pretty much justified by my actions. The police might not have been rocket scientists, but they were hardworking and smart enough to keep an eye on me. The trouble was I didn't stick around long. I bounced from city to city, following leads. Most of them never panned out, and I'd come home to rest for a while.

Twisting my wrists to test the tension on my restraints, I noticed Susan watching me. "You don't have to stick around for this part."

She smiled. "Afraid I'll rat you out to the police once you're gone?"

I stopped. "Of course not. I just don't want my life to keep tossing junk at you. You shouldn't have to lie for me, Sue. Heck, you shouldn't have to do any of this."

"Mind that tongue or I'll mind it for you, young lady," she scolded. Even though heck wasn't really a swear word, Sue thought it was ill-fitting for a lady. She was the only reason I never swore. I respected her too much.

I couldn't help but smile at her stern look. Or the way she tried to press out the wrinkles in my hospital gown. It felt good to be mothered. I'd missed that while I'd been on the road. "And don't you be worrying about me none. I know how to handle myself."

"That I don't doubt."

She leaned in and kissed me on the forehead. "Promise me you'll be safe."

"I'll try." That was the best I could offer.

She rose, patted me on the head, and moved toward the door. Before it closed behind her, she was already working her charm on the cop. No one could resist a cup of hot coffee from a sweet southern lady like her.

The instant the cop's attention shifted, I focused on my wrists. The tingling came a split second before smoke rose from my restraints. I had to focus to keep the flame minimal or I'd risk setting off the fire alarm.

Ridding myself of my IV, I leaped out of bed and tore open the closet in search of my clothes. They hung in a small blue plastic bag and stank of Fluffy's urine and smoke. I scrunched up my nose as I put them on. Urine was better than letting my butt hang out as I escaped the hospital. I'd find somewhere to wash later.

As soon as I snapped the final boot buckle in place, I headed for the door. The cop was leaning against the wall now for support. His eyes looked heavy.

Focusing my attention on the glass door, I created a small beam of heat to melt a hole in the glass. The instant I was through, I shoved the heat toward the nurse's station. A computer burst into flames, sending two nurses into a flutter. Papers flew into the air as they tossed their charts and hurried for a fire extinguisher.

Laughing to myself, I redirected the heat to another patient's closed curtain. The fibers lit and smoke began to billow out into the hall.

"Fire!" the cop yelled and raced to pull the alarm.

Patients woke all around the ward. Nurses shouted as they worked to put out the fire. Patients performed an awkward IV pole shuffle as they fled. Susan grinned. She shot me a thumbs up from where she stood at the instant coffee machine.

She called out, and I turned to see a small wad of cash flying through the air. I grabbed it and shoved it deep into my pocket.

"Don't you be skipping any meals, you hear?"

"Yes, ma'am." I waved goodbye.

My heavy footfalls echoed in the vacant stairwell. On the first floor, I slipped into a supply closet when the fire trucks rolled into the hospital lot. Several masked men rushed by. Before the sliding doors closed, I was on the move.

Never before had it felt so freeing to escape. For the first time, I had Susan's permission. That helped lighten the guilt load. But knowing the man I'd hunted for so long was nearby made every sacrifice worth it.

I would find him, no matter what it took. He was going to pay.

CHAPTER 4

hile some girls wasted their teen years chasing boys, I perfected a few life skills. Like hot-wiring a car. I'd lost count of how many times that came in handy. Susan had insisted that my momma's dream of a good education not die with her. So I'd gone to school like she asked. But showing up and sticking around were two very different things.

Slipping behind the wheel of a Jeep, I worked fast to shut off the alarm. Sweet silence filled the air. The needle showed three-quarters of a tank of gas. Luck was finally smiling on me.

Crime scene tape roped off the alley when I arrived. I rolled past and parallel parked a few cars away. Pieces of government equipment remained behind.

"I guess they can't find the source of their gas leak," I muttered.

Keeping my head ducked low, I hurried to reach my hiding spot. I grabbed my stashed bag and did a quick check to make sure everything was safe. Even with the scent of day-old trash clinging to its fabric, it still smelled better than I did.

I searched a several-block radius from the condo to locate a place to get cleaned up. Slipping inside the Greedy Hamster, I passed a frazzled bartender. There was little space to move during the booming lunch rush.

With the bathroom lock engaged, I washed in record time. The water turned grimy as smoke and wolf urine leached out of my clothes. I made an attempt to use the hand dryer on them, but a pounding at the door told me time was up.

A tray of steaming food caught my eye as I passed the kitchen. I gave in to the temptation to steal a fry. The mixture of grease and salt told me it'd been far too long since I ate.

But the small wad of cash in my pocket had to last.

Back at the Jeep, I sunk low in my seat, determined to watch the street. Cars rolled by at regular intervals. Couples with small children came and went from the condo, headed for the park at the end of the road. The doorman directed a delivery van to the rear of the building.

It was business as usual. All apart from one important detail: a Rolls Royce sat parked in front. Its silver paint gleamed in the sunlight. I would have bet the interior still had that new-car smell. Judging by the other cars parked in this neighborhood, the Rolls was a rarity.

Cars didn't do anything for me. One man's priceless baby was another man's target of mayhem. I wasn't interested in the underbelly of Denver. Not the human side, at least.

What did interest me was how fast that car was replaced. Only someone with a great deal of money and connections could pull that off. I doubted there were many dealers in the area.

I didn't know for sure that it belonged to my momma's killer, but my gut told me to follow that car. I'd learned to listen to my instincts. Sure, there was that one time that it led me to a nest of hungry vampires, but I was a silver lining kind of gal. I lived. That was good enough for me.

Ripples of heat rose from the hood of the Jeep. June was a nightmare no matter where you lived. Growing up in the Deep South taught me to deal with high humidity and bugs the size of Frisbees. Denver had nothing on Savannah or Alabama.

I ignored the growling in my stomach and moved to the back seat. That helped minimize my exposure to the sun. Even with the windows cracked, I panted like a freakin' dog.

Not long after school buses took to the streets, a cop car rolled to a stop at the alleyway. I peered between the seats. One of the men was from the hospital that morning.

I'm so busted.

If there was one thing I'd learned, it was that paranoia kept you alive and out of jail. Digging through the cargo area in search of a cover, I groaned.

"Of course my luck would dive straight into Crapsville." I lifted a wool blanket and glared at its offensive texture. "Talk about a sweatbox from hell."

The cops hung around long enough for me to turn into a puddle of sweat. The instant they pulled away from the curb, I burst free. Pressing my face to the window, I sucked in great gulps of cooler air.

I allowed myself small breaks outside of the car as the afternoon turned to dusk. The Rolls didn't move. No one came to check out the crime scene. I watched to see if any of the fight-club crowd would return. Some were sure to be nosy. The explosion had been all over the news. It wouldn't surprise me if Fuzzbert showed up to find any cash he'd stashed away.

When the last threads of light bled from the sky, I couldn't deny my stomach any longer. I snagged a hot dog from a food truck. The remaining sixty-eight dollars wouldn't get me far, but I'd stretch every penny of it.

The rumbling in my stomach abated, and a new weariness set in. I'd spent a good part of my day trying to heal. Resting in the back of a sweltering car wasn't as easy as it sounded, but it helped restore a bit of my energy. Enough to seal my final wounds, at least. The bruises would take time.

Pressing into the headrest, I fought against sleep. I was a night owl by default, which came in handy when hunting state to state. I bummed rides off more truck drivers than I cared to count. Most of them were nice. The others earned their missing fingers for trying to mess with me.

My eyes grew heavy as the cooler night breeze slipped through the narrow gap of my window. I was nodding off when the doorman's voice called from across the street, "Let me get that door for you, sir."

Popping my head up, I saw my momma's killer slide behind the driver's seat of the Rolls Royce. The doorman tried to close the door for him, but it yanked right out of his hands. No tip was given.

"So you're a cheap bastard, too," I said.

I tapped the wires together, and the Jeep roared to life. I eased out of my spot and followed the Rolls. By the time we hit the edge of Denver, it was full blown night. That black-eyed bastard spent an hour guiding me on a tour of a suburban nightmare.

"Looks like I'm not the only one who's paranoid," I said, easing behind an older model SUV.

He wasn't my first mark. I knew to keep my distance and blend with what little traffic there was. Off-roading vehicles were a dime a dozen in this state. I wouldn't stand out.

Entering the interstate six cars behind him, I kept my pace slower than his. At times, I allowed the distance to reach half a mile. I eyed each exit to make sure he didn't take a sudden turn. Instead, he seemed quite content to cruise at only five miles over the speed limit. Wherever he was going, he was in no hurry to arrive.

He pulled over for gas one time. I eased the Jeep into a station across the street. Keeping him in my sights, I put a few gallons into my own tank in case he decided to take off across the country. I wasn't about to lose him because I was a poor planner.

The farther we drove from Denver, the more distance there was between exits. From time to time, I spied the glow of a town against the cloudy sky. The mountains grew more impressive as we headed south on state highways. I blasted the AC almost as high as I did the speakers. Belting out eighties rock helped me stay awake.

Half an hour later, the Rolls took a side road. A quick glance at my phone's GPS showed nothing in that direction. No town. No rest stop. Nothing but uninhabited mountains. At least, I hoped they were uninhabited. Who knew what creatures lurked in the dark out here?

"Where are you going?" I eased the Jeep off the highway.

With the traffic almost nonexistent now, I had to maintain a greater distance. Coming out of one bend, I saw the Rolls drifting into another. With each turn, the gradient increased. Stress wound me tighter than a jack-in-the-box. It would be easy for me to lose him up here.

My headlights didn't feel powerful enough to cut through the inky night. I spotted eyes shining from the woods, but passed by too fast to get a second glance.

"It could be anything," I said. "A harmless coyote. Doesn't mean it has to be something supernatural."

The clouds parted, and for a moment, the forest shimmered with moonglow. The dappled light filtered through tall pines, firs, and aspens. But in the thickest parts, it enhanced the eerie darkness.

I laughed. "Maybe I need to tone down the paranoia a bit."

But the farther I drove, the more I felt like I was being watched. Hairs rose on the back of my neck. I kept a close watch on my rearview mirror, sure that something darted across the road behind me.

As I turned a sharp bend, the light of the moon vanished. A dark shape flew over the hood of the car, and I slammed on the brakes. The tires skidded, and the Jeep fishtailed. The brakes locked down and sent me careening toward the guardrail. I closed my eyes and threw up my hands to protect my face. Sparks and the grinding of metal filled my world.

Then an ear-piercing screech filled the car. My eardrums vibrated as the car tipped.

I'm going over!

Inches above my head, great talons pierced the roof. I cried out as the car lifted into the air and then dropped back onto all four tires. The shock absorbers took the brunt of the impact. The chassis groaned. The car fell still.

My hands shook as I peeled them off the steering wheel. "What was that?"

With a powerful flap of its wings, a bird appeared from the valley below. It climbed into the sky with impossible speed. I leaned hard enough against the steering wheel to earn a new bruise come morning.

"The wingspan has to be at least thirty feet," I whispered. I used my hand to try to measure it against the distant road. "That thing could carry off a baby elephant."

Or a car. I shuddered at the thought.

The bird soared on the wind with a grace that betrayed its enormous size. Distinct color variations in its feathers appeared in the moonlight. The patterns reminded me of an eagle, but far more intricate.

The bird was mesmerizing to watch as it dipped toward the tree line. Then it burst back up into the air with terrific speed. Each flap of its wings bowed the trees toward the ground with a force to match that of a small cyclone.

I knew that I needed to go. I'd already let far too much distance come between us. But I couldn't make myself move.

There was something about this bird that called to me. Though the creature had sent me into a panic, it had also saved me from falling into the ravine. What sort of intelligence did it have? What did it feel like to command the skies?

For several minutes, the bird circled. It appeared to have no destination in mind. Nothing else moved. No sounds, apart from the life-changing guitar riffs of Metallica, disturbed the peace. Then, just as suddenly as it had arrived, the bird was gone. I craned my neck to search the skies, but the bird never reappeared.

"Beautiful," I whispered. That one word summed up so much, and yet it didn't feel large enough to capture what I was feeling.

After one last look at the vacant skies, I pulled the Jeep back onto the road. The ride was not so smooth. The tires pulled a bit to the right. But when I gunned the engine, it followed my command.

"Where are you?" I said.

By now, the man I pursued could've disappeared completely. After several miles, I noticed a distinct downward slope to the road. The turns became sharper, the dropoff more perilous. Near the bottom of the mountain was a pair of headlights.

"That'd better be you." I urged the speedometer on.

Several miles separated us now. No matter how hard I gunned the engine, I couldn't catch up. With each sharp bend, I had to slam on my brakes or risk flying off the edge. The night's shadows stretched on, making it harder to judge distance. It took a half hour before I reached the bottom. I white-knuckled the wheel as I blew by a babbling stream alongside a straight but narrow road. The stream grew into a river, fed by the melting snow of the mountains.

Lights appeared up ahead, and I eased off the gas pedal.

"Havenwood Falls," I read aloud as I passed the sign. Glancing at my GPS again, I saw nothing. No town name. No road apart from this one. "Well, that's not weird at all."

As I drove over the town limit, warmth seeped into my chest. It was like what I felt while watching the bird. There were no words to describe it. It was more of a feeling of coming home. Which was absurd, since I didn't actually remember what home felt like.

Ignoring the speed limit, I passed a high school on my left, a turnoff for a ski resort on my right. Street signs with ascending numbers caught my eye before the town center came into view. It looked quaint. There was an array of boutique shops, a couple coffee houses, consignment shops, and more. There was even a cute little gazebo next to a fountain. It was the sort of place where good things happened to nice people.

A large banner with the words "Midsummer Night's Festival" hung across Main Street. Large posters with a Shakespearean feel were hung in several of the windows.

"Wow. I really don't belong around here," I said. Rolling down my window, I breathed in deep the clean mountain air. "But it's not a half bad place to rest up."

Havenwood Falls was larger than I would've imagined when entering the town. I searched for the missing Rolls for an hour, but it had disappeared. I checked out the cemetery and drove through a development with a country club, searching driveways for the missing car. I spotted several motorcycles parked out front of a building named Swords of the Infernal Night, according to the sign over the door. SIN for short—that seemed appropriate.

"Cute name," I chuckled as I passed the Get Buffed! business sign. Not that I would ever step foot in a place like that. Sweaty men ogling themselves in the mirror while they pumped iron wasn't my thing.

"That bites," I grumbled, admitting defeat. He was gone.

There was no sign of taillights on the road leading away from Havenwood Falls. I visually searched the mountainsides for several minutes to be sure. Convinced that he remained in town, at least for the night, I made my way back to the big park with a sign that said Danzan Park. Snatching my bag off the back seat, I found a community bathroom. It surprised me when the door swung open.

"Well, look at that." I locked the door behind me. "I didn't even have to pick the lock. People around here must be way too trusting."

With my shirt hung over the sink, I stared at myself in the mirror. Every way I turned, my flesh showed a patchwork of nasty bruises. The one over Fluffy's last bite was an angry purple.

I dabbed cool paper towels over the bruises. I cleaned away the sweat. I'd lost count of how many times I'd done a strip wash like this one. Teenagers should be at home, draining every drop of hot water from their parents' tank. Not standing in some strange bleached public restroom.

My hip bones pressed against the skin. My cheeks looked less plump than when I had lived back home, getting three square meals a day. The loss of body fat gave me a six-pack, though.

"It's worth it." Leaning over the sink, I splashed water on my face. "I found him."

The water ran between the layers of scar tissue that covered the right side of my face. I stared at my burns without emotion. The burns were a part of me, whether I liked it or not. My momma died the night I got these. Walking away with a few scars seemed a small price to pay for my life. Losing my momma . . . well, that was just about the most any gal could pay.

Of all the wounds I'd survived and healed, my tears were helpless to reverse this damage.

Standing there under the blinking halogen lights, I poked at the wounded flesh. The skin was puffy and pale. It never tanned like the rest of me.

"What do you care how it looks?" I asked my reflection. "You're never around long enough to hook up with a guy."

Wasn't that the truth?

There was a time my burns were an embarrassment. People stopped and stared. Kids were cruel. But every snide remark made me stronger. They were a daily reminder of my purpose.

With a sigh, I braided my tangled hair and donned my clothes again. The leather pants were a pain to pull on with my skin still damp. I could probably get another day or two out of this set, as long as I didn't get into any more fights.

Once back at the Jeep, I made one more drive around town just to be sure, then turned the car toward the town center. Waking up in front of the police station in a stolen car didn't seem like the smartest idea, so I made my way to the southern side of the square.

Pulling into a parking spot in front of Coffee Haven, a hipster sort of coffee shop that looked way too trendy for my liking, I turned off the engine. Despite the quick wash I had earlier in the day, I needed to inspect my wounds again. I reclined the driver's seat and searched the sky through the sunroof one last time. Clouds concealed the moon, and a light mist had begun to fall. I turned onto my side and sighed. Sleeping in cars had never been my forte, but there was no other option. My measly stash of cash wasn't enough to cover even one night at that cute little inn at the end of the block.

Balling the blanket into a pillow, I closed my eyes. "You escaped me tonight. I won't let you get away a second time."

CHAPTER 5

*M*ornings sucked. So did the people who loved them. I hated all those perky smiles and chipper greetings, as if six a.m. was the best freakin' time of the day. News flash, folks. The rest of the world dragged until someone took pity on them and passed an espresso.

Teenagers didn't do mornings. Period. Since I was still nineteen for another two days, I considered myself an expert on all things moody, melodramatic, and insomniac. So when a pounding on my car window sent me into panic mode the next morning, I came up fighting.

"What the heck, man?" A spike of heat flared in my palms, scorching the bottom of the steering wheel. I snuffed out the flames and hoped the guy didn't notice the small puff of smoke.

His shadow fell over me when he stepped up to the window. It relieved my temporary state of sun blindness long enough to reveal that I'd sworn at a cop. Or rather, a rent-a-cop, by the looks of it.

"Perfect." I rubbed my hands over my face. This was not how I wanted the day to begin. Especially since I was sitting in a stolen car.

"Ma'am, are you aware that you're in a no parking zone?"

I blinked. It was hard to focus with a massive crick in my neck and a hole in my stomach the size of the Grand Canyon. It took me a full minute to process that he wasn't accusing me of falling asleep in someone else's car.

See? I could find the silver lining even at the butt crack of dawn.

"This isn't a handicapped space," I called back through the gap at the top of my window.

The shiny gold letters on his badge told me his name was Lloyd. He turned and pointed at a paper sign stapled to a wooden stake at the front of my car. I couldn't read the words, as the sides folded in on themselves in the wind, but I got the gist of it. I was in a temporary unloading zone for some stupid town festival.

That's when I remembered the festival signs and groaned. Some days I had the worst luck.

"I'm going to have to ask you to vacate the premises." He placed one hand on his hip, and with the other, he jerked his thumb back over his shoulder.

Lloyd looked determined to stand right there and watch until I moved. This posed a slight problem, considering I had to hotwire my ride.

"Can't you give a girl a second to wake up?" I yawned and stretched my arms as high as the ceiling of the Jeep would allow.

The young man pursed his lips in response.

He didn't look much older than me. Mid-twenties at the most. The closer I looked, the more I began to suspect that he was a greenie. He definitely wasn't a real cop. Probably just hired on a part-time basis when the real cops were too busy to deal with the small stuff. His shirt was wrinkle-free and the seams of his pants were pressed. His badge didn't have a scratch on it. The holster at his hip was still shiny with polish.

I could take him if I wanted to.

"I'm afraid you're going to have to finish waking up somewhere else, ma'am." His voice even cracked a little as he tried to sound official. "The vendors will be setting up shortly, and I have to clear the area."

I turned to look out the passenger window. Main Street and the park across from it looked empty. Not a single soul, vendor table, or vehicle was in sight.

"The place is a ghost town. Looks like you can spare me five minutes."

Lloyd's jaw flinched. From the corner of my eye, I saw his hand travel to rest on his Taser.

"Exit the vehicle, ma'am."

My hands tightened on the bottom of the steering wheel, concealing the burn marks. If he called me ma'am one more time . . .

"Now." He backed away three steps so I could open my door. I paused to consider my options.

I could do as he said and let him puff up with self-importance. Then he would threaten me with a ticket that I would never pay.

I could take him out. That option sounded pretty good right about now.

Or I could sit right here and see how far he would take this.

When he grabbed the Taser, I sighed and reached for the door handle.

Might as well play along. I couldn't get run out of town before I found my momma's killer.

"I'm coming. I'm coming." The Jeep door creaked as it swung open.

I arched my back to ease the stiffness as I stood. Everything ached. On top of that, I looked like a mess. After a night of tossing and turning, my braid was ruined. A wild mane of fire surrounded my face. When the wind changed directions, it revealed my burns.

He gave me a once-over. "That's quite a scar you've got there."

"I could say the same about your crater face, but I'm not rude." I gritted my teeth. I sure would have loved to punch him in the throat right about now.

As a child, I was a sweet little thing. I'd spend my weekends picking flowers and making necklaces with them for my momma. I baked cookies and made sweet tea. I smiled a lot back then, too. Even had proper manners.

Now I had a chip on my shoulder. One that I usually didn't stick around long enough to apologize for.

Lloyd narrowed his gaze. "You a runaway or something?"

"That's none of your business. I'm an adult. End of story." This guy was tap dancing all over my rising bad temper.

Thin lines appeared around his eyes when he squinted against the sunlight. I snorted. The rookie hadn't even earned sunglass marks on the sides of his face yet.

"Step aside."

"Excuse me?" I crossed my arms over my chest. This guy was starting to piss me off. I had to work to control the tingling in my hands.

"I said, step aside."

"Not going to happen." I stood my ground. I'd had about all I was going to take from him.

His eyes widened. Apparently, he'd never been told no by a suspect before. Or whatever the heck he thought I was. "No?"

"You have no probable cause or evidence of criminal activity against me to give you the right to search my car. Judging by your attire, I'd say you aren't even a real cop. I happen to know that if you are nothing more than private security, you have about as much authority as I do right now. So the answer is no. You do not have my permission. In fact, you have the complete opposite."

Lloyd wiped at a bead of sweat on his brow. He looked baffled.

"And furthermore," I took a small step toward him and smiled when he flinched. "I don't appreciate you treating me like a common criminal. Sleeping in my car is legal. I was not parked in the wrong spot, and that sign was not there last night."

Looking toward the sidewalk, I spotted a mallet, wooden stakes, a stack of signs, and a staple gun.

"It is my job to—"

"Yeah, I get it, Barney Fife. You've got a duty. Don't we all. But you need to learn some people skills, or you'll wind up on the wrong end of that Taser one of these days."

His finger flinched against the Taser. "Is that a threat?"

"Of course not." My words dripped with poison-laced honey. "I'd call it friendly advice."

He shuffled his feet, seeming unsure of what to do next. When he scratched the back of his neck, I almost burst out laughing. This guy was a real piece of work. If the real law enforcement in the area was anything like Lloyd, I didn't have anything to worry about.

A sudden blast of a car horn startled me. I looked over my shoulder, but not before seeing Lloyd rush to put his Taser away.

A sleek sedan paused at the street corner before turning our way.

"Is there a problem here?" a smooth voice called from within the darkened interior.

The windows were as black as the paint job. I couldn't imagine that was legal, but one look at Lloyd told me that he'd be the last person to say anything about it. The driver kept his face in the shadow of the vehicle.

"What's it to you?" I asked.

The vehicle was not a marked police car. In fact, I couldn't see any visible form of identification on the vehicle from where I stood.

"I'm a concerned citizen. Nothing more."

"How sweet, but I can take care of myself."

"Yes," the man drew out the word like the hiss of a snake. "I can see that. Seems to me that Lloyd here might not understand that quite as well as I do."

The rent-a-cop straightened his shoulders. "I have orders to clear the area, Mr. Laroc. What with the festival and all happening today."

Unlike Lloyd, I didn't cower back from the hard once-over that came from the blacked-out car. The man turned his attention back to me. From the depths of the darkness, I caught the glint of a golden eyeshine.

"You're new to Havenwood Falls. I haven't seen you around town before."

I shrugged. "Arrived last night."

A string of smoke escaped through the open window. "Are you here for work or pleasure?"

"I don't see how that's your business."

"A girl who sleeps in her car doesn't seem all that keen on sticking around long. It is my business if you intend to stir up any trouble."

Well, now that was interesting. This concerned citizen had a reason for nosing around and wanted to be sure I knew it. I made a show of wiping my nose so that I could conceal my inhale. I caught the scent of a vampire and the foul stench of an ogre. But there was a strange odor in the air. One that I couldn't place.

"A bit of both, then." With another shrug, I leaned back against the Jeep. This conversation needed to end.

The engine of the car gave a sudden throaty roar. I tried to see into the interior, but it was almost as if a veil of night lay between me and the driver. I recognized it as a glamour requiring a mage to be present. That must have been the final person in the vehicle.

Whoever this guy was, he didn't want to be seen.

The hairs on my arm began to rise. My gut clenched as I fisted my hands at my side. Something wasn't right. The only time I ever saw a blending of species like this was at a fight. Or in the underbelly of some criminal organization. Havenwood Falls hardly seemed the place to find a crime boss. But if my momma's killer was hiding out here, then I was dead wrong. The peaceful little rural town could be a front for something far more sinister.

What other evil lurked within these town limits?

Turning to glance at Lloyd, I knew right off that he was human. No supernatural could be that big of a bumbling idiot.

"Well, I'm sure Lloyd here will be happy to let you off with a warning. After he collects a few minor details for his records, of course." The man's voice was as smooth as a razor's edge now. "I'm sure you understand."

I had zero intention of handing over a single ounce of detail about myself.

"Isn't that right, Lloyd?" Another puff of smoke exited the car. This time I realized it didn't have the scent of a cigarette or cigar. Instead, it smelled of brimstone.

My stomach clenched. Was the driver a demon of some sort? Or perhaps a dragon shifter phasing in and out of his form?

Lloyd stood to attention, breaking into my thoughts. "Yes, sir! I won't let you down, Mr. Laroc. You can count on me."

I rolled my eyes. What a pansy.

"As for you, missy, I'd be careful of that tongue while you're staying in Havenwood Falls. Folks around here don't take kindly to veiled snide remarks. Especially from outsiders."

A smirk tugged at my lips. "Who said I was trying to veil them?"

A deep chuckle emerged from the car before the window rose and the sedan rolled away. Lloyd breathed out a sigh of relief from behind me. Whoever that man was, he held some power in this town. Or at least over Lloyd.

"You always wet yourself around that guy?" I asked.

Lloyd blinked and then refocused on me. I was actually impressed when his boyish features settled into a scowl. "You don't know what you're talking about. Mr. Laroc is an important man."

I pushed off from the car. "Whatever. I know fear when I smell it."

He stiffened. "Did you say smell?"

"Yeah. Smell." I laughed and turned back to slide into the driver's seat. "You'll figure it out someday."

And that was it. No threats of a ticket. No additional warning or huffing from Lloyd. After I slammed the Jeep door shut, I looked back to see Lloyd staring down the street.

That guy really messed with his head.

Lloyd hesitated before moving to collect his signpost items from the sidewalk. With his back turned, I connected the wires. The Jeep thrummed to life, and I threw the car into reverse.

"Watch out!"

After years of training for the unexplained, I'd developed lightning fast reflexes. They didn't save me this time. One push on the gas pedal and I ran into something. The car rocked as I slammed on the brakes.

"Crap." Throwing open my door, I raced around the back to find a man sprawled on the ground. It looked like he'd been clipped and spun clean around.

"Oh, my god. You killed him!" I looked up to see horror written all over Lloyd's face. "We're dead. We're so, so dead."

The urge to punch his ugly pockmarked nose rose up again. "He's not dead. He just got knocked out when he landed."

Lloyd looked between me and the man with such utter disbelief that I almost chuckled. Who would hire a guy like him to be weekend security?

"That's going to hurt in the morning." The fallen man groaned and rolled onto his back.

Smudges marred the front of his shirt. The fabric showed a few tears. Minor road rash markings littered one side of his face where his five o'clock stubble ended. Other than that, he looked fine.

Scratch that. He was way better than fine. His hair was a sandy blond, with fascinating streaks of white. The coloring was a stark contrast to the warm tawny eyes that stared up at me. Though I was sure he was the sort of guy that girls would do a double-take for, I didn't get the sense that he was cocky.

"Well, hello to you, too." He smiled, interrupting my assessment.

I snorted. Maybe a little cocky.

Lloyd spluttered when the man pushed up to his feet, shoved the cop aside and offered me his hand. "The name's Atticus, and you're welcome to run me over any day you like."

Calluses lined the palm of his hand. His skin was kissed by the sun. I guessed him to be some sort of day laborer, judging by the sheer size of him. The telltale angle of a once-broken nose, paired with his lopsided grin, made him look younger than he probably was.

"That's quite a grip you've got there," I said when he continued shaking my hand. "I'm impressed."

He beamed back at me.

That smile could do bad things to me.

Atticus was hot. That might not be the manliest sentiment, but it was true nonetheless. Right down to his flannel shirt, dusty work boots, and the large scar that peeked out of his rolled sleeves.

If I'd known guys like him lived in Colorado, I'd have come out this way sooner.

Lloyd waved a hand in front of Atticus's face. "Are you feeling okay? Any concussion? Head trauma is completely common in hit-and-runs."

"I didn't run." I rolled my eyes. "I'm standing right here."

"Go away, Lloyd," Atticus said.

"Go away? Well, I never." The cop bristled. "Are you pressing charges against this girl, Mr. Laroc? I can call the sheriff to write her up right here and now, if you'd like. I saw it all. She was definitely at fault."

"Go away," Atticus and I said at the same time.

Lloyd's ears went red. His hands fluttered around him, unsure of what to do. Finally, he threw them in the air and walked away.

"Is he always like that?" I asked, watching the rent-a-cop fumble with his armful of materials. He dropped a few, tried to balance them on the top of his foot, and then gave up trying.

"Yeah. Rumor has it his mom dropped him a few times on his head. I prefer to think he was hexed."

"Did you say hexed? As in voodoo or witchcraft?"

Atticus's wink told me that he was joking. Thank god for that. I'd run into my fair share of witches, and some of them were as mean as rattlesnakes.

"Why'd he call you Mr. Laroc?"

"Well, that is my name. But I assume you're thinking about my uncle. I thought I saw his car pull away when I rounded the corner." He sighed. "I hope he wasn't rude. My uncle can be a bit abrupt at times."

That's an understatement.

"It's fine," I said instead. "He was just making sure Lloyd wasn't harassing me."

"Right. He's thoughtful like that." But the furrow of Atticus's brow deepened.

Not wanting to get dragged into a family affair, I glanced at the small dent in the back of the Jeep and winced. "Sorry about taking you out like that. You came out of nowhere."

Atticus waved me off. "It was my fault. I heard raised voices and came over to snoop. Guess I was standing a bit too close."

It was almost refreshing how open he was about his attempts to eavesdrop. I'd have done the same thing. Curiosity killed the cat . . . or ran him over with an SUV.

"Are you okay?" This time I took my time looking him over. For medical purposes, of course. He was a good sport and turned to give me the full view.

"Sure thing. A few bumps and scrapes. Nothing I can't handle."

Now that he mentioned a bump, I noticed a nasty one starting to form on his forehead. The split skin leaked a small trickle of blood spreading into his eyebrow.

"You'll need to get that looked at." I motioned to his head.

His fingertips were painted with blood when he pulled them away from the bump. "I'm a fast healer."

I didn't doubt that. I could sense that he wasn't human. Not by a long shot. But his scent—it was foreign to me, and yet somehow familiar. Like a lost word teetering on the tip of my tongue, but held out of reach.

"Right. Well, I should probably—" I hiked my finger over my shoulder at the open driver's side door. "I'm parked in the wrong spot on the wrong day."

Atticus glanced at Lloyd, who had moved to post another sign. "Yeah. Havenwood Falls may be small, but our festivals are mighty. It can get kind of hectic."

I laughed. I couldn't imagine anything about this sleepy little town being hectic.

"It was nice running into you." I started toward the car but fell still when his hand brushed my arm. I had a thing about people touching me, but I gave him the benefit of the doubt before I took him out.

"Do you like food?"

"Food?" I smirked.

Atticus rubbed at the back of his neck and shrugged. "Yeah, you know. The stuff that takes care of that obnoxious growling your stomach is doing right now."

Mortified, I pressed a hand to my stomach. He was right. I'd been too preoccupied to notice that my hunger level had reached DEFCON 1.

"There's a place I know that serves the best waffles in town. My treat."

I shot him a suspicious glance. "Waffles?"

"I get that it's kind of weird to share a waffle with a guy you just hit with your car, but when you stop and think about it, you owe me."

"I owe you?" I laughed. Wow. He had some balls to go with those muscles. "How do you figure that?"

"Well, you see there's this thing . . ." He pretended to think it over. "Yeah. I've got nothing. I just want to talk to you a bit longer."

The laugh lines around his eyes told me that he liked to have a good time. His smile was sincere. His eyes were clear of any visible hidden agendas. Atticus looked like a good old boy. Which made it hard to place him with the nosy guy from the sedan. Atticus didn't have any of his uncle's creep vibes, but he might know something worth hearing.

"Thanks for the offer, but I—"

"One waffle, that's all I'm asking for. Then I promise I'm out of your life, if you want."

If I want . . . oh, boy. That could easily turn into the loaded question of my day.

I could imagine a great many things I'd like to do with Atticus Laroc, but none of them brought me any closer to finding my momma's killer. So I glanced back at the idling Jeep. Atticus was a distraction—one that I wouldn't mind entertaining on any other day, but I had plans.

"You're new here, right?" he hurried to add when he realized he was losing me. "I know what it's like to be in a new place. No friends. No family. I get it."

"Who said I'm alone?" Atticus glanced at the lone backpack in the passenger seat of the car. He'd spotted my blanket as well. I sighed. "Fine. You caught me. I'm passing through."

He tilted his head to the side, pursing his lips to give me a hard stare. "Nobody *passes through* this town. It's not exactly on the way to anywhere."

"Right?" I nodded. "What's the deal with this place, anyway?"

Atticus took a step toward me. "An answer for a waffle. That's the deal."

Oh, he was good. And I was starving. Plus he was a local with obvious connections.

Am I really agreeing to this?

Pushing my hair back out of my face, I waited as his gaze flitted over my scars. There was no look of disgust or horror. His smile didn't fade an ounce. Maybe he really was a nice guy.

It wouldn't kill me to give him one meal in exchange for information.

"Make it a chocolate chip waffle and I'm in."

CHAPTER 6

One bite into my triple layer chocolate waffle told me that I'd never truly lived before. It melted in my mouth and made me think of sinful things. Atticus slumped into his chair, arm slung over the back, and gave me a knowing smile.

"It's a good thing we didn't put a bet on these." I wiped a dab of chocolate off my chin.

Atticus grinned and shoved a tall glass of milk my way. "Trust me, you're going to need this, too."

I wasn't much of a milk drinker. In fact, I wasn't much on anything that even resembled health food. Give me a bag of chips and a candy bar and I was set. But, yet again, he knew what he was talking about. The milk washed down the chocolatey goodness with perfection.

"All right. I'll admit it. These are the best waffles I've ever had." I sat back to give my stomach a chance to expand so I could shovel in a bit more. "Double brownie points for the location, too."

Atticus had brought me to the country club for breakfast. The interior looked like a log cabin fit for an HGTV show. There was a beautiful stone fireplace, with a woman perched on the hearth playing an acoustic guitar. Two plush couches sat a few feet away so that during the winter months you could snuggle by a roaring fire. The bar, brightly colored with hundreds of bottles seated on glass shelves, stood off to my left.

Lifting my face, I stared up at the huge chandelier overhead. Electric candles sat unlit under hurricane glass. Floor to ceiling windows stood no less than thirty feet high and spanned the entire far wall. Not even I could deny the beauty of an early morning overlooking a golf course. From where I sat, I could see a team of greenskeepers trimming the fairways. One man bent low to check on the sprinklers. The water hung like a fine mist in the air, giving this place an almost magical feel.

"So you want to tell me why you're in my town?" Atticus asked.

Digging into my waffles again so I didn't have to give him a full answer, I shrugged. "No real reason."

"That line might have worked on Lloyd, but I'm not such an easy sell. I know you're in trouble."

My knife clattered to the plate, making me jump. A couple at a table nearby glanced our way.

"I'm not trying to out you. Heck, I don't even know your name yet." Atticus leaned closer. "But I can tell that you're in a bad way, and I want to help."

"Why?" My defenses kicked in.

He seemed almost hurt by the question. "Because I'm a nice guy."

I snorted and picked up my knife. Even though it was nothing more than a butter knife, it felt good to have it in my hand. I missed my dagger. Fuzzbert must have run off with it during the chaos.

Stupid troll. I saw him eyeing it before my fight with Fluffy.

"Nice guys don't get far in this world," I said.

He cocked his head. "That may be true in some towns. But Havenwood Falls isn't like other places."

Though I was only halfway through my waffles, I sat back and pushed the plate aside. Not so far that I couldn't sneak another forkful or two if I chose, mind you.

"Fine. I'll bite. What makes this place so different?"

Atticus placed his palms on the table and smoothed out the tablecloth. When he spoke, it was in a hushed tone. I got the distinct feeling he didn't want anyone else to hear our conversation. "Do you believe in ghosts?"

I stared at him for a moment before I burst out laughing. "The town's haunted? Is that it?"

"Shh." He motioned for me to lower my voice. "No. But also yes at the same time."

I stopped laughing when I saw that his smile had faded. "Wait. You're serious?"

"Havenwood Falls is special." He glanced around. I followed his gaze and saw that no one was paying any attention to us. I was starting to get a vibe about this place, but I focused on Atticus instead. "There's an energy here that draws certain people to it. People who have their eyes wide open to what the world is really like. Who are willing to believe in the impossible. Someone just like you."

Thinking back to the odd tugging sensation that I'd experienced the night before, I frowned.

He spoke now in a lower whisper. "I know you can feel it."

"And?"

He leaned so far that he breached the center of the table. "You're here for a reason. We all are. Some come to expand the town through business and whatnot. Others to cause trouble."

"So you think I'm trouble?"

Atticus smiled. "I know you are."

He had a fair point there.

"And the people who are drawn here? What are they like?" I said.

"Nonhuman."

"Huh." I hadn't expected him to come right out and say it. Most creatures that I'd met on my travels liked to keep such things private.

"Let me get this straight. Because some mystical force supposedly called me here, you think I'm a freak?" The table hid my hands from sight so he couldn't see my nails digging into my palms.

Atticus offered me a kind smile. "Some might call us that."

"Well," I snorted. "I wouldn't put that particular detail on your town's tourism brochures any time soon." With that, I pushed up to my feet, not bothering to say my next words in a whisper. "The waffles were good. Shame the company was lacking."

"I didn't mean to offend you," he called as I started to walk away.

"Offend me?" I laughed and turned back. It was only when I noticed several pairs of eyes looking in our direction that I hurried back.

"You just implied that I'm a freak," I said in an angry whisper. "What's to be offended about?"

"Please." He motioned to my empty seat. "Let me explain. I'm not saying this as well as I should be."

"Is this how you pick up the girls in town? By insulting them?" I shot him a withering glare. "Sorry. I'm not that kind of girl."

He shook his head. "Look, I get it. You're not used to being around your kind in such large quantities. It can be a little disconcerting at first."

"There are no others of my kind," I bit back.

Realizing I'd spoken too loud, I shoved into my chair to glare at him. The last thing I needed was to make a scene where people would remember my face. What with the burns and all, I was pretty easy to spot.

Atticus nodded. "We all felt that way when we first came here. Havenwood Falls is a sanctuary for supernaturals, or supes for short. The outside world is a harsh place, but we can live in peace here. Shifters, mages, fae, and the like. We can be normal."

Normal. I couldn't remember the last time I felt like I was.

"Look around you. The truth is right under your nose. You just have to really look," he said.

Glancing around, I noticed people watching me. For the first time, I realized several of them were not human. A girl with a feline scent sniffed the air and turned away. One man sitting in the far corner piqued my interest. He was enormous, with an extensive growth of hair covering every part of his body not hidden by the trench coat he wore. A wide-brimmed hat sat low over his eyes.

"Is that a . . ." I trailed off, feeling silly for even thinking something so outrageous.

Atticus glanced over his shoulder. "His name is Sherman. And yeah, he's a Bigfoot. Or a yeti, I think he prefers. He's new to town. Here visiting a friend that hides out in the woods, I've heard. They aren't very social creatures, as you can imagine. I'd never actually met one before Sherman. Havenwood Falls draws in all sorts. Pretty cool, huh?"

My mouth gaped at the thought of how this town would react if a camera crew from some TV show rolled into town. Man, would they get a rude awakening!

"Yeah. Cool." I spotted no fewer than six humans sitting in the room. Not a single one paid Sherman any mind.

"It's a glamour," I whispered as I discovered the majority of the busy room was nonhuman. A pair of vampires sat in a recessed corner. They returned to their conversations over cups of blood rather than of plates of food.

"I've never seen so many species mingling together. They aren't fighting," I whispered. Then I shook myself and looked at Atticus. "And what about you?"

"What about me?" He smiled.

"I can't quite figure out which supernatural you are."

"Ah." He grinned. "I'm a man of mystery."

I snorted. "Well, don't you go thinking that I don't see what's happening here. You assume that since I'm one of you that you can pour me a big ole glass of Kool-Aid. Figure I'll be eager to sign up for the crazy train."

Atticus grinned and sat back. "I knew I'd like you. From the moment I heard you giving crap to Lloyd, I knew."

I rolled my eyes and sank back into the seat. This was too much. The idea that an entire town of supernaturals existed blew my mind. How had they managed to bring peace and order to so many species? Thinking back to his uncle's black sedan that morning with the mixture of creatures, it made sense now. The blending was a natural occurrence here.

"I'm not saying the town is perfect," he added in his hushed tone. "Some of the personalities can be a bit strong. And there are skirmishes sometimes that break out. No one is perfect. But that's why our registry is important. It helps keep people in check."

That didn't sound good. "Does everyone have to register?"

"Sure do. Humans live here as well, but they don't know about us. We either assume human form while in town or use a glamour to conceal our real identity. Sometimes a memory charm is used if things get out of hand, but for the most part, it works. Some of the humans have relatives who come to visit. Others show up and decide to stick around. For them, it's a matter of a little paperwork and a background check. But for those of us with extra abilities, the registration process is a little more in-depth."

Ideas began to spiral through my mind. If everyone had to register, that meant there had to be a record of my momma's killer.

"You want to tell me why seeing that registry means so much to you?"

I blinked and looked up to meet his piercing gaze. *Crap.* I must have let my excitement show.

"You're right. I am here for a reason. I'm looking for someone."

When he nodded, a bit of sandy blond hair fell over his eye, and he brushed it away. "I figured as much."

"Everything all right over here?" Our waitress returned, balancing a steaming pot of coffee on her tray. She directed the question toward Atticus.

"We're good," Atticus said. "You know I'm a sucker for your waffles, Harlow."

The girl's long hair was pulled back from her face, revealing stunning eyes, cheekbones worthy of envy, and flawless skin. Her smile was just a shade too wide when she spoke to Atticus, twirling her hair around her finger like a pro.

I decided right then that I hated her. Not because she was beautiful, or charming, or god knows a gazillion things different than me. It was because she did it all with perfect ease. I hated people that could breeze through situations that made me cringe.

"Why don't you grab our check and bring it to me?" Atticus

flashed me a smile. "I'm treating our new guest to the finest Havenwood Falls has to offer."

Harlow cut her eyes toward me. She did a poor job hiding her look of annoyance, but Atticus didn't take notice.

"Sure thing." Her heels clicked on the wood floor as she walked away.

"I don't need charity. I can pay my own way," I snapped the instant she was gone.

When his eyebrow hiked high enough to dust the ends of his hair, I knew he saw straight through that lie. "It's the least I can do, since I blackmailed you into joining me."

"You seem pretty good at that," I grumbled. Harlow had gotten under my skin for no good reason.

Sunlight caught the white streaks in his hair when he nodded. "I've had a bit of practice."

"I bet you have."

A man like Atticus was sure to have more than a few admirers in town. Not that I cared. Not one little bit.

"Our waitress likes you."

"Who? Harlow? She's a nice girl." Atticus smirked. "And you're changing the subject."

"So are you," I shot back.

For a moment, I thought he was going to jump into a battle of wit and words, but instead, he fell silent, watching me. Why did everyone around this place have to keep sizing me up?

"Who is he?"

"Huh?" I was confused.

"Your mark. The guy you're hunting."

"How do you know he's a he?" I challenged.

"Is he a lover? A long-lost soul mate?" He tapped his chin. "No. You don't seem the type for that."

"You're batting zero on the whole not offending me thing," I said.

His tawny gaze glowed pure gold when he leaned forward. Maybe it was a play of the sunlight streaming in through the windows, but I'd have bet money it wasn't.

"No," he mused. "You're looking for someone you hate."

Well, that's a bit too close for comfort.

"You know, for a super-secret town, y'all sure pry into people's business too much."

He reached out to take my hand. I flinched, but didn't rip my hand away. "You do a good job of hiding it, but I can sense your pain. This man took something from you. Something you loved."

I looked away, afraid he might stare long enough to see the terrified little girl still trapped there. Sliding my hand out from under his, I clasped mine together in my lap to stop them from shaking.

"My business is my own. Take a hint and butt out." I stood, and this time I didn't look back.

CHAPTER 7

*I*t wasn't until I reached the sidewalk out front that I remembered I drove both of us to breakfast. I wasn't about to hop in a car with a stranger. Apparently he didn't have the same qualms.

"Bugger!" I stomped my foot. "Way to ruin a perfectly good exit."

"It's a lot easier to storm off when you don't have a passenger." Atticus chuckled from behind me as I marched toward the Jeep, but his long stride overtook me. "You could have left me behind. Thanks for sticking around."

"Like I really had a choice." I groaned. "Taking a hint isn't one of your strong suits, is it?"

"Nope. Well, I mean it usually is, but I like you."

"Gee. Lucky me."

He sank into the passenger seat beside me. Nice homes of varying shapes, sizes, and landscaping passed by as I picked up speed. It didn't take long to realize I would have been lost without Atticus guiding me. Why did they have to make the houses look so similar?

As I turned back onto Main Street and headed toward the town center, I realized those waffles were starting to fight me. The school parking lot we passed on the way was packed with cars. I weaved through the traffic.

"Where did all these cars come from? It's not a school day."

"The festival, remember? We have something every month. You'll love this one. The town goes all out with their costumes."

"Costumes?" When I glanced at the busy sidewalk, I realized several people were dressed in old-world style dresses. One man even had breeches and stockings on. "Oh, that is too funny!"

"Hey, don't knock the style. If you stick around long enough, you might just buy a dress."

"Not likely," I snickered.

The sleepy little town square had become a bustling mecca of trade. I hated crowds, but what better place to do some reconnaissance than right there? Turning into one of the last spaces available behind a row of apartments, I threw the car into park and distracted Atticus while I disconnected the wires.

"Is that guy carrying a lance?" I asked.

"Sure. Later this afternoon they will have a mini jousting tournament. My brother Orlon and I won it last year."

"Of course you did." I slammed the Jeep door behind me. "Is that . . . turkey legs I smell?"

Atticus grinned. "It wouldn't be a Renaissance faire without turkey legs. Come on."

His excitement made me smile as he ushered me toward the square. We passed by a quaint art studio and Pyntz Butcher Shoppe. Both had closed signs for the festivities. I noticed Lloyd's No Parking signs lined with anal perfection around the square as we crossed the street.

"Wait!" Atticus called as I darted out into traffic. Horns blared, and a few people shot me their middle finger, but I made it to the other side unharmed.

"Well, that was fun," he said a second later.

"Are you kidding me right now?" I turned to see him grinning. "Why did you—no. Never mind. I don't care. Please don't feel the need to escort me around. I'm perfectly capable of seeing the sights on my own."

"Of course you are." He raised a hand to wave at a couple decked out in their Renaissance attire. The little girl with them looked precious with ribbons tied into her hair. "But what's the fun in that?"

As we passed by a Tacos for Daze truck parked out front of the Haven Saloon, I winced and held my breath. There was no way I could eat another bite. A long line outside Coffee Haven told me that I'd been right about the clientele and how popular it would be.

"You weren't kidding about the crowds." I whistled as we joined a herd moving toward the park. Last night I'd slept to the peaceful sounds of the water fountain. Today, all I could hear was laughter and music in the air. I realized it was coming from speakers set up around the area.

"Wait until tonight. That's when the real fun starts."

Tonight? Well, it was official. I was stuck with Atticus. That much was clear. What wasn't clear was why. I was a nobody. A total stranger who had established I had a chip on my shoulder. Yet Atticus stayed glued to my side. He pointed out some of the vendors, rattling off details about who they were and what businesses they ran, most of which I refused to admit were actually interesting.

He introduced me to Rhys Graywalk, the owner of the Dirty Knuckle, who was passing out a few samples of libations despite the fact that five o'clock was a long way off. Atticus offered me a frothy beer in a plastic cup, but I turned him down. No sense revealing that I was still underage.

Next, we came to a booth ran by Rhiannon Underwood, gardener extraordinaire from Fairy Tale Florists. Even though flowers weren't my thing, hearing Rhiannon talk about the predatory aspects of a Venus fly trap to a little girl was pretty cool. She'd just started giving a presentation about plants used to make deadly concoctions in the dark ages when Atticus dragged me on.

Charlotte Ramsay ran a booth for Shear Magic, situated just out front of her shop. Atticus got a good laugh when Charlotte offered me a discount on a waxing. Bastard.

Havenwood Falls Medical Center had a booth set up, but I steered clear of that. No sense tempting fate. But the staff did look hilarious in their jester costumes.

"What about this one?" Atticus asked.

"Oh, heck no." I practically ran from the Tragic Ink booth.

"Got something against tattoos?" Atticus didn't even try to hide his smile.

"That's none of your business," I huffed, annoyed that I'd let him see my weakness. I didn't care how childish it was. Needles were evil!

As the hours went by, it was easy to see how ingrained Atticus was in the town. He knew everyone, and they certainly knew him. His easygoing manner was popular with the buxom ladies. He was the target of a couple obvious advances, but he was a gentleman in his rejections.

I found myself watching him as we wandered through the crowds. He stood a head taller than most, and his broad frame cleared a path for me.

"It's ok to stare," he said over his shoulder as we passed the turkey drumstick food truck that smelled like heaven on wheels. I was pretty sure I smelled funnel cake too.

"At what?" I asked.

"My butt. I know you want to."

That sent me into a fit of giggles. I couldn't remember the last time I laughed like that.

"There it is." He wagged a finger at me. "I knew it was there, hidden under that sexy little scowl of yours."

I stopped walking. "Sexy?"

"Well, yeah." He scratched at the thin layer of beard growth. "You have looked in the mirror, right?"

More times than I cared to admit. I knew what was there, and it was nothing special.

"Hey," he whispered and gently took hold of my chin. "I know that look. I've seen it before."

He brushed my hair back from my face and let his gaze fall over my scars. "Why must it always be the good ones who never see their true beauty?"

I wanted to scoff and crack a joke about his lame pickup line, but somehow I knew it wasn't one. His smile was too genuine and his eyes sincere. It made me wonder who in his life had taught him such compassion.

"Well." I blew out a breath. "You just made this awkward."

"I did, didn't I?" He laughed and let his hand drop away. But when I caught him watching me, I couldn't help but smile. He had that way about him.

We made the rounds of the festival vendors three times before I allowed myself to admit defeat. My momma's killer wasn't here. But it sure seemed like everyone else in town was.

I allowed myself to be dragged to a play set up on a small stage placed in the gazebo. It would have been mind-numbingly boring if not for the fact that one of the bumbling characters reminded me of Lloyd. I hid my smile until Atticus bumped my arm.

"I saw that."

"Did not." But I didn't mind that he'd seen. The day had turned out to actually be nice. Far better than what I'd expected.

As the crowds dispersed, many people rushing to line up for the food trucks again, I sank down onto a bench to people-watch. Atticus sat with me, content to be silent for a while.

"So what's the deal with tonight?"

He glanced at me. "What?"

"You said that there was more." And more might mean a sighting of my momma's killer.

"Oh." He nodded his head at an older woman. I think he'd told me she was Mabel, who worked at Broastful Brew. Somehow the kind woman, and her less trendy coffee shop, seemed more Atticus's style. And mine, for that matter. "The daytime activities are for everyone. The ones that happen tonight, well . . . let's just say it's a bit of a free-for-all."

My eyebrow hiked. "Meaning?"

He leaned in close. His arm, slung over the back of the bench, brushed along my back as he whispered in my ear, "You ever see that movie *The Purge?*"

I snorted. "You're kidding."

"Nope." He moved back but didn't remove his arm. "Now I'm not going to say that it's that bad, but things can get pretty wild around here."

"Wild?" I laughed. That seemed hardly the sort of thing that would happen in a place like this, but then again, I now understood what lived here. "You going?"

This time, Atticus hesitated. "Maybe."

I shifted to look at him. "You scared?"

He laughed and shook his head. "No. I can handle myself. It's just . . . it's not my thing."

I watched him for a moment, trying to decipher his meaning. "It bothers you, doesn't it?"

Atticus kept his gaze focused on a shop called Room across the street. It was located just behind Broastful Brew and had a dove-gray awning. The front was a clean white brick with two lovely trees planted in wooden boxes. There was nothing noteworthy about the building that would require his candid study. That's when I noticed that he was watching a woman pacing in the window.

"Someone special?" I asked.

He blinked and then looked at me. "Who? Melissa? Nah. She's just been through a lot recently. My aunt loves fine art, and Room has the best in town. Melissa's son Harry is—was—a godsend." Atticus's expression grew somber as he clasped his hands in his lap. "I can't imagine how hard it must have been on Melissa to lose him. Especially knowing her new baby was due not long after."

"You know, I don't know many guys who would care about someone that much." And that was the darn truth. "You've got this knack for putting other people, even strangers, first, don't you?"

He smiled. "Trust me, some days it's a curse."

"Maybe." I offered him a small smile back. "But the world needs more men like you."

"Is that a compliment I hear?"

I laughed and shrugged. "Maybe."

He leaned back into the bench, folded his hands over his chest and grinned. "I'll take it."

A man entered the shop, and I heard the small tinkle of a bell over the door. I watched as Melissa moved to greet her customer. Room was one of the few shops that hadn't chosen to have a vendor table for the fair, but I supposed she wouldn't want to risk damaging her son's art.

She looked to be around forty, with long legs, perfectly blond hair and a tiny waist that made me feel even more insecure.

"I bet yoga is her miracle cure for post-pregnancy weight," I muttered and instantly felt a stab of guilt. Hadn't Atticus just told me that this woman had experienced a great deal of pain recently? *I am a terrible person.*

"Want a snow cone?" Atticus said, breaking into my thoughts.

"You've got a thing for food, don't you?"

He shrugged. "There's a high probability that I have a sweet tooth. Besides, it's sticky hot."

He was right about that. The humidity levels had risen since that morning. One glance at the clouds told me that there was a storm brewing. "I'm good."

"You sure? I'm buying."

"Go," I laughed.

"Fine. Your loss." He moved to stand in a long line outside a colorful stand.

The scent of sugar and ripe fruit was heavy in the air. Closing my eyes, I breathed it all in. If this had been a real Renaissance faire, there might have been animal feces lining small paddocks. Thankfully, this town went with the more sanitary bunnies in cages and a few chickens for sale.

That's when I caught the sound of a voice I recognized. My eyes popped open, and I searched the crowd.

It was him.

Standing at a booth on the other side of the street, I saw my momma's killer stooped low in conversation.

"Got you." I darted through the crowd, wishing I was as big as Atticus as I tried to push my way through. Several people cried out when I shoved them aside. A little girl burst into tears when I hit her from behind and she lost her grip on a red balloon. Guilt wiggled through me as I watched it rise into the sky.

"Sorry!" But my apology meant nothing to that little girl. I wanted to stop, to go back and offer to buy her a new one, but I didn't have time. The man was already walking away, heading toward the long line of cars that weaved down the street.

"Stop!" I yelled.

Though several people around me paused to watch as I rushed past, my momma's killer did not.

"Get out of my way!" I leaped over a booth that had been set on its end to tear down for the evening. The tablecloth flapped in the wind and caught my foot. I hit the ground hard, knocking the wind out of me.

"Are you okay?"

I groaned and looked up into Atticus's face. "Why do you always show up during the embarrassing moments?"

"Well, you do have quite a few of them." When he helped me to a seated position, I fought to see around his shoulders, but it was too late. The man was gone.

"No!" I beat my fist into the ground.

Atticus's eyes narrowed. "Care to tell me what that was all about? You tore this place apart like it was nothing."

I shoved my hair back out of my face and glared. "I saw him. Thanks to you and those people in my way, I lost him."

"Whoa." He held up his hands. "I don't seem to remember standing in your way when you took off like a bat out of hell."

"Not then." I rubbed the raw skin on my elbows. "Earlier. You were distracting me."

Atticus's mouth opened and closed. When he chuckled, I rolled my eyes. "Oh, don't let that go to your head. I meant you were talking too much, made me lose my focus. Not that you're hot or anything."

"So you have noticed then?" That perfect grin was back.

"Is everything okay over here? That girl took quite a fall," Mabel asked, giving me an out. I hadn't managed to run very far at all—I was still in front of Broastful Brew. *Well, that was pathetic.* Not to mention embarrassing. I glanced up to see Melissa looking out at me from the window of her shop.

"She's fine. Her hard head broke the fall." Atticus helped me to my feet and used his body to shield me from sight. "It might help if I had something to call you when I'm chasing you. 'Hey you' doesn't seem to work too well."

"Ember," I muttered, still wallowing in frustration and no small amount of embarrassment. I really had made a scene.

"Ember? That's hot."

I glanced back at him and saw that his familiar lopsided grin was fixed in place. "Congratulations, you tricked me into telling you."

He tugged on the collar of his flannel shirt. With a puffed-up chest, he did a little strut that made me laugh. "Stick around long enough, Ember, and you'll realize I've got skills."

I glanced past him to the tearful little girl and sighed. "If you really want to help, take this and get that girl a new balloon."

He stared at the crumpled dollars I'd placed in his palm. "Well, aren't you a softy."

I snorted. "Hardly."

A light rain began to fall as I waited for Atticus to buy a new balloon. I didn't notice it at first. But as the sky began to darken and the winds increased, rolling off the mountains, I knew we were in fact in for a good storm. All around us, people rushed to cover their tables.

"Hey," he said when he hurried back over. "I'm sorry you lost your guy. It's a small town. We'll find him again. But I'd advise against doing it tonight."

"Right. The whole Purge thing. But wouldn't that be the best time?"

"Nope." He steered me back toward my car. "Trust me. You don't want to be anywhere near town for that. We'll find him tomorrow."

"I've been hunting him for six years. He's not an easy man to catch."

"Six years?" He whistled. "He must have hurt you pretty bad."

Droplets of rain pattered my face as the heavens opened. Atticus took my hand and led me through the chaos of vendors tearing down. Before my foot could land on the sidewalk, Atticus pushed me against the side of a food truck. He stepped in front of me to block my view.

"What are you doing? It's pouring!" I said.

"Look."

I stopped grumbling at him when I saw a boot clamp on the front tire of my Jeep. Lloyd was no longer alone. Several other cops wearing rain ponchos now surrounded the vehicle. The driver's side door was open, and one officer was poking around, searching under the seat.

Atticus glanced at me, but I said nothing.

"Here." He pressed a set of keys into my hand and pointed down the street. "Take mine. It's that black Subaru two blocks down. Ignore the cloud of smoke that'll follow you. The muffler is junk."

I opened my fingers to see a car key surrounded by several others. "You're loaning me your car?"

He nodded. "The gold key is for my cabin. It's not much. Just a small place up Miles Mountain. Take the main road back out of town. Take the first right after the town sign. You'll find the cabin about three miles up on the right. It's an A-frame set out on a rocky ridge."

"Why are you doing this?" I stared at him, trying to commit his directions to memory. "You don't owe me anything."

Atticus nodded. "I already told you. I'm a nice guy. Besides, I'd rather know you make it to morning. Sticking around town isn't a good idea. Especially for someone like you."

CHAPTER 8

Waking up in a strange place had a way of messing with my mind. Especially when the waking came as a pounding on the cabin door that rattled my brain. Oh, and then there was the fact that I had to maneuver a rickety ladder as my only escape from the sleeping loft.

My foot slipped, and I dropped a couple of rungs before I caught myself. Pain flared when my chin smacked into the wood.

"Son of a—" I gritted my teeth.

From the other side of the door, there came a throaty laugh, and I groaned. I should've known it would be Atticus. I was shacked up in his home after all.

The door creaked as I opened it. "I'd tell you to go away, but I know you won't."

"Of course not."

He gave me an appraising glance as I rubbed my chin. I'd been soaked by the time I arrived. With my spare set of clothes trapped in the backseat of the stolen Jeep, I'd had no choice but to go digging through his drawers. I'd found a faded Led Zeppelin shirt and claimed it. But now, standing in front of him wearing only that, I realized how little it covered.

"That shirt looks way better on you than it does me." He winked and pushed past me into the room. He'd definitely noticed that it barely covered my backside.

He kicked the door closed with his foot, while somehow managing not to spill a single drop of coffee. His display of coordination skills at this time of the morning royally ticked me off.

"I brought coffee and doughnuts," he said with an upbeat tone.

Of course, he's a morning person.

I slumped into one of the two wooden chairs and buried my head in my hands. Atticus bustled around the small kitchen. The clatter of metal plates made my head hurt. I squinted at the cups of coffee in front of me and lunged, knocking the table back a few inches.

"Whoa!" Atticus slid into the seat across from me and braced the table. "Heaven help the person who comes between you and your caffeine."

I glared at him, but his smile never faltered. He really seemed to enjoy taunting me.

"Sleep well?" he asked.

Taking a long, scalding sip of my liquid mojo, I shrugged. "The bed is lumpy."

"Huh." He frowned and glanced at the loft. "I never noticed."

Setting aside my cup, I sighed. Thanking people wasn't something I was good at.

"Thanks for not asking questions yesterday and for lending me your car so I could crash here. And I guess for breakfast, again."

"Wow." Atticus chuckled and shook his head. "That must have hurt to say."

"You have no idea." I scowled and gripped my cup tighter.

He grinned, seeming quite pleased with my reaction. Then he made a show of plating up our gourmet breakfast of sprinkle donuts and bear claws. The funny thing was that they actually did resemble a real claw.

"Did you buy me pink on purpose?" I glared at the offensive color. I hated when guys assumed that because I had different anatomy, I was fond of pink.

"What? Oh." He reached over and shoved a chocolate donut in my direction instead. "Sorry. That one is for me."

It was a good thing I wasn't trying to drink at that moment, because I spit all over myself. Although I hadn't known him long, I'd come to realize that I didn't have one stinkin' clue how his mind worked.

"What?" he said with a giant mouthful of glazed dough. "I'm man enough to admit that I like a little pink in my life."

As I watched, he downed the whole pastry in two bites. Now that was impressive. I took longer with mine. Although sugar and I were good friends, my stomach had no desire to wake up this early.

I looked around the cabin as the sky began to lighten. Wooden planks lined the walls, some straighter than others. The floors were roughly hewn. A sliding glass door to my right looked out over the valley. Puffy spray can insulation peeked through the cracks around the unfinished door. No curtains or blinds hung to conceal the view of the town below.

Next to the door was a small kitchen with the bare essentials. A rack hung from the ceiling, stocked with a couple cast iron pots and pans. The remaining camp plates and mugs stood on a handmade shelf. The small countertop led my gaze to a cozy seating area with a well-used couch and a wood burning stove.

The kitchen table we sat at filled the center of the space. A ladder led up to the sleeping loft. It held one bed, a nightstand, and a lantern that I hadn't bothered to light the night before. I'd been so exhausted by the time I arrived at his cabin that I'd only taken time to check the perimeter. Then I barricaded the doors, stripped out of my wet clothes and passed out. I wondered where Atticus had spent the night.

"You built this place, didn't you?" I asked, fiddling with the hem of his T-shirt that I wore. It smelled of him, like everything else in this place.

"Sure did." Atticus wiped frosting from his lips.

His day's growth looked good on him this morning. I was glad that I'd bunked in his house long enough to prevent him from shaving.

There was something so irresistibly sexy about a man with a bit of scruff.

"It took me most of the fall and winter to get the frame up. That's a slow time for me at work, so I had more time to spare. There are a few things that still need doing. I don't have electricity or any running water, either, so you'll have to forgo a shower. But I can haul up some water if you'd like a bath."

"I'm good," I hurried to say. The idea of him being close at such an intimate time stained my cheeks with a blush.

"The outhouse is back by the tree line," he continued. "I know that's not what you're used to—"

"Fine by me," I cut him off. "I just used a tree."

I wasn't some soft city girl who needed luxuries. I'd slept in my fair share of bus stops, public restroom stalls, and a few abandoned subway cars. I knew how to make do, and for some reason, it mattered to me that he understood that.

"Well, I guess that's the tour then. You can stay as long as you need to." I shot a quick glance up at the sleeping loft with its compact bed and then looked away again. "I'll take the couch. No sense making this awkward."

When he stretched his arms over his head, the bottom of his flannel shirt parted enough to reveal a tease of muscle. I smirked and looked away, knowing that he'd given me that eyeful on purpose.

"I know this is your place and all, but why exactly are you here?" I asked, pushing away the remaining crumbs of breakfast. I'd lost what little appetite I'd had.

"Oh." He grabbed my plate and spun toward the sink. It was only a few feet away, so it wasn't quite as an impressive feat as his coffee balancing act earlier. "It's Sunday, so I've got the whole day off for a bit of sleuthing."

I groaned. I knew he was going to say that.

"Now, don't you go griping at me." He shook a small scrub brush in my direction. I realized with a great amount of surprise that he was actually doing dishes.

Wow. This guy was the whole package.

"You need help, and I'm the man for the job."

"And if I say no?"

He shot me that sexy lopsided grin of his, and I knew it'd become my kryptonite. "You aren't the only stubborn one in town. Besides, I know people. Good people with tracking skills."

When he turned back to cleaning our two plates, I tapped my fingers against the coffee cup. Maybe it wasn't a terrible idea. He knew everyone. And he did want to help.

"Are you on friendly terms with any demons?" I asked.

Atticus went still. "No."

"Sure about that?"

He glanced over his shoulder at me. "Few people are. At least not the kind of people you want to hang out with."

I nodded. That was true enough. I'd heard rumors there were some demons that were actually halfway decent. They were a hybrid of sorts that somehow enabled them to maintain a sliver of their soul. That was hard for me to wrap my mind around. A demon was bad, no matter how you looked at it. And by bad, I meant BAD. I usually avoided them at all costs.

When I looked up, he was watching me. "You think this guy you're after is a demon?"

"To be honest, I'm not sure what he is. I haven't been able to pin anything solid on him, and believe me, I've tried."

Atticus sank back into his seat, drying his hands on a small rag. "So what do you know?"

"He killed my momma on my birthday."

He closed his eyes and shook his head. "I'm sorry, Ember. If I'd known—"

"It's fine." I looked away, feeling the familiar tightening in my throat. Even after all this time, it was still hard to talk about it. "It wasn't a good death. She burned alive in front of me. At night, I can still hear her screams when I'm drifting off to sleep."

I paused, needing a moment to get my emotions in check. "Southern gentlemen and proper belles surrounded me as a child in Savannah. My momma raised me to be a lady, to make her daddy proud, I'm sure. I'd attended the finest schools and trained with the best ballet company in Georgia. Dancing has given me an edge when fighting these days, but I'd never admit to it."

Atticus grinned at that.

"High society taught me that people could be kind to their own when they chose to be. Which was mighty fine until my thirteenth birthday. That's the night my momma died and I became an orphan. Then I learned how cold and unfeeling my momma's 'friends' could be."

"I'm sorry." And I knew he meant it.

"That was also the night I entered this new world. One where monsters hid in the shadows, waiting to take me out. A girl learned a thing or two mighty quick when she had to." I paused. I didn't think I'd ever told anyone this story before. "My momma's death left my emotions a bit unstable. Several other fires occurred over the months that followed. I guess my granddaddy figured I was the reason his little girl was gone. He blamed me, disowned me, and turned me over to the state. I never saw him or his money again. Disreputable foster care families were the least of my worries after that."

His eyes grew wide. "And this demon started the fire?"

"I've asked myself that same question more times than I can count. No matter how hard I try to remember, I just can't."

Back then, I hadn't been aware of my abilities or that supernaturals were even a real thing. After that, I spent days digging into lore. I was desperate to piece together the shards of memory that I had from that night. When I'd learned that a traumatic event could release dormant powers, I'd begun to suspect that I was to blame.

"What little family I had left after Momma died didn't want to deal with my oddities. I bounced from home to home after that. None of them fit well. I seemed to cause trouble everywhere I went, so after a while, I stopped caring. Then I found a few people who were different, like me. Some were kind and taught me the way of things. Others put a dagger in my hand and tossed me into a fighting ring. I learned real quick how to defend myself."

Atticus's mouth fell open. "They forced you to fight? That's barbaric."

"I didn't have a Havenwood Falls to grow up in. The real world isn't like this place." I shrugged. "My first fight was when I was fourteen. I'd been placed in a foster home with an angel."

His brow creased with lines of confusion. "Wouldn't that be a good thing?"

"They aren't all cute little harps and rainbows, Atticus." A bitter laugh rumbled in my chest as I scooted to the side on my chair. He glanced over as I lifted the T-shirt to reveal a ten-inch scar that ran up my thigh. "That Seraph blade nearly took my leg clean off. Cut clear to the bone faster than I could react. I got a few good swipes in on my own. It took almost a full week of intense healing before I could walk again. Needless to say, when I skipped out of the hospital, I decided that home wasn't for me."

Atticus didn't react to the speed with which I'd managed to recover from such a severe wound. That betrayed that he knew all about healing powers. I wondered if he possessed them himself or had seen them in action.

He remained silent with his hands clenched into tight fists on the table. The muscle in his jaw clenched as he ground his teeth. The depth of his concern touched me, but I reminded myself I didn't care.

"The next place, a small town in Florida's panhandle, ran me smack dab into a witch's coven. I stuck around there for a while. They took a liking to me. After a while, I moved on. I knew I wasn't going to find my momma's killer there, and having them take care of me was making me soft."

I looked toward the glass window. The mists had finally begun to burn off, and the sun shone brightly, but it did nothing to lift my mood.

"I traveled around the Deep South for several years. When the cops would catch up with me, I'd find myself bounced into a new home. School had its uses, but I never stuck around long enough to make friends." I fell silent for a moment. Some of the things that'd happened to me weren't relevant, so I kept those to myself. "New

Orleans was a scary place. Why tourists think voodoo is cute is beyond me. I saw things there that will haunt me until I die, but that's where I found my first clue two years ago."

"How'd you end up here?" The chair creaked as he leaned back on two legs.

Rubbing at the scar on my hip, I laid out the details of how I'd come to live with Susan after my brief stint in New Orleans. Of hearing rumors about other children going missing. Most of those cases turned out to be the results of sick-minded humans with a thing for kids. Then I'd stumbled across a troll in Albuquerque who'd told me about a snitch for a fair price: my momma's gold watch. It broke my heart to hand it over, but I knew it'd be worth it if the information rang true.

I amended the finer details about my fight with Fluffy, choosing to leave out the parts where he was a three-headed wolf and that he'd put me in the hospital. Some things were best not known. That included the details about my abilities.

After I skipped the gruesome parts, I caught him up to when I ran him over with the Jeep. He laughed when he realized that Lloyd had actually gotten something right. "So you really did steal that car?"

"Of course I did. Do I look like a Jeep kind of girl to you?"

He gave me a long look that made a warm blush rise to my cheeks. "Nah. But I could see you on a bike."

Now that was an idea I could get on board with. I'd always had a thing for black and leather. Adding a motorcycle on top seemed like a good next step.

When his hand fell over mine, I flinched and jerked my gaze up to meet his. "I'm sorry that your life has been so hard. I can't even imagine what it must have been like. I promise I'll help you find the scumbag who killed your mom."

For the first time, I was at a loss for words.

"But first," he shoved up to his feet and held out his hand to me, "we need to get you registered."

CHAPTER 9

*R*egistration wasn't as bad as I thought it would be. The paperwork went fast enough once I figured out a new false identity to roll with. I'd used many over the years, but a few of those covers were blown. Atticus told me the fake name wouldn't work, but what did he know about lying low from the law? He was Mr. Perfect.

While I waited for the test results to confirm that I wasn't human, I wondered if it could tell me my species. The thought both excited and unnerved me. I'd gone so long without knowing that the idea of finally discovering the truth made me almost nauseous.

"What's got your panties in a twist?" Atticus asked from behind a magazine. He flipped the page, but didn't look at me.

"Who says they are?" I countered.

"Your knee is bouncing ninety miles an hour. FYI, that jangling your boots are doing is making it hard to focus on this fascinating article."

I looked over at him and smirked. Yanking the magazine out of his hands, I turned it over. "It helps if you hold it the right way up when you're pretending not to check me out."

He didn't look the least bit embarrassed. We both knew he'd been eyeing me up all day. I guess seeing me scantily clad in his Led Zeppelin T-shirt had made quite an impression on him. I wished that I could say his flannel shirt was a total turnoff. I usually wasn't into that whole lumberjack thing, but he made it look good.

In need of a serious derailment from those thoughts, I focused on my surroundings instead. A nondescript maintenance door had led us to the registry office. It was a good cover-up. I hadn't expected this part of City Hall to look so normal. A few swords on the walls, maybe a steaming caldron or toads in jars would have felt more realistic than this waiting room.

"You're doing it again." He set aside the magazine and forced me to drag my thoughts back to him. When he placed a hand on my knee to stop the bouncing, I had to force myself not to swat him away. That would be childish. Not to mention it would have given me another reason to touch him.

"How much information does that blood work give?" I asked, pushing aside the thoughts of where else I'd like to touch him.

He watched me for a moment. "Afraid your blood is going to rat you out? I told you that fake name wouldn't help. Blood doesn't lie, especially when Addie is back there, working her magic."

I sighed and slumped into my chair. His statement wasn't a figure of speech. I'd smelled magic in the room the moment I walked in. "The opposite, actually."

"Wait a second." Atticus leaned toward me.

"You really don't know what you are, do you?"

My scowl was already firmly in place before he finished his sentence. "I told you that I'm the only one."

He shook his head. "No way. There's always more than one."

"Yeah?" I poked him in the chest. The muscle was firm and way too tempting, so I pulled back. "Well, I've been a lot of places, and I've never met anyone like me."

"So what can you do? Shift? Fly? Talk to the dead?" Atticus turned toward me in his seat. "Wait! Are you already dead? I'm not into that sort of thing, but I could make an exception for you."

He sniffed the air like he'd be able to smell the rot right off me. I smacked him on the arm, making sure to connect with bare skin for the added sting effect.

AMY MILES

"What was that for?"

"For sniffing me without asking."

"Fair enough." He laughed and waved an invisible flag of surrender. "But you still haven't given me any hints."

"Huh." I looked away from him and stared at the cat poster on the far wall. Cats creeped me out. Especially the cute cuddly ones. Somehow the girl who worked here didn't seem the sort to like stupid cats either. I'd bet money that someone stuck it up there as a joke. "I wonder why that is."

"Oh, come on, Ember." He nudged me with his shoulder. "I'll show you mine if you show me yours."

From the corner of my eye, I saw him wiggle his eyebrows suggestively, and a small laugh escaped me.

"Ember Ramsey?"

My head shot up at the announcement of my real name. Atticus muttered a "told you so" under his breath as I stood and walked through the door. I followed behind a girl a few years older than me. In her mid-twenties, she knew how to rock wide leather bracelets. With her ripped-up jeans and a diamond nose ring, I knew she was my kind of girl.

"How you doing, Addie? Haven't seen you in a while. Is the Court keeping you locked up?" Atticus asked as we entered what appeared to be a large courtroom and headed toward a desk in the back corner.

"Oh, I'm still around." Addie grinned and moved toward the far wall. "It's you that's a no-show these days. How's the landscaping business keeping you, now that summer is here?"

"Busy as always. You know Orlon, always cracking the whip. I'm lucky to get a day off."

A twinge of guilt hit me. Atticus had made it seem like it was no big deal to spend yesterday and today with me. Was he skipping out on work for me?

Addie turned to look back at him. "How is your brother doing? I saw Orlon yesterday, but he kept to himself. He downed his fair share of beers over at the Dirty Knuckle last night. When I went over to say hi, he grunted and stumbled away."

Atticus's shoulders took on a distinct slump. "Thanks for keeping an eye on him. It's been tough, but he'll find a way to move on when he's ready."

Addie smiled and reached out to squeeze his hand. "It's been tough for you, too. If you ever need to talk, you know where to find me."

"Thanks."

A tingling in my palms flared to life in response to Addie's friendly offer, and I closed my fists.

Did I almost fry that girl because she was nice to Atticus?

No. She'd touched him and made it seem so effortless. Like they'd done it countless times before.

Jealous much?

A puff of smoke burst from my palm. I coughed and waved my hand to conceal the evidence.

"Sorry. Is it a bit warm in here to you guys?" It was a totally lame way to disperse the smoke, but it worked when they both shrugged and shook their heads.

I winced when they turned away. I was turning into one of those girls. Ugh.

The more time I spent with Atticus, the more I began to realize that he wasn't like other guys. There was something between us. I wasn't into that love at first sight crap. I'd stopped believing in fairy tales a long time ago. But I knew chemistry when I smelled it, and we had a lot of it.

Addie motioned for me to sit in a chair beside a desk. "Sit there. I'll just be a minute."

As soon as my eyes fell on her tattooing tools, I was done. There were few things that made me nervous in this world. Creepy dentists and tattoo artists were among them. Another glance at her tray of tools and ink told me that I was in the wrong place.

"Oh, heck no!" I was out of that chair and trying to push past Atticus in a heartbeat. "You never said anything about getting a tattoo."

Addie snickered at me as Atticus rolled his eyes. "This again? Are you telling me that the girl who took down an angel can't stand a little needle?"

"Whoa." There was a splash of liquid behind me as Addie whipped around. "You took on an angel? What was that like?"

I glared at the girl. "It wasn't a full takedown. More like a mutual truce after we got pretty bloody. I managed to land a few good blows."

"Wicked." She grinned and handed me a cup. "Drink this."

I sniffed it first. "What is it?"

"It's water. You look like you could use something a bit stiffer, but it's the best I've got."

Atticus gave me a quick nod, so I knocked it back. The liquid was about as tasteless as water, but it had a silky texture to it. A soothing sensation started to come over me. My grip on Atticus's hands loosened. The hammering of my heart slowed, and my gaze sank to the floor.

"Hey! I like your boots. I always thought combats were the best," I said with a slurred voice. Atticus smiled at me as he led me back to the chair. "What's wrong with my words? Did you drug me?"

"Of course not." But by the way he said it, I knew I'd been suckered.

"That's not cool." I glared at each of them in turn, but only innocent faces looked back at me. Four of them, actually. This stuff worked fast.

When a set of straps latched over my wrists, I realized that Atticus had tied me to the chair. "What are you doing?"

"The calming tincture is only temporary," Addie spoke with a soft tone. She moved toward the wall, and the lights dimmed around me. "Sometimes it's best to make sure you can't go anywhere, in case you try to bolt before I'm done. It's for your own safety."

I pressed my head back into the headrest, vowing that if this hurt as much as I thought it would, I was going to burn them. Nothing major. Enough to leave a mark. The trouble was I wasn't sure which one of them to hit first.

The sound of the tattoo pen humming to life made me dig my nails into the armrests. I hated that sound.

"All right, Ember." Addie's face appeared in front of me. "What would you like?"

"For you to get the heck away from me." My lips had started to go numb, and my head was definitely heavier than normal.

She grinned and tapped her chin. "Something fierce and deadly like you."

Atticus's head bobbed in agreement. "Got any good ideas?"

Addie's instant grin worried me. "I've got just the thing for you. Don't sweat it."

But I did. A lot. Sweat dripped into my eyes. It collected in the scooped neck of my tank as the pen pressed against my skin. Addie was much stronger than she looked. One hand clamped hard on my wrist while Atticus stroked my free hand. He acted like he would've liked to hold that hand, but I kept it gripped to the seat.

"It will all be over soon. I promise." His touch might have been soothing if I wasn't left wishing I could singe his pants for putting me here in the first place.

"All done." Addie sat back and placed the silent pen to the side.

"What? Already?" I blinked. My vision was a little fuzzy as I looked around. Atticus had somehow switched sides to stand with Addie. "How did you—"

"Why did you choose that design?" Atticus cut through my question.

"I don't know." Addie's shoulders rose and fell with a shrug. "It just came to me. You know, sometimes I get these feelings."

The two shared a long look at my tattoo before they turned toward me. As she unbuckled the strap around my left wrist, fear rose up in me. Fear that I couldn't quite contain under their sharp gaze.

"Go on then." Addie smiled, but it didn't look quite so confident now. "Tell me what you think."

Lifting my arm, I stared at the colorful new addition to my body. A beautiful firebird now took up half of my inner forearm. Its wings were the color of my hair, tipped in gold and vibrant oranges. Shock stole my breath away when the tattoo suddenly opened its wings wide.

"It moved!"

"What?" Addie reached for my hand, but Atticus beat her to it.

He yanked on my arm, and together we watched the bird ruffle its feathers. It turned its head, the brilliant fiery plume fluttering as if touched by the wind. Then its feathers began to shimmer. The gold became blinding, and I had to look away.

Atticus yanked Addie to her feet. "What the heck did you do to her?"

Her brow creased in confusion. "I don't see anything."

"What do you mean you don't see anything?" The planes of Atticus's face went rigid. "That tattoo burst into flames."

I rubbed my finger across the tattoo. He was right. That's exactly what the bird had done. But before that, it had shimmered with the same glittering color of my healing tears.

My breath caught. I recognized this creature from my search into lore. "This is a phoenix, isn't it?"

Addie and Atticus both turned to look at me. Addie nodded. "It is. The first I've ever done."

Atticus's face was pale. His hands shook where he still held Addie.

"Does it mean anything?" I whispered.

"No." Atticus said at the exact moment Addie said, "Yes."

He glared at her and then seemed to come to his senses. He released his grip on her arm and backed away. Small red markings where his fingers had been were highlighted against her pale skin.

I stared long and hard at him, but he refused to meet my gaze.

"I'll be outside." With that, he turned and hurried out of the room.

"What was that all about?" I asked.

Addie stared for a good minute in silence at the door. "He's still trying to get used to magic. Even for those raised knowing about the supernatural, it's sometimes hard to accept."

"And my tattoo? You didn't see it move?"

Worry creased the corner of her eyes. "I wasn't meant to see it."

"Meaning what?" I unbuckled my other hand and slid out of the seat.

I watched as she tugged at the sleeve of her hoodie. It was a bit frayed there, evidence that she liked to worry in that spot. "Infusing magic into our tattoos to uphold the town's warding isn't a science, Ember. Sometimes things just happen. Things that even I can't understand. Like the vision I had of your phoenix."

I looked at the bird. It seemed to be as agitated as I felt.

"You said a moment ago that my tattoo means something."

"Usually people tell me what they want. Like a clan emblem or something. But then other times I have to get a sense of a person from their blood to determine what fits best. Magic is about intent, Ember. I have to infuse the right kind of magic into the ink, and that requires working with the facts. With you, I saw fire." She looked a bit flustered when I stared back at her. I bet I looked as confused as I felt. "You do know why that is, right?"

"No."

She rubbed the back of her head and thought for a moment. It looked like she was working to choose her words. I wished she would just spit it out already. "With each tattoo that I give comes a magical benefit based on your species—"

"And what is my cool new gift?" I interrupted.

"For vampires, it allows them to be out in daylight. For you, it will be something different. Something that can help guide you with your own personal abilities."

"Great." That's when I realized she knew. She had to know. What with all of her talk about intentional magic and blood work. Addie knew full well what my species was, and for some reason, she wasn't sharing. "What am I?"

Her image swirled as a few rebellious tears snuck through, but not before I caught her hard glance. "You really don't know, do you?"

I shook my head. "There was no one left to tell me."

Addie sighed and placed her hand over my tattoo. "The truth is inside you, Ember. Sometimes people know deep down what they are, but they aren't ready to hear it. My guess is that you're scared. You want to know the truth but are too afraid to admit it. It's just like how you must sense why only you and Atticus saw your tattoo move."

"I don't. Sense anything, I mean." I wiped at my nose with a spare tissue she handed me.

Addie sighed again. I was pretty sure right about then she was ready to give me a good knock on the head to get me thinking straight. I would have welcomed that if I thought it would help. "Have you ever stopped to wonder if maybe all of the facts you need are right in front of you?"

I blinked. "I think I would have figured it out by now if that were true."

"One would think." She turned to write a couple of notes on my forms. Then she paused to look at the door. A somber expression fell over her face, and I wondered if she was thinking about what had upset Atticus so badly. "My job requires that I reveal your identity to the Court, which I'll be doing as soon as I leave. They are pretty strict about knowing who and what is walking our streets. Just in case anyone decides to cause trouble. I'm also supposed to tell you your species if you are unaware, which I'll admit is a rarity." She paused, giving me a once-over. "But I suspect you'll be figuring that out much sooner than you think all on your own. Good luck, Ember."

That was it.

I wished that she would say more. Anything that would clear away the clutter in my mind. Instead, she just smiled and turned away. I hesitated, hoping that she would add something else, but it became obvious that she was done. She really was refusing to tell me the truth. A truth that I apparently wasn't ready to accept. Whatever the heck that meant.

Turning the door handle, I opened the door but paused to turn back.

"Thank you for this." I held up my tattoo. "I can't explain it, but I feel somehow more at peace now."

She offered me a weak smile. "I'm glad. And I hope you find what you're looking for. Just keep an open mind. Not everything is black and white. Sometimes it's the gray areas where we find ourselves."

I nodded my head in farewell and stepped through the door. The waiting room was empty.

"Atticus must be waiting outside." I hated that I'd somehow upset him. But it would be a lie to deny the feeling I got when I realized he'd seen my tattoo come to life. Did that have something to do with our growing attraction? Was there some sort of a bond that we shared?

"Ember!"

I turned back to see Addie running toward me. Her gaze flitted around the empty room before she leaned in close.

"I know why you're here in Havenwood Falls," she said in a rush. "The man you're looking for is called Mehki."

"What?" I blinked, shocked. "How did you—"

She clasped her hand over my arm, and I felt my tattoo begin to grow warm. "I can't tell you any more than that. Just watch your back. This town may seem nice enough, but there are plenty of ears listening."

"Wait, Addie!" But she turned and ran back the way she came. When she reached the doorway to the room where I'd received my tattoo, she ran through.

"Mehki," I whispered, staring at the wall across from me. I finally knew the name of my momma's killer. "I'm coming for you."

CHAPTER 10

I found Atticus waiting for me next to his Subaru, his hands shoved deep into his jeans. He was staring at the dormant ski lift that rose up the mountain, but I doubted he saw it.

"Want to tell me what that was all about?" I asked. He didn't react when I walked up.

"Nope."

"You've done nothing but dig into my business since we met. And the one time I ask you a question, all you can say is nope?" Crossing my arms over my chest, I shook my head. "That's not how this works. You asked me to trust you, and I told you things no one else has ever heard before. So it's time you start talking. Trust goes both ways, buddy."

It was true that I'd extended a bit of trust to him this morning. Beyond that, he was on a need-to-know basis. Anything more, and I might have to kill him.

When he turned to look at me, I faltered. There was an emptiness in his gaze that made my heart seize up. An irrational desire to wrap him in my arms and tell him that everything would be okay gripped me. I knew that pain all too well. It was the sort that only came from death. One you felt guilty about, at that.

"You want to know the truth? Fine." When he looked down at the tattoo on my arm, his lip turned up into a sneer. "One of those killed my parents."

"A phoenix?" This time I stepped back. "How?"

Atticus looked back to the mountains. "About six months ago, my mom and dad went on a trip to Denver for their anniversary. I guess they stayed longer than they'd planned and were coming back well after midnight. Had a few extra drinks on top, I'm sure. My dad always did like a good whiskey." A muscle flexed in his jaw as he paused to rein in his emotions. "The attack happened on their way home."

His words didn't feel right. From what little I knew about phoenixes, they seemed like gentle creatures. The lore claimed they loved nature and its creation. I couldn't imagine one attacking someone. Heck, I couldn't imagine one actually being alive, for that matter. They were supposed to be extremely rare.

"What happened?" I asked.

He blew out a breath. "I was out of town when it happened. My brother, Orlon, had sent me after a shipment of fertilizer. On the way back, my truck blew a tire. Normally I would have changed it and gone on, but we had removed the spare to make extra space for the bags. I had to sleep in the truck until the tow company opened. When Joshua Breen came to tow me back to town the next morning, he told me they were gone."

"And no one tried to call you?"

"Sure they did. Trouble is, some of these mountain passes have a crap signal. Had to climb halfway up the mountain to get through."

Maybe that's why Havenwood Falls didn't show on my GPS. Atticus would blame it on the mystical force or some crap like that.

"Did anyone see the accident?"

"No."

I frowned. "Well, maybe the secondhand account got it wrong? I've spent my fair share of time in jail for disorderly conduct or other lame complaints filed against me. No two people ever see an event in the same light."

"It was a phoenix. I know it was."

I didn't want to press him too hard, but I needed to know more. "How?"

"My uncle said he saw it. Like a huge fireball shooting across the sky. He's always been fascinated with phoenix lore. Used to talk to me about it when I was a kid. Back then, he made it sound so magical and elusive. A creature of immense beauty and power that could live for hundreds of years, and then begin again." He shook his head. "I think it was the immortality aspect of the bird that fascinated him so much. That and its healing powers."

I blinked. "Can a phoenix heal itself?"

"Maybe. How else could it live so long? That's not so hard to believe. Many of us supes have that ability. But the phoenix is different. It can cheat death using its tears. There's a special kind of magic hidden there. But it does have one enemy. A roc."

I had a vague memory of reading about this giant bird from my studies. It made me wonder about the bird I'd seen soaring over the valley the night I arrived. Was it a roc? It was certainly big enough to be one, but it had looked too peaceful to be a killer. But looks were always deceiving.

"And that was all important to your uncle?" I asked.

Atticus frowned at my probing question. "He has his reasons."

When he went silent, I knew not to push the issue. But I had a gazillion questions racing through my mind when he did choose to speak again.

"When he saw that bird lit against the night sky, he took off to follow it. I guess he thought if he could capture a picture of it, then it would be real to people. Kinda like how some folks hunt Bigfoot, like Sherman. They need proof."

I could understand that. Legends and lore were rooted in cultures across the world. People liked to consider the "what if" of their reality. Most, if they knew the real truth, were better off staying in the dark.

"My uncle saw the explosion on the mountainside. He hurried to reach the spot, but when he arrived . . ." Atticus paused to carve his fingers through his hair. When he spoke again, there was a quake in his voice. "I don't know why that bird chose my parents as its target. They were good people. Kind and generous to everyone they met. The only thing remaining from their car was the license plate. It tore off when they crashed into the tree."

"What about the car? There had to be something left of it," I asked, thinking back to the molten heap of metal that I'd turned that Rolls Royce back in Denver into. Sure, it'd burned, but there was still something left.

"Nothing. Not even a single tire skid mark. I guess the blaze burned away the evidence."

The feeling of unease continued, but I didn't speak of it. It wasn't my place to contradict his story further or to insert my own personal feelings into it. But in my gut, I knew something was off.

"And the bird?" I held my breath, torn between feeling sorry for his loss and desperate to know what happened to the phoenix.

"Gone." His voice lost all emotion. "Sheriff Kasun was the first on the scene. He told me later that they found claw marks high in the trees after they sniffed around for a bit. That bird must have perched up high to watch my uncle fall apart over losing his kin."

A tremble began to spread through me as I let that imagery sink in. It ran far too parallel to what my momma's killer did. It was terrible to imagine another creature being so cold and heartless.

Addie's earlier comments about his brother Orlon's heavy drinking started to make sense. The man was trying to drown out his pain. That was another thing I knew about. But I used fighting to release the bitterness.

"And your brother? Was he here when it happened?"

"No. He was on a date. The last one he may ever have, thanks to this." Atticus shook his head. "He's really torn up about it. Blames himself, not that there was anything he could have done."

"And you?" I reached out and placed a hand on his arm. The instant we connected, I felt my tattoo come to life again, but I ignored it.

He turned to look at me. A sad, heartbreaking smile touched his lips as he placed his hand on mine. "I keep telling myself that if I ever find that bird, I'll gut it for what it did to my parents. But guys like me never get that chance. I'm no hunter like you. Havenwood Falls is my home. I doubt that phoenix would dare come back again."

It was hard for me to offer condolences when it felt like a betrayal to even speak the words.

"Besides," he said with a forced a smile, "if there's a way I can help you avenge your mom's death, it might help me find peace, too."

"So that's why you've been such a pain?" I laughed, trying to lift the mood. "You're using me as a distraction?"

A flicker of some unspoken emotion flashed across his face, and my breath caught. In that split second, heat swirled in my hands, and I knew I could lose control with him. But the emotion vanished just as quickly as it came, and the heat faded.

"Nothing wrong with a good distraction now and then." He winked.

Clearing my throat, I stepped back to put some much-needed space between us. "I may have a new clue for us to go on. Feel up to doing some digging?"

"Yeah, I am." His smile returned. It didn't reach its full charm, but it was a far cry better than his earlier hollowness. "Point me in the right direction and I'll—"

Before he could finish his sentence, his hand slammed into my chest and shoved me backward. I landed hard on the concrete, my tailbone cursing his name before I could get back to my feet.

"What the—"

"Sheriff Kasun," Atticus called. He waved at the driver of the unmarked black Chevy truck pulling into a parking spot a few feet away. Atticus rounded the front of his SUV. "Nice to see you."

Hurrying toward the driver's side tire on his Subaru, I pulled my legs tight into my chest.

"Atticus." The cop's boots ground against the rocks lining the edge of the road, fallen from the landscaped path. Ducking my head to look under the car, I was surprised to see the sheriff decked out in casual attire. "Don't you mow the cemetery on Sundays?"

"Sure do." Atticus leaned back against his car across from where I crouched. He probably thought he was helping to hide me. If anything, he'd drawn the cop's eyes to my location. "I needed to take a day off. Been working too hard lately. Addie mentioned that Orlon hit the tavern pretty hard last night. Thought it might be a good idea to stick around town in case he needs anything."

"Tate mentioned seeing him in there. Said he looked a bit rough." There was a long pause, broken by the cop clearing his throat. "I'm sorry about your parents, Atticus. Not sure I ever got around to saying that, what with the investigation and all. Wish we had more to go on."

"The town and your family keep you busy. I know that, Ric."

I closed my eyes, hating that the sheriff had dredged up those feelings again. Atticus at least sounded more in control now.

"Is there anything I can do for you, Sheriff, or are you passing through?"

"I was on my way out to your cabin to talk to you. Found a stolen car abandoned in town yesterday with a new girl passing through. Lloyd mentioned that the girl clipped you. Hinted that you'd taken a liking to her and decided not to press charges. I'd like to have a chat with her."

I heard Atticus scratch at the stubble on his cheek. "Is she in some kind of trouble?"

"Well, that depends on how she came to be in that car. Lloyd seems to think she stole it."

"And you?"

The sheriff shifted his footing. "Her scent was all over the vehicle, as were her prints, but that makes sense if she was sleeping in it. We're waiting for the report to get back on the car's registration. You know how things are after the Midsummer Night's mess. It's hard to get people focused again."

"I bet last night kept you busy."

"Yes." His disgruntled agreement almost made me smile. I could only imagine the things people got up to.

"Thinking about it, maybe she found the car abandoned and needed a place to crash. It wouldn't be the first time that's happened around here."

"You always were too positive to be a cop, Atticus," Ric said. "If you see the girl, let her know I'm looking for her. I've got Tate and Conall sniffing around, too."

That was the second time he'd mentioned using scent to track me. Lifting my face, I did a bit of sniffing myself and caught the distinct scent of dog.

Ugh. I hated wolf shifters. Especially when they had my scent to track. That made them hard to evade. Thankfully, the cloud of ozone-killing crap coming out of Atticus's muffler was probably enough to keep me hidden.

"Good to know," Atticus said, pushing off the car to shake hands with the cop.

I held my breath as the sheriff returned to his truck. The man did a three-point turn and headed in the opposite direction. Atticus waited until the Chevy disappeared before he rounded the car. "Did I hurt you?"

"Nothing a hot bath wouldn't cure." I winced, rubbing the throbbing in my hip where Fluffy's bruise was still healing.

He offered a hand. "I can arrange that."

"Atticus?" I said, stopping him before he moved to open my car door. "Thank you."

"For what?"

"For covering for me back there. You didn't have to. I know I'm putting you in a bind with the people around here, and I just . . ." I rubbed the back of my neck. "Thanks."

He smiled. "I'm a nice guy, remember?"

The ride back to his cabin was silent. I slumped in his front seat in case one of Kasun's men spotted me. We didn't talk about the wolf pack or the fact that Atticus was going to be watched over the next few days. Whatever hopes he had of trying to help me had gone out the window. I wasn't going to let my presence cause him any more trouble than it already had.

"Go on inside and start the fire. There's kindling and wood next to the stove. I'll bring some water from the stream." He put the car in park when we arrived at his front door.

I looked all around. "I don't see any water."

"It's a bit farther down the mountain. The hike sounds worse than it is." He came around to open my door, but I sat there staring up at him. "What?"

"I can't figure you out." And believe me, I was trying. Every time I turned around, he did something sweet and totally unexpected. I'd been around strangers for so long that I had become accustomed to callous looks or snide remarks. But Atticus was different.

"So I'm a man of mystery?" He rubbed his chin and nodded. "I can live with that."

I laughed. "I'm serious. What sort of man offers to haul heavy tubs of water halfway up a mountain just for a complete stranger to take a bath?"

"The sort that wants to see you in his Led Zeppelin shirt again." He winked, then grabbed two large buckets off the front porch and headed away. There was a little extra swagger in his walk that I couldn't help but appreciate.

As I watched him disappear, I chuckled to myself. "A guy like that could make leaving Havenwood Falls a hard thing to do."

Turning to shove open the unlocked door to Atticus's cabin, I saw movement from the corner of my eye. A figure emerged from behind a tree. He stood as tall as Atticus, but had more of a lean build. Ropes of muscle lined his bare arms. His beard held a reddish tint as he stepped into the sun. The resemblance to Atticus was striking.

"Orlon? You're Atticus's brother, right?" I said. "He went to get some water and will be . . ."

"So it is true." His hands clenched into tight fists, still wrapped in leather work gloves. There was a crazed look in his eye as he stared at my phoenix tattoo. "You killed my parents!"

I was so shocked by his accusation that I didn't react until he'd closed the gap and circled his hands around my neck. A garbled cry burst from my lips when he squeezed. I beat at his hands and brought my knee into his groin. The reflex to the pain loosened his grip enough for me to break free. But Orlon tackled me from behind with enough force to send us toppling over the porch railing.

The instant I landed, I jabbed my elbow into his side and scrambled to my feet. "Atticus!"

I clenched my fists to keep my flames contained. I didn't want to hurt Orlon. He was confused, desperate to find someone to blame. I couldn't fault him for that, but I also couldn't let him hurt me.

Orlon snagged a handful of my hair and yanked me to the ground. I screamed and fought back, twisting around to rake my nails across his face. My cheek exploded in pain at his backhand, and several strands of hair ripped free.

"Don't make me hurt you," I warned. The tingling increased, the flames begging to be free.

"I knew one of these days you'd come back to gloat." Spittle hit my cheek as he growled into my ear.

"Orlon, I know you're hurting and this feels right, but I'm not who you think I am."

He yanked me to my feet and slammed my face into the car window. The glass spiderwebbed under the impact. My temple was sliced open, and blood trickled down my face. Darkness edged my vision as I fought against the need to let it take me. "Don't you say my name!"

The man was beyond reasoning with, but I had to try. I'd been where he was. I didn't want him to make the same mistakes.

"Please," I struggled to say around the rapid swelling of my split lip. I tasted blood. "Don't do this."

"Is that what my mom said before you lit her up?" He pressed his body against mine. I blinked back the tears as the barrel of a gun pressed against my back. When it nestled into my spine, sheer panic hit me. He was too blind to see the truth.

"You've got the wrong girl. I swear. I've never been to Havenwood Falls before."

With a growl, he whipped me around to face him. "You expect me to trust you? A murderer?"

I closed my eyes. The heat in my palms had reached excruciating levels, even for me. My body had begun to tremble. "Orlon, stop! I'm warning you."

He pressed the gun to my abdomen. "I know a few things about your kind. About how you can heal all wounds. How death is laughable to you when you've got centuries spread out before you, but I'm an excellent shot. All it takes is one little bullet to immobilize you. A spinal wound would take a bit to heal. I reckon I've got a place I can hide you away to make sure no one finds you again."

"You want to kill me?"

He laughed. "Oh, no. There's someone you need to meet first. I just need to keep you from finding a way to escape."

"What about Atticus?" I needed to keep him talking. Atticus had to be back soon with the water. Maybe he could talk sense to his brother before this escalated.

Orlon spat to the side. "If he knew what I know about you, he'd have done the same thing when he first met you."

My breath caught. He was right. I'd seen the rage that lingered beneath Atticus's calm exterior at the sight of my tattoo. He may not have been drinking away his sorrows at the local tavern, but he was far from handling his parents' deaths well.

"Filthy phoenix," Orlon spat at me and twisted us around so that he was pressed against the car, giving him extra leverage. "I'll kill you for what you did."

The firebird on my forearm fluttered its wings. The tingling from my hand traveled up to my heart, spilling liquid flames into my chest.

What if I am a phoenix? Addie told me that I already knew, that my tattoo was meant for me. And Atticus said that a phoenix had healing tears. Not to mention I was drawn to fire. But I couldn't be. I wasn't thousands of years old. Heck, I wasn't a bird at all.

"Any final words?" Orlon's breath reeked of cheap whiskey as he leered at me.

"Yeah." I focused on his glazed eyes and knew I had no choice. A thirst for murder had darkened his heart. It was a perfect reflection of my own. "Screw you."

Orlon pulled back as I opened my hands. A brilliant glow of flames burst between us, sending him flying back through the air. The impact crumpled the hood of Atticus's Subaru. I landed on my hands and knees, dazed by the intensity of the explosion. It made my head swim and my stomach clench with nausea.

"Whoa." I shook my head to clear it. "Never felt that before."

The ground around me was scorched black. The last of the flames died out when I trampled over them in a dead sprint in the direction Atticus went. He hadn't been clear on how far that stream was.

"Get back here!"

A bullet whizzed past my head. I screamed and ducked, veering onto a new course. A second bullet grazed my cheek, but I kept going. Pumping my arms and legs, I headed straight for the downslope only to realize that it wasn't a slope at all. It was a cliff.

"No!" My scream echoed around me as I tried to slow my momentum, but it was too late. I slid right off the edge and fell.

CHAPTER 11

The wind whipped my hair into a frenzy as I plummeted from the cliff. Bits of dirt crumbled at the edge and pelted me. My heart clenched at the sight of the ground rushing up to meet me.

This was it. The moment my life should be flashing before my eyes, but all I could see was Atticus. How freaking annoying was that? I could have at least spent my last seconds on this earth thinking of something great. Like the saltwater taffy my momma used to buy me, or one of her hugs.

Instead, the image of Atticus's lopsided grin actually made me smile. The fact that I was about to splatter all over the rocks below didn't seem quite so terrifying.

"Oomph." I crashed into something soft and warm, and my eyes flew open. Instead of the ground being on swift approach, the sun was. All around me, the soft down of feathers flapped as a great bird carried me into the heavens. "Holy—!"

Terror seized me as the bird took a steep ascent. I gripped onto its neck with all my might. It rose higher, and the air became cold and thin. I buried my face in its back, willing my heart to not give out on me from shock.

"This can't be happening," I whispered as the bird dipped and swooped, gliding with grace on the wind. My teeth stopped chattering as we sank back toward the earth.

Daring to open my eyes again, I saw the trees passing by at frightening speeds mere inches from the bird's belly. The force of the wind dried out my eyes, but I couldn't look away.

"It's beautiful," I said, staring in awe.

I felt a great rumble in the bird's breast before it released a bone-rattling cry. It rotated its head so that its eye watched me.

"Did you just agree with me?"

Its head bobbed, and I laughed. That's when I noticed the fine white lines that traced through amber and chestnut tones on the crown of its head. "Atticus? Holy crap. Is that you?"

I eased off my death grip and sat back. I was safe with him. Also a bit mortified that I'd needed him to save me. Lord, what I must have looked like as I fell!

"I knew you were a shifter all along," I announced. This time the rumbling from beneath my arms was a laugh.

The view was breathtaking. The mountains stretched out before us. With two powerful flaps of his wings, Atticus shot straight for them. Then he spiraled into a dive just before we hit.

I laughed and threw out my hands on either side as he leveled. "Show-off!"

As we glided back toward Atticus's house, I remembered why I'd needed saving in the first place.

"Oh! Atticus." I leaned down to speak where I thought his ear might be. "Your brother was there, at your cabin. I don't know how to say this, but he attacked me. That's why I went over the cliff."

The bird trembled beneath me.

"I'm so sorry. I should have told you sooner. Orlon—" My words cut off as Atticus suddenly dove to the ground. He pulled up at the last second, folded his wings and glided to a stop in front of the cabin.

Dipping his wing, he allowed me to slide to the ground. I cast a wary glance at the forest but saw no movement. Atticus's bird eye followed my gaze.

"I'm sorry," I whispered. It was a little unnerving talking to a giant bird. "He wasn't thinking straight. He saw my tattoo and thought . . ."

He dropped his head.

"Sorry about your car." I glanced at the extensive damage. "I'll pay you back for the damages."

He flapped his wings in agitation. The great gust sent me sprawling to the ground.

"This would be a lot easier if you were human again," I muttered, bracing myself in case he decided to flap again. I'd spent far too much time already having my backside handed to me today.

With a small twitch of his wing, I got a distinct impression that he wanted me to turn around.

"Let me guess, you're naked after you shift, aren't you?" The temptation to turn around and check him out was strong, but I resisted out of respect to him.

When he pressed his chest against my back, I chuckled at the obvious answer. "I guess I asked for that one."

"You could be naked too if you wanted."

There he went with that whole "if I want" thing. If there was ever a more loaded question to answer, I sure didn't know what it was.

"Nice to see you still have your sense of humor. Does that mean I'm forgiven for your car?"

Atticus went rigid behind me. For a moment he didn't speak. I wanted to, but wasn't sure what to say. "I'm sorry about my brother. I know Addie's tattoo put me in a bad headspace, but she should've known how you sporting that tattoo would make our family feel. It hasn't been easy for us. The wounds are still raw. But if I'd thought that Orlon would . . ."

"Hey." I eased around to face him but kept my eyes chest height and above. It didn't seem right to check out his junk without permission. Though I got the feeling that he was testing me to see if I would. "It's okay. I'm a big girl. I can take care of myself."

"Says the girl who tossed herself off a cliff!"

I laughed and nodded. "Okay, that might not have been my best move, but to be fair, I was being shot at."

"My brother shot at you?" Atticus blinked, trying to process it all. That's when he noticed the healing mark on my cheek. He cupped his hand around my neck and pulled me close. "I'm so sorry he hurt you."

"It's just a scratch."

"It could've been so much more. Orlon is a skilled marksman, Ember. He never misses his target."

"Well, I guess I got lucky then."

Or that concussion I gave him screwed with his aim a bit. I kept that thought to myself.

I shuddered as he wrapped his arms around me. Never before had I felt such a strong burst of power. What happened between Orlon and me was more than a usual flame. It had been electric. My arms still ached from where they shook with effort as I tried to hold it back for so long.

Something was changing inside of me. I could feel an energy pulsating.

"Are you okay?" He pulled back to look down at me.

I started to give him the obligatory response but stopped myself. Atticus cared. He deserved more than that.

"He thinks I'm the one who killed your parents."

"I assumed as much." Atticus winced. "I thought the same thing when I saw your tattoo."

That admission stung more than I wanted it to.

"You know I'd never . . . I couldn't . . ." But I didn't finish that statement because I knew that I could. I'd killed before. Not without reason, but the stain of death was on my hands.

"Of course not." He tucked my head into his chest again. "Orlon needs someone to blame. You're an outsider bearing the wrong mark. I should have anticipated how he might react."

But it didn't feel like the wrong mark. In fact, it was the total opposite. For the first time in my life, something felt right.

"It's not your fault." I leaned up to kiss him on the cheek but froze. Where his cheek touched my lips, a warm tingle began.

Now, I wasn't the swoony romantic sort, but there was no denying this physical reaction. It was like the initial tingling in my palms before the ball of fire would appear. Kissing Atticus's cheek resonated within whatever part of my soul connected me to the flames.

Whoa.

"Did you feel that?" I whispered.

Atticus cleared his throat. When his hands settled on my hips, I realized that he was still very naked and there wasn't a sliver of space between us. "Yep. Pretty sure I'm feeling something."

I laughed and slapped him on the arm. "Way to ruin the moment."

"That's what you wanted, right?" He stared at me with a sudden intensity that I felt both drawn to and terrified of. I was getting in over my head, and he was trying to give me an out.

"Sure." I shrugged and kept my eyes fixed on his until I'd turned around and it was safe to look down. "You should probably find some pants."

"I'll be back in a minute. I want to check things out. Make sure Orlon is gone."

"And if he's not?" I asked, wrapping my arms around myself.

"I'm not going anywhere tonight. I promise I'll never let him hurt you again."

As he shifted back into the great bird and took to the sky, I sighed. "But what if I hurt you?"

WE ATE dinner in silence a few hours later. Both of us were lost in our thoughts. Atticus's search hadn't turned up anything. Orlon was gone, but I knew he would be back. And this time, I wouldn't hold back. He'd threatened my life. No amount of grief could excuse that.

I didn't tell Atticus how close his brother had come to paralyzing me. Laying that guilt on him wasn't something he needed. By the droop of his shoulders, he was already placing enough guilt on himself for the both of us. It would seem the blame game was a family trait.

I barely tasted the fillet of fish and roasted broccoli that I pushed around my plate. The scent of butter and herbs lingered in the air.

Under normal circumstances I would have been thrilled with his cooking skills, but not tonight. All the same, I made sure to thank Atticus for the effort he put into making it for me. After we cleaned the dishes together, I moved to stand at the glass doors and stared out at the valley. Havenwood Falls disappeared as the shadows grew longer and night claimed the sky.

A shiver ran down my spine.

"You okay?" Atticus stood behind me, close enough for me to feel safe.

"Yes," I said in a whisper. "And no."

"Do you want to talk about it?"

I turned to look at him. His face was lost to shadow, but I could see the golden glow of his eyes. The same glow I'd seen before.

"It was you that I saw flying the night I arrived in town, wasn't it?"

"That was you in the car?" He laughed and moved toward the couch. "Sorry if I scared you. I didn't expect to see anyone on the road so late and cut the curve closer than I should have."

I sank next to him, my knee touching his side. The loveseat's oversized cushions pressed us closer together. "Have you always known that you're a giant bird?"

He shifted to face me. "Yeah, I guess. I mean, my whole family is, so you sort of grow up knowing that someday you'll be like them."

"When was your first time?"

He arched an eyebrow at that, and I laughed. "I'm trying to have a serious conversation, and your mind is in the gutter."

"Sorry," he muttered and lowered his gaze. I was wearing his favorite T-shirt again. The hunger I saw in his gaze each time he looked at me was starting to become mine as well. "I guess it was when I was a teenager. Maybe a bit earlier. My brother was older and a bit of a know-it-all. Orlon used to taunt me about having his wings long before I did. One night, he coaxed me into jumping off City Hall."

"What happened?"

Atticus shot me a sheepish grin and rubbed his hand down his left leg. "I broke a few ribs, this knee and shattered one arm. But the second time I flew."

I laughed. Despite my encounter with Orlon, I liked the way Atticus talked about his brother. Sibling rivalry was something I'd always seen but never experienced. Rivalry in foster homes was totally different.

"Mom wanted to clip his wings over that one, let me tell you." There was a note of sadness in his voice at the memory. "You would've liked her. She was one of those people that lit up the room. Always ready with a quick joke or to lend a hand to someone in need."

"I see where you get it from. Always the giver, even when it's annoying." I smiled.

His eyes grew wide for a second, but then he laughed. "Yeah, I guess you're right. I never really thought about it much. What about you? Are you anything like your mom?"

I lowered my gaze. The skin around my nails was raw and bleeding from when I'd tried to stop my fall.

"I don't remember much. After Momma died in the fire, I went to a few doctors. Some tended to my burns, but the others wanted to dig through my brain." I didn't expand on that, because to do so would be to admit that there had been a time that even I thought I was crazy. "There was one man who was kind. Dr. Darcy tried to explain to me that sometimes when a child undergoes a traumatic event, the mind shuts down. Sometimes it does that by splintering off pieces of memory. Then it shoves them into some locked box in the back of your mind."

"Sure." He nodded. "It's a way of protecting yourself."

"Exactly. Dr. Darcy believed there were strings of events that got all tangled up in my head. Like that game kids sometimes play where you hold a string and wind through the big tangle to try to find the end. Well, he said I was still trying to find my ending and that's why my memories are all jumbled up."

Atticus laid a comforting hand on mine. "So you don't remember anything?"

"Sometimes I get these flashes of images. Like a scent will trigger a memory. Or a place will feel familiar. I remember my momma's smile most of all." I lifted my gaze. His tender smile broke through whatever defenses I thought I still had against this man. "I don't think about her much. It's easier not to."

"Hey." He pushed in closer to me and rested his hands on my shoulders. "I understand. Believe me, I do. There were days when I didn't want to get out of bed, or wondered if I'd ever laugh again. I felt guilty when something good happened, because it was a reminder of what my parents missed out on. That they'd never get the chance to experience joy again. I feel that way with you."

I turned away to wipe at my eyes. "You do?"

"Ember." His breath washed over my cheek. He was so close now. "I know life hasn't been easy for you. I can see it in the way you carry yourself. You push everyone away so you don't have to feel. I get it. But I swear to you that I would never do anything to hurt you."

I wanted to believe him.

"I'm here for you. No matter what."

A part of me wanted to laugh, crack some joke about how sappy he was being, but I knew he meant every word of it. That scared the ever-loving crap out of me.

I wasn't ready to fall for a guy. Least of all one I could hurt. What if I was a phoenix? How could he ever look me in the eye without wondering? Without condemning?

"Atticus, I—" He stopped me with a kiss. It happened so fast, I barely realized that his arms had come around me and drawn me into him.

The kiss wasn't filled with heat, but instead tenderness, as his lips moved against mine. I stared at his closed eyes, shocked by how right this felt. I never kissed with my eyes open. Heck, I never kissed, period. It was too personal.

But with Atticus . . . I wanted to.

"Sorry," he whispered when he finally pulled back and opened his eyes. "You looked like you needed that before you went full tilt logic on me. Sometimes letting go is the only way to heal."

"Letting go can be dangerous, too," I countered. He'd left me breathless and a tingling mess. The sensation wasn't limited to my hands now. The electrical charge reached my toes. It wound around my belly and straight up to the tip of my nose. I'd never felt so alive before.

He smiled. "Not if you do it with the right person."

"And you think you're that guy for me?"

Cupping my face, he drew me close again. His gaze lingered on my lips before his lopsided grin drew me in. "There's only one way to find out."

CHAPTER 12

The candlelight flickered from the main living area below. I focused on the shadows they cast on the ceiling as Atticus pressed his lips to the hollow of my throat. His breathing grew ragged, like my own, as I traced my nails along his back. My legs felt weak as he hovered over me.

The neck of his shirt hung low, giving me a teasing hint of what lay beneath. He flinched when I ran my hands up under his shirt but soon settled into my touch. The planes of his stomach were rigid, rippled with muscle that came from years of manual labor.

His fiery kiss ran along my shoulder then back up toward my ear. A low moan rose from my parted lips when he tugged my earlobe between his teeth. His hot breath washed over me. Goosebumps raced down my body beneath the kneading touch of his hands as he gripped my waist.

The hem of my shirt rose high enough for him to explore the length of my angel scar. I wondered if he would see the scar in its entirety before the night was over. Or if I wanted him to.

"Ember," he whispered against my lips.

I closed my eyes to the sensations hearing him speak my name lit in me. His voice was deep, sultry. I wanted him more than I'd ever wanted another man, but I felt his restraint.

"We shouldn't—"

I cut off his words with a kiss, plunging my hands into his hair to hold him close. I wasn't ready for reason to return. If given the choice, I'd rather stay here, in his arms, the whole night through. Here was safe and warm. So very warm.

I lengthened the kiss until our lips were bruised and I panted for breath, but still, it wasn't enough. He tasted of mint. He smelled of fresh dew on grass and flowers newly budded on a spring morning. I couldn't get enough of him.

"Don't," I whispered, breaking the kiss only long enough to breathe.

His eyes were tender as he held my face in his hands. The calluses along his palm brushed against my cheeks as he leaned in for another kiss. This one was soft and gentle. "You know I want to, right?"

I nodded. I could see the truth of his desire burning in the depths of his eyes.

This man could be the end of me. I stared back, memorizing every detail of this moment. From the sheen of sweat on his brow to the flare of his hips encased in jeans.

"I don't want to take advantage of you when you're feeling vulnerable," he said and eased back.

I loved the way the white highlights in his hair seemed to glow in the moonlight. Now I knew they were a part of his feather pattern, soft and beautiful. But there was also a reminder of the events earlier in the day.

"You think this is about your brother?" I asked. He cut his gaze to the side to look out the window, but I reached up and pulled his chin back around to look at me. "Atticus, I didn't kiss you because I'm scared. I kissed you because . . ."

"What?" He propped himself above me so that his weight didn't crush me.

"Nothing," I rushed to say. "Never mind."

"Ember." He brushed my hair back from my face. "Sweet, beautiful Ember. It's okay to admit that you are hopelessly attracted to me. I know I'm irresistible."

I burst out laughing and yanked him back down to me. Our lips crashed together, but I didn't care that he'd smashed my nose or that it was hard to breathe under his big frame. All that mattered was his taste, the feel of him against me, and the obvious press of his need against my thigh.

With each moment that he consumed my lips, the temperature in the room rose. Kicking his bent knee out from under him, I rolled until I was on top. His hands settled on my waist. His eyes drifted low to take in my exposed thighs.

"I didn't think you could look any more beautiful, but I was wrong."

I smiled down at him before I leaned in to take his lower lip between my teeth. He inhaled sharply. Reaching up, I took hold of his wrists and placed them over his head. Holding them with one hand, I explored his stomach with the other.

"I'd say the same to you," I teased, trailing my fingers through the soft hair that led into his waistband. "But it would just go to your head."

He groaned when I moved my hand higher. "You're doing that on purpose."

"Of course I am."

He resisted my hold as I licked along his jaw. Heat swelled around us as I teased and taunted him. Steam fogged up the windows. I explored his chest and nipped at his neck. His fingers tugged against my grasp as he tried to remain in control. Ever the gentleman, though I could feel how much he wished he could give in.

The sheets lay crumpled beneath him. His head pressed tight against the pillow, teeth buried in his lower lip as I ground my hips against him. His body was taut with need. I knew that it wouldn't take much more to weaken his resolve.

When I released him and his hand fell to the side of my hip, I couldn't help but flinch in response. Atticus went still.

"Are you hurt?"

"Don't stop," I said, but he was already shifting to try to look.

"Holy—" He rolled me off. When his hand lifted the hem of my shirt, I closed my eyes. I knew what he saw. Fluffy's bite mark had sealed over, but the bruise was still extensive and ugly. "Who did this to you?"

I sighed and yanked the shirt out of his hand. "The question you should be asking is what did this to me. It was a skinwalker. That snitch I told you about wasn't human."

Atticus's eyes bulged. "You're lying."

"Nope." I shoved my hair back out of my face. "Kinda wish I was, though. His teeth were sharp."

He stared at me for a minute. Long enough for me to wonder if I'd suddenly sprouted three heads of my own.

"Who are you?" he said.

Realizing that any hope of time spent with him under the sheets had vanished, I slipped to the edge of the bed. "I told you already."

"Well, you failed to mention this little bit of information about facing off with a skinwalker."

My skin felt clammy when I ran my hands along my arms. It was way too hot in here.

"Kinda like you forgot to mention that you're a giant bird," I said.

He raised his hands in defense. "That's fair. I did. But you can't drop a bomb like this on me and not say more. How did you run into a skinwalker?"

I shrugged. "It was a fight club in Denver."

"A fight club." He laughed and shook his head. "Of course it was. Because that's something normal people do."

I narrowed my eyes at him. "I never claimed to be normal."

"No. In fact, I'm starting to realize that you're anything but." The heat under his gaze became stifling. "First you take on a skinwalker, which is insane, by the way. Then you steal a car, which I helped cover for you, so now I'm involved. You're here to find your mom's killer. I'm assuming you don't intend to give him a slap on his wrist and send him on his way. This means I may end up an accessory to murder. You've already told me that you've been in and out of trouble your whole life."

"So?"

Atticus looked taken aback. "Doesn't any of that bother you?"

I frowned. "What choice did I have? This is the life I was handed."

"It doesn't have to be." He turned to face me fully. I tried not to notice how his shirt had ridden up. The sight of his glorious abs was a distraction. "You can start over here."

"What? With you? Is that what you were going to say?" I laughed. "Who are we kidding, Atticus? Your brother wants me dead. The sheriff is after me. And as soon as I do track down my momma's killer, I'm going to take him out one way or another. So whatever you think we have between us . . . don't. You're better off without me in your life."

"What if I don't want to be? Out of your life, I mean?"

I pushed up to my feet. "This was a mistake. I have a rule: don't get close to anyone."

"Wow." He shook his head. "I think I understand now. That chip on your shoulder is to make sure you don't care about anyone but yourself."

"Whatever." I didn't like how close he'd come to pegging me. There was more to it than that. There had to be.

"Ember." Atticus grabbed hold of my arm when I tried to move toward the ladder.

"Don't!" But it was too late. Shimmering light consumed my firebird tattoo a split second before two fireballs burst from my palms. One lit the hem of the bedding. The second brushed past his arm and set his shirt on fire.

He scrambled back as the flames rose up between his legs, lighting his jeans. He tumbled off the other side. When he got to his feet he began yanking off his clothes until he was down to his boxers.

He stared in wide-eyed disbelief at the damage. Then he looked at where I stood with a pillow in hand over the smothered flames.

"How did you—"

I closed my eyes. "You're really going to have to learn how to finish those sentences."

"But how?" I heard him swallow. I could hear the thundering of his heart in his chest. I could even hear the bead of sweat that fell from his brow and hit the hardwood floor.

"I told you. I'm not normal."

"Did you . . ." He shook his head. "You didn't try to hit me with those fireballs, did you?"

My eyes popped open. "Of course not. I would never."

"Then what happened?"

I didn't know. I knew he wasn't trying to hurt me. Why did I lose control like that? I hadn't even felt the tingling in my hands before.

"Crap." I tugged on a swatch of sweaty hair. "I was hot."

Atticus stared at me.

"It's this thing that happens before I, you know, go all pyro and whatnot." I turned to stare at the charred bedding where I'd lain in his arms only moments ago. "It was you."

"Excuse me?"

I spun to face him. "You're my trigger. Why I lost control. I was so focused on you that I lost myself, and when you grabbed my arm, it must have thrown me into a fight response."

His brow furrowed. "You're blaming this on me?"

"No. That's not what I—" I growled out my frustration. "I'm not making any sense."

"No. And neither is your hair."

"What?" Freaked out by the intensity of his stare, I snatched my hair and gasped. Running my hands through the strands, I saw a wide black streak had formed from near my right eye to the tips. Nothing like that had ever happened before, and I'd wielded fire countless times.

When I looked back at Atticus, I saw he'd backed away. "Atticus?"

"You glowed," he said, his gaze looking beyond me. "Just before you threw the fire at me, it was like your aura caught on fire. Everything burned."

My mouth fell open. I wanted to say something, but the storm clouds darkening his handsome features stopped me.

When his gaze shifted to meet mine, I recoiled. His eyes were far too like those Orlon had glared at me with earlier in the day when he looked down at my tattoo.

"Atticus, I can explain—"

"Is it true?" He cut me off. I tried to cover the bird on my forearm, but heat waves continued to radiate from it. "I think I'm starting to understand now. Addie didn't pull that phoenix tattoo out of thin air, did she? She knew you could control fire."

There was no sense denying the evidence in front of him. "Yes, I can. But this is the first time I've lost control like that."

That wasn't true, though. I'd lost control back in Denver, and it'd cost Fluffy his life.

Atticus began to shake. His fists clenched at his sides. "Why didn't you tell me you could wield fire?"

"Why?" I scoffed and wrapped my arms around myself. Only a moment ago I had felt free in his arms, but now I was a freak. "Because I knew you would look at me like that. With condemnation and hatred in your eyes. Just like your brother!"

The floor creaked when he came to a sudden halt. "You can toss fireballs, Ember. I've never met a supe that can do that!"

"Don't you think I know that?" I yelled back. My voice quaked with anger and frustration. "I have spent my entire life being different from everyone else. God help me, but you made me believe that you might be the first person to overlook that."

Atticus growled and turned away. Every muscle in his back went taut as he fought to control the emotions raging through him.

"Was my brother right about you?"

My arms fell to my sides. "So it's like that, is it? I control fire so that makes me a murderer? Someone you think is capable of killing your parents in cold blood?"

Atticus hung his head. "You just admitted that you're willing to avenge your mom by whatever means necessary. Doesn't that make you capable of that?"

"He took everything from me!" My hands quaked at my sides, and I clenched them for fear of another fire burst.

"So that justifies murder?" he whispered.

I stopped short. If I said yes, that would condemn me, but if I said no, it would be a bald-faced lie.

Atticus slammed his fist into the wall. The wood creaked, and for a moment, I wondered if it might give way. The sheer power of him took me off guard and reminded me that even in his human form he was strong. All this time he'd been holding back with me.

And yet I'm the one condemned for lying. I snorted.

"Fine." I threw up my hands. "If you want to think I'm such a terrible person that I could kill your innocent parents, fine. I can't stop you. But you're wrong, Atticus. I may have had a hard life, and yeah, I've done a few things I'm not proud of, but I would never kill an innocent. And if you want to think I'm a phoenix, well, that's on you. I don't know what I am. I just know that when I'm with you, I feel things that I shouldn't, and it scares me. All of this." I waved my arms at the bed. "That was me. The real me. You said you didn't want to take advantage of me because you thought I was vulnerable. Well, news flash, Atticus. Orlon didn't make me feel vulnerable. You did. That's why I lost control."

With that, I headed for the ladder with every intention of storming off in epic fashion. The trouble was, I forgot that he was a freakin' bird. By the time my foot hit the bottom rung, he'd leaped from the loft and scooped me into his arms.

"Get off me!" I beat at his arm, but he held me with a vise-like grip.

"Where do you think you're going?"

"I still have a murderer to find, remember? That's why I'm here. And if you're done helping me, then I'll find my own way."

A dark glint crossed his eyes. "So that's it? You're just going to run out on me like that?"

"You haven't exactly given me a reason to want to stay." I tried to yank my arm out of his grasp, but he was too strong. "Let me go, Atticus."

"Or what? You'll burn me, too?"

His callous words burrowed deeper than any had before, and I gasped at the sudden stab of pain.

"Of course not. I'd never hurt you. Don't you get that?"

The hard lines of his face softened for a split second, but then firmed up again. "How do I know anything you've said is true?"

"Because I said it's true. That should be enough." A single tear slipped from my eye. He stared at it, appearing as confused as I was by its presence. Then I realized what he saw. The tear shimmered a crimson orange. A tear he would associate with a phoenix.

When he turned and raced for the door, I knew the only way I could get free of his grasp was to burn him, and I would never do that. Not because I promised him I wouldn't. Because I couldn't bear the thought of hurting him.

The instant we were free of the cabin, I felt him beginning to shift. His bones moved, popped, and elongated.

"Where are you taking me?" For the first time, I felt fear.

"To my uncle. Mehki will know if you're lying." His human form shifted away. The giant eagle-like bird stood before me, fierce and beautiful. I could run, but he would catch me.

As I stared into the black of his eyes, I considered the pain to come. Both mine and his. I took my place on his back, knowing that Atticus had no way of knowing his uncle was my momma's killer. But that didn't matter.

Mehki wouldn't live to see the dawn.

CHAPTER 13

*T*held my breath as the doorbell echoed through the darkened house. If the interior was anything like the extravagant exterior, I knew I'd hate it. The show of wealth didn't fit Atticus's personality or his tiny handmade cabin in the woods. I suspected his uncle had far loftier goals in life.

Atticus's grip on me was just shy of painful as he tapped his foot with impatience. After the third ring, footsteps approached from the other side of the door. Squinting against the sudden brightness of the porch light, I made out the figure of a young girl.

"Atticus?" She sounded sleepy as she rubbed at her eyes. A mess of raven hair fell over her shoulders when she leaned on the doorframe. "You do know that it's like four a.m., right? Now I'll never be awake for my calculus test in the morning."

The girl cut off when she looked at him for the first time. "Why are you naked? And who's the girl you're holding?"

He pushed past her. "Where's Mehki?"

"In bed. Duh." She hurried to follow behind us. It was hard to take in my surroundings when they passed by in a blur of darkness.

"Go and wake him up, Bex. Now!" Atticus left no room for complaint.

A light flicked on, and I found myself carried into a study. Or maybe it was a library. There were enough books lining the shelves to make it one.

"What's your damage?" the girl asked. The uncertain look she shot me was promising. At least, I wanted it to be.

"Bexley, I'm in no mood. Go get your dad."

Never mind. There was no way she was going to be on my side if she was Mehki's daughter.

I half expected Atticus to dump me on the small settee, but instead, he lowered me with care. I refused to meet his gaze, or check out his junk when he stood and began to pace.

"Would you put something on? You already gave your cousin a heart attack showing up like a crazed naked guy in the middle of the night."

"What?" He turned and blinked, appearing confused until he looked down. He crossed his hands to cover himself.

There was nothing in the room that would work in the way of clothing. I saw him look toward the door, but he decided against leaving me alone. That was the first smart thing he'd done all night.

"Use a curtain. Pink flowers suit you." I brought my knees to my chest.

"Cute," he muttered, but did give them a second glance.

"So Mehki's your uncle, huh?" I asked, needing a distraction while we waited. Or at least to make him think I was distracted. I had every intention of being in control when that man walked through the door.

Atticus turned to look at me. "Why?"

"Addie told me about him."

"What? When?" He frowned. "What'd she say?"

I met his gaze. "That he's the one I'm looking for and that I should be careful who I trust. Looks like she was right about one of those so far."

Atticus stopped pacing. "My uncle wouldn't hurt a fly. He's just a normal guy."

"That's what they all say about serial killers," I said under my breath, but knew he heard me when he flinched.

"That's not funny, Ember."

"Not trying to be." I glanced toward the hallway. "Not that it matters. It's pretty obvious you don't trust a word I say."

"That's not . . ." He trailed off, rubbing the back of his head. "I don't know what to think."

"Sure." I nodded as I listened for footsteps. "You know what's funny? Addie must know what your uncle is all about. And yet you stand there, ready to defend a murderer's honor after calling me out for the same thing." I shook my head. "I'm not gonna deny there's irony in that."

He turned and paced a few steps before stopping again. "Addie warned you against me?"

"Well, this whole taking me prisoner thing does kinda make that warning seem legit, doesn't it?"

He swallowed hard and averted his gaze. *Well, I bet that pill sure tasted pretty darn bitter!*

"You're not a prisoner, Ember." He sounded tired. "I just need answers."

"Right. And I gave them to you, but you'd rather think I'm the monster that killed your parents."

He winced at that, refusing to look me in the eye.

"You'd better have a good reason for waking Dad," Bexley said when she entered the room. When she tossed a pair of shorts in Atticus's direction, she didn't notice the tension. Or assumed that it was a normal byproduct of this whole messed up situation. "He's been cranky. I guess his trip to Denver didn't go well."

Atticus paused with one leg in the shorts. "Uncle Mehki was in Denver? I thought he was in Atlanta."

"Yeah. Plans changed, I guess." Bexley sank into the plush seat behind the desk and kept her gaze far from him until he was dressed.

Under the lights she looked pale, her skin taking on an almost jaundiced tint. Now that I really looked, I noticed that the dark circles under her eyes were very pronounced for a teenager. One sniff told me this girl was sick.

"Mom flew into a rage when he showed up in the middle of the night. Even tossed her favorite vase at him."

Atticus frowned and watched me from the corner of his eye. He knew that's where I'd been hunting. "What was he doing in Denver, Bex?"

"How should I know? Dad never talks about family business with me. He thinks I'm too fragile." She scrunched up her nose. As an afterthought, she yanked a box off the bookshelf and pulled out a medical mask. She looped it around her ears. There were several boxes around the room. "Not that I'd care anyway. All that landscaping convention stuff is boring."

I snorted and shook my head. Both sets of eyes turned to look at me. Atticus's demanded an explanation. "What?"

"Are you that blind? A landscaping convention? Please. No one would go to one of those."

Atticus's expression soured. It hurt that he shut me out again, but knowing to expect it this time around made it easier to deal with.

"That's it!" Bexley's outburst from behind her mask startled me as she snapped her fingers. "I knew your girlfriend looked familiar."

"She's not my—" But he cut off as Bexley hurried back through the doorway. "Teenagers."

Atticus slumped into a chair. When he covered his face with his hand, I was grateful to be hidden from him. Even for a moment. Being around him made it hard to focus. Knowing that I planned to kill his uncle, a man Atticus cared for, wasn't an easy pill to swallow. Knowing just how sick Bexley was made it that much harder.

But I couldn't let my conscience get in the way.

A banging sounded on the other side of the wall, followed by a rather unladylike grunt. A moment later, the girl waddled back in with a large golden frame.

"Dad brought this home from Room the other day. I guess he'd had Melissa's son Harry paint this back before he died. When he gave it to Mom yesterday, it didn't go over so well. I'd never heard her swear so much."

Atticus removed the hand from his face. "Your mom swore?"

"Sure did." Bexley balanced the heavy frame on her foot. "I

thought the neighbors were going to call the sheriff on them. Never seen Mom so mad."

Atticus stared at the back side of the painting. The artist signed and dated it only a few months ago.

"What's this got to do with Ember?"

"You're not going to believe it. It's like looking in a mirror, if that mirror turned back time, I mean." She shifted the frame onto one corner so she could slip her foot out. Then she rocked it from side to side. Leaning it against the desk, she paused to make sure it wasn't going to topple over and then stepped back.

"What the—" Atticus leaped up from his chair.

Bexley was right. It was like looking in a mirror. I rose from the settee to study the painting. The artist had a skilled eye. He'd captured my features with perfect strokes, including the blistering skin around my eye.

Words tried to form as they fell from Atticus's lips, but I ignored him.

"It's you, isn't it?" Bexley whispered. "Sorry, but your scars are kinda intense."

"Yes." I stared at the young girl who stood in the center of a blazing inferno. She wore a white nightgown, her hair draped in two braids. My gaze fell over the floral wallpaper behind the flames. This painting depicted roses instead of lilies, but it was close enough to reality. My gaze fell to the right-hand corner of the painting, and a sob caught in my throat.

"Momma." I collapsed to the ground and ran my fingertip over the image of the fallen woman. Her face was turned from sight, lost behind the wall of flames, but I knew it was her.

"That man." Atticus's words broke through my pain. I looked up to see him pointing. "Bexley, who is that?"

"Heck if I know. Looks a bit like dad, though." She squinted and then frowned. "Wow. It really looks like him. That's weird. I didn't think Harry knew Dad all that well. Maybe it's a coincidence? Trying to personalize his art for a paying client?"

"No." Atticus turned to look down at me. "That's no coincidence."

When his hand fell on my shoulder, I reacted without thinking. Atticus screamed as I twisted his hand. It took every ounce of willpower I possessed to hold back the burning in my hands.

"I'm sorry." His whisper tore through the waves of rage radiating through me at the sight of the painting. I tried to remember that I didn't want to hurt him. But there was something inside of me that was screaming for vengeance. For pain and darkness and death.

"It was my fault she burned," I sobbed, staring at the fireballs depicted in the girl's hands. My shimmering tears splattered against the floor.

"Ember, let me—"

"No!" I yanked back on his wrist until there was a sickening pop. His eyes bulged, and a gargled cry of pain escaped.

"Dad!" Bexley shrieked and started for the door. I shot out my free hand and sent a flame in her direction. She dove to the side at the last second.

"Don't hurt her," Atticus grunted. He'd dropped to one knee, fighting against my hold. "She's innocent."

"Innocent?" I laughed, sounding a bit crazed. I could only imagine that I looked it as well. "She is his daughter, Atticus."

"Yes, a girl like you. Forced into a life she didn't ask for."

Heat spiraled around me as I glared down at him. Another tingle in my palms intensified the heat, and Atticus began to squirm.

"Hurt me if you have to, but leave her out of it."

A reddish tint tainted my vision. Flames licked at the edges of my sight. Rage swirled in my heart and sank heavily into my stomach. In the back of my mind, I could hear the screams of my momma as she burned alive. "Mehki took everything from me."

"And for good reason," a voice said from behind me.

I whirled around, yanking Atticus with me as I turned to face the man I'd been hunting for years. He glanced to where his daughter cowered behind a chair. I spotted a woman backing away from the doorway over his shoulder. She was older, but shared Bexley's features.

"I knew you would come." He stepped into the room with a calm that unnerved me. "It was only a matter of time."

"Uncle?" Atticus grunted when I yanked on his arm again.

Mehki tsked and shook his head. "Leave it to you to fall for the enemy."

"She's not my enemy," he ground out. My hold on his hand eased as his words worked to help me see reason again.

"This girl killed your parents, Atticus. Orlon was at least smart enough to see the truth."

Atticus's eyes narrowed. "You're the one who told him about Ember?"

"Of course." He circled around me, keeping a fair distance between us, and then sat on the edge of his desk. His casual demeanor didn't fool me. I knew he'd chosen that spot for a reason. He most likely had a weapon hidden there. "I'd hoped he would rough her up enough so that he could bring her to me. Seems someone else decided to rescue her instead."

Realization began to dawn on Atticus. I watched the lines around his eyes soften. When he looked up at me, regret spilled in to take the place of his anger.

"Don't apologize," I said through gritted teeth. "You saved my life."

He nodded and remained silent. Mehki's laugh grated on my nerves as I turned to face him again. "Why?"

"That is the ultimate question, is it not?" He folded his hands in his lap. Black leather gloves covered them. I realized he was dressed. As if he'd been planning for this moment long before Atticus brought me to his doorstep.

"I'm sure you have a lot of questions. Most of which I don't care to answer. Your mom was in the wrong place at the wrong time. I never wanted her. Not after I found out you were adopted. I'm sure you already guessed that by now, since she never had your abilities. But you . . ." His smile made the hairs on the back of my neck stand up. "You were the ultimate prize. I have traced your lineage through the ages, followed your many lives. It's all quite fascinating. I have yet to actually find your origins. I'd ask you, but then I suppose you don't actually know."

"So just because I was adopted, my momma was useless to you?"

Mehki shrugged. "Yes."

My nails dug deep into my palms as I fought to hold back my rage.

"You son of a—"

Bexley peeked out from behind the chair. At his admission, she rose. "You killed her mom?"

"Bex, darling, sometimes sacrifices are made for the greater good." He held out his hand to his daughter. "I did it for you."

She stopped short of his hand. "For me?"

"Of course," a new voice joined the group. I turned to see that Mehki's wife no longer cowered in the dark. She stood in the doorway, her silver hair shining in the light. Her coffee-colored eyes were large behind the glasses perched on her nose. She looked frail and gaunt in the nightgown that hung loosely over her slight frame. "Ever since you were diagnosed as a child, Mehki has been obsessed with phoenix lore."

"What's wrong with her?" I asked Atticus and released my hold on him.

"She has a rare sickle cell disease." He rubbed his hands together. "The human doctors don't have a cure for it yet. Even Jared Lewis gave it a shot and failed. He has the ability to fix any disease, but it's almost like her body rejects any form of healing. We suspect that since she developed the disease at such a young age, her human side left her in a weakened state. Now it's preventing her shifter abilities from awakening."

"So Bexley is dying," I finished for him. "And you figured I could cure her."

"We were desperate." Atticus's aunt stepped into the room. "I couldn't lose my baby girl. Not when there was one last chance to hope."

Flames shot out from my palms and lit the fringe of the rug. Atticus hurried to stamp them out, wincing at the pain in the soles of his bare feet.

"Elora," Mehki called to his wife. "We don't have to explain ourselves. Our reasons are our own."

I took a step forward, but Atticus grabbed my arm and held me back. With the flicker of his gaze, I turned to see Mehki had a shotgun in his hands now.

"I realize you're blessed with immortality and this gun can't do a whole lot against you, but it sure can hurt." He set it on his lap. "I taught Orlon how to shoot, knowing one day that skill might come in handy. He almost succeeded with you. But I won't need this gun, because you're going to give me what I want without a fuss."

I snorted. "There's nothing you can do to make me."

"Oh, I reckon I'll be able to change your mind. You care for my nephew. It's easy to see. And I have something that's very dear to him." Mehki's smile stretched so wide, it became plastic. "I have his parents."

CHAPTER 14

For the span of a breath, the room fell into shocked silence. But just as quickly, it erupted into shouting.

"What do you mean, you have my parents?" Atticus raged. "Who did we bury?"

"I thought a phoenix killed Uncle Ridge and Aunt Jaelyn," Bexley said.

"You faked your own brother's death?" Elora gasped.

I remained silent, watching Mehki. He did the same with me. No one else in the room mattered to him. Not his dying daughter, grieving nephew, or distraught wife. And in that moment of clarity, I knew his entire family had been duped by a master manipulator.

"He wants me for himself," I said.

Atticus turned to look at me. "What?"

"This was never about healing Bexley or using your parents as a cover-up. He wants me. Wants what I can give him, isn't that right?"

Mehki's smile was cold. "Survivors do what they must, Ember?"

"Is she telling the truth?" Elora turned on her husband. "None of this was about healing Bexley?"

His silence was answer enough. So was the crazed look in his eye.

"It wouldn't have mattered," I said to his wife. "I can't heal others. Only myself."

A sob escaped Elora as she collapsed to the floor. Bexley rushed toward her mom and wrapped the shaking woman in her arms.

"It's okay," the teenager soothed, but the tears falling from her eyes told a different story.

"And my parents?" Atticus said, lifting his gaze from the women of his family. "They're alive?"

"Ridge may be a thorn in my side, but he's still blood." Mehki waved his hand as if the matter was trivial. "He still has his uses."

"You destroyed Orlon—made him feel like this was his fault—and for what?" Atticus threw out his hand toward me. "So you could kidnap her? What good does that do you if she can't heal anyone else?"

Mehki surged to his feet. "You always were too short-sighted to see the bigger picture. That girl isn't a walking doctor. She's a gift. Her tears contain the secret to immortality. If we can collect enough of her essence, then I can live forever."

Elora sniffed. "How could you do this to us? To your only daughter?"

"Immortality is everything, my dear. Once I discover its secrets, I can save you and Bex."

"And my parents?" Atticus pressed. He shifted his stance. When he did so, I realized he was maneuvering his way between me and his uncle.

"Yes, they can live, too," Mehki said in a flippant tone. "Under my rule, of course. Ridge doesn't deserve to lead our family. The Roc Aerie needs a strong leader."

"He was strong before you murdered him." Atticus took another step.

I grabbed hold of Atticus's arm, and he looked back at me. "So you are a roc."

"We changed our name to Laroc ages ago, but that's our species." He looked confused for a split second before realization dawned on him. "Ember, it's not what you think. I would never . . . I didn't . . ."

"But you already have betrayed her, Atticus. It's in your blood, that thirst for hers." Mehki laughed. "You know well enough that we're the only known mortal enemy of a phoenix. The only being

247

capable of killing her. The guns just make the process a little more fun."

Atticus stiffened and looked back at me. "I'm not like him."

"Of course you aren't, boy. At least not enough to finish the job for me. But Orlon is." When Mehki looked over my shoulder, I turned to see Atticus's brother standing in the doorway.

"Oh, crap." I took the brunt of his tackle hard to the chest. My head slammed into the hardwood floor, and the room started to grow dark as his hands found my neck again.

"Get off her!" Atticus appeared over me, yanking against his brother, but Orlon was crazed. The maniacal look in his eye told me that I had no choice but to fight back.

"Atticus," I coughed, fighting to speak. "Run!"

The instant Atticus's hands slipped from his brother's shoulder, I slammed my hands into Orlon's chest. The man erupted into flames. His screams rose into shrieks. Bexley cried out when Orlon shot to his feet, flapping his arms as they shifted into wings. By the time he hit the large window and took flight, the flames had engulfed him.

"Orlon!" Atticus screamed into the night, hanging out the window in search of his brother.

I coughed and rolled to my side. Elora sat staring at me with horror. She ignored Bexley's pleading to run.

A violent tug on my hair sent me flying up into the air. I found my footing just before Mehki dragged me from the room. I twisted and fought back, but he remained out of reach of each flame that I threw at him.

The wallpaper in the foyer caught fire. The drapes began to smoke. I carved deep scorch marks into the floors.

"Ember!" Atticus appeared in the doorway.

"Atticus, no!" But my cry of warning was too late.

Mehki turned on his nephew as Atticus leaped. His hand shifted into talons and raked across his nephew's chest. I watched as Atticus's shirt and flesh split, spilling blood onto the floor. When he fell, he didn't move.

"No!" I reached back and took hold of Mehki's hand. The scent of his bubbling flesh burned my eyes.

A hard backhand with his claw sent my head spinning as I collapsed to the ground. Lifting me as if I weighed no more than a bag of feathers, he slammed me repeatedly into the wall. Shimmering gold and crimson tears fell from my eyes as my nose cracked and the skin over my temple split.

Something smooth and cold touched my cheek. Fighting against my swelling eye, I spied the small glass vial he used to capture my essence. His grin made my blood boil.

"Get off me." Heat burst from my hands, and Mehki flew backward. He hit high on the wall, shattering a mirror, and then fell to the floor.

I dragged myself over to where Atticus lay in a pool of blood. His chest was sliced open, the torn skin flapping when I rolled him over.

"You have to shift." I took hold of his hand. "It's the only way to heal."

He groaned as he nodded. I watched as his right arm flopped against the ground, trying to extend into a wing. A few feathers sprouted and then nothing.

"I can't." When he wheezed, his words sounded wet from the blood filling his lungs.

"Don't you die on me," I pleaded. Tearing my tank top over my head, I pressed it to his wounds. Mere seconds was all it took to soak through. There would be no stopping the bleed out. His wounds were too severe.

"I'm . . ." He gasped as bubbles of blood burst at his lips. "I'm so sorry."

"Shh." I pressed his hand to my face. "It's okay. I understand."

"No." He tried to roll to his side, but the effort was too much. "I know you. You're . . . a . . . good . . ."

"Atticus!" I shook his shoulders when his eyes fell closed. "No. You can't leave me!"

I pressed my cheek to his chest. The blood didn't matter. Only the fading sound of his beating heart did. My tears fell as I felt his life draining away.

"He can't save you now, girl."

I screamed as Mehki's hand latched around my calf and dragged me away from Atticus. I twisted and fought, kicking and screaming, but he didn't relent. He was in mid-shift, and his strength far outweighed my own.

His feathers were far darker than Atticus's, black and etched with the silver of his hair. His talons were razor sharp as they tore into my leg and shredded muscle. His beak had a wicked curve to it, sharp enough to tear flesh from my bones as he tossed me out the front door.

By the time he reached his porch, he was full roc. If I had thought Atticus was big, he was nothing compared to Mehki.

"How can you kill your own family?" I screamed at him. The hole that had opened in my heart grew with each passing second. The only relief I could find was that Atticus's suffering was over. But it killed me to not be there with him in the final moments.

Mehki twisted his head around but didn't answer. I didn't know if he even could. Fluffy had been able to speak when he was in his wolf form. I suspected that even if Mehki could speak around his beak, he would choose not to.

I screamed as he grabbed me in one talon and took to the air. This flight was nothing like what I'd experienced with Atticus. The beating of his wings stole the air from my lungs as we shot high into the air. I feared my neck would snap from the force.

My ability to wield fire was useless in the face of certain death from a fall at this height. So instead of fighting, I held on for dear life. With each flap of his wings, my stomach dropped and spun. Nausea gripped me as I closed my eyes, but the instant I did so, I realized that made it worse.

When a terrible cry echoed around me, I clasped my hands over my ears and yelled. The cry filled the air, permeating every inch of space around me and in me. It was only after something huge slammed into us that I realized the cry hadn't come from Mehki.

"Atticus!" I stared in disbelief at the white-streaked bird that clung to Mehki, digging his claws in. Streaks of blood lined his feathered breast, but when he looked at me, I saw life in his eyes. "But how?"

Anchoring himself on his uncle's back, he lifted one wing. I stared in disbelief at the golden shimmer of my tears threading through his feathers. I laughed through my tears. "I healed you."

I didn't know how it could be possible. My tears hadn't worked as I clung to my momma's smoldering body. Or kissed Susan's cheek while she lay recovering from a heart attack in the hospital a year ago. But why didn't matter. He was alive.

Mehki's talon loosened its grip when Atticus raked his claws across the length of his back. I screamed as I fell, tumbling end over end. Screeching erupted in the air. The rushing of wind soon drowned it out.

I'm going to die. Again.

"Umph," I groaned when I landed hard on the back of a bird. This one had chestnut markings with a brilliant white head. The side of the bird was black and scarred.

"You're alive!" The instant relief rushed in, I remembered why I'd had to burn Orlon in the first place.

Orlon dove straight to the ground, pulling up at the very last second. I saw my dinner for the second time as he skidded to a stop and ruffled his feathers, sending me rolling to the ground.

"Why is my brother attacking Mehki? Is it because of you?" His human hand wrapped around my throat within seconds of landing. I could see the extent of his burns. His skin peeled back to reveal raw flesh. "Answer me!"

I pried at his fingers, gasping for air. He seemed to take a hint and relaxed his grip enough for me to be able to speak.

"Mehki lied." I sucked in another breath. "Parents . . . alive."

"What?" He yanked me so hard, I worried my hip would shake right out of its socket. "Explain."

"Killed . . . my momma. Faked your parents' deaths. Still . . . alive."

His eyes flashed a dark gold, then he turned to stare at his brother's desperate attack on Mehki. "If you are lying, I will shred you where you stand."

"If I'm not . . . Atticus will die . . . while you stand here . . . threatening me," I ground out.

With a disgusted snarl, he tossed me away. He shifted and shot up into the sky. I rolled onto my back to watch him join the fight.

Great droplets of blood fell from the sky. It was impossible to tell who was winning. The three birds spiraled in a ball of feathers and claws. Their cries echoed off the mountains.

Struggling to my feet, I hurried to wipe my damp cheeks, spreading my healing tears on the worst of the wounds in my leg. Spreading the second dose on my eye, I regained vision in that eye. The healing warmth spread through my body.

Taking in my surroundings, I realized that Orlon had dropped me off on the slope leading to Atticus's cabin. The climb was steep and arduous as the ground gave way beneath me. I fought to climb as I tried to keep an eye on the fight in the sky.

A teeth-rattling shriek nearly sent me rolling to the bottom. I searched the skies and spotted a dark figure plummeting to the ground. Trees cracked, and a great cloud of dirt rushed into the air where it landed.

Desperate to know who it was, I wrapped my hand around a tree and leaned out over the ravine. Circling in the sky were the two remaining birds. One black. One light.

"He's still alive." Sweet relief swept in as I hugged the tree. "Come on, Atticus. Make him pay!"

The final hundred feet of the climb left me panting on the ground at the top. Dust clung to my bloody legs.

From behind me, the roof of Atticus's cabin exploded. Splinters of wood sliced my skin as I covered my head. The walls groaned but held firm. The windows shattered under the impact of the birds suddenly plummeting from the sky.

Peering through the dust cloud, I stared at the front door. "Come on, Atticus."

I leaped to my feet when I heard a shrill scream followed by a sickening crunch. "No!"

Racing toward the cabin, I skidded to a stop at the driveway when the door opened, and Mehki stepped out. Scratches, torn strips of muscle, and blood clothed his nakedness. So much blood.

"Atticus!" I screamed.

Mehki's gaze shifted to meet mine. When he did, he smiled. It was the same smile he wore when he stepped over my momma's body. Triumph.

"You bastard!"

The phoenix tattoo on my forearm spread its wings, and a scorching heat spread along my body. Tongues of fire danced over my skin. The fibers of Atticus's Led Zeppelin shirt shriveled and became ash. The light radiating from me pulsated. My vision darkened despite the intensity of the light. Like a roaring wind, I felt the power surge through me and then burst free.

Mehki raised a hand to shield himself. I screamed at the jolt of released power, and my vision exploded into flame.

CHAPTER 15

*T*he world around me burned. A vibrant orange glow lit the expanse of the night sky and forced the stars into hiding. The temperate air made the oxygen feel thin in my lungs. I rolled to my side and brushed singed leaves from my naked body. With each labored exhale, the rain of ash drifted like feathers on a gentle breeze and then spiraled away.

I coughed and took a quick inventory of my condition. The throbbing in my head made my thoughts hazy. Weariness weighed on me as I sat up. Nothing within my body appeared to be broken.

There was no sound apart from the crackling of fire all around. No wolf's cry to the moon or the hoot of an owl swooping overhead. The sudden absence of insect song was eerie.

"Atticus?"

My voice resonated in my chest, sounding both unnatural and louder than I'd expected. The call trailed off when I saw that I was surrounded by some sort of a shimmering gold force field. It was visible only from the corner of my eye. The hairs on my arms rose. My fingertips tingled as I traced the ground in search of an end to this mysterious force. I discovered that it arched over my head, completely surrounding me.

"Whoa," I whispered, in awe of the raw power emanating from the barrier. "Well, that's new."

My hair floated off my shoulders, drawn to the current of electricity when I tried to push against the barrier. The few stray hairs caught my eye, and I gasped. Each strand had shifted to onyx.

"At least black is my color." I coughed.

When I moved to brush my hair back, I stopped. Where my fingers brushed against my face, smooth skin lay instead of scar tissue. I traced the edge of my eye and around my lip, but there were no ridges from my burns.

"Oh, my god," I wept as I explored my new and perfect face. "I'm healed."

But with this new joy came a profound sense of emptiness.

"Atticus? Please tell me you're still alive in there." I waved my arm to try to clear away some of the ash falling from overhead so that I could see the cabin. I realized with a start that none of it touched me. It was blocked by the shield surrounding me.

That's when I noticed the obvious shaking of my hands. Not from shock, though that would be justifiable at the moment, but from power. It was unlike anything I'd felt before. It rippled through me like an electrical current, charged and ready for use at a second's notice.

I clenched my hands. The sensations were too much. I needed answers, someone to explain what happened, but I was alone. An inferno raged all around me. Lifeless trees were uprooted and tossed thirty feet away. Those that remained were nothing more than burnt stumps. The grass was blistered. This part of the mountain was a landslide of devastation.

My knees were weak at the sight of it when I stood. As I turned in a full circle, I knew that I was standing in the epicenter of something truly terrible. A suffocating sadness dragged at me at the thought of so much loss. The animals that survived wouldn't have a home to return to. The forest would take years to regrow.

As I moved toward the scorched cabin and stepped over a pile of charred bone dust, I knew why Mehki was gone. There was no one left alive. No one apart from me.

I looked down at my naked form. I was completely unsoiled by the flames. My skin was washed clean of the blood and healed of all wounds. It was almost as if I'd become a new person.

My breath caught. "Like I was reborn from the fire."

Twisting my arm to look at my phoenix tattoo, I saw a small baby bird lying in a pile of embers. It fluttered its wings and then nestled down to sleep.

"From the embers a new phoenix will rise," I whispered, repeating the phrase I'd read during my search into the lore. "Atticus was right. I am a phoenix."

Though my transformation didn't come in the way the lore spoke of, I knew I'd found my kind.

Maybe sometimes legends and myth get things wrong. I hoped so, because that might mean there was someone else like me out there. Someone who could help me understand who I was.

My fingers began to tremble as I closed my eyes so that the shimmering of the force field was hidden from sight. I breathed in what felt like my first real breath of air. I knew what I was finally. And no matter how scary that might be, it was right.

"If only Atticus could have seen this transformation," I whispered. My eyes shot open. "The cabin!"

The thought of his final moments sent me racing toward the charred steps. They crumbled underfoot, but I didn't fall. My force field held me up.

"Please be alive." I kicked aside the smoldering remains of the door and clambered over the fallen timbers.

I stopped short when I caught sight of a burnt corpse. It was kneeling on the floor, its hands raised against the wall of flame that had consumed him.

"No!"

I collapsed at Atticus's side. The feeling of loss was too great. Though his facial features were unrecognizable, I knew it was him. My heart couldn't deny the truth of it, and my eyes would never be able to erase this horrible scene.

"You can't leave me," I begged, reaching out for him. My fingers hung in the air less than an inch from his face. "You were right about me. I need to believe that there's good in me, but there's something more now. Something dark and angry. I need you to show me how to come back from this!"

I hung my head, unable to look at his scorched form any longer, while violent sobs racked my body. I did this. I killed the only man that I'd ever let myself care about.

Wrenching back my head, I released a soul-shattering scream into the night. It overshadowed the crackling of the fire and the splintering of trees. My fists beat against the wood floor that he'd built with his own hands. With each hit, a surge of shimmering gold raced across the floor. The wooden boards split and groaned. The cabin began to lean.

"No!" I lunged forward to try to catch Atticus.

His form began to crumble in a slow tide. His nose dissolved first. Then his cheeks and forehead. His right arm fell away, followed by part of his left side. As I tried to hold him together, his embers slipped through my quaking fingers, nothing left but a pile of ash.

In that moment, I forgot how to breathe. The numbness that I felt wasn't a complete lack of feeling. Instead, it was a volatile overload of so many emotions that I couldn't process them all at once.

Atticus was dead. Because of me.

The swirl of my emotions funneled into suffocating despair. My heart splintered into a thousand pieces. My hands glowed a brilliant red. My hair sparked with electricity as my vision exploded in an array of color.

Stretching out my arms, I felt a dark power pulsating through and around me. I became one with the dying trees. The frantic heartbeats of the animals fleeing my destruction echoed in my ears. Then I became aware of the screams from the valley below.

An invisible force lifted me into the air through the hole in the cabin's roof, and I glimpsed the extent of the damage for the first time. Half of the mountain was obliterated. Cars were overturned on countless streets, their wheels spinning and on fire. The ski lift was decimated and the lodge engulfed in flames. I saw several figures fleeing from their ruins, their clothes alight.

The firestorm I'd unleashed had made its way to Havenwood Falls. The roads leading into town oozed tar. The high school was trapped by the landslide, buried by several feet of molten earth. The main street was lit with an unquenchable blaze as the shops burned.

The roof of the motorcycle club had collapsed. The clock tower of City Hall was a rising pyre into the night. I glanced down at the burning remains of Broastful Brew and a sob caught in my throat. What if Mabel was still in there? Smoke billowed out of the shattered windows, but I couldn't see any movement.

Beside it, the dove-gray awning of Melissa's art shop was scorched. Tears streamed down my cheeks when I saw her sitting on the street, huddled over a wailing child in her arms. Her blond hair was matted with soot.

The gazebo where I'd watched the play was demolished into splinters, the fountain charred black. The painted front of Shear Magic where I'd been offered a free wax was blistered. I rose higher and saw several bodies with smoke rising from their torsos outside of Coffee Haven.

"What have I done?" My voice quaked as numbness raced through me like a cold rain.

Dozens of screams rose from the apartments by the ski resort. I could see people waving pillow cases out the windows, desperate to be saved before the fires reached them. Several people stood in shock outside Whisper Falls Inn.

Everywhere I looked, I saw pain, fear, and desolation. It hit me like a wrecking ball to my gut, and I closed my eyes as my stomach heaved.

As countless alarms blared, creatures of all sorts took to the air and streets to fight back the fires. Humans sat in front of smoldering homes, mourning the loss of their loved ones. I wondered if the little girl I'd bought a balloon for was among the children I'd killed tonight.

Those supernaturals who had survived worked their way through the town giving aid. The community, both human and nonhuman, came together. Their sheer love for one another made me want to hurtle myself out of the sky so I could be rid of my guilt.

How could I have allowed my grief to bring me to this point? To harm so many innocent people?

My grief battled with a new sensation, one that reveled in this death. Voices filled my mind, sinister in their whispers. They weren't done with me.

"No." I closed my eyes to the pain. "This isn't me. These people didn't deserve this. Atticus cared for them, and for good reason. They are decent, loving people."

At least they were before I arrived.

"What about Bexley and Elora?" I whispered, turning to see if I could spy their house, but it was too hard to see through the smoke. I still had no clue if Orlon had survived the fall. If he didn't get out of the woods in time, I sealed his fate for him.

I searched for Sheriff Kasun's vehicle but couldn't find it. But there, near the fire department, I spotted the shine of Lloyd's badge. He was trapped halfway under a mangled car. The skin on his face was melted.

"No," I sobbed, wrapping my arms around myself. "This can't be happening."

Rising high enough to see the waters of the falls boiling, I peered into its distorted reflection. I saw myself, a naked girl surrounded by the fiery image of a magnificent flaming bird. Though I couldn't say for sure at this height, I would've sworn that my eyes glowed red.

Currents of power swirled around my hands, fighting to be unleashed. This new rage thirsted for blood, for revenge. But as I looked at the cabin, I saw the pile of ash where Mehki once stood. He was finally dead. I got what I'd wanted for so many years.

But looking out over the valley, I knew the cost of my revenge was far too great.

I threw out my hands and stopped rising in the air. "This can't be. I won't allow it."

My body hummed with energy as I began to spin. I didn't know what I was doing, only that I had to do something. A golden vortex appeared beneath me as I focused my powers inward. It tore at the ground, ripping aged trees up by their roots and spitting them out as the funnel whipped around.

My bones rattled and my stomach lurched as I pushed myself faster. The light around me grew so intense that it was almost as if I'd become the blazing inferno of the sun. The heat blistered as if I had landed on the star's very surface, and in that split second, my inner being burst apart.

Then everything stopped.

I hung, suspended in air. It was neither warm nor cold. It felt like nothing at all, and on the same hand, it was everything. Every beating heart, every laugh and child's cry. It was every kiss shared between lovers and tear shed for those that'd died.

This place was an infinite stream of time. Shards of light floated around me. Each one glistened with colors no human eye had ever glimpsed before. There was no sound of the vortex or the screaming of the dying. Time stood still as I reached out to touch the nearest shard. It glittered with power. With life.

"It's beautiful." My voice echoed around me without end.

The shards jingled like a glass wind chime as they floated into each other. It was peaceful here. Then just as quickly as I entered this strange place, time and my life force ricocheted back into my body. I was flung from the sky. Like a falling meteor, I fell in a blaze of flame. A crater formed when I hit, and darkness consumed me.

WHEN I OPENED MY EYES, I swayed in place, blinded by the light that emanated from me. Mehki stood less than five feet from the cabin steps, his hands raised to ward off the light. Through the glass door, I saw Atticus was shifting back into a man.

"He's not dead!" I gasped. A tear fell. Then another.

I've been here before. The sensation of déjà vu was too strong to ignore as I blinked and tried to remember. Something terrible was about to happen. But what?

When Mehki took a step toward me, I knew that I could kill him. I raised my hand, intending to take revenge for what he'd stolen from me, but I stopped. My fingers refused to open, though I was desperate to release this newfound power. Strands of onyx hair tangled in my eyelashes. The transformation had begun.

"I remember this." My voice echoed and bounced back at me. That's when I saw the force field beginning to form, and panic sent me into action. "Not again!"

I yanked my hand back. Pressing my palm against my chest, I focused the full brunt of the firestorm on myself. Mehki's cry of alarm faded as the light exploded and I flew back into the woods. Trees cracked and fell with each impact. The force field shimmered but remained intact as my world exploded into flame. The fires ate at my skin, melting it away until I was sure nothing more than bone remained.

Never before had I experienced such pain. It stole my breath away as thousands of tongues of flames licked across my body. Gold and crimson shimmered around me, and then with a brilliant burst of blue, it vanished.

I don't know how much time passed as I lay trapped in torment. It felt like days before I deciphered a shout.

"Ember!"

I couldn't move when Atticus's arms wrapped around me and cradled me against his chest. His skin was sticky, matted with blood and feathers. My head lolled to the side. Before the darkness swept in for the second time, I realized that I was lucky to still have a body for him to pick up.

EPILOGUE

$\mathcal{W}$hen I awoke, I wasn't surprised to find myself tied to a hospital bed. Or to see a rather grim looking sheriff staring back at me. What did surprise me was to find a few other familiar faces at the end of my bed.

Bexley stood hugging her mom, Elora. I wasn't sure which one was holding the other one up. Orlon leaned on a crutch. His right arm was tucked into a sling and his left leg trapped in a cast that went almost to his groin. Bloody gauze was wrapped around his head, covering a bump. But he had a wry smile on his face when he noticed that I was awake.

"Looks like Sleeping Beauty finally decided to join the party after all." He chuckled. Then he winced when Bexley jabbed him with an elbow in his side.

"How do you feel, Ember?"

I turned to see Atticus sitting right where Susan should be. His face was more black and blue than skin-toned. His arm was in a matching sling to Orlon's, but the smile on his face was perfect.

"You're alive!" I shot up in bed, but the restraints stopped me.

Sheriff Kasun smirked. "You won't be sneaking out of this hospital any time soon."

"Want to bet?" Atticus and I said at the same time. I laughed and felt a sharp pain in my ribs. Apparently, I still had a bit of healing to finish.

Atticus eased me back. "The doctors said you should be dead. Turns out you had other plans."

I smiled. "I could say the same for you."

His brow dipped in confusion. "Yeah, about that. You kept mumbling that I was dead while you were sleeping. Planning on finishing the job later or something?"

I looked at each of the people standing around my bedside. "You don't know?"

"Know what?" Sheriff Kasun stepped forward.

"The town . . . the fire . . ." I shook my head. "I killed everyone."

Atticus and the sheriff exchanged a long glance before Ric snorted and shook his head. "If that's not the ramblings of a concussion—"

"No, it's not—" I stopped when Atticus squeezed my hand. "Sure. Yeah. That must be it."

Ric Kasun's eyes narrowed at me, but then he shrugged and headed for the door. "Tate is on watch, in case you try to make an escape. I've given him orders to bite on sight. What with you being immortal and all, we figure it'd just be a flesh wound."

"Good to know." From around the corner, the younger officer flashed me a grin.

"We should get Orlon home to rest," Elora said. She patted the blanket over my foot and pulled Bexley along. "I'm glad you're alive, Ember. If I had known—"

"You didn't," I said. I gave her a nod. A small but awkward smile lit her face before she nodded back. We had an understanding. Mehki had hidden the monster well, but all evil gets found out eventually.

"Hey!" I called, and Elora turned back. "When I get out of here, I'd like to try something with Bex. I might be able to help your daughter."

Her eyes widened, and she looked to Atticus, who smiled in return. "I told you she was something special."

Elora smiled and nodded. "Any help you could give would be very much appreciated."

She didn't need to apologize for Mehki's actions. It wasn't her place to do so.

Deep down, I knew the price I'd almost paid for my revenge. A mother's love ran deeper than even that. I couldn't fault her for wanting her daughter to live. I'd have probably done the same thing if given the chance to bring my momma back.

"Rest up, little firebird. When you're feeling better, we'll teach you how to fly." Orlon smiled.

"Seriously?" I blinked. "I can do that?"

Atticus laughed. "After what I saw in the woods last night, I doubt there's much you can't do."

"Wait!" I called as Orlon turned to leave. "What about your parents? Mehki said they were still alive."

A shadow fell over his face. "Yeah. Well, Mehki's not doing much talking now that he's been turned over to the Court, but word will spread. People will help us look. We'll find them."

"Count me in on that search party. I'm pretty good at tracking," I said. He shot a pointed glance at my restraints, and I laughed. "Well, when I'm free, that is."

"I'll take it. And thanks for not letting me kill you. I'd have felt pretty bad about that after this came to light." Orlon waved his good hand and then hobbled out into the hallway.

"I told you he's not a half-bad guy when he's not trying to kill you." Atticus leaned over and rewarded me with that lopsided grin I'd come to love so much.

"Yeah. Funny how that changes a person." I leaned my forehead against his chin and breathed him in. I didn't think I'd ever find another scent that I liked more. "You going to tell me what happened after I passed out?"

"Not much to tell. Ric showed up with the cavalry right after you went all flame ball. I guess a three-bird brawl in the sky caught a few people's attention, and the Court had to do some cleanup work. They sent Ric to investigate. I was just getting my feet under me again when I saw Mehki make a run for it. I yelled out to Ric that Mehki faked my parents' deaths, and that was all it took. Personally, I think Ric enjoyed taking my uncle down. He wasn't the most popular man around town, if you hadn't guessed."

I smiled. "And you don't remember a firestorm or dying?"

Atticus's frown returned. I hated to steal away his smile again, but I needed to know. "It's time that you tell me what really happened out there, Ember."

I relayed to him as much as I could remember. It wasn't much more than the feeling of total desolation followed by peace. I couldn't have explained how I altered time if I wanted to. And then came the flames. Those I remembered.

"My face!" I yanked my arm up to try to check for my scars, but the bindings held tight.

"Easy." Atticus reached behind him and then lifted a mirror for me to see. "Look."

I couldn't believe my eyes. I was beautiful. Perfect and whole, the way I'd been after the firestorm. "I don't understand. I fixed everything back to the way it was."

Atticus set aside the mirror and took my hand in his. "When I found you lying in the woods, you looked like an angel, all glowing and shimmering. I was almost afraid to touch you, but I couldn't help myself. That's when I saw your scars were healing. And there was something else . . ."

"What?" I twined my fingers through his.

"You were calling my name."

"I was?" A blush rose to my cheeks, and I started to look away, but he stopped me.

"It meant the world to me," he whispered. But then he gave me his lopsided grin. "And don't you go thinking that you look any better than you did yesterday. I never saw those scars, remember? You've always taken my breath away."

The tenderness in his gaze as he brushed his fingers across my newly healed skin made my heart swell with love.

"Wow," I whispered.

"What?"

"I just realized that I kinda like you." I grinned.

"It's about time you figured that out." He smirked. "My being the only one able to see your tattoo come to life should have been your first hint. Guess you're a bit slow on the uptake."

"Oh, you—"

Atticus crushed his lips against mine. The fluttering of wings on my forearm told me that my tattoo was preening. I almost laughed, knowing he was right, but this kiss was too good to ruin.

I didn't know what would happen to Mehki or how the Court would make him pay for his crimes. I only hoped that I'd be around to see it. In the coming days, I knew that I'd have to account for my own actions. Sheriff Kasun seemed like a decent guy, and I vowed that I would pay my time, however long that was. After that, I figured I'd stick around Havenwood Falls for a while.

Atticus would wait for me. I knew that. Just like I knew that I'd need to speak to Addie about adding some extra warding to my tattoo. Something that would help prevent me from ever setting off another firestorm again.

But that could wait. This kiss, this moment with Atticus, was all that mattered. And for the first time in my life, I felt whole.

ABOUT THE AUTHOR

Amy Miles is the author of multiple published novels, including her bestselling young adult immortals books, The Arotas Series. Unwilling to be defined by any one genre, she has written paranormal romance, science fiction/fantasy, post-apocalyptic, romance, inspirational, and plans to continue to explore new genres. She is the co-Founder of Red Coat PR, a firm helping indie authors build a marketing base for their career.

She is also the co-Founder of Penned Con, an annual two-day convention held in St. Louis, Missouri, bringing readers and authors together with industry professionals to learn, grow, and give back. She and her husband are heavily involved in charity work through Action for Autism, a St. Louis–based organization aiding families with autism, and founded the Penned Con scholarship to benefit area families. She is an avid reader, urban homesteader, weekend golfer, and Netflix binge addict who lives with her husband and son in South Carolina.

ACKNOWLEDGMENTS

For every book that I write, there is always a team of people working on the sidelines to support me.

I'm first and foremost grateful for my husband, Rick Miles, and son, Landon, for giving me the time and headspace that I need to get through another project. I know that when I'm in the writing cave I can be insanely focused, and it's hard to pull myself out of that to have family time. Heck, sleep and a shower seem optional some days. Far too many days I tend to get these mile-long stares into nothingness when I'm struggling with a particular section of a book, and they kindly leave me be until I have it sorted in my head. They are my rocks.

My endless thanks go out to Danielle Bannister, for not only being with me every step of the way through each of my books, while listening to me moan and whine and cry over frustrating plot lines or characters that refuse to behave, but also for being my chip gal. She is always there to tell me that any time is chip time. And believe me, that's a real life saver. She also beta read *From the Embers* before anyone else. The fact that she liked it was a HUGE win, since we are polar opposites. Your comments are invaluable to me, Danielle. I couldn't stay sane without you.

To my Badass Betas, words cannot express how you have helped me over the years. Just knowing that my book doesn't suck before it goes to edits gives me hope that when it's all polished and shiny, it will be worth reading. Thank you for taking this wild ride with me.

A huge thank you goes out to all of the Havenwood Falls authors. You guys are the best. Seeing all of your excitement over the project mingled with a bit of crazy that I know all too well is inspiring. Thank you for letting me be a part of this journey.

Thank you to Kristie Cook, Liz Ferry, and Regina Wamba for being the powerhouse team behind this project. You guys make us look good.

And lastly, I wouldn't be where I am today without amazing readers. You guys get my own personal weird, and I love you for it. Thank you for supporting Havenwood Falls and making it a blast.

DEFYING GRAVITY

KALLIE ROSS

~ A Havenwood Falls New Adult Novella ~

Havenwood Falls

Defying Gravity

Kallie Ross

ALSO BY KALLIE ROSS

Written in the Stars: A Havenwood Falls High Novella

Descent: A Lost Tribe (Book 1)
Defend: A Lost Tribe (Book 2)

Evelyn: A Cupid Chronicles Novella
Unbreakable: The Cupid Chronicles

Defying Gravity is dedicated to Jessi.

CHAPTER 1

ALEX

*T*echnically, summer was a week away, but it appeared the winter still had a hold in the shadows of the forest along Mount Alexa. I'd never experienced what I considered cold weather in June, since I'd never before traveled to Colorado. I explored beyond the trail, feeling comfortable on the mountain because we had something in common. Our names were the same, only I went by Alex.

My good sense of direction and constant attention to my compass should have had me at the ridge of the mountain in another hour. Navigating around the trees and patches of snow wasn't too difficult—I'd prepared and conditioned for the outdoors back in Arizona.

I hated to admit it, but my last breakup had inspired my trip. The guy hadn't been that bad. In no way was I running away. I'd just finally realized I was wasting away while waiting for him to commit, and so was my work.

I would be better off with a dog anyway.

Driving to Colorado had always been the goal, and I'd decided I wouldn't let a dead-end relationship get in the way of me getting my doctorate. It was time to see if what I had inside me could change the world, or at least *my* world.

Buds of green had begun to dot the bare, gray bark sprawled

overhead. The branches fractured the last of the day's sunlight, and my chest burned from breathing in the brisk mountain air. All the locals in the last town I drove through wore shorts and tank tops like there was a heat wave, but growing up in the desert had me donning a jacket and jeans everywhere I went.

I had one month to finish my research, two months tops, then I'd be defending my dissertation. I didn't know what would come next, but it would definitely not include dating. I wanted to make sure the next guy I invested myself into was a best friend. Someone who would invest in me, and not only his own academic aspirations. Sitting in classrooms for six years, researching hundreds of case studies, and hiking through these "haunted" forests had all been in hopes of helping people like me.

Snap.

The sound of a twig breaking interrupted my train of thought, and I made a sharp turn to find the woodland creature who'd crossed my path. Nothing was there. The sound of crunching leaves underfoot brought me to a stop. My heart pounded in my chest, and I took in a deep breath.

A low purr drifted toward me, followed by an extra-large tawny mountain lion. He had golden eyes and black edges around his ears and at the end of his lowered tail.

"Shoo," I commanded in a panic. "Back off."

He raised his head and sniffed the air.

"You're a nice kitty, aren't you?" I rambled. "I'm Alex Newton, and you are? You look like a Mr. Kitty. You don't have to call me Ms. Newton. Alex is fine. Are you feeling peckish?"

The mountain lion's tongue curled over his top teeth as he prowled toward me. A gust of wind rustled the leaves above us and blew my dark curly hair into my eyes. After tucking the strands behind my ears, I peeled the straps of my pack off my shoulders and held the bag between me and the cat like a shield.

"Okay, you don't have to go if you don't want to, Mr. Kitty." My voice shook.

I began to back up, and moved my hands behind my back. My feet dragged along the ground in slow motion, not wanting to startle the big cat. A few feet behind me, my fingers brushed up against a tree. There was no place to run without having to dodge a giant tree trunk or pass a wild, hungry animal. I'd wandered into his trap.

"You can have my bag. There's some beef jerky and trail mix." I slid another few inches, bringing my back flush against the tree's rough bark. "It'll taste way better than me."

I did remember reading about mountain lion attacks, but the article focused on how non-confrontational the cats were. Maybe I could escape while he tried to figure out the tricky zipper.

I tossed my bag a few feet in front of me. Mr. Kitty approached the backpack and pushed at it with his paw. My keys jingled against each other inside. And that's when it dawned on me—my car keys would be the mountain lion's new cat toy.

It's what I deserved for wandering off the trail. I thought I remembered leaving one of the backseat doors unlocked. If only I could get inside the car, I knew I could out-wait the mountain lion.

Suddenly, the cat's ears flattened and a low growl vibrated in his chest. One of my thumbs hooked into my back pocket, where I'd been carrying a decent-sized pocket knife. I'd have to worry about getting my car started later.

"Whoa, big guy, I don't want to hurt you." My gold thumb ring glinted as I swung my knife in front of me and flicked a notch on the side of the gadget. The blade popped out. I doubted the knife would stop the mountain lion, but it could do some damage and maybe buy me some time.

With a glance at my surroundings, I still had nowhere to run. I'd have to distract the mountain lion somehow, but I wasn't about to throw away my one defense. I searched the patch of grass around my feet for a rock or a stick.

The sound of dry leaves crackling surprised me. Hope rose in my chest, but when I looked up, a black wolf stepped out into the open. The presence of another predator caught Mr. Kitty's attention, too.

"Just my luck," I muttered. There wasn't any sign of a pack, only the one wolf. "Lone Wolf, meet Mr. Kitty. Maybe the two of you can have dinner together."

I took my eyes off the mountain lion to try to figure out what the wolf was up to. His coat was peppered with silver around his neck, and he looked bigger than the wolves I'd seen at the zoo. His golden eyes met mine, and I could have sworn he was staring at me. I closed my eyes for a second longer than was safe, and he barked, startling me. Something inside told me to run.

Weird.

The mountain lion bounded toward the wolf. I took a chance and reached for my backpack. Before I turned away, I saw the wolf crouch down in a submissive position. The cat flew over him, creating more distance between us. Then, Lone Wolf attacked the big cat.

Unsure of who to root for, I took off.

One of the creatures yelped, but I fought the desire to look back. My feet pounded against the ground as I zigzagged through the forest. Shallow breathing caused a stitch in my side, but I pushed myself to keep the pace. My face stung from being whipped by low-hanging branches.

What had been an hour climb turned into a twenty-minute sprint down the mountain. I'd gotten off course, twisting and turning around the trees, but only by a couple dozen yards. My well-worn green station wagon waited patiently for me. I'd lovingly named the vehicle Samwise. He groaned and complained, but always came through, like the fictional character in *Lord of the Rings*.

The feeling that one, if not both, of the animals had followed me kept me panicked. I didn't waste time rummaging through my bag. I ran straight for the back door and pulled the handle. Before the door was fully open, I was inside, yanking it back closed. My hand slammed down on the lock.

Why I thought a mountain lion or wolf could open a car door was beyond me. Locking the door gave me some peace of mind.

Trying to slow my heart rate, I took several deep breaths. My backpack sat in my lap with a gaping slash across the front. I unzipped the pocket and shoved my hand into the bottom. My keys were still there. My cell phone was gone.

I couldn't call the local police department about the animal attack, and I'd lost my navigator, Siri. In reality, I knew I'd be okay. But I needed a few minutes to gather myself. I squeezed my five-ten frame between the driver and passenger seats, only to drive my left knee into the steering wheel.

"Crap!" I hollered.

My hand covered my mouth, afraid the outburst would call attention to my location. I hadn't seen any signs of the mountain lion or wolf, but I didn't want them to be able to locate me. I closed my eyes and rubbed my temples in an effort to still my mind.

I decided I didn't want to wait long enough for Mr. Kitty and Lone Wolf to find me, so I inserted my key into the ignition. Samwise grumbled in irritation.

I set my hands up on ten and two, and they were trembling. I sensed something or someone nearby, but I didn't want to look up. If the mountain lion had found me, I would run him over with my car. But the wolf had saved me. It sounded crazy.

I shook my hands in the air and squeezed my eyes shut one more time. I could find my way back to my run-down motel, and then I'd get another phone. I'd report the incident, take notes for my research, and move on to the next trail tomorrow.

A few minutes passed before I worked up the nerve to shift my car into drive, and as I pulled onto the main road, I caught a glimpse of black fur and golden eyes.

CHAPTER 2

TATE

*B*eing a wolf shifter had its benefits and its drawbacks. Being a Kasun, and the second son of the town's sheriff, had mostly benefits. I could roam the woods and protect the borders undetected, but I always shifted back into my human form in my birthday suit. Last night, while in my wolf form, I'd scooped up a lost woman's cell phone into my mouth, after chasing off a mountain lion I didn't recognize, and ran to where I'd hidden my clothes. No one had called the phone, and I toyed with the idea of trying to crack the passcode. By morning, I'd decided to rush to the station, even though I wasn't on duty, and take advantage of my connections.

The calm, small-town pace of the Havenwood Falls Police Department was an illusion for the humans. Under the veil of paperwork and khaki uniforms, our supernatural community kept things interesting. I hadn't recognized the mountain lion last night as a local shifter, so I'd need to report an attack if the cat or the woman hiking had not set off any of the magical wards when wandering across the Havenwood Falls border. The Luna Coven had made it so a fly shifter couldn't sneak across the town line without them knowing, but if the creature were merely a house fly, it could buzz wherever it wanted with none of us any the wiser. I hadn't heard anything on the police scanner all night, and as I walked into the office, everyone was business as usual. So, I figured running the plates I'd memorized the night before would be the best way to find out who the woman was.

It had taken me hours to fall asleep last night. I couldn't get the tall brunette from the forest out of my head. From the moment I saw her, I'd felt the need to protect her, but I told myself it was my job. So I'd texted my brother her license plate number. I'd almost gone to the station in the middle of the night, but running into my father, the sheriff, would only get him riled up about why I was out in the woods to begin with. We had a rotation that rarely changed, and you'd think the order of the town teetered on the patrol our wolf pack had been doing for over two hundred years.

My dad and I'd had it out earlier yesterday, and he'd reached his breaking point. Ric Kasun had finally given me an ultimatum. At the end of the summer, I would have to honor our pack's agreement and protect the town full time as a deputy at the Havenwood Falls Police Department or I'd have to leave Havenwood Falls. My dad had made a pact with the founding families centuries ago, and I was expected to hold up his deal by serving them like a guard dog. The thing was, it was in my blood to want to protect. I just wanted to set my own terms. Up until now, I'd gotten away with a part-time volunteer position as a cadet for over fifty years.

Of course, for the past seventeen years I'd been helping my dad raise my little brother and sister. When we lost Mom after the twins' delivery, I stepped up, since my older brother had already taken a leadership role at the sheriff's office. As wolf shifters, our lives would last more than ten times longer than a human's. Losing Mom was a shock to everyone. At the time, my father let me help, but he didn't expect or understand when I changed my mind about working at the sheriff's office. Instead, I wanted to be a guide for tourist hikers—a service we provided through our family's outdoor supply store.

"Hey, Tate," Conall called from his desk. He waved me over with a slip of paper covered with his chicken-scratch handwriting. "The plates I ran are registered under Alexa Newton. She's a student at the University of Arizona, and she's gotten three speeding tickets—"

"Thanks, that's all I need." I held up my sorry excuse for a cup of coffee brewed at the station.

"Wait, do we need to go to the Court—" The corners of Conall's mouth turned down in panic.

"Nah, she's probably long gone by now. Plus, the Court has enough on their hands. Anything called in last night? I know everyone is on alert for information about the Collector." I tried to change the subject.

Conall smirked. "I know what you're doing."

"The Court would have notified you or Dad if they'd heard any warning bells. It's no big deal." I waved my hand in the air, dismissing the inquiry as casual.

"But you felt something?" Conall asked with raised eyebrows. He'd been happily married for over twenty years, and consistently tried to set me up with other supernaturals.

"Maybe? I don't know." I shrugged. "It's not worth getting into. I think I'll go enjoy the rest of my weekend outside, but first I need a real cup of coffee." I let my cup drop into a trash can. I'd come to the conclusion that the perfect Americano would never be produced by the department's coffee maker the same way I knew the perfect woman for me would never come from Havenwood Falls.

Maybe I'd be better off leaving town. I'd never been away from my family, but I wouldn't feel the pressure to join the force, and I could look for that woman from the forest.

"Don't forget Father's Day dinner at the cabin," Conall reminded. "Everyone will be there."

Ugh.

That's all I needed, a family dinner. My dad discussing town troublemakers, my older brother with his perfect family in tow, and my younger brother, Kase, going on and on about his summer conditioning. The only family member I looked forward to seeing was Willa, but she'd probably bring her boyfriend, Tarron.

I needed caffeine.

I left the department and made my way around the town square toward Coffee Haven. Choosing the longer route potentially included

Ruby Howe casting a spell on me while she swept the sidewalk in front of her herb shop, but it was better than running into Ana Novak, my little brother's ex-girlfriend. She was nosy and outright conniving, and exiting the butcher shop.

Luckily, Ruby didn't stop me, and as I crossed Main Street, an old green station wagon pulled in front of Coffee Haven. It was the same car from the forest yesterday. How had she gotten past the wards and driven into town? I glanced around the square, looking for one or more members of the Court of the Sun and the Moon.

No one came.

Alexa Newton, or Alex, as she had introduced herself to my wolf, stepped out of her car and took in her surroundings. Honestly, Havenwood Falls looked like every other small town I'd been to, but that wasn't saying much. No one in our family had ever left the town for longer than a week. The townspeople were strutting around the square in shorts and T-shirts, enjoying the warmer temperatures, and they walked with purpose. Some crossed the grassy area at the center of the square, moving from Howe's Herbal Shoppe to Soothing Sips. The pedestrians seemed to rotate around the fountain standing in the middle of it all. Teenagers were messing with each other on the steps of the white, wooden gazebo sitting on the corner of the knoll.

As though I'd suddenly joined the Havenwood Falls welcome committee, I walked over to greet Alex. She had a natural, exotic look and wore twice as many layers as everyone else, making her stick out like an owl in a flock of flamingos. The *feelings* I had when I first laid eyes on her grew with each step I took. Something in my gut pulled me to her. I couldn't tell if it was merely attraction or more—magic. Wolf shifters mated for life, and had an undeniable pull to their mates. But I had no idea who this woman was. I hadn't even had a conversation with her.

Before I could get her attention, Alex turned and tripped on the curb, face planting into my chest.

"Hi, there," I welcomed with a chuckle. "Nice ride." Her station wagon looked as old as her.

She inhaled, then looked up. She froze. My jaw clenched when our eyes met. My heart had always been my own, but in an instant, it belonged to her. The same way my feet had always met the ground, I knew my heart would always seek Alex. It was like gravity. The same way the town spun around the fountain, this stranger became my center.

Alex backed away slowly, but misjudged the distance between me and the curb. She tipped backwards, and I darted toward her and wrapped my arms around her waist, pulling her to me.

My pinky finger grazed her skin, and a spark shot up my arm. It hurt a little more than a static shock. I gritted my teeth and steadied her.

After her feet flattened on solid ground, she mumbled "Hellooo" into my shirt.

Careful to make sure she wouldn't fumble again, I slid away from her hesitantly.

She breathed, "Thank you."

I held a hand out for her to shake, and she moved to wave. Awkward.

Her hand froze mid-wave, and her cheeks turned pink. I was a head taller than her, but that only meant she was a few inches shy of six feet. She examined my backwards baseball cap, then her eyes turned to my T-shirt. It read:

Take a Hike
Backwoods Sport & Ski

Her eyes were a warm chocolate brown, and when she grinned at me, I couldn't help but smile back.

"I guess you're new here?" I tilted my head with a frown when she didn't shake my hand, and shoved it in my jeans pocket.

"Yeah, new, I mean passing through, that is." She nodded down and said, "I'm sorry." Alex pointed at my hand. The one in my pocket. But it looked more like she was pointing at my crotch.

My smile widened.

Alex moved her pointer finger to pinch the bridge of her nose. "I'm in desperate need of caffeine."

I chuckled. Her bashfulness was endearing.

"Me too," I agreed and walked over to the coffee shop. She followed, and I opened the door for her. "I'm Tate, Tate Kasun."

"Thanks. I'm Alex Newton." She smiled when the smell of espresso and fresh bread met us. "Are you British intelligence or something? Tate, Tate Kasun." She furrowed her brow and spoke my name in a British accent.

"No, it's just that everybody knows everybody around here, except for the tourists, of course. And I figured since you're new to town, you wouldn't know my last name. Usually, when I'm introducing myself by my last name, I'm giving someone a speeding ticket." I bit the inside of my cheek, hoping she would move on to a more interesting topic.

"Oh, you're a policeman?" she asked.

I felt my lips thin, and I nodded. That's typically not what I led with when I met a pretty girl. I lifted my arm in the direction of the shop's espresso machine in hopes of changing the course of our conversation.

I walked behind her, and continued to explain, "I also work as a trail guide for my family's store, Backwoods."

"Clever name for a store in the mountains." She giggled. "It would be more accurate if we were in the Smokies."

I laughed out loud.

The coffee shop was buzzing with customers. Original art lined the walls, and the wooden floorboards squeaked underfoot as we approached a long marble counter. Paisley, a teen with blue streaks in her nearly white hair, stood behind the register.

"Good morning," she greeted. "What can I get you?"

"Hi, um, I'll take a large Americano with an extra shot and a splash of milk." Alex ordered her drink, but looked lost when she inspected the case filled with bakery items.

"If you want to know my favorite, the blueberry scones are killer, and if you don't snag one now, there probably won't be any left this afternoon. We always sell out," Paisley informed her.

"Thanks for the suggestion. I'll take two. One for now and one to take with me."

"And what'll you have, Officer Kasun?" Paisley looked over Alex's shoulder.

"Oh, we're not together." Alex stopped her. "I'll get my own."

"I just thought—" Paisley started, then pouted in confusion.

My eyes widened, and I started making a slicing motion at my neck with my hand. Alex turned to find me mid-swipe.

"What did she think?" Alex looked down at my wallet in hand. Then I lifted my shoulders, attempting a look of innocence, but failing. She turned back to Paisley. "Please, fill me in, you just thought what?" Her voice raised an octave at the end of her question.

"Oh, nothing, it's just that you're obviously a tourist, with Tate, on a Sunday morning, looking a little disheveled." Paisley's lips twisted as her eyebrows slid up her forehead.

Alex's chin dropped.

"Paisley," I growled, and stepped around Alex, handing her a crisp bill. "I'll have my usual."

When I turned to Alex, I placed my hand on the small of her back, over her shirt. She'd been ready to insist on paying for her own food, as well as set Paisley straight. I'd hoped with a more direct approach she might let it go.

As I led Alex to a table, Scottlin waved at me, her other hand balancing a drink carrier. I waved back at the cute young woman wearing her usual scrubs. Dodging a chair that had been left in the middle of the walkway, I directed Alex to a table at the front window, looking out on the square. I pulled out her chair, but she hesitated, glancing back and forth between me and the door.

"Who was that?" she asked suspiciously.

"Oh, Scottlin?" I smirked, thinking Alex might be jealous. "She's a nurse at the medical center."

"I wonder who does her hair? It's beautiful," Alex gushed.

Alex probably had no idea what it was like living in a small town. There were probably two places Scottlin might go for a haircut, while there was no shortage of baristas who'd make assumptions about your personal life. Not to mention the bystanders pretending not to listen in and looking over their shoulders.

As I sat down across from Alex, she reminded me of a goddess: bronze skin, exotic beauty, and statuesque. She inspected the shop's tables and their occupants while we waited for our order.

"Sorry about that," I said, looking down at her hiking boots, a little nervous to meet her eyes. My confidence dwindled, because I was worried something I'd say or do would drive her away.

She waved a hand in my direction. "There's nothing to be sorry for, except maybe that 'disheveled' jab Paisley made. Do I really look that bad?"

I inspected her messy curls piled on top of her head, the countless freckles scattered across her nose, and her full lips.

"You look pretty." I gave her a half smile.

Pretty? That was the understatement of the year, and where had my vocabulary run off to? You'd think I could form more than a three-word sentence.

Alex wasn't pretty. She was gorgeous, and it left me wondering how I could have found any other woman attractive. She stood out, and it wouldn't be long before someone realized she didn't belong here.

Our blue-haired barista arrived at the table with two coffee cups and two plates of pastries balanced on one arm. As she placed them in front of us, her eyes darted from me to Alex. One of the plates teetered, but I swiftly grabbed the dish.

Before Alex could make a comment about my reflexes, I straightened in my chair and gave Paisley a stern look.

"I'm sorry," Paisley offered Alex flatly. "I didn't mean to say that you looked bad. It's just that Tate doesn't date much—"

Ahem. I cleared my throat.

"I mean, I'm sorry for alluding that anything would happen between you and Tate that would result in you looking disheveled—"

A-hem. I interrupted more forcefully.

"Gah." Paisley pressed her palm to her forehead. "Help me out here. Did you sleep in your car?"

"Paisley!" I smacked my leg. "I think you've done enough apologizing for one morning."

Alex reached for Paisley's hand before she could turn away. Her gold thumb ring glinted when she touched Paisley. "I probably would have slept better in my car."

Alex winked and let Paisley assume the worst, or best.

My head tilted to the side. I had no idea what Alex was up to with that comment.

"The place I stayed last night was a dump." Alex twisted her ring around her thumb. "If you could recommend a local place to stay tonight, I'd appreciate it."

"Huh. Well, the Whisper Falls Inn might have a room." I took a long sip of my coffee, then looked over the rim of my mug. "So, what are you in town for?"

"I'm working on my doctorate, and doing a little research in the area." She tore off a piece of her scone and popped it into her mouth.

"Wow, your doctorate. I have my undergrad degree, but if I knew I could study out in the wild, I might have four doctoral degrees by now. Is your dissertation on plant life or forest animals?" I was intrigued and leaned forward in my chair.

"You can't be much older than me, and I'm struggling to finish this doctorate on the psychology of the paranormal by my 25th birthday." She shrugged and picked up her mug.

"Paranormal?" I asked cautiously. If someone overheard our conversation, we'd have half the town to deal with.

"You know, like when someone thinks they've seen a ghost or they believe in werewolves. I'm studying the psychosis of individuals who say they've had a paranormal encounter. Hopefully, my results will encourage people to consider therapy instead of seeking a psychic."

Most people didn't see what was right in front of them, and if Alex knew she was surrounded by wolf shifters, fae, and vampires, who knew how she'd react.

"Why are you up in the mountains, then?" I asked, arching an eyebrow.

"There are rumors about haunted rivers and trails all over

Colorado. When I started driving here from Arizona, I decided I'd let the interviews and tips lead me. My goal is to finish my research in time to present my findings before the fall semester starts."

"A paranormal shrink, huh? But you don't believe in all the hocus pocus mumbo jumbo." I grinned. The irony wasn't lost on me. "Where would you set up your practice?"

"I'm not sure yet," she answered.

A cool waft of air blew in with a customer, and Alex choked on her coffee. I turned to find the high school history teacher.

"Do you know her?" Alex stuck her thumb out and gestured to Savannah.

I wasn't sure if there was a right answer. My lips twisted in thought. I knew of the teacher, but I didn't *know* her. Even though I considered a white lie, something in me wouldn't let me follow through with it.

"I think that's my sister's history teacher, Ms. Bash?" I rubbed my chin. "No, that's not right."

"Ms. Bast," Alex called out hesitantly, but her face lit up with hope.

I looked back and forth between them. The teacher did a double take, and then rushed to the table and embraced Alex.

"Alex Newton? Is that really you?" Ms. Bast asked. "It's been at least three years."

"Probably closer to four," Alex corrected.

"Well, if it's been four years, then you can call me Savannah." The teacher smiled, then looked over at me. "What's brought you all the way to Havenwood Falls?"

"I'm writing my dissertation."

"Wow, that's amazing. I think your final paper in my Women and Addiction class is still one of my favorite. You were a psych major, right?" Savannah asked.

"Yeah," Alex answered. She gazed at her former professor. "You haven't changed one bit."

The rumors surrounding Savannah Bast when she first arrived were vague, but her teaching credentials had landed her a job at the high school. I'd thought I'd overheard my dad saying she'd be the best history teacher the town would ever have, last fall. It seems she'd lived through everything she taught firsthand.

"Oh, you're too kind." Savannah looked over at me. "So, how do you two know each other?"

"We just met," I explained. "Do you want to join us?"

I stood up before she could say no, and offered her my chair. As she sat down, I grabbed a chair from the next table and sat closer to Alex.

I nudged Alex with my shoulder. "You know, I haven't even gotten the full story of how Alex arrived in Havenwood Falls."

The teacher's eyebrows rose. She was an attractive woman, with high cheekbones, a slender neck, and regal posture. She reminded me of an Egyptian statue I saw on one of those museum television shows. Some of the artifacts they researched were ancient, but I'd heard gossip about Savannah being older than the pyramids at Giza.

"That's actually a wild story." Alex's face lit up. "Yesterday, I lost my cell phone on a hike near Mount Alexa. I had a little run-in with some wildlife and must have dropped it. Anyways, I made it back to my motel, tried to find a place to get a new phone, but couldn't find anything open this morning. I thought I was going to have to get out of my car and push it up the mountain, but Samwise, my car, chugged past the Welcome to Havenwood Falls road sign, and here I am. I need coffee and a cell phone, then I'll move on to the next haunted trail on my list."

"You named your car after a hobbit?" I asked with a laugh.

At the same time, Savannah asked, "You ended up here by accident?"

"Yes," she answered both of us and smiled.

Savannah and I looked at each other, both in awe of Alex. I knew it was improbable for anyone, human or paranormal, to accidentally reach our town without magical help. There was definitely something different about Alex, and I wanted to find out what it was.

"I bet I could get a phone for you. You probably want to call your family." Savannah broke my train of thought. "You could be on your way this afternoon, but we definitely need to stay in touch."

Savannah was handling Alex like we would any outsider, but I couldn't let her go yet. I had to figure out why I felt a pull toward her. So I laid my hand over Alex's hand on the table. Her ring tingled under my skin, and where my hand brushed against hers, I felt a sharp prickling. In a moment, my hand had retreated back to my cup of coffee.

Alex bit her bottom lip, then admitted, "Actually, my parents died when I was ten. My Aunt Kay raised me. "

Savannah went on without a blink, and I couldn't tell if she was avoiding dwelling on a sore subject or if she didn't want me to know about Alex's past. "Well, I'm sure she—"

"You know, we have a couple of trails in the area that are rumored to be haunted." I gave her my most sincere smile. "Maybe you could take a detour and stay here a few days. I'd be happy to guide you while you're in town."

Alex smiled back at me and nodded, but when I glanced at Savannah, her mouth had fallen open.

CHAPTER 3

ALEX

I spent my first day in Havenwood Falls catching up with Savannah and transcribing notes from my last few hikes. Nothing supernatural, only a little ominous. Savannah encouraged me, saying that a few months of research may not be glamorous, but someday they would add up to breakthroughs with patients, and hopefully some answers for me.

Monday morning, my car wouldn't start. I was determined to be back on track within the week, and I told myself it had nothing to do with the guy I'd met when I arrived. Tate Kasun had his charms, but I had work to do. No matter where I ended up in town, somehow he appeared. Once, I saw him in the corner of my eye driving through the square in his squad car, and another time, he stopped by Savannah's house to check and see if I needed anything.

My academic career was almost finished, and I should have been thinking about working on my research or applying for jobs. Instead, I spent Tuesday morning daydreaming about Tate. After I rolled out of bed and inhaled two cups of coffee, I snapped out of it. I spent the rest of the day meeting the most intriguing people.

One of the women I bumped into, Ruby, was destined to make an appearance in my dissertation. She rambled on about talking to a dead girl after I asked her for some peppermint oil at their herb shop. Luckily, her granddaughter stepped in and helped me.

Tate called Savannah that night to check if we were still on for a hike Wednesday, and I figured it wouldn't hurt, since my car would be fixed soon.

All Wednesday morning I struggled to keep my eyes on the trail with Tate walking in front of me. His broad shoulders, tan calves, and what was in between distracted each of my steps. I stumbled so often, Tate slowed down. The slower pace wasn't helping.

So I decided to watch out for mountain lions and wolves. Anything to keep me focused on what I'd driven so far to study.

"What type of haunted things are you looking for exactly?" Tate cocked his head to the side.

"Nothing supernatural has caught my attention, just as I'd expected. I'm just enjoying the hike." And I was.

"I'm glad," Tate said. "I'll admit, when you mentioned you were just passing through, I was a little bummed, but now you get a few days to enjoy our town while Joshua works on your car."

I also get to enjoy more time with you, I thought. I was so cheesy. Of course I'd traveled over eight hundred miles and started crushing on a small town police officer. I thought I'd seen the same plot in at least four Hallmark movies.

"I'd love to know more about Havenwood Falls. Do you know much about the town's history?" I asked. Savannah hadn't known much, since she'd only moved from Arizona a year ago.

"My family's been in the area for generations, so I've heard a lot of stories." Tate straightened his backpack and stepped to the side of the trail. "How about we take a break?"

"Sure, but only if you tell me one of those stories," I challenged, trying not to sound like I was flirting.

"If I tell you a story, you have to tell me one. Preferably about yourself," he retorted with a grin.

"Deal."

Tate walked over to a large boulder and patted the top. "We can sit here."

As I pulled off my pack, he took it and set it higher on the rock, a gentleman. I hid my smile as I hopped onto the flat edge and made myself comfortable. The sun shone on the rock and warmed it.

"My family traveled here before Havenwood Falls was a town. They discovered a mine before the gold rush was a rush." Tate rubbed his hands together and began pacing. "What do you want to know?"

"Is there a reason the town isn't on any map?" I asked. It seemed the town wanted to stay hidden in the mountains. The way I'd been greeted and made a fuss over, I couldn't imagine that many tourists came into town from the surrounding national parks or ski resorts.

"I'm pretty sure that decision is above my pay grade. But with the roads only being two lanes and the town's Court—I mean council— being a little set in their ways, they probably don't want the outside world to come in and destroy all this beauty," he explained, dampening some of my curiosity.

Tate looked up at the sky. There were a few puffy white clouds drifting in the light blue sky, framed by a canopy of green. Tate was right—this place felt untouched by technology and trends, but so did he. I knew there was more to this town's Stars Hollow-esque vibe. There was more to Tate Kasun. I felt like I'd been introduced to a cast of characters in the town. The blue-haired teen had even memorized my order at Coffee Haven.

"Your turn," I said. "Ask me anything."

"Why don't you believe in the paranormal?" he asked. His brows furrowed.

"Do you?" I asked. Tate's demeanor suddenly lightened, and his mouth spread into a smile.

"Ah, ah, ah. You have to answer first." He waved a finger at me.

"It's not that I don't believe in something bigger than all of us. I just need an explanation. When I was ten, my family was in an accident. My parents were walking, and I was riding my bike. As we crossed a bridge, a car swerved and hit us. My parents were declared dead on impact, but I was thrown over the side of the bridge and into a river. When the rescue workers pulled me out, they pronounced me dead and put me in a body bag like my mom and dad. My Aunt Kay arrived at the scene and asked to see me. When they unzipped my bag, they said I just *woke up.*"

"You mean you came back to life?" Tate's face scrunched up in confusion.

"No one really knows, but I thought I'd been dreaming. The medics explained that the cold water must have slowed my heart rate, and I woke up with this hand in my aunt's, gold ring and all." I waved my hand in the air, and the ring on my thumb caught the sunlight. "For about a year after the accident, I believed the entire event was a nightmare. My aunt never left my side, and it wasn't until I spent time with a therapist that I could wrap my mind around it all. I thought I'd been walking into a beautiful light, but it was really a searchlight on the bank of the river. My parents were with me, then they weren't. Ultimately, I want to help people who struggle with why they believe supernatural powers are at work when they're involved in a traumatic event. They deserve to find peace," I said softly, turning the gold band on my thumb.

"Wow, I'm so sorry for your loss." Tate stepped closer to me. His body was only a few inches from my knees, and I held my breath with anticipation. "My mom passed a little over seventeen years ago."

His words stilled my heart. "That must have been tough," I said, avoiding eye contact. I'd never met a guy who could relate to my loss.

"Not as tough as losing both your parents. I had my dad and my siblings. Is your Aunt Kay still around?" he asked.

"If you mean is she still living, then yes, but I never see her anymore. She's kind of a gypsy, and it was hard on her to stay in one place while raising me. Every now and then, I get a phone call or an exotic postcard in the mail with a brief description of her latest adventure." I twisted my lips, not really sure how it made me feel. She wasn't my mother, but I missed her. I leaned back on the boulder and propped myself up with my hands. "I've lost count. Whose turn is it now?"

Tate took another step closer to the boulder and me. I took a deep breath, but he sidestepped and pulled himself up onto the other side. "I think it's your turn to ask. Want to lean against me?" He'd sat down, with his back to me, and I scooted closer. Like two bookends, with no books between us, our shoulders rested against each other. His body radiated heat, and I could feel it through my light jacket.

"Hmmm . . . I'd like to know why everyone is so interested in me," I said, before realizing how it sounded. "Not that you're interested in me—"

Tate chuckled, and I could feel his laughter vibrate against my spine. "What if I am interested?"

I froze. "Um, well, you can, be interested, if you don't have a girlfriend, but you have to answer my question first." I smiled to myself, proud that I hadn't completely melted into a puddle. "Did you know that I ran into three different city officials yesterday? Savannah said it was a coincidence, but they were drilling me with questions like I was a suspect in a murder. I figured, since you're a policeman, you might know why."

He groaned. "I'm not exactly a policeman. I'm meant to be a deputy. And don't let any of the guys in uniform hear you calling them a policeman. The whole law enforcement career path is not by choice, but more of an obligation." Tate nudged back with one of his shoulders. "By the way, I'm not aware of any murder cases being worked currently, so you're in the clear. I personally think several of our townies have too much time on their hands. Without a life of their own, they gravitate to new blood."

I sat up slowly, not wanting Tate to fall back onto the rock. He twisted at the waist and met my eyes. I wanted to confront him about what I was feeling when we spent time together, but it seemed silly since we'd only known each other three days. For two of those days, he was on duty at the station, but every time he showed up somewhere, I couldn't help but wonder if he felt the same way.

"What's the matter?" he asked. Like he could tell I was conflicted, his eyebrows pulled together in concern.

Could I really just tell him? Every other relationship I'd been in consisted of me being *fine*, or of everything being *okay*. I didn't want to be in that kind of relationship ever again.

"Nothing, I'm just trying to figure out how to answer your question from before. You know, what if you're interested?" I smirked.

Tate grinned, but when I didn't say anything else, his smile faltered. "Do you have a boyfriend?"

"Nope, not for a few months. I've kind of sworn off dating. Do you have a girlfriend?" I asked, not sure I wanted to know the answer.

"The last girl I went out with was married, but it's more complicated and less sinister than it sounds," Tate admitted with a shrug.

I wasn't sure what to think, but I believed him. Tate didn't come across like a cheater, or the type of guy who liked complicated.

Before he could retreat, I leaned forward and brushed my fingertips across his cheek. I wanted to make it clear—I was interested too. But he flinched. His grin had turned down into a frown, and his hand rubbed at the place on his cheek I'd touched, as if I'd slapped him.

"Are you okay? Did I do something wrong?" I asked, scooting closer.

He jumped off the boulder and stood. Then he started strapping his backpack over his shoulders. "Yeah, I'm good. Sorry, I just—I mean—I should be acting more professionally. You did schedule this guided hike through the store."

"Oh-kay," I said, determined to ignore the heat rising up into my cheeks. A mixture of embarrassment and anger churned in my gut as we finished the hike. My car would be fixed soon enough, and I wouldn't have to see Tate again, as long as I didn't speed on my way out of town.

CHAPTER 4

TATE

*T*he afternoon I'd spent with Alex was perfect, until she touched me. We finished our hike in and out of an awkward silence. My mind raced trying to figure out a way to fix what she must have perceived as me dissing her. When her fingers feathered over my skin, it felt like my face had been set on fire. My muscles contracted in an effort to escape, but my instinct left pain etched across Alex's face.

At the end of the day, I'd asked her out for Saturday, but she was hesitant. My heart sank when she told me she'd have to get back to me. I would have the day off, and when I invited her to join me at the farmers market, she didn't say anything about continuing her research or ask if the place was haunted. I couldn't help but wonder if I'd ruined everything. If Joshua fixed her car before then, I'd be forced to ask Willa for her help. Maybe she would have an idea for how to keep Alex in town.

It wasn't until after I told Alex goodnight that I realized I didn't want her to leave. I wanted her to stay with me, so I could explain how I felt. But I couldn't understand why it had been painful to touch her. As I watched her close the front door of Savannah's house behind her, I wondered if I should talk to Conall about these *feelings*.

The street lamps lit my way back to the town square where I'd parked my Jeep, and I took note of Tarron's car in front of Backwoods.

It wasn't too late for him to be at the apartment my sister stayed in, but the store was closed, and I decided to run in and say hi. What good brother wouldn't check on his baby sister?

It might be a good excuse to ask her for that advice.

Willa moved into the loft apartment last year around this time. Our dad kept close tabs on her, and slept most nights on the couch, while Kase and I stayed at our family cabin. Ric Kasun didn't speak teenage girl fluently, but he hadn't given up on Willa. Her future would be to become our pack's alpha.

It was crazy to think my little sister would be leading the Kasun pack someday. Our family migrated from Croatia a couple hundred years ago. Back then, it had only been my mom and dad, and my mom led the pack as alpha. Like our mom, my sister would be expected to serve our people, and whoever chose to live life as her mate would take her name the same way my father took Kasun. Tradition ran deep in our blood.

I strode up to the front door and reached in my pocket for the store key. Out of the corner of my eye, I saw movement behind a rack of Havenwood Falls hoodies. I ducked and focused my heightened wolf eyesight to get a better look. Mathilde Augustine, in her broom skirt and messy white bun, appeared to be perusing our selection of thermal underwear.

Unsure of what the member of the Court of the Sun and the Moon was up to, I unlocked the door and entered to confront her. But Mathilde wasn't alone. Savannah Bast and my dad, Ric, were standing under the shadow of the faux rock climbing wall. The bell hanging from the door's hinge dinged, alerting all of them to my arrival. My father turned in my direction first.

"Finally. Son, we've got to talk." He was in sheriff mode, serious but calm.

"What's going on?" I asked. Then I looked Savannah in the eye. "Alex is at your place. What are you doing here?"

"I texted her that I'm running late. She'll be fine," she answered. "This is important."

"Tate," my father started, "the Court wants Alex out of town."

"No," I growled as I gritted my teeth and took a step forward. I hadn't stopped to think about my response, but that protective instinct had taken over. I'd have to remember to keep it in check, especially if I wanted to stay on the Court's good side.

"Whoa!" Savannah stepped between myself and my father. "None of us want to see Alex leave, Tate. You should be thanking Mathilde and your dad for keeping me in the loop, and for having my back when I explained that she needs to stay."

"Wait, what? They want her gone?" I rubbed my forehead, confused. I couldn't remember the last time my dad and I were on the same side of any argument.

"Yes, son. The wards at the borders didn't faze Alex, and you've just confirmed Conall's and my suspicions. But there's more to Alex than you know. Savannah tried to explain how Alex is veiled, but the other Court members need more convincing. That's why we need your help."

I looked from my dad to Savannah, then over to Mathilde. She had a pair of long thermal underwear in her hands, and slowly placed them back on the clearance rack. It was like she'd been keeping busy until it was her turn to speak.

"I'll have to come back tomorrow for those." She grinned at me and reached for one of my hands. She wrapped her slender, trembling hands around mine. "Dear, I've had a vision of sorts, and it's very clear to me that Alex, or something in her possession, is essential to our town surviving a new threat. The Court is scared of Alex and how magic can't reach her. She's an anomaly we've never had to consider, because she's one of a kind. Savannah?" Mathilde didn't let go of my hand, but gripped it tighter.

"I've been watching over Alexa since she was a little girl. It has been my calling as an Egyptian protectress to see her to her destiny. Alex lost her parents at a young age—"

"I know," I interrupted. "She woke up to find them dead after they were hit by a car, and her aunt took care of her until she went to college."

"Tate, Alex didn't merely wake up. Alex comes from a long line of

Romani on her mother's side. They don't appreciate being referred to as gypsies, but for lack of a better way to explain her power, it will have to do."

"Like Callie Montgomery?"

"We think so, yes. And when Alex fell into the river, her power to astral project took over. It saved her life. Only, she hadn't been trained or even aware of her abilities. I bestowed one of the links from an ancient chain I carry to Kay Boswell, Alex's aunt. The single ring has the power to bring someone back to life, or in Alex's case, to connect her soul to her body. Kay placed the ring on Alex's thumb before her soul had returned. Alex cannot live without the ring because it is the only thing tying her soul and body together. Technically, her soul is not at rest inside her, because she's never learned to control her magic, but her projection is creating a veil around her." Savannah sounded worried.

"The ring on her thumb?" I asked, furrowing my brows.

"Yes," my dad answered. "The problem is the Court believes we should remove the ring. With her soul and body being disconnected, magic doesn't have a way to make a connection. Think of a gift box. Alex's body is the gift inside, and her soul is the box. Backwards, but the ring the Court is so afraid of is the bow holding everything together. Savannah tried to explain the ring's power, and its importance, but they want to banish her if they can't take the ring." He crossed his arms over his chest, and his biceps tensed. He was trying to control his frustration, and his wolf.

"I believe the ring brought her to me, and I plan to reach out to Alex's aunt, Kay Boswell, to let her know." Savannah pulled at a gold chain around her neck. A few rings threaded on the chain clinked together as they fell over the collar of her blouse. "If these rings were to be linked together with the rings I've gifted over the past three thousand years, the wearer would be given eternal life and unlimited power. I came to Havenwood Falls last summer to protect the last few rings I have in my possession. There are rumors someone is working to collect them all. And, if the rings have the power to call to each other like I believe they do, anyone who wears or has inherited a ring will not be able to resist the rings' calling to each other."

I turned to Mathilde, and pleaded, "Doesn't the Court want the power of the rings close by? You guys granted Savannah citizenship, so why not Alex?"

"Darling, she doesn't know about the supernatural. And with her being veiled, we can't charm her memory away or cast a spell to make her stay. The Court would rather Alex walk away, never knowing the difference." She shook her head sadly.

"Son, you have to try to defy your feelings. We need to think of the town," my dad said and rubbed the stubble along his jawline.

I shoved my hands into my pockets and looked him in the eyes. "Dad, I'm not sure how to explain it, but that would be like defying gravity. You said I confirmed your suspicions?"

My feelings for Alex were foreign to me. Conall didn't talk much about when he met his wife, and my dad never talked about my mom. They'd both mated with wolf shifters, and their feelings were reciprocated, but I was dealing with a human. So, how was I supposed to be sure Alex was my mate?

"I gave you a choice the other day. If we were to have the same conversation today, would there be a choice?" Dad asked, referring to his ultimatum.

"No," I admitted. "Without her ring, she'll die, and without her, I won't want to live. I'd leave with her, no question."

My dad ran his fingers through his hair and rubbed the back of his neck. He hated not getting his way, and I could tell he was trying to work out a solution in his mind where everyone would win. He finally exhaled a long breath.

"Joshua says her car will be ready tomorrow, and we need your help to convince her to leave. If you want to save her life, you have to let her go. But if you want to follow her, I won't stop you." My father was letting me go.

I'd practically ensured Alex wouldn't want to stay in Havenwood Falls when I went from acting like boyfriend material to the most boring trail guide on the planet. I'd attempted to strike up a conversation about different types of pine trees.

The wooden floorboards creaked at the foot of the staircase leading to Willa's loft. She stood, eyes wide, staring down at our dad. Savannah and Mathilde looked at each other and excused themselves through the front door, promising to call Ric later. Tarron wasn't anywhere to be seen, but I could hear the television on upstairs. It was smart of him to stay out of Kasun family business. Not only was our dynamic altered recently with Willa flexing her alpha power, but the feelings I had for Alex bonded me to her as tightly as I'd ever been with my pack.

"Dad, I think you're underestimating the Kasuns' influence in this town," Willa said sweetly and moved to stand next to me. "There has to be a better way to deal with the Court."

"We don't deal with the Court, Willa. They delegate to us. Our job is to protect the town first," he said, annoyed. I'd grown up hearing that line on a weekly basis.

"You made a pact to protect the town a couple hundred years ago, but was it at the expense of your family? What if we can keep Tate here, make sure Alex stays safe, and satisfy the Court?" Willa threaded her arm around my elbow.

"How do you propose that?" I turned to face my sister. "Didn't you hear? She can't live without the ring." I hoped she had answers and not only questions.

"We live in a town full of witches, fae, and shifters. Someone has to know how we can keep her alive without the ring. I mean, it's that or you can propose? The Court wouldn't banish your wife, would they?" She propped her hands on her hips.

I rolled my eyes. Then I felt a soft wave of magic brush over my cheek. My initial reaction was to be on alert, but it soothed my growing impatience. Could Willa have a power related to being alpha I didn't know about?

"No," Dad answered, "they'd banish you both. But you might be on to something, Willa."

I frowned in disbelief. "She might?"

Our father started pacing, a sure sign he had an idea.

My sister picked up an oversized coffee mug. "Ya know, if we're *proposing* ideas, you could—"

"I'm not proposing," I said. "She'll think I'm crazy!" I raked my hands through my hair. "To be honest, I can't even touch her. Every time I do, I'm shocked, literally." I rubbed my cheek, where I'd first felt her touch.

"I'm not sure, but that sounds like a standard protection spell gypsies use. You should talk to Callie about it. She may be the same kind of gypsy as Alex, and if so, she'll have an idea of how the spell was cast. I'll ask around about keeping Alex alive without the ring, and if it's possible she'd no longer be veiled. I'll have to make a few calls, but hopefully we can have a plan in place by this weekend." Dad sounded relieved, almost at ease. It was the first conversation I'd had with him in weeks that hadn't escalated to a yelling match.

"Okay, I can work with that," I agreed, thinking to myself that it wouldn't get awkward talking to Callie, even if she was technically the last woman I dated.

Dad walked to the front door, and before exiting said, "I'll get back to you in the morning. Don't forget to lock up behind me." He smiled, but before he closed the door, he paused and shook his head. "Willa, I know you're trying to help, but don't allow that to happen again." He growled without looking back.

My brows knit together in disbelief. I glanced from the door to Willa, back to the door. "Did you just do *that*?"

Willa smirked at me like she knew a secret.

"What?" I asked.

"I might have asked Tarron to use a little of his magic on you and Dad for the last five minutes. He can influence moods." She giggled and started for the staircase.

A growl vibrated through my chest in frustration. I understood why Dad was irritated when he left. Willa being in my head wasn't much different than her overhearing conversations when she was a kid. She also made it difficult to stay mad at her. But knowing Tarron was in my head made me feel exploited.

"Don't be angry. He never uses his charm, but I begged him to help. Come upstairs, and he'll explain how it works." Willa moved up a couple steps, then turned and looked at me expectantly.

"I don't like the idea of being manipulated," I started, "but I'll go upstairs anyway. It's my brotherly duty to make sure Tarron isn't manipulating anything else." I raised an eyebrow.

"Tate!" Willa slapped my arm when I reached her. "Don't forget who's alpha."

She winked at me with a smile, and pulled me up the rest of the staircase.

CHAPTER 5

ALEX

*I*t had been almost a week since I'd wandered into Havenwood Falls and I'd agreed to hang out with Tate again. That is, without Savannah hovering. Even though Savannah was the one who convinced me to stay in town and give Tate another chance, it felt like the universe didn't want Tate and me to be alone during the past two days.

Honestly, I hadn't been sure I wanted to spend another day with Tate. I'd been telling myself I was staying for Savannah, but in the back of my mind, I knew Tate had more to do with my interest in the town. My feelings were building for Tate, and I feared they would create a wall that blocked me from pursuing my dreams.

Everyone I met in town asked me about Arizona, constantly reminding me of the life I had waiting for me. But when shopping for tea at Howe's Herbal Shoppe Thursday, a lady named Rose said something that made me question the future I'd planned. She'd said, "You won't really live until you release the things that bind you. This blend should help."

She may have been referring to digestion, but I'd taken her words more personally. Rose handed me a bag of mixed tea leaves and went on humming a tune to herself.

My car had been fixed, and the due date for my dissertation was looming, but Rose's words gave me peace about staying a few more days. I had to figure out why my feelings for Tate were so strong or find a fault in him that would make me want to leave. The latter was more likely, considering my relationship history.

"Hi, Alex." Sedona Mathews waved as she passed me on the sidewalk, jarring me from my thoughts. The day before, Sedona and I had hit it off while I perused her book shop. I smiled and waved back, but was at a loss for words when I made eye contact with the guy walking beside her. He was beautiful. They walked hand in hand and appeared to be smitten with each other. She pushed her long colorful hair over her shoulder and whispered something to him. If a bookworm like her could find love, there had to be hope for me.

While I had been perusing the bookshelves, a girl, Holly, had her nose in a text about the Victorian Era. When I asked if Sedona had any reading material on the supernatural, they both gave me a look of surprise, but I'd been receiving similar looks most of my life. After settling at a bookshelf lined with novels about vampires, ghosts, and werewolves, Sedona spouted off the most random fact. Something about a two-thousand-dollar bounty for vampires in India. I responded with my own fact about a study done at the University of Texas: a belief in the paranormal can be a shield from harsh truths and the brain's way of organizing chaotic events. We both laughed, and she pointed out a few books I might like.

Everyone in Havenwood Falls made me feel at home, but it could never be boring. I felt like I recognized a few other people as I continued meandering down Main Street. They all smiled or waved as I made my way over to the gazebo. Tate and I had planned to meet instead of him picking me up. I feared that Savannah would invite herself along and hijack our date. I hadn't been able to get a moment alone, unless it was in her guest bedroom.

"Good morning," I said as Paisley, from Coffee Haven, passed me.

"Hi! Will you be coming in for your usual this morning?" she turned around and asked. Her head tilted as she took in my appearance. Paisley had become more familiar with me, since I'd been in for caffeine at least three times in the last 48 hours, but I could tell she was struggling with whether she should say what she was thinking.

I stopped to answer. "Not today. Well, maybe later, but I'm headed to the farmers market."

Paisley smiled and asked, "Are you going with a certain *someone*?" Her eyebrows bounced up and down.

"Why would you ask that?" I asked in a high pitch, sounding guilty.

"Two reasons. The first is because you look super cute, not that you don't always look cute—" Her eyes widened as she tried to dig herself out of what could have been taken as an insult.

"And the second reason?" I asked with a laugh.

"You're looking around like you're hoping to find someone . . . like a guy."

"Fine, I'm meeting Tate. Are you happy?"

She beamed. "Yes, but don't worry. I'll keep it on the down low."

"I hate to break it to you, but it's not a secret. We'll be walking through town together in a few minutes." I hooked my thumbs in my jacket's pockets.

Paisley twisted her lips in thought. "Ya know, it's okay. If someone thinks they've got the scoop and tell me later, I can say I already know. It'll be satisfying, especially if it's one of those blue-haired gossips who sit in the shop all morning." She glanced down at her watch and frowned. "I'm late. Gotta go. Have fun!"

"Thanks," I offered, but she was already a few yards away after breaking into a jog.

Glancing around the town square, I noticed Ruby sweeping the sidewalk in front of Howe's Herbal Shoppe, and a younger version of her walking away with a box of jars and plants. Maybe they had a booth at the farmers' market.

As I started to cross the street, I looked both ways, and Tate's Jeep rumbled up to the stop sign. He lifted two fingers from his steering wheel and smiled. A car pulled up behind his, so I didn't stop to talk. The square was buzzing, and it wouldn't be easy for Tate to find a parking spot.

I made my way across the lawn, and tucked my hands in my jacket pockets. The cool mornings still amazed me. In Arizona, the temperatures would have already been in the nineties.

I glanced around the square in search of Tate, but he must have had to find a parking space on one of the side streets. As I turned to avoid tripping into the fountain, I met a wall made of muscle and leather. The six-and-a-half-foot man didn't budge, and when I stumbled backward, he caught me. His tan Adam's apple bobbed after he steadied me.

"Hello there," he purred. His glossy dark hair was combed back, and his dark eyes wrinkled at the outside corners.

"Hi," I replied.

"I'm Monte, and you must be a magician." His bright smile contradicted the scruffy beard covering his jawline.

My eyes squinted in confusion. "Huh?"

"Because everyone else just disappeared."

I giggled. The cheesy pickup line would have normally fallen flat, but nothing about Monte's appearance was cheesy. He wore a black leather jacket over his skull-and-crossbones T-shirt, a pair of dark worn-in jeans, and black boots. His aesthetic was the opposite of the quaint town's, and while he stood out in the picturesque scene, he still fit somehow.

"I'm Alex." I held my hand out to shake his. "Nice to meet you."

"Nice ring." He tapped my thumb with his. He'd been the bajillionth person to comment on it this week. It's like no one had ever seen a thumb ring before.

"Can I interest you in a ride?" he asked, and one corner of his mouth pulled up into a sly grin.

My eyes widened.

He waited long enough for me to feel awkward, then pivoted and waved to a motorcycle parked twenty feet away. "I bet you'd enjoy riding around town with me. I could show you sights in Havenwood Falls most tourists don't get the pleasure of seeing." Monte's voice purred, then he winked.

Ew. I bit the inside of my cheek to keep from gagging or laughing. I couldn't decide if this guy was for real, and I had the urge to do both.

"I'm actually meeting someone." I tried to let him down easy.

I felt a hand glide across my lower back, over my jeans, and wrap around my waist. "She's meeting me," Tate's voice warned.

Monte offered Tate a nod, but frowned. Monte's jaw clenched, and he faced me. "When you get tired of holding this guy's leash, come find me." He winked at me, then snarled at Tate before he started to walk away.

I'd only seen Tate in his police uniform once, but he didn't need it to make himself understood. He stepped in front of me and broadened his shoulders.

Tate reached for Monte's arm to stop him. "Someone needs to put you and your crew on a leash, and I'm happy to be that someone."

Monte laughed, but when a low growl emanated from Tate's chest, Monte choked on his guffaw. The cavalier confidence Monte had with me had disappeared and been replaced with stooping discomfort. Tate stepped closer to Monte, blocking the other man from my view. Grumbled words were exchanged, and Monte turned and walked away without another peep. He straddled his motorcycle and revved his engine.

"Pathetic." I crossed my arms over my chest and turned away from Tate.

Tate followed close behind. "I know. Where does that guy get off?"

I rolled my eyes. "I meant both of you are pathetic. I can take care of myself, and Monte was harmless."

"You haven't seen his record, or the crew he rides with. Anyways, I was just—"

"Marking your territory?" I asked, pausing at the steps of the gazebo and giving Tate a stern look.

He smiled at me.

Good grief, he was handsome, and it was so frustrating. I furrowed my brows, trying to hold my ground. Tate moved in, making the air around me feel heavy and warm. His attempt deserved some credit, but I knew I couldn't let him get away with his machismo-measuring ways or he'd always act that way when other men were around. As attractive as it sounded, it felt like an insult.

His smile faltered. "You're right, but—"

"Oh, don't ruin the moment," I interrupted. I pressed a hand to his chest and said, "Say it again."

"You're right?" He placed his hand over mine, but scrunched up his nose.

I giggled.

"What's so funny?" he asked, stepping back and shoving his hands into his pockets.

"If you plan on hanging out with me, you'd better get used to saying that." I grinned.

Tate leaned in and whispered, "You're so right." His warm peppermint breath brushed over my lips, but he wasn't close enough.

"You're impossible," I whispered back.

Tate pulled back to look me in the eyes and smiled. "You've never been more right."

I wanted to push myself up on my toes and kiss him. But after reading him wrong on our hike, I'd decided Tate would have to make the next move, if there was a move to be made. He stepped to my side and wrapped his arms around my waist.

I noticed a few eyes in the square on us. Tate pulled me in a little closer and apologized.

"It's an occupational hazard," he explained. "Not only clearing out the riff-raff, like Monte, but I'm always watching out for them." He nodded out toward the square, where people were shopping, catching up with neighbors, and watching us. "So, they must think it's their turn to keep an eye on me."

"Small-town life is so different than what I'm used to," I admitted.

Tate frowned, and I wondered if he felt as strongly for me as I did for him. Living in a small town was different, but I couldn't help but wonder if it would be worth getting used to for him. I had a feeling our conversation was about to get a little too serious too fast, so I stepped forward, out of Tate's grasp. When he caught up, I wrapped my arm around his elbow and pulled him in the direction of the farmers' market.

Tate didn't ask for an explanation, but he let me lead as we walked through the historic neighborhood surrounding the square. Havenwood Falls was made up of a grid of streets with the square at its center, and I'd become familiar with the major landmarks after my car broke down. Savannah's neighborhood was quiet and tucked away past the square. She lived near the corner of Mills Avenue and Twelfth Street, and walking from her place to Joshua's garage to pick up my car Thursday had given me a clear lay of the land.

"So, what's the plan today?" I asked. We'd remained quiet, in a good way, for a few minutes, but I was curious if Tate had the whole day to spend with me or merely a few hours.

"We're going to shop for lunch, then have a picnic near Wylie's Gulch," Tate said with a laugh.

"What's so funny?"

"I was just wondering why it's called a *gulch*. Anyway, I thought we could do some climbing after we eat," he explained and pointed to some carabiners hanging from a loop on his backpack.

"Sounds like fun," I replied. "And for future reference, a gulch is bigger than a gulley and is prone to flash flooding. There isn't any rain in the forecast, is there?" I gave him a wary look.

"Nope, we should be safe. And by the way, I know what a gulch is. I just meant it's a funny word." Tate walked a little closer. "I knew you were smart, but where did you learn about geography?"

"I took a survival course before heading up here." I shrugged. "I'm all about being prepared."

The problem was, I hadn't been prepared for Tate. I hadn't expected to be so confused about a guy after a week. This had been the first time in a long time that I'd ignored logic and let my heart guide me. I just hoped my heart could handle where Tate Kasun was leading.

CHAPTER 6

TATE

*T*he day was only beginning, and I'd already stuck my misogynistic foot in my mouth. So, when Alex wrapped her arm around mine, I fought the urge to jerk back from the pain of her touch, but there was none. She had worn a jacket, and the fabric between us kept the protection spell from shocking me. I'd asked Callie the day before if the spell could be broken, but she said she'd have to get back to me. Regardless of the protection spell, I'd planned for us to have a great day.

The bright green foliage and buzzing townspeople made Cook's Corner Park unmistakable. As Alex and I walked out of the Havenwood Falls historic neighborhood, I noted the regulars setting up their goods on tables. The weekly farmers' market gave everyone an opportunity to do their shopping in one place. The Howe family sold their herbs and oils, along with some local honey and handmade jewelry. A local farmer had covered his table with vegetables. The butcher shop had coolers filled with meat lined up in front of their table, as well as on top. Another booth stood empty, but I knew from experience it would be filled with freshly baked breads before the market officially opened.

Charming vine-covered archways invited us into the green space, and we followed a stone pathway leading to the fountain at the center of the manicured grounds. I passed the small field lined with tent-covered tables and nodded toward the bronze statue in the middle of the fountain.

I dug my hand into my pocket and retrieved two pennies, and held them in the palm of my hand.

"Here," I offered.

Alex picked one shiny coin up with two fingers, and her touch left a pop of static electricity. I'd mentally prepared for the sharp sting and successfully kept myself from flinching.

"What's this for?" she asked and twisted her lips skeptically.

"I'm not superstitious, but as long as I can remember, I've been making wishes at this fountain. It was something I did with my mother, and after she passed away, I've felt compelled to keep the tradition alive." I surprised myself when the story tumbled out. I hadn't told anyone before.

I placed the penny I held on my thumbnail and flicked it into the air. I quickly caught the coin before it could fall to the ground.

"Do you think I need luck?" She looked up at me through her dark eyelashes.

I couldn't tell if she was flirting, but I knew I needed to remove any doubt about how I felt. Maybe Alex's disbelief in the supernatural carried over to superstitions as well. Her logic acted as a safety net, and I hated the idea of revealing the truth about our paranormal town and decimating any trust we'd built. But I didn't need to get ahead of myself. There was no way Alex could feel as strongly for me as I did for her.

"You may not need luck, but I might when it comes to you." I gave her a half smile, while trying to ignore the doubt creeping into the back of my mind.

"I don't know about that." She tossed her penny onto the first tier being held by three metallic mermaids. "But, for you, I'm willing to test my luck."

She smiled back at me and winked. I thought my heart would burst.

"What did you wish for?" I asked.

"I can't tell you that! It would make the wish null and void if I said it out loud." Alex nudged my bicep with her shoulder. "You focus on making your wish, mountain man."

I closed my eyes and squeezed the penny in my fist. *I wish for Alex to find real happiness.* Before I opened my eyes, I tossed the penny into the air, and as it flew through the air, I listened. The sound of metal clattering against metal startled me out of my trance. The penny had bounced off the edge of the top tier and plopped into the same basin Alex's had landed in.

"Our wishes can keep each other company," I said, and it took everything in me to stop myself from threading my fingers between hers. "Now, let's pick out our lunch."

Alex's purchases threatened to bust the seams of my backpack. She'd been intrigued by each vendor, and asked everyone questions. Her sincerity and ability to listen helped her gain the trust of everyone she encountered. Townspeople opened up about why they loved what they did.

She would make a wonderful therapist someday.

I'd noticed two people at the farmers market who avoided Alex. My father, the sheriff, spent the morning staking out the park from his black pickup truck, and Millicent Mathews spoke to everyone except Alex at the market. The older woman was a Luna Coven member, and probably meant for her slight to be a warning. If Alex hadn't been new to town, most people wouldn't have noticed.

As we stepped up to the Howes' table, past Millicent, Alex whispered, "If Mary Poppins and Loki had a daughter, that's what she'd turn into after fifty single years in a house full of cats."

I covered my mouth to keep from bursting into laughter. "Are you sure you're not psychic?"

"No," she answered. Her eyebrows wiggled up and down teasingly.

"My dears, living *veiled* makes it impossible to see the future." Ruby Howe prattled on with a small bunch of yellow flowers in hand. "All will be set right, of course, then you'll know the future, because you'll be there. Knowing is only half the battle."

"G.I. Joe, the great American hero," Alex sang under her breath.

Ms. Howe held out her flowers to Alex, ignoring her pop culture reference. "This rhodiola will help you fight."

Ms. Howe placed the yellow flowers in Alex's hand, but didn't seem to feel a shock. Yesterday, I'd explained Alex's and my electric connection to Savannah, but she said she needed to contact Alex's aunt before she could understand why it was happening.

I reached for my wallet to pay for the flowers.

Ruby Howe had been rambling for years, but no one paid her much attention. Her family hadn't been in Havenwood Falls as long as mine, but I'd heard my father say something about the Howes' ancestors having something to do with the magic that filled the falls.

Ms. Howe walked away to rummage through a box behind her table. I lifted my hands, palms up in question, at Alex when she looked at me dumbfounded with a handful of money. I chuckled as I searched the table for a money jar or box. Then, as I was contemplating stuffing a five dollar bill under a small pot of sprouting mint, Scarlet walked over to work the table.

"Can I help you?" Ms. Howe's granddaughter asked. Her long red hair had been twisted and spun into two buns on top of her head. "Sorry if Gram said anything awko-taco. Normally, she likes to recite love poems, but lately she's been a little more imaginative."

"Oh, it's okay," Alex assured her.

"This morning, Gram has been going on and on about how we're all links in a chain." Scarlet shook her head and rolled her eyes.

Alex tilted her head to the side. "Interesting, has she been diag—"

"How much do I owe you for the rhodiola?" I asked, quickly cutting Alex off from saying more. The Howe family had taken offense more than once when someone tried to diagnose Ruby's forgetfulness or rambling. Who knows how many curses and jinxes they'd whispered over townspeople and tourists who thought they were helping?

Scarlet inspected the plants on display and the flowers in Alex's hand. "If she gave them to you, then you don't owe me anything."

"I insist," I said.

"Well, if that's the case, then three dollars." She held her hand out.

I gave her a five-dollar bill and told her to keep the change. I quickly walked to the next table before Scarlet could refuse. Bale Grayson, Scarlet's boyfriend, walked past me and greeted Scarlet with a kiss. I really hoped Savannah would come up with a fix or at least a reason why I couldn't touch Alex soon. It almost hurt as much not to take her into my arms.

My wolf hearing picked up on Scarlet and Bale whispering about another rumored mountain lion attack. As dragon shifters, Bale's family helped with patrols along the town's border. Before I could make out any details about the location of the attack, Alex stopped me in my tracks and kept me from eavesdropping. She had placed her hand over my heart, only my T-shirt protecting me from my human defibrillator. She pointed at the table covered with cookies, pies, cakes, muffins, and scones.

I smiled, and my mouth started to water. "Alex, before we pick out dessert, I wanted to apologize. First, for cutting you off back at the Howes' booth. They're a little sensitive about Ms. Howe's mental state."

Alex twisted her thumb ring between two fingers. "You don't need to apologize for that. I appreciate you interrupting. I forget that some people don't want or need answers, and sometimes I'm envious of them. I'm sorry if I overstepped asking about Ms. Howe." She looked at me wide-eyed, searching my face for a reaction.

I wasn't sure what to say, if anything, but I didn't want to have to lie more than I already had. Ms. Howe was a witch, an old one. Her gifts and powers had become less controlled over the years, similar to how an Alzheimer's patient struggles to live in the present. Ms. Howe hadn't turned anyone into a frog or cast a love spell— that we knew of. She merely rambled on vaguely about frogs and love.

"Was there something else you felt like you need to apologize for?" Alex asked, interrupting my thoughts. She turned and started toward the dessert booth, rambling, "It's just that you said *first*, implying that there might be a second, but it could have been a Freudian—"

"I guess having a brilliant girlfriend means I won't be getting away with much," I said.

My eyebrows raised expectantly. I'd hoped to get a reaction from Alex that would help me gauge how she felt about me.

Alex froze mid-step and turned around slowly. She placed her hands on her hips and searched my face. "I'm not—"

"Please, don't finish that thought. Maybe my second apology should be for calling you my girlfriend? But I was planning to apologize for sending you mixed signals. I want you to know how much I like you." I rubbed the back of my neck, worried she would say she's not my girlfriend and she never would be.

"I like you too. And I appreciate you apologizing. I guess I'm just curious why you've been keeping me at arm's length physically. It doesn't match up with the way you talk to me." She looked to the ground, and then the corners of her mouth turned down.

Alex's honesty was refreshing, and heart-wrenching.

I wanted to be honest, too. The problem was that I heard my father recite his mantra about protecting the town in my head. I would only omit what I had to.

"I'm not good at relationships. I struggle with balancing the emotional and physical, so if you're willing, I'd like to try something a little more old-fashioned. When I think of the way my dad loved my mom . . . I can still feel that love from him when he talks about her." I took a deep breath and met Alex's eyes. "I want to capture your heart."

"I'm willing." Alex beamed up at me. "Now, let's pick out our dessert before all the good stuff is sold."

That afternoon, Alex and I ate a delicious lunch, climbed one of my favorite boulders, and laughed. Before dusk, I rushed to shove everything into my backpack. The previous night I'd been on duty, Havenwood Falls had been celebrating Midsummer Night, when magic, and sometimes a little mayhem, reigned over Havenwood Falls until sunrise, while the humans slept under a light spell. The town should have been tame that night, but Savannah and I had agreed it would be safest to get Alex back home and order takeout for dinner. Especially since I hadn't heard back from my father about the Court's decision.

As Alex and I walked back to Savannah's house, north on

Fourteenth Street, a familiar face approached with purpose. Alex looked up at me with concern. Millicent Mathews, with her nose up in the air, took short and determined steps in our direction. She'd appeared as well manicured as the front lawns, but less colorful.

"Good evening, Tate," the older woman's voice greeted, but she sounded more annoyed than welcoming. "You must be Alexa. My niece, Sedona, mentioned you were new to town. I'm Millicent Mathews."

Millicent didn't need Sedona to tell her about Alex's arrival. The stern witch knew everything and everyone in town. Her eyes lingered on Alex. Alex's feet shuffled self-consciously. Finally, Millicent reached her long, bony hand out to Alex. Before taking it, Alex glanced up at me in question. My mouth flattened into a thin line, but I gave a curt nod.

"It's nice to meet you, but you can call me Alex." She forced a smile.

I watched as Millicent's fake smile morphed into a sneer.

~

ALEX

EVERYTHING WENT BLACK.

The last thing I felt was my thumb ring sliding off as Millicent's hand slipped out of mine and Tate scrambled to catch me. The last thing I heard was Tate screaming.

CHAPTER 7

TATE

One hand connected with Alex's face and the other caught her at the waist, where a sliver of skin was exposed between the hem of her shirt and the top of her jean shorts. The initial contact shot pain up both arms, and as Alex lost consciousness, I couldn't hold her up. The electricity from her body didn't let up, so I had to. I laid her down as softly as I could on the sidewalk.

She had to be alive. Otherwise, the electricity between us would have relented, right?

Millicent Mathews had only been doing the Luna Coven's bidding, but in that moment, I'd wanted to shift and rip her to shreds. It had taken every ounce of self-control to keep the wolf inside me from attacking the witch in the middle of the street. It was the message she carried that saved her life.

Millicent's disapproving look didn't waver as she handed the slip of paper to me. She briskly walked away, and I didn't wait to see where she went. I unfolded the note and began reading.

Tate Kasun,

The Court of the Sun and the Moon request your presence at the City Hall immediately. They have reached a verdict regarding the town's latest visitor. Arrangements have been made for Alexa Newton.

Respectfully,
Adelaide Beaumont

As I read, a van screeched to a stop in front of me and the side door slid open. Monte Tayute jumped out and scooped Alex into his arms before I could stop him. Another one of his biker buddies sat in the driver's seat, and as soon as Monte stepped back inside the van, they sped off. For a millisecond, I hesitated. Then, I chased them. I growled, and my wolf stirred, ready to go after Alex. The neighborhood was quiet, but that didn't mean someone wasn't looking out of their window. It did mean I couldn't shift without making matters worse. As the van sped up and ran through a stop sign, I debated whether to follow them or beeline it to the impromptu meeting. Heads would roll in either case.

My boots pounded the pavement in a rapid, steady beat. When I turned to cross the square, I surveyed the area. A group of teenagers were messing around at the fountain's edge and couples were strolling on the sidewalks.

I had my eyes peeled for a white unmarked van. If Monte and his gang were following orders, they probably parked behind City Hall. I changed my course.

I didn't answer Paisley when she called after me, and the protector in me didn't even pause when I noticed a few guys catcalling one of Willa's friends, Elle. I had a feeling she could take care of herself.

I needed to find Alex, and I had to get her ring back on her finger.

Bypassing the front door, I made my way between the police station and City Hall. The clock tower bells, perched above the second floor, rang out eight times. I knew exactly where the Court's entrance was located. I turned to the left and reached for the door, but it swung open for me before I'd gripped the handle.

My dad stood in the doorway, and when I tried to push past him, he gripped my shoulder tightly.

"Son, she's fine. I promise." His voice rumbled low and tense.

"I have to see for myself!" I used my forearm to shove him to the side.

My dad didn't resist. "I know, and I'm sorry for asking you to ignore your feelings."

"What?" I shook my head in disbelief.

"I saw you together at the farmers market, and I heard you with her," he said softly and patted my back.

"I can't do this right now. I need to find her." I clenched my teeth and took a few steps.

"Go. I'll be in soon." He moved outside.

I didn't wait for the door to close behind him. The Court of the Sun and the Moon ran the town, and the backside of City Hall was proof of it. Havenwood Falls had a way of taking any visitor back in time, but the Court's offices appeared ancient. I darted down the stairs and through a long hallway that entered into a small reception area. I passed a couple of chairs and approached the courtroom. Dark wood accented the rustic stonework, and a magical vibe emanated from the candlelit glass globes suspended from the wood-paneled ceiling overhead.

Shadows loomed behind murals hanging on the wall, each depicting the history of a different era of the town.

As I walked into the room, the representatives appeared restless, perched on the dais at the front of the room. Savannah stood at the right of the room with a woman I didn't recognize, and the left side of the room was empty. An empty long table sat in front of the representatives, forming a barrier.

"Where's Alex?" I asked, moving to stand in front of the tall platform. One step on either side of the courtroom could have been perceived as an allegiance, but I would only be on Alex's side.

Addie Beaumont, the business manager for the Court, from one of the oldest families in Havenwood Falls, looked down at her watch before answering.

"She should be here any minute." Addie glanced from Savannah to Mathilde. "Will you be ready to try?"

"Try what?" I asked with determination, balling my hands into fists. I took a turn looking from Savannah to Mathilde, the one Court member I thought I could trust, and then moved a few steps to stand directly in front of Addie.

Savannah spoke first. "Tate, this is Alex's aunt, Kay." She used her thumb to point at the woman with tight, dark curls behind her.

"Hi, Tate, I've heard a lot about you." She waved in the air.

How could Alex's aunt know anything about me? They only communicated through postcards, and Alex had only been here a week. The puzzle pieces wouldn't fit together in my mind. Did they need Alex's aunt to give permission for her thumb ring to be removed? Would Kay take Alex back to Arizona?

I reached for the back of my neck with one hand and started rubbing, hoping the knots would loosen and make things clearer. "Can someone please take me to Alex? I'm not sure how much longer I can hold myself together." I gritted my teeth. "I know she's alive, but without the ring, she feels further away."

"We're well aware of your *connection*," Elsmed, the fae representative, said. His voice sounded almost amused.

My eyes darted to Addie, hoping for an explanation. That's when my father entered the courtroom through the same tall wooden doors I'd walked through. Alex was limp in his arms.

"Someone put that blasted ring back on her finger!" I yelled as I rushed over to her. I took her hand in mine, not caring about the inevitable shock. I felt a weak buzz, but her hand felt cool. "Hurry!"

Tears welled up in the corners of my eyes.

No one moved, except my father. He nodded in the direction of the table at the center of the room. I took his lead and followed, then he gently placed Alex on the table. Kay joined us and examined her body, then looked over at me.

"She doesn't have long," I said.

Kay tilted her head and replied, "I know, but I need to remove a jinx placed on her when she was a little girl, before we try to force her projection back into her body and replace the ring." Her words were rushed, and she sounded panicked.

Kay went to work. She pulled a small pouch out of her pocket and dangled it over Alex's heart. Foreign words flowed from Kay in a rhythm, like an old song she'd been singing all of her life.

When she fell silent, she nodded at Mathilde Augustine, and the older woman, a witch and one of the leaders of the Luna Coven, slowly pulled herself out of her chair. Once she reached the table, she pulled a few dried herbs out of her tunic's pocket. Mathilde wrapped the dried leaves and stems together with a thin piece of twine and set the bundle on the table next to Alex's head.

I took Alex's hand in mine, not caring if it shocked me. I'd hold it forever and deal with the pain, if it meant she could live side by side with me. But the electricity never shot from her skin into mine.

My brows furrowed, and I glanced over at Kay. She smiled at me knowingly. Mathilde snapped her fingers, and a flame sparked to life in the bundle of herbs, demanding my attention. The witch picked up the small bouquet and waved them over Alex's body, so the smoke floated over her.

Mathilde recited a few words, but frowned.

Then she spoke the words again with more gusto, the way a witch would cast a spell in the movies. Her frown deepened, and she shook her head. "The girl is stubborn."

"What does that mean?" I asked.

Kay interrupted. "She won't—or doesn't know how to—place her projection back into her body. She'll have to remain veiled for now, but I can help her."

Savannah walked over to me, and held out her hand. The gold ring rested on her palm. I didn't waste any time and slid the ring onto Alex's thumb. Alex didn't move.

I looked from Kay to the Court members. Each of them leaned forward in their chairs, all witnesses and judges.

"What happens next?" I asked, worried and anxious.

The question applied to everyone in the room. I wanted to know when Alex would wake up. I wondered if Mathilde could try her spell again. I wished for the Court to grant Alex sanctuary in Havenwood Falls so she could learn about her powers.

Kay answered first. "The ring will awaken Alex soon, and her touch will no longer cause you pain. But her projection will continue to keep her veiled from all magic," she warned.

Saundra Beaumont, from her seat on the platform, added, "We have accepted Kay Boswell's request for citizenship, under the condition that Alexa Newton remain unaware of the town's supernatural presence for as long as she is veiled."

I bit my bottom lip to keep myself from arguing a case for telling Alex the truth. I knew it would be a better idea to wait and make a solid case later. The stipulation that Alex couldn't know about the town didn't mean her aunt couldn't tell her she was half gypsy.

After Saundra stood, the other Court members followed her lead and exited. Savannah checked on Alex, then told me to bring Alex home in a half hour. She planned to surprise Alex with Kay's arrival when I dropped Alex off.

After everyone but my father had cleared out, I asked, "Dad, can I take her to Backwoods until she wakes up?"

"I don't see why not, unless Kay wants her back at Savannah's right away," my dad reasoned.

"We agreed it would be a bit of a shock for Alex to wake up to Kay suddenly being in town. And after she wakes up, I can walk her home."

Dad nodded. "Willa will be out with her friends, and I can park my truck in front of the back door. I'll leave the keys in the glove box." He patted me on the back and offered me an encouraging nod.

My dad hadn't been so helpful in years.

"What changed your mind about Alex?" I asked, immediately regretting the question.

My dad's eyes glistened, but not one tear was shed. He admitted, "I was reminded of how it felt to lose your mother. I had my doubts about how serious you were, but seeing you keep yourself together for her, and putting her first, made me realize she's the one for you. I'd do anything if it meant you could love someone the way I loved your mother."

He cleared his throat, and I took that as my cue to move. Scooping

Alex into my arms, I was thankful not to be throttled with a shock. Dad held the door open for us.

I stepped out into the cool night, and turned to ask, "Dad, do you know what kind of spell Alex's aunt did?"

My dad, always vigilant, scanned the back of the building for anyone eavesdropping. Our hearing was heightened as wolf shifters, and if there had been a couple of teens making out two blocks over he'd have heard them. I'd picked up on some tourists and townspeople walking the square, enjoying the warmer weather. I'd have to take side streets and gain access to the loft from our private entrance.

"She explained that when Alex was a little girl, their family traveled with Romani who had a tradition of blessing their children with a protective spell." Dad lifted his fingers up to create air quotes. "Those were Kay's words. Sounds more like a curse the way you were tortured, getting zapped every time you touched Alex. Kay thought the ward had been broken during the family's accident, but Savannah checked in with Kay after you told her about your little predicament. Maybe I should ask her about having a similar jinx put on Willa."

We both laughed, but I got the feeling my dad was half serious.

"At least with Kay here, I know Alex will stay a while. But when it's time to present her dissertation . . ." I shook my head. I didn't want to think about losing her.

Dad looked from Alex, who lay across my arms, to me. "Enjoy the time you have. I have a good feeling about her."

My dad turned and walked away in the opposite direction I had planned to go. He'd always been a no-nonsense kind of man, and while that mentality was difficult for me to grasp at the age of ten, now I had a better understanding of why he'd chosen to come across that way. Opening oneself up is a lot like rock climbing. The farther you make your way up, or into the relationship, the scarier it can be. But it can also be exciting, exhilarating even.

I took my time walking to the store, not wanting to jostle Alex. Getting the back door open was tricky, but once we were in the loft, I laid Alex on the couch in the living room. I untied and slipped off her boots, then spread a blanket over her body.

My body ached from being so tense all evening. I needed a quick, hot shower. So I leaned over Alex's head and placed a kiss on her forehead. "I'll be right back, my little gypsy," I whispered.

The whole family kept clothes in the loft, even though only Willa technically lived here. Not to mention there was an entire store filled with clothes downstairs if I couldn't find anything.

I tiptoed over the creaky floor boards and made my way to the only upstairs bathroom. Willa didn't keep any manly body soaps in stock, so I came out of the shower smelling like a fresh flower. I wrapped a towel at my waist and darted to the dresser in Willa's room. Each drawer I pulled out had been stuffed full with Willa's clothes, and there wasn't anything of mine, Dad's, or Kase's in sight.

So I started to dart back to the bathroom, but when I paused to check on Alex, she wasn't lying on the couch.

"Alex?" I called out.

The bathroom door squeaked as it opened, and there she stood, only she looked like I'd been the one to shock her.

CHAPTER 8

ALEX

I woke up with a gasp. Aunt Kay barged into my room while I'd been having the best dream. It hadn't been the first time I'd dreamt about Tate in a towel. I'd been having them all week, since I'd seen him at the loft above his family's store. In the past seven days, the doctor had conducted every test imaginable, and my aunt was testing every nerve. I looked forward to the afternoons when Tate would come by or take me to dinner. We were still taking things slow, but I had a feeling it had more to do with the recent addition and constant presence of Aunt Kay.

My shock at being roused surprised my aunt, and the coffee she carried threatened to splash over the lip of its mug. Kay's reflexes were unreal, and once she handed over the hot liquid wake-up juice, we laughed.

"Were you having a nightmare?" she asked. It was nice to have Aunt Kay at Savannah's house. "We can go back to the medical center and get you checked out again if you want."

I felt heat crawl up my neck. "Nope, it wasn't a bad dream, and the only way I'll allow anyone to do more tests on me is if it's at Coffee Haven, and Nurse Scottlin is doing them."

I smelled my coffee before taking a sip.

"Do you like it?" She sat down at the edge of the bed.

"Mm-hmm." I smiled and took another swig.

"Good. You keep drinking, and I'll talk." Aunt Kay made herself more comfortable and pulled a knee up to her chest. She looked like my mom, and my heart ached when I thought about it.

Aunt Kay had an eccentric style, but under the mixed patterns, she was a lean, average-sized, middle-aged woman. Her skin was a shade or two darker than mine. Her hair hung longer, but the curls were tighter. I'd thought of her as an exotic beauty since I was a little girl. Her light hazel eyes had always mesmerized me.

"What's up?" I smiled, feeling more like myself after having coffee.

"I'd like to look for a place after our training today," she started.

"But—" I tried to interrupt. We'd been arguing this point all week. Our bickering negated the meditation she insisted we do each morning. I had to agree with her that the time we spent at the waterfalls helped me feel better after collapsing, but every time she mentioned buying a house and settling down, I questioned if she was the one who'd really suffered some mental trauma.

Aunt Kay held her ground. "We're imposing on Savannah, and it won't be long before she needs to be focused on school."

"I guess I should be glad you're planning to be here long enough to get a place, but I'll have to go back to Arizona before you know it." I reasoned with the same logic I'd used every time the topic came up.

My aunt rubbed her temples, and for the first time, I noticed how tired she looked. It had been a week since she'd arrived. She claimed she'd been on a meditation retreat and wanted to share what she'd learned with me. When she'd found out about me passing out the night before, she insisted I go to Havenwood Falls Medical Center. After being poked and prodded, we found out I was perfectly healthy, and I found a new friend, Nurse Scottlin. Every morning since, we'd been sitting criss-cross-applesauce on yoga mats near the falls. And because of more mountain lion sightings, I couldn't hike by myself. We were both getting on each other's nerves.

Aunt Kay exhaled, "Alexa."

I knew she meant business when she pronounced the *a* at the end of my name.

"Okay, fine," I grumbled. "I concede. We get a place. Then what?"

"We keep up the meditation, and you go back to Arizona for a few days to defend your dissertation. Then, I want you to come back here. Who knows, maybe you can start a practice in Havenwood Falls?" Aunt Kay shrugged.

I shook my head at the idea.

"Why are you so against moving here? I thought you liked it." She crossed her arms over her chest and fell silent, waiting for me to answer.

"I can't put my finger on it, but the people are secretive. Someone might act like everything is normal, then I hear them saying something paranoid." I twisted my thumb ring while waiting for my aunt to tell me I was the crazy one.

But instead, she said, "Your reasoning supports my argument. They need a professional to talk to."

I'd thought about being that professional for the town, before I'd blacked out and lost five hours of my life. If my aunt hadn't been waiting at Savannah's house when Tate dropped me off, I might have raced out of town in the middle of the night.

I couldn't ignore my connection with Tate. We grew closer every day. But I couldn't ignore what I'd heard that night either.

I'd been skeptical of my aunt's meditation exercises on the first day, but once I'd cleared my mind, everything that had happened the day before became less fuzzy. I remembered walking through the farmers market with Tate, our picnic, and even climbing around Wylie's Gulch. But our walk to Savannah's house was hazy. Then I woke up at Willa's loft, with Tate in a towel.

Sketchy much?

My gut told me Tate was telling the truth, but he'd been vague, and I could tell he was holding something back. I knew I heard voices echo around me. As hard as I'd tried, I hadn't been able to will my eyes to open, but I had made out some of the muffled words. A woman had said my aunt's name and mine. Then, I clearly remembered the words *supernatural* and *veiled.*

After falling back into blackness, I woke up in what I thought was a stranger's home, only to find Tate with a towel wrapped around his waist, and nothing else. I hadn't complained or asked a ton of questions because, well, Tate in a towel.

Instead, I'd told myself that the whole thing was a dream. I let Tate take me back to Savannah's house, and he made me feel safe. But when I saw my aunt sitting in Savannah's living room, I knew something was going on.

Aunt Kay had a way of taking charge. She'd made me hot tea and tucked me into bed that night, and every night since. As secure as I felt in the routine, something changed after I'd blacked out. Apprehension lingered at the edge of every conversation I had with the townspeople. I sought out women to speak with, in search of the voice I'd heard that night.

"Don't feel like you have to decide today." She patted the comforter laying over my leg. "I think you could help a lot of people in Havenwood Falls. Now, you need to get dressed. We have work to do," Aunt Kay said, and left to start cooking breakfast.

I rolled out of bed, brushed my teeth, changed clothes, and met her and Savannah in the kitchen. Every morning since her arrival, we'd gone for a jog up to the falls. After an hour or two of stretching and meditation, we'd walk to Coffee Haven and run into Scottlin during her caffeine break. Routine was my security blanket, and Aunt Kay knew it. She'd been the one to encourage it in my life after my parents died.

But no matter how hard she tried, something still felt off.

That afternoon, Tate met me and my aunt at a house with a For Sale by Turner Real Estate sign, with Jeanine Turner's name and number on it, off Tenth Street. The quaint fixer-upper had a brick façade that had been painted white. Its natural wood shutters framed the windows on either side of a sage green front door. It would be perfect for a small family.

We also looked at a large yellow Victorian home on the corner of Twelfth and Mills Avenue. The home was used as a vacation rental during the busier winter months, but the owners wanted a renter through fall. One of the bedrooms had been painted pink, and it contained a bookshelf lined with porcelain dolls. The place was too big, and creepy. When I explained to my aunt that renting a loft in the square made more sense, she insisted on buying a home and settling down.

In an effort to avoid saying something I'd regret, I decided to bail and take Tate with me.

As we walked out of the Victorian house, I said, "So, Tate and I have plans. Can we finish house shopping tomorrow?" I asked, and squeezed Tate's hand. Hopefully, he'd go along with my fabrication. We did have plans, for later tonight.

"Oh." Aunt Kay looked down at her watch. "Sure, I have a few things I need to do. Savannah is planning to meet us at the next showing, and I'm sure the two of us can handle it. Then, we'll be going out for a bit." She gave me a tight-lipped smile and leaned in to kiss me on the cheek. "See you two later."

"Bye, love you," I said. I turned to head for the town square, and pulled Tate behind me.

"Is everything okay?" Tate asked. His full lips were pouted, and his brows pulled together. "You're acting kind of weird."

"I could say the same about Aunt Kay. She's never owned anything that wouldn't fit in her car. Do you believe in alien abduction?" I asked with a laugh.

Tate didn't laugh with me.

He'd stopped walking, and I only walked a step ahead before feeling resistance from where our fingers were weaved together. When I turned to face Tate, he was rubbing the stubble along his jawline. He pulled me to move closer, and when he took a deep breath, his chest rose and brushed against mine. My heartbeat stuttered. He looked up for a few seconds, then made up his mind to meet my gaze.

He slid a curl behind my shoulder with a finger and softly traced the crook of my neck down to my collar bone. He definitely wasn't acting old-fashioned. Come to think of it, we'd been surrounded by chaperones whenever Tate could get away from work. We'd only been able to see each other for minutes at a time, but he'd grown more affectionate, even if my aunt or Savannah were with us.

Tate licked his lips, and suddenly I couldn't remember what planet I lived on.

"Are you doing okay?" he asked.

I blinked a few times, startled by the question. I'd hoped he was finally going to kiss me.

"I mean, I want to talk to you about something important, but if there's something bothering you?" Tate leaned forward and kissed my forehead.

The gesture was sweet, and it triggered a memory. He'd done that before, but for some reason I couldn't remember when. I took a step back, doubting the man who stood in front of me.

"You've kissed my forehead before, but—" I shook my head, like I could loosen the memory, and held up my hands to create some space between us.

Tate's brows furrowed, and he searched me for understanding. "I don't—Wait, I did kiss you like that once before, but you were still blacked out on the couch. How do you remember that?"

I relaxed a little. Tate didn't seem to be trying to hide anything, and he'd expressed he wanted to tell me something important.

"Technically, I don't remember." I folded my arms over my chest. "You said I blacked out, and Ms. Howe checked on me, but I think I heard another woman's voice. And, then a while later, I felt you kiss my forehead," I said, moving my hand to rub the spot.

"How about we go back to Savannah's house? You can rest, and when your aunt gets back, we'll talk through all of this with her." Tate took a step closer, then hesitated. When I didn't refuse, he wrapped his arms around me.

His body was hot, literally. He radiated heat. He'd worn his old jeans, a black T-shirt, and his baseball cap backwards. My arms snaked around his neck, and my head rested on his shoulder. I fit perfectly against him. The dark curls escaping his hat were fun to run my fingers through.

Tate rubbed my lower back with his palms, and whispered, "Promise me, no matter what, you'll go on a hike with me tomorrow morning."

I looked up at him and smiled. "You don't have to convince me. It's that overprotective aunt of mine you'll have to sweet talk."

"I think I can handle her." His arms squeezed my waist, and butterflies stirred in my chest.

"But can you handle me?" I bit my bottom lip and batted my eyelashes a few times, in full flirt mode. "If Aunt Kay has her way, I'll be moving here permanently. Does that scare you?"

"You know what would scare me? If you said you were leaving." Tate reached up and tucked one of my curls behind my ear. Then his finger traced down the sensitive skin, giving me goosebumps, to my jawline. He drew a line with his finger to my chin and lifted it slightly.

He exhaled slowly, and his breath smelled like cinnamon. I searched his face, looking for his intention. His thick eyelashes were lowered, he'd clenched his jaw, and his bottom lip pouted just enough for me to figure out he wasn't going to get what he wanted.

I was determined not to make the move. I'd been humiliated when he dodged my attempt to kiss him on our first hike. Instead of caving, I slid my hands down the front of Tate's shirt to his chest. I'd intended to create some space, but Tate pulled me tighter.

"I want to kiss you." He grinned.

I smirked back, and said, "I know."

"You're torturing me." He chuckled, and we were so close I could feel the vibrations in my hands. "Is that you giving me permission or you warning me to keep my distance?"

"Hmmm," I teased. "Permission grant—"

Tate's lips were pressed against mine before I could finish my thought. His mouth was soft, and instead of pulling away, he dotted gentle kisses across my bottom lip over to my ear. He hovered there, his breath warm, and a tingling sensation shot down my neck.

"I want to keep kissing you," he whispered, "but we're standing on the sidewalk. And I think one of the neighbors is staring."

We both laughed.

He took my hand in his, and we started to walk away from town square. I followed with a giddy grin plastered across my face. When we passed the neighbor who'd been watching us, I waved.

"Please, tell me this rest you speak of at Savannah's involves food," I whined.

"It does, don't worry," he assured me.

I tugged on Tate's hand, and said, "Wait! Didn't you want to talk to me about something?"

"What I wanted to talk about can wait until tomorrow, but right now food is the priority. How about we raid Savannah's kitchen?"

"You're cute. You think I can cook," I quipped. "I don't think she has any ramen noodles in the pantry. You forget, I've been in college for six years." I winked.

"Well, lucky for you, I can cook," he said with confidence.

We walked hand in hand all the way to Fourteenth Street, and as we turned to make our way to Savannah's house, we both noticed the front door was wide open. No one was outside watering the lawn or pruning the hedges. The street was eerily quiet.

Tate glanced from the house to me, and back. "I need you to stay here while I check the house." His tone turned serious.

"No, I'm going with you," I insisted.

He pressed his lips together in frustration, but didn't let go of my hand. As we entered the house, my other hand covered my mouth. The living room had been ransacked. The couch cushions were sliced and diced. The bookshelves had been thrown over, and books were strewn across the floor. There were even holes in the wall.

When we turned into the kitchen, I asked, "Who would do something like this?"

All of Savannah's dishes were shattered on the tile floor, and the contents of her pantry were scattered across the room. Food and glass crunched under our boots as we made our way through the hallway to the bedrooms. I prayed my aunt and Savannah were still gone.

"Someone was definitely looking for something," Tate answered with a hint of confusion. "Don't touch anything. I could get into trouble for letting you come in here with me."

"Letting?" I raised an eyebrow.

He shook his head.

The guest room I'd been staying in looked similar to the front room, but instead of couch stuffing, the mattress fluff had been thrown everywhere. All of the dresser drawers had been removed and emptied on the floor. Tate pulled me with him to the second guest room, where my aunt had been sleeping. It had been treated the same as mine.

"I need to call this in," Tate said.

I pulled my phone out of my back pocket and dialed 911, then passed it to him. When Tate attempted to let go of my hand and walk farther into the house, I gripped tighter. He looked back at me, and I waved him forward.

"I'm not leaving," I said dryly.

Tate explained that there had been a break-in at Savannah Bast's house, and as he turned into the last bedroom, he lowered his voice and growled, "We need an ambulance."

~

TATE

SAVANNAH HAD BEEN alive and clearly breathing, but Alex struggled with seeing her friend beaten and unconscious on the floor. She entered the wrong code on her phone twice when trying to call her aunt. Alex started rambling about needing to be back in Arizona, as soon as her aunt arrived. She was in shock. I'd seen it several times, but at one point, Alex pulled me aside with tears streaming down her face.

"Would you go with me?" she asked. "I mean, I'll stay in Havenwood Falls until I know Savannah's okay, but if I went back to Arizona, would you consider coming with me?"

I was shocked, but my chest filled with warmth, knowing she wanted me to stay with her. A few weeks ago, I would have jumped in my car and never looked back.

"Alex, I would do anything or go anywhere for you, but I need you to calm down. We don't know what happened. And until we talk to Savannah, we can't assume anything." I tried to reason with her, but she began to pace.

"I heard someone say *supernatural* when I was blacked out," she blurted.

I froze, and she noticed.

"You know something about that, don't you? I also heard a woman talk about a *veil*." She crossed her arms over her chest and waited.

My heart felt like it was in my throat.

I tried to swallow the worry churning in my gut. "Can we clear the scene and get you and Kay to my family's cabin, then talk about this? I swear, I'd planned to bring this very topic up tomorrow on our hike. I've never lied to you, and I don't plan to, ever."

Immediately, I knew that was the wrong thing to say. Alex's shoulders slumped, and she turned and walked away without a word. I wanted to go after her, but I needed to find out who was behind Savannah's attack.

For all I knew, Alex could be next.

CHAPTER 9

ALEX

*T*ate Kasun infuriated me. He made me feel exhilarated and doubtful all in the span of ten minutes, but because of that, I couldn't bring myself to leave. I'd stubbornly spent the night in Savannah's hospital room, where she was still unconscious. Thankfully, Scottlin was working a shift and kept me company. When my aunt came to relieve me, Tate was waiting in the hallway. It seemed he'd never left.

I couldn't believe I'd asked him to go to Arizona with me. What was I thinking? I should have been worried about Savannah, but I'd spent the night worrying that I'd scared Tate away.

As promised, he took me to his family's cabin, where a hot shower and a clean outfit greeted me. Sheriff Kasun had commandeered a hoodie and pair of leggings from Backwoods. When I walked into the living room, Ric and Tate were cooking in the kitchen. Tate was frying bacon, and Ric was cracking eggs.

"Breakfast will be ready in about fifteen minutes." Tate nodded to the leather couch. "You can take a nap, if you'd rather."

"No, thanks," I muttered. "If I go to sleep now, it will throw off my day and night. I think I'll go for a walk."

"Do you want some company?" he asked.

I noticed Ric trying not to listen in on our conversation, if you could call it that. I didn't have the brain capacity to hash things out with Tate. I needed to find out the whole truth, and I wasn't sure who I could get it from.

"No, thanks." I shuffled to the front door and slipped my boots on, then walked out into the forest. A trail led behind the cabin, and I decided to follow it.

Something about being in nature opened my mind, and I'd hoped taking a walk would help me work out everything that had been happening around me. I wasn't trying to be arrogant, but it seemed like there was some sort of gravitational pull I had for trouble lately.

I took a deep breath and pushed forward. The tree branches had filled with leaves, and the sunlight filtering through made a hopscotch pattern on the trail. I made a game of only stepping on the light. With each move, I calculated up to four steps ahead. Someone had been doing the same thing with me and my friends' lives. But who? And why?

I glanced at my wrist and realized I'd left my watch and cell phone on the bathroom counter. The guys had probably finished cooking, and by the time I'd make it back, the food would be cold. I really needed to snap out of my mood.

Searching the woods around me, I couldn't find the trail. But the sunlight steps remained. I turned to follow them, less enthusiastic than when I first saw them. A stiff breeze swept beneath the canopy the trees provided, and my whole body shivered. I pulled my hood up over my head and tugged on the strings to secure it.

I lost some of my peripheral vision, but I told myself all I needed to see were the lights. The wind continued to blow stronger, and the trees creaked and swayed above me. Soon, clouds rolled in, and I found myself lost.

My survival class had taught me to stay put if I ever wandered into the unknown, but I knew I couldn't have gotten too far. I chose a tree in the distance and walked to it, then repeated the process three more times. The fifth tree looked oddly familiar.

I turned to survey my surroundings, and that's when I noticed I was being followed. A tawny big cat, with gold eyes, prowled around the trunk of a tree twenty feet away.

I didn't have a backpack to offer the mountain lion or a car to run to. Mr. Kitty froze and glanced to my right. I chanced a look and saw Tate approaching. Hopefully, he'd carried a weapon out here. But then the scent of bacon wafted toward me.

"Tate," I whisper-yelled. "There's a mountain lion!"

Tate walked over to me and protectively stood between me and the cat. His broad shoulders blocked my view, but I heard the mountain lion growl. Tate peeled his shirt off and tossed it to the side, then he kicked his boots off.

"What are you doing?" I asked through my teeth. "I don't think he needs you to model the meat."

"Stay calm," he whispered, his eyebrows raised, and he forced a smile. "I need you to trust me. What I'm about to do might freak you out a little, but remember to stay calm."

Tate stepped toward the big cat. I wanted to reach out and stop him, but I told myself to stay calm. He had probably been playing in this forest all his life.

Without warning, Tate began talking. "I commend you on getting past our borders without sounding the alarm, but it's time for you to leave."

I searched the area around us, trying to see who Tate was talking to. He took another step away from me.

"You know that I won't let you harm her. No matter how fast you are or how powerful, you will not leave Havenwood Falls as easily as you entered."

The mountain lion roared, then a low growl emanated from Tate.

Then, silence. The calm before the storm, or in this case, the mountain lion attack.

"Alex, I want you to run in the direction I came from. My father is on his way." Tate's voice sounded like he had gravel in his throat.

"I'm not leaving you. I won't," I cried. As I took a step closer to him, he raised his hand to stop me.

"I'm sorry you had to find out this way," he said, sounding resigned.

And that's when my life turned into a Netflix Original. Tate's form shifted, magically with lights and swirling, into a huge black wolf. His transformation shredded the clothes he'd been wearing, and I realized that's why he'd taken off his boots and shirt. Tate had become the same wolf I'd seen in the woods a little over two weeks ago.

"Holy—" I yelled, but stopped short at the sight of the two animals attacking each other. Fear, anger, and worry flooded my senses. Everything I'd been studying to disprove for the past several years, and what I'd been fighting to believe in myself, had all been true. The man I was falling in love with had transformed into an oversized wolf, and the realization left me feeling nauseated. I wrapped one arm around my waist and fought the urge to run.

The wolf, Tate, jumped toward the mountain lion, sinking his teeth into the cat's neck. He shrieked in pain, but fought back with his sharp claws. Then Tate whimpered. I felt so helpless, but my fear was quickly replaced by the instinct to protect him.

A rock the size of my palm caught my eye, and I squatted down to pick it up. Squeezing the stone in my hand, it pressed against my thumb ring. I raised it in the air, and a desire to hit the mountain lion overwhelmed me. If I could wait until Tate broke away from him, I'd have a better chance of striking.

The two barrel rolled, and they were only a few feet away. Tate sprung back to position himself in front of me again. Another wolf, silver with a gray neck, bounded from the trees behind the mountain lion, momentarily distracting the cat. I took advantage of the distraction and threw the rock as hard as I could, wishing he would fall over and die.

The stone struck the cat along the side of his neck, and I immediately started looking for another one to throw. But when I looked back at the mountain lion, he had crumpled to the ground. The silver wolf looked up at me, and then Tate turned to face me. He was a wolf, but when I looked into his golden eyes, I could see Tate, the man.

I fell to my knees, and within a few seconds, Tate was kneeling next to me with his shirt wrapped around his waist.

"Are you okay?" he asked.

I looked up at him with tears streaming down my face. "I don't know. How could you— Are you? I just don't know." And then, I laughed. I don't know where it came from, and it didn't make sense, but none of it did.

"Whoa, I wasn't expecting that." Tate looked over his shoulder, and I followed his line of sight to find his dad walking toward us.

I pressed my palms to my cheeks and wiped the wetness from my face. I'd been so scared and shocked that I hadn't realized I'd been crying. When I finally met Tate's eyes, he looked down at the ground. I wasn't sure if he was nervous about my reaction or embarrassed about being practically naked.

So, I wrapped my arms around his neck and hugged him. I wanted to thank him with a kiss, but Ric reached us, holding a pair of jeans. He waved them in the air with a smirk.

"Son, I hate to interrupt, but we'll need to report this to the Court." Ric nodded to where the mountain lion had fallen, but instead of a cat, a man lay on the ground with a bloody wound on his neck.

I stood and covered my mouth with both hands, and stuttered, "D-did I k-kill him?"

"I'm not sure," Ric answered. "But, if you did, you saved my son's life." He sounded proud.

CHAPTER 10

TATE

"So, you're telling me your entire family has the power to shift into wolves?" Alex asked. Her fingers massaged her temples as we sat on the sofa in the cabin.

I nodded.

She wouldn't let me help support her as we walked back, and when I sat next to her, she scooted away from me. The small distance she'd created between us stung more than her touch ever had.

"And you're the same wolf who saved me a few weeks ago?" She looked up at me with pleading eyes, desperate to find some truth to hold on to; a logic to this new reality.

I nodded again.

"What else don't I know?" Her brows pulled together in determination.

"I'd planned to tell you about my condition," I began, waving my hand up and down in front of my torso, "but there's a lot about Havenwood Falls I can't tell you without the Court's permission."

"Permission? You sound like you're in the military and this is some secret base. You're not military, are you?" she asked, irritated with the same traditions and rules I'd been trying to break for years.

I shook my head. "Not technically, but it is my family's job to protect the town and the people in it."

KALLIE ROSS

"Protect them from what? Mountain lion shifters?" Alex pointed over her shoulder with her thumb, toward the front door. "I hope you realize that until you start spilling, I'm going to be drilling you with questions."

I nodded, and Alex clenched her jaw tightly. She was frustrated, and I didn't blame her. At least she wasn't running away. The situation I'd been put in seemed impossible, but I understood both sides of it. If I expected Alex to trust me, I needed to tell her everything. If I told her everything and she decided to leave, the town would become compromised. The memory spell cast on tourists as they crossed the border wouldn't work on Alex.

I sighed, trying to keep her focused on what I could reveal. "How about I start with you and me? Then, if you don't want to bail, I'll explain whatever you want to know."

She nodded, and started fidgeting with her thumb ring.

"I just hope your aunt doesn't curse me," I mumbled. My hand moved to take hers, and with some hesitation, she let me twist her ring between my thumb and pointer finger.

Alex tilted her head and raised her eyebrows expectantly.

"Your aunt *is* Romani," I said.

"I know—" she started to argue.

"Listen to me." I tugged her hand. "Your mom, her sister, was a Romani gypsy. You're at least half gypsy."

Alex shook her head.

"I don't think your mom or aunt knew you could tap into the same power they possessed, but you could. You can. It's part of what saved your life when you fell into that river." I squeezed her hand, hoping she could embrace this part of herself.

"*Part?*" she asked.

"Your ring." I tapped the gold band. "Your aunt acquired it from a friend, Savannah, and it gives your physical body life."

"So much of that last sentence is confusing!" Alex pulled away from me and stood. She began to pace. "Savannah knew my aunt before? My physical body? Does that mean my emotional or spiritual body is dead?"

346

I stood up, stopping Alex in her tracks. I placed my hands on her arms to hold her still. "Your aunt would be better at explaining the details, but you astral projected just before your body died. It was your soul's way of trying to survive the trauma. Kay did her best to reconnect your projection to your body, but you didn't have much control. This week, she's been trying to teach you how to tap into your Romani gifts through meditation. The Court—that is, the group who makes decisions for our supernatural community—decided, when you blacked out, to keep you figuratively in the dark until you could manage your powers. The thing is, you're veiled. Your spirit or projection is acting like a slipcover and blocking magic from having an effect on you. It scares the crap out of the Court." I'd spoken slowly, to make sure I explained everything clearly.

Alex's mouth fell open.

"And I don't know how Savannah knows your aunt. You'll have to ask them." I watched for any indication that Alex was processing this new information.

Her eyes widened, then she met my concern with another question. "What part of that has to do with a mountain lion man trying to attack me?"

"I think he's after your ring." I pointed. "Supposedly, it's one ring from a set that Savannah protects. Considering it has the power to bring the wearer back to life, I'm surprised no one has come after it before now."

"Maybe the guy was after Savannah all along, and he happened upon me?" she asked.

"Or you led him to Savannah," I thought out loud.

Alex's shoulders slumped. "Oh my—"

"Don't," I interrupted her guilt game. "There's no way you could have known. You thought you were simply conducting research. Savannah has a theory that your ring drew you here."

Alex pulled away from me again and headed for the front door.

"Where are you going?" I asked.

She reached for the handle, and didn't look back. Her head hung low. She was exhausted. "I need to get back to the hospital and straighten things out with Kay."

"I'll take you," I offered.

She shook her head. "No, I need some space to work this out."

"Please, don't walk away. Let me help you," I begged.

"You've known about me and didn't say *anything*." She finally turned to face me, and tears had welled up in her eyes. "I've been talking about how I don't believe in the supernatural since we met, and you let me ramble on like an idiot for weeks. I was . . ."

She swallowed back whatever she'd been about to say. Before I could assemble the right words, if they even existed, she'd turned the doorknob and walked out. I followed and found my dad giving orders to a group of pack members.

"If you're going to leave, at least let me get one of the guys to drive you to where you want to go," I said loud enough for my father to hear. I had the procedures memorized for circumstances like this. The sheriff would want to keep tabs on a witness.

She stopped, but didn't look back. "Fine."

My dad looked over at me, then glanced at Alex. When I nodded for him to make his move, he gave me his *I'm sorry* grimace. I hated to see Alex leave, but at least I knew my dad would be by her side.

I went back into the cabin to put on a shirt, then decided to check in with my brother, Conall. Determining who had attacked Alex in the woods would help us figure out if anyone had seen him break into Savannah's home. The pack had formed a line about fifty feet wide, and they walked at the same pace, combing the forest floor.

When I spotted Conall, I called out, "Kasun!"

A few guys turned curiously, but my brother knew it was me. We'd been calling each other that way longer than some of them had been alive. I jogged over to him, and we walked side by side.

"What's with the grid search?" I asked. "When I left, the guy was dead."

"He's still dead, but he doesn't have any ID, and the necklace taken from Savannah wasn't on his person. This John Doe is clean, and I don't think we'll be able to trace him to the break-in." Conall growled in frustration, but never stopped searching the ground as he talked.

"Are you talking about a gold necklace threaded through a handful of rings?" I asked.

Conall grunted as he nodded. "That's kind of how Dad described it."

"Why didn't he tell me it had been stolen?" I stopped in my tracks. "If there's more than one person after the rings, Alex could be in trouble."

"Dad thought it would be a good idea to search the area in case he dropped something that could help us figure out who he is, but you and I both know that's highly unlikely."

"Could we get Big Mike out here? Maybe he's seen the guy before," I suggested.

"That's not a half-bad idea, Kasun." My brother's voice was thick with sarcasm. Even though he gave me a hard time, Conall was a great deputy. I should have known he'd already contacted the McCabes.

I looked at my watch. "How long until he gets here?"

"Should be here any minute, but depends on if he shifts or drives."

I rolled my eyes. "I hope he drives, otherwise I'm giving him some of *your* old clothes to put on."

Big Mike arrived minutes later, strutting up to us in his work jeans and a T-shirt that read McCabe & Sons Construction. "What's so important that I had to drop everything and drive over here? I have work to do." Mike puffed up his barrel chest and shoved his hands in his pockets, sounding bored.

"Sorry, Mike." My brother switched to deputy mode. "I have a body, and I'm hoping you can help identify it for us."

"Body?" His weather-beaten face scrunched up in confusion. "Now, I don't know anything about a body—" He pulled at his ear with the missing lobe nervously.

"We know how he died, Mike. I just need an ID," my brother assured him.

"I'll do my best," he said.

Mike followed us farther into the forest, where one of the officers was taking pictures of the scene. I hadn't really looked at the dead guy before leaving with Alex. Blood pooled around his neck, where I'd bitten him, but another wound caught my eye. A red mark, the size and shape of a small rock, colored the man's skin an inch below his ear.

Mike took a good long look and shook his head. "I can't believe it."

"What?" Conall looked from Mike to the body.

"I've seen him before, and the Court should have his information on file. He arrived last summer, and when our den reached out, he kept to himself. Our kind typically prefer to live out on our own." Mike rubbed at the stubble on his cheek. "I think his name was Dave, or Don. I can't remember. But I do recall offering him some work when he first arrived, and he told me he already had a job, with someone he called the Collector."

"Thank you, Mike," I said, and patted him on the shoulder. I cut my eyes over to Conall. We'd been told to keep an ear out for any mention of the Collector.

Mike looked at my hand and frowned. I slowly pulled away, then Mike guffawed and slugged me on the arm. "I'm just messin' with you."

I laughed half-heartedly.

"I appreciate you coming out." Conall shook Mike's hand. "If I have any more questions, I'll be in touch."

Conall turned and headed back to the cabin.

I followed.

"We need to fill Dad in. This may be about the issue regarding the Petrans and Rocas. I'm wondering if it has to do with Micah and his niece Holly, too." Conall pulled out his cell phone and started moving his thumbs across the screen.

"I agree, but something isn't sitting well with me," I admitted. "That guy was probably only after the ring because the Collector sent him, and the Court had no clue he was up to no good."

"True, but do you really think we have a supervillain pulling all of our strings and living in Havenwood Falls?" Conall asked sarcastically.

"If we do, then Alex is still in danger." I grabbed his forearm in panic.

"Calm down, bro." Conall patted my hand in an effort to console me. "Dad's with her. And, get real, do you think someone could really pull a fast one on the Court of the Sun and the Moon?"

"Alex did." I glanced at Conall's phone screen. My dad was about to reply to his text. "And if the way this guy left Savannah is any indication of how the Collector operates, he'd take Alex's ring and leave her to die," I said, determined to find her, and quick.

CHAPTER 11

ALEX

*H*avenwood Falls Medical Center, an old renovated home across from the high school, was quiet, but not as awkwardly silent as the drive over with Sheriff Ric Kasun. The only words he'd uttered were about stopping for coffee, and I insisted on going straight to Savannah and Aunt Kay. I wanted answers.

I'd taken all of my shock and frustration out on Tate, but deep down, I knew he was walking a fine line between following orders and protecting me. Ultimately, he'd chosen me. He had the choice to shift before approaching me, when the mountain lion attacked, but he'd shifted right before my eyes. He'd been determined I know the truth.

"Are you going to go in?" Sheriff Kasun asked.

I resolved to find out why my aunt and friend wanted to keep me in the dark and unbuckled my seatbelt. "Yeah, sorry. I'm still trying to wrap my head around this." I waved my hand in front of me, motioning to the supernatural town in general.

"Can I give you a piece of advice?" he asked. "Don't be too hard on them." Ric looked down at the steering wheel and rubbed his hand over the leather. "I've had to do the single parent thing for a while now, and it's not easy. Making decisions for family members isn't about taking over their life, but about helping them get to a place where they can make the decisions for themselves."

I wanted to understand where Ric was coming from, but I related to Tate and his side of their relationship better. Tate was an adult, and he'd put off making those decisions for himself so he could help his father with his siblings. Someone needed to help Ric see Tate's perspective, and I cringed knowing it would have to be me.

I swallowed down the emotions swirling inside me, and spoke in the calmest voice I could muster. "Can I give you some advice?"

"I'm not sure—"

"Why are you making Tate work at the station when you know he thrives at Backwoods?" I interrupted. "He's been putting your family and this town first in his life for a long time, and his loyalty and dedication will always result in him defying his own happiness. Have you ever considered that his calling could complement the work you do for Havenwood Falls?"

"Ms. Newton, I don't think this—"

I reached for the door handle and smiled. "Take it or leave it." I slid out of the truck and landed on my feet with a thud.

Before I shut the door, Ric leaned over in my direction and said, "I'm going to grab a coffee and be right back. Can I get you something?"

He may not have liked my advice, but I could tell his gesture was a peace offering. I wouldn't refuse the olive branch or the coffee. It had been a long night.

"I'd love an Americano, and if you go to Coffee Haven, Paisley knows just how I like it." I grinned.

"Got it." Ric nodded. "I'll give you a few minutes alone with your aunt and Ms. Bast."

I closed the truck door, and Ric drove off toward the square.

The town's medical center was a white house with blue trim, and when I entered, the receptionist recognized me and waved me past her to the room Savannah was being treated in. As I entered, I found Savannah reading while my aunt slept on the chair next to her bed.

Savannah reached over and tapped Kay's arm. "Wake up, sleepyhead. Alex is back."

I walked over to them, but stopped a few feet away. The distance

353

would help give me the courage to say everything I'd been reciting in my head on the way over.

"I know," I started.

My aunt choked in the middle of a groggy yawn, and her eyes widened. Savannah promptly closed her book and set it at her side. They looked to each other, then back at me.

"What do you think you know?" Aunt Kay asked.

I ran my fingers through my hair and let out a slow breath. "I *know* that I'm a gypsy, that you're a gypsy. I *know* that a mountain lion tried to attack me and my boyfriend shifted into a wolf to save my life. And I *know* that the ring on my thumb is somehow holding me together and granting wishes, because I *think* I may have killed a man earlier."

My rant caught me by surprise, especially the fact that I'd referred to Tate as my boyfriend. I wanted to keep going and drill the two of them with questions, but my aunt gasped and Savannah started a rapid fire questioning.

"Are you all right? Was the mountain lion a shifter? What did he look like?" She pressed a hand against her forehead in a panic.

And that's when I noticed her bruises had disappeared. She'd been in the medical center less than 24 hours, and her body looked to be completely healed. "What are you?" I blurted.

Savannah's mouth formed a small o.

"She's an Egyptian goddess," Kay answered. "Your father—"

"Whoa! My dad was supernatural?" I asked, shaking my head in disbelief.

"No," Kay said, "and we won't clear anything up unless we agree to stop asking new questions until the first ones are answered." She folded her arms over her chest.

I nodded in agreement.

Savannah leaned forward and reached for my hand. "Your father was a descendant of the people I served. All of my existence has been dedicated to protecting their welfare. When I felt his departure from this world, I gave your aunt that ring to save you."

I walked to her bed and sat on the corner, then took her hand. "But why me? I'm half gypsy."

"You're special, a beautiful combination of two ancestries over three thousand years old. Your Romani blood is powerful, and I could tell when you were ten. And my purpose is—was—to protect all women and children." She sounded sad.

"What do you mean *was*?" I asked.

"The rings." She tapped my thumb. "I've spent centuries gifting them to women and children in need, and they've been handed down through family lines. You're not even the only person wearing a ring from the chain in Havenwood Falls. Last summer, I was called here to protect the remaining rings, but now I've failed." A tear fell down her cheek. "If you killed the man who took the rings, there still may be hope."

"If you're feeling better, maybe Sheriff Kasun can drive you to identify the body," I suggested.

She nodded.

"Alex," Aunt Kay started softly, "I'm sorry. Everything I've kept from you has been to protect you. I didn't know if you shared any of our family's gypsy gifts, and until I knew, I thought it would be pointless to tell you about them. Most Romani children show signs of power by the age of eight, but it seems you're a late bloomer." Her lips spread into a tight smile.

"Honestly, I don't know if I want to have anything to do with that power. I just want things to go back to normal. My dissertation is almost finished, but I can't present it now. I can't defend something I no longer know to be true. My mind will always wonder if the people I meet and the places I go are normal or paranormal."

"You don't have to go anywhere," Aunt Kay declared. "You know who we are, and you know what this town is. That's a start, and it's why I was so adamant about moving here. You'll be protected here, and your studies will contribute to your work whether you counsel humans or supernaturals."

"I'm the one who needs therapy," I said half-heartedly.

Savannah cleared her throat and looked me in the eye. "I know if you left, you would be leaving your heart here. Alexa, your work would be valuable here in so many ways. You could help so many people. And if you really want to finish your doctorate, I could make a few calls to the university and help you." She sounded hopeful.

Knock, knock.

Ric Kasun stood in the doorway with two coffee cups in hand. "I hate to break up this party, but I just got word from Conall and Tate. It seems we aren't out of the woods yet. No pun intended."

"Is everyone okay?" I asked, worried about Tate. I stood up and took the coffee from Ric.

"Everyone is fine, except the dead guy in the woods." Ric placed a consoling hand on my shoulder. "Someone from the Court is on their way to determine the cause of death, but Big Mike already ID'd him. It seems our mountain lion was a loner registered with the Court, doing odd jobs for someone else."

"You don't know who?" Aunt Kay asked, moving across the room to stand next to me.

"Not sure yet," Ric admitted. "Maybe someone called the Collector, but while my department works on finding the identity of the culprit, you two have been called in for an emergency meeting with the Court."

Aunt Kay let out a sigh.

"They aren't going without me," Tate's voice echoed from the hallway.

"Or me." Savannah started to get up.

Aunt Kay darted over to help her, and I walked into the hallway to meet Tate. His father's eyebrows furrowed. Ric shoved a hand in his pocket and took a long sip of his coffee.

"What are you doing here?" Ric asked.

Tate took my hand in his. "I'm not leaving Alex's side until we've caught this guy. You know as well as I do that until he gets her ring, he won't be satisfied."

"I promised you I would look after her," Ric argued.

"And I appreciate that, but you're needed on the case. You have more history with the people in this town than me, and you know I wouldn't be able to focus with Alex in danger. I'd be better suited to a security detail watching after her."

"I agree, but—"

Tate stepped forward, towering three inches over his dad. "Dad—"

"Let me finish, son," Ric growled. "I won't be giving you that detail, because you won't be working for the department anymore. I've decided, with the guidance of a new friend, that you'd be a better asset in the field. Or, in our case, the forest, guiding and protecting tourists."

Tate's mouth fell open, and he blinked slowly twice before responding. "Oh-kay."

"Now, can I trust you to get these ladies to the Court safely?" Ric asked.

"I have a patrol car outside." Tate jingled his keys in the air.

Ric's lips twisted. "I guess I can't fire you until you return the car." He smiled.

"Well, we could always trade," Tate suggested. "I'd be extra careful with your truck."

Tate grinned, still holding the keys up.

Ric rubbed the back of his neck with his palm, and said, "Nah, how about you take the car, and then you can put your resignation letter on my desk after you turn in those keys to your brother?"

Tate nodded, and my aunt and Savannah joined us in the hallway.

"We're ready." Savannah pressed her hands against the front of her skirt nervously.

"I'm not sure anyone is ever really ready to meet with the Court of the Sun and the Moon, but I have a feeling you'll give them a run for their money," Ric said. "I'll meet you there after I get word about the cause of death."

"Thanks, Dad," Tate said, and released my hand to hold it out to his father.

Ric took it, and pulled him in for a hug. They patted each other's backs, Ric whispered something to Tate, and then both were back to business.

"Tate, stand your ground in there," Ric warned.

"Don't worry, Sheriff Kasun. I'll take care of him." I smiled and reached for Tate's hand. When he wove his fingers between mine, I felt stronger. Not because I had a man by my side, but because I had love on my side.

CHAPTER 12

TATE

*T*he courtroom was filled with nosy supernatural citizens. I'd rarely ever been allowed in the reception area, let alone the courtroom, and there were dozens of people waiting for the proceedings to begin. My dad had mentioned character witnesses being called, but the crowd was impressive. The red fabric hanging behind the founding family representatives muffled the noise, but as people realized we'd arrived, the volume lowered. As we moved closer to the table at the front of the room, each row we passed fell silent. I recognized everyone, but a few faces surprised me.

At the back of the room, Monte sat with the collar of his jacket turned up. Paisley had a seat at the middle of the room, and she sipped from a cardboard Coffee Haven cup. Next to her, Sedona sat with a book propped open in her lap. One person I'd expected, Millicent Mathews, sat with a sneer in the front row, and when I stopped to let the ladies pass a short partition, I gave Millicent the widest smile I could muster.

As I held Alex's seat out for her, I glanced up at the town's leaders sitting behind the dais. Mathilde Augustine winked at me and then went back to a conversation she was having with Elsmed. I made sure Kay and Savannah were settled before taking my own seat.

Once we'd all made it to our places, Mathilde rose the gavel into the air and smacked it on the desk. "It is with fear and skepticism the Court has called this emergency meeting. It has come to our attention that the ruling agreed upon in regards to Alexa Newton's being privy to our town's supernatural presence has been breached. The consequence is banishment."

The crowd's oohs and ahhs filled the room. Alex nervously twisted in her seat.

Mathilde tapped the gavel three times. "Order, order." Once the noise died down, she continued. "Due to Ms. Newton's immunity to magic, we cannot risk her knowledge of Havenwood Falls. She will put our town, or herself, at risk. So I am proposing we waive the banishment and provide sanctuary for her and her aunt. Before the Court votes, we open the floor to any of your concerns." She nodded to the crowd.

Buzz filled the room once again. One soft voice stood out, but it wasn't the one I'd been expecting to hear. One of the ladies I'd noticed Alex talking to at Coffee Haven, Scottlin Glover, stood and proclaimed, "I have something to say!"

A pile of strawberry blond braids crowned her head, and she wore scrubs like she'd come straight from the medical center. She was known for giving impeccable care to her patients, but I couldn't imagine what she'd say. Alex nudged me with her elbow and shrugged.

"Healer," I whispered, but didn't explain further so I could hear Scottlin talk.

"I met Alex when she came in for some tests, then we'd run into each other at Coffee Haven. She spent some time one day listening to me drone on, and her advice helped me with a problem I'd been dealing with. She's even been kind enough to ask me about it since then. I find her trustworthy and agree with Ms. Augustine that she should be approved for citizenship." She smiled at Alex.

"I agree," a blue-haired teen said. Paisley had popped out of her seat to stand. "Alex is the best, and she didn't hold it against me when I was totally rude to her the first day she came into town."

Beside Paisley, Sedona Mathews stood and said, "Alex Newton and I have spent a little time together at my shop, and I believe—"

"Do you hear yourselves?" Millicent stood and turned to face her niece. "Alexa Newton may be a good person, but someone is dead because of her, one of our own. The ring she wears makes her veiled, and protects her from magic, but who will protect us from her!" Her veins looked like they would pop out of her forehead.

A few people looked at each other in confusion, then the doors opened, and my dad walked in. Ric Kasun strode to the front of the room, up to the dais, and motioned to Saundra. She leaned forward, and he whispered something up to her. She nodded at him.

In true Kasun form, Ric faced the crowd and folded his arms over his chest and waited. He wore his take on a small-town sheriff's uniform—black boots, jeans, and a flannel shirt.

The room fell silent with expectation. Alex set her hand on mine, and I threaded our fingers together.

"Sheriff Kasun, if you would please share your findings," Saundra Beaumont prompted.

My dad cleared his throat. "Early this morning, Alexa Newton was attacked by Donald McElroy in Kasun Pack territory. Tate Kasun shifted in an effort to save Alex's life, revealing himself. During the fight, Alex used her own power, as a gypsy, to distract the attacker. There were traces of magic as well as two deadly gashes along Donald McElroy's throat."

Saundra nodded, and said, "Thank you, Sheriff." Then she looked over the audience in the courtroom, and her eyes stopped on Alex. "Miss Newton, would you care to say anything?"

Alex squeezed my hand and stood. "Hi, everyone, I'm Alexa Newton. A few weeks ago, I found myself driving into Havenwood Falls. I had no map, no ulterior motives, and no idea this place would feel so much like home." She turned to face the Court. "I know you'd rather have me in the dark, and I'll concede to the decision you make, but my power, or my veil to magic, doesn't have to be feared. In fact, I believe honesty and transparency are honorable. I can't be tainted by your charms. No one here can jinx me to make me hurt someone or cast a spell to make me lie. I'm figuring out there isn't anything to fear in this town, but there are a few people to feel sorry for." Alex locked eyes with Millicent.

Alex had enraptured the audience. Her words weren't hurtful, but truthful. She didn't plan to use her power to gain more power, but to use it to help others.

"If there's nothing else—" Saundra said.

My legs straightened, and I stood next to Alex. "I'd like to say a few words."

Saundra nodded, and I looked at each Court member, really looked at them. They had obtained their position by being born into a certain family. Their job to rule and guide the people of this town had to be an act of service if they wanted to it to be done right.

"We don't know enough to understand Donald McElroy's motives, or who might have employed him. I won't rest until Alex is safe. I'll stay by her side, whether that means staying in town or leaving town with her. I don't expect my actions to influence the Court's decision, but I want each of you to understand that protecting her is our job because she *is* one of us."

A few people clapped awkwardly as I finished, and Mathilde's gavel raised into the air. "We will deliberate and return with a verdict within twenty-four hours."

Crack. The wooden hammer hit the desk a final time.

Alex turned to face me, and said, "Thank you, for what you said and for standing next to me."

"I hope you'll let me stand by you for a long time." I smiled and wrapped my arm around her waist.

"We probably shouldn't celebrate yet." She frowned.

"I have a good feeling that either way, we'll be able to live with the verdict, because we'll be together."

She pushed up on her toes and kissed me. Her lips were soft, and as I leaned into the kiss, I heard someone whistle.

Paisley.

"My intuition is never wrong," she bragged, and her violet eyes sparkled. "I knew you belonged together the first time I saw you, all disheveled."

Alex and Savannah laughed as Paisley exited the room, and Kay looked lost.

"Disheveled?" Kay's head tilted to the side. "Do you need to fill me in?"

"No, promise," Alex answered. "It was a misunderstanding." She laughed.

I tugged Alex closer to get her attention, and asked, "What do you want to do while we wait?"

She rubbed her eyes and yawned. "Sleep, eat, I don't know."

"How about I cook?" I offered.

"And I'll help," my dad said as he walked up behind me. "Savannah, Kay, I hope you'll come too."

"Sure," Savannah accepted. "I guess my house is still a crime scene?"

Ric nodded. "Yes, but we'll put you all up at the Whisper Falls Inn. I'll make a call on the way to the cabin."

Ric led the group out of the courtroom, and once we stepped outside, he offered to give Savannah and Kay a ride in his truck. He winked at me before Alex and I made our way to the patrol car. Alex still wore her clothes from yesterday.

"Do you need anything?" I asked, opening the passenger-side door. "I can stop wherever you want on the way."

After making my way around the car, I slid behind the steering wheel.

Alex reached over and took my hand in hers. "This is going to sound cheesy, but I've got what I need right here. No matter what the Court decides, I'm thankful I have you. And I know our circumstances have fast-forwarded our relationship, but if you want to slow down or revert back to a more *old-fashioned* way of doing things, I'm okay with that."

I wasn't sure how to respond. She'd been overwhelmed with so much crazy, and I didn't want to push her over the edge by revealing my magical connection to her. I could hold on to this one last secret, and hope the right time presented itself, or I could tell her and trust that she was strong and patient enough to understand.

"I'm sorry," Alex apologized. She wore a frown and scooted a little closer.

"For what?" I asked. "I'm just trying to figure out how to word something, because it might freak you out." I rubbed at my temples.

"Oh." Her eyes widened, and she bit at her bottom lip. "Well, I don't want you to get in more trouble with the Court or your dad."

"My dad already knows, and I think he offered to take Savannah and Kay so I could tell you."

"Then, go for it." Alex turned her body at an angle to face me.

"It's another level to this supernatural world, and I don't want you to think I'm throwing you into it too fast," I explained, wrestling internally with the thought of potentially scaring her away.

"I'm a Romani with a magic ring and you're a wolf shifter. How much weirder can it get?" One corner of her mouth lifted, challenging me. She was about to find out just how weird it could get.

"I have a connection to you—"

"I feel connected to you too." Alex smiled, and she leaned forward.

"Hmm." I wanted to kiss her, but I had to tell her first. I ran my fingers along the outside of her arm. "Wolf shifters, like so many other pack-like shifters, mate for life. When they meet that person, they *know*, and there isn't much that can break that bond."

"Wow," she breathed. "So it doesn't have to be with another wolf shifter?"

"No, and there have been a few cases when the other person doesn't return the feelings." I pinched the bridge of my nose, terrified Alex would pull away. "But usually the magic isn't wrong."

"The magic? It isn't an animal instinct?" Alex's brows had pulled together.

I smirked at her. "There is definitely attraction, which seems more animal, but the magic is what pulls me to you, like gravity."

"Gravity, huh?" Alex tilted back slightly and smiled.

I leaned forward to match her angle and brushed my hand across her cheek. The motion lured her forward, and as my lips touched hers, I answered softly, "Gravity."

EPILOGUE

ALEX

FRIDAY, JULY 13TH

*B*eing with Tate for five days on a road trip had sounded heavenly, but when his dad and the Court heard about the trip, they'd assigned Tate's sister, Willa, to go with us as backup. With an unknown villain—this Collector person—still out on the loose, I appreciated everyone wanting to keep me alive, but the idea of Tate's little sister going with us had dampened some of my plans for the week. Once we hit the open road, and I'd gotten to know Willa, I embraced the opportunity to spend time with another person who could fill me in on Havenwood Falls, and Tate.

We'd arrived back from Arizona early in the afternoon, and Addie Beaumont was waiting at my aunt's new house on Tenth Street. Before all of my worldly possessions could be carried inside from the car, Addie insisted on welcoming me with her tattoo kit in hand. The Court figured, with Savannah's counsel, they would try to mark me with the same magic every supernatural citizen wore. A tattoo. The purpose of the magic wasn't to penetrate my veil, but to protect me. So, in theory, it should work.

I'd seen Tate's tattoo, the night he'd walked out in his towel, and knowing it represented his family and the Kasun pack inspired me to choose something special for my tattoo.

"Are you sure you want to give me creative freedom?" Addie asked, the corner of her lips pulled up with a hint of excitement.

I looked to Tate, and he nodded with a grin. "I trust Tate, and he says you're the best. As long as it resembles a compass, you can do whatever you feel inspired to do."

"Okay." Addie smiled. She began unpacking her case at the dining table. "Now, you just have to decide where you want it."

"My shoulder," I said. I'd been thinking about it all week while we'd been in Arizona.

I spent two hours sitting perfectly still, straddling a dining room chair. When Addie finished the tattoo, I slowly stood up.

"It's beautiful," Kay said, as Addie smeared a clear ointment over my shoulder.

By then, Tate, Willa, Savannah, and Kay had finished bringing my boxes into the house. I'd insisted they wait for me, but being under Addie's needle, I was in no position to protest when they started. Everyone sat waiting with anticipation for Addie to finish, except for Kay. She'd wanted to watch.

"Do you have a mirror hanging anywhere close by?" Addie asked.

"There's one in the entryway," Kay answered.

Addie held out a hand mirror for me. "Go take a look."

I walked through the living room in my shorts and sports bra, suddenly aware of how little clothes I had on. The others stood up to follow me. Willa bounced behind me, with an approving grin. Savannah's eyes widened when I turned my back to the mirror and the compass was in full view. And Tate waited patiently behind them.

"Did it hurt much?" Willa asked. "Mine barely hurt at all, but I think I have a higher pain tolerance. I guess that's part of being a wolf shifter. Do gypsies have a high pain tolerance?"

"I'm not sure, but it didn't hurt that bad," I answered.

"I love it," Savannah offered. She glanced between me and Tate, then took Willa's hand and walked into the other room to join Addie and Kay. "Addie, you've outdone yourself."

"It really captures what brought me here," I said, smiling and holding the mirror up to see the reflection on the wall.

A golden ring encircled the face of a compass, and was nestled in a forest of trees. Mountains surrounded the compass, along with the night sky. The moon and stars adorned the curve of my neck and created an asymmetrical frame for the artwork.

The unusual quiet, after Willa left the entryway, made the space feel smaller. Tate approached me and took the mirror from my hand. He set it on a side table, then slipped his arms around my waist.

"Do you like it?" I whispered.

Tate's chest vibrated against mine. "Nooo." He pressed his lips against mine in a soft kiss, then trailed kisses along my jawline to my ear. His hands rubbed my lower back, pulling me closer. His fingers made my skin tingle. "I love it," he whispered.

I pulled my head back and searched his eyes. I had only begun to understand the depths of his feelings for me, but he made it easy to reciprocate them. "I think I love it too."

"Okay, lovebirds, I gotta jet," Addie said with a grin.

Tate and I jerked apart.

Addie came up behind me and taped a sheet of plastic wrap over my shoulder. "Leave that on for a couple hours, then make sure to put the ointment I left with your aunt on twice a day. You'll get a little scabbing, but that's a good sign. Tate knows how to find me if you have any problems."

As Addie exited, she picked up her hand mirror. Willa, Savannah, and Kay filed into the living room to meet us. They each examined Tate and me, but when all of their eyes landed on me, I realized I was still standing around in my bra. As I stepped toward my new room to escape and find a shirt that wouldn't irritate my shoulder, Kay held out a short silky robe. I wrapped it around myself and tied the belt.

"Thanks," I said bashfully. How was it I could be a supernatural and super embarrassed? The awkwardness in the room thickened the air like humidity after a storm.

"I should probably get Willa home." Tate shoved his hands in his pockets. "Then I'll be back here to pick you up tonight around seven."

Willa gave me a quick hug on her way across the room, and said, "I'll see you tonight."

"Oh, and don't eat dinner," Tate said, and opened the front door for his sister. "I'll have that covered. See you soon." He winked at me.

When I turned to start unpacking, both Kay and Savannah had wide grins spread across their faces. Even though I didn't know how long Aunt Kay would stay in Havenwood Falls, I loved having her here to help me get settled in. She and Savannah had already started a few little renovations in the kitchen, and she described a plan to turn the extra bedroom into an office for me while I unpacked. I had about four hours to finish and get ready for an event held once a year, always on a Friday the 13th. The Super Hunt was one of Havenwood Falls' oldest traditions.

Tate picked me up a few minutes early. Somehow, he made jeans and a plaid shirt look less lumberjack and more GQ. He'd parked his Jeep in the driveway, and carried a picnic basket. A quilted blanket hung folded over his arm, and when I greeted him, I took it from him.

"You don't have to—" he said.

"I think I can handle carrying a blanket." I kissed his cheek. "And if I get cold, I can just wrap it around me."

"I planned for us to sit on the blanket." Tate smirked. "But I'll be happy to keep you warm."

I stepped out into the night, and Tate took my hand. As we walked to the town square, other people in the neighborhood joined us, everyone headed in the same direction. It seemed I'd underestimated the draw of superstition.

"So, this really is a big deal?" I asked. My eyebrows lifted as I took it all in.

"Yeah, it's like the counterpoint—or a spoof, to some—to our Wild Hunt every June, when the supernaturals are doing the hunting. This human version is for fun and raises money for a different charity or fundraiser every year. Everyone pays a few bucks to play, and one person is selected to be *it*. This year we're doing a werewolf hunt." Tate smiled knowingly. "Before we start the hunt, they'll tell us who's *it* and give the so-called *werewolf* some time to find their hiding spot. The winner gets a gift card and bragging rights."

"Interesting." I nodded. "And everyone plays?"

"I'll admit, the interest level for some of the teenagers is less about the prize and more about the potential makeout sessions." Tate winked and pulled me close as he turned left on Stuart Street.

The crowd gathering in front of the gazebo was bigger than any I'd seen in town so far. There had to have been more than a hundred people waiting for the festivities to begin. The lampposts around the square were lit, but some people already had their flashlights on. I glanced at Tate's hands and pockets, and twisted my lips in confusion.

"Are we not playing?" I asked.

"Oh, we're playing. I have flashlights for us in here." He held up his hand holding the basket. "I just thought it would be fun to give our competition a little head start while we enjoy a picnic."

"I love that idea," I said. "Where are you thinking we'll eat?"

"That's the best part. Once they start the hunt, the square will clear out. We can spread our blanket out on the lawn in front of the gazebo, and we won't have to worry about anyone walking up on us for at least an hour." Tate smiled proudly.

The crowd's roar dulled to a hum. A tall woman tapped a microphone, and the speakers let out a ringing sound. Everyone cringed, and then settled again. A few people were still in line at a table set up near the fountain, signing up to participate. Tate set his basket down on the edge of the fountain and motioned for me to stay there while he waited in line.

He leaned in and explained that the woman with the microphone was the mayor. She explained the evening with enthusiasm, and her blond bouffant hair bounced as she spoke. "Tonight, the quarterback for our Havenwood Falls High Dragons football team has been selected to act as our prey. The proceeds from this event will be going toward new equipment for the high school. With Kase Kasun's athletic advantage, we'll all need to be extra diligent. Our acting werewolf has already left to find his hiding spot, and as always, the perimeters are from Mathews River to Blackstone Road and from Havenwood Falls High to Bels Creek. The sheriff and his men will be on patrol, so no wandering out of bounds or pranks. The game will end when Kase is found, or if he's not, we'll meet back here at eleven p.m. to draw a random winner. Is everyone ready?"

The crowd cheered.

Tate made his way back to me with two armbands. The woman at the table waved at the man on the stage.

"On your mark, get set, go!" The man's voice echoed through the square.

Tate placed one of the bands around my wrist. "In two minutes, we'll finally have some alone time." He smiled and took the blanket from me.

After one minute, the square was abandoned. Tate spread the blanket over a patch of grass between the gazebo and the fountain. In two minutes, the lampposts turned off and the stars twinkled in the sky.

"It'll be difficult for anyone to find Kase with it being a new moon," Tate said. He'd walked back over to me and grabbed the picnic basket. "Come on."

He took my hand and led me to the blanket. I sat down and watched as Tate pulled two flashlights, two water bottles, and several small containers out of the basket. He looked up at me and shrugged.

"I wasn't sure what you'd be hungry for, so I brought a little of everything." Tate started to peel the lids off each container. "I hope you're hungry." He winked.

I ate a few different kinds of cheese, some salami, olives, cantaloupe, and chocolate-covered pretzels. We joked about how Tate really had brought everything, and we ate it all, because whatever I didn't finish, he polished off. The basket was full of empty plastic tubs, and we folded up the blanket, ready to start our hunt.

"It'll just take a sec for me to run this upstairs," Tate said, as he worked to unlock the front door of the Backwoods store. "Do you want to go up with me or wait here?"

"I'll walk up with you," I answered with a frown. "It's creepy-quiet out there." I pointed with my thumb behind me as Tate waved me inside.

Tate immediately perked up, and straightened an arm out in front of me. I thought I heard something upstairs, and I could tell Tate definitely had. He set the basket and blanket on the counter next to the register and moved to stand in front of me. We walked slowly to the staircase, and Tate turned his ear toward the loft.

He whispered, "I think it's the television."

I nodded.

We crept up the stairs, and when we arrived at the loft's door, Tate twisted the knob. It hadn't been locked. Tate looked back at me and held up one finger, then two, then three, and punched the door open. His brother Kase was sitting on the couch, but jumped up at our intrusion. He was watching a cooking show.

I started laughing.

"Bro, you nearly gave me a heart attack!" Kase said, holding his hands to his chest.

"What are you even doing up here? You're supposed to be hiding," Tate reprimanded.

"I know. I figured I'd try Conall's trick from that one time a few years ago." Kase smiled. He looked so much like his father. "Please, don't say anything."

"I won't, but you better pick a good place to hide since people have been hunting for an hour," Tate said, crossing his arms over his chest.

"I will. I figured everyone would try the football fields first, but I plan to hide near—"

"Don't tell us," I exclaimed. "It's my first time playing, and I don't want spoilers."

Tate smiled at me.

"What?" I asked.

"You're cute." He leaned toward me and pressed a quick kiss on my forehead.

"Thank you, I think." I frowned.

I faced Kase. "Now, we'll give you five minutes, but then the game is on." I stepped to the side and pointed to the stairs.

Kase smirked at me, then said to Tate, "I like her." And then he rushed out of the room.

Tate picked up the TV remote and pushed the off button.

"So, do you want to learn how to bake while we wait?" I pointed at the blank screen. "I could probably use a lesson or two," I joked.

Tate stepped between the television and me, and he tucked a piece of hair behind my ear. He searched my face, and his eyes lingered on my lips for a split second too long. I placed my hands on his chest and slid them up and around his neck. He closed his eyes and wrapped his arms around my waist.

"I'd rather do this while we wait." He grinned.

"We can do this, but don't think that I'm not planning to hunt your brother down in four minutes and thirty seconds," I said with a chuckle. My hand rubbed along his hairline at the nape of his neck. "I want that gift card to Burger Bar."

I felt Tate laugh with me as he pulled me close, but then he grew quiet.

"Alex?" Tate asked in a more serious tone. He pulled back and locked eyes with me.

"Yeah? What is it?"

He pulled my hand in front of him and twisted the ring on my thumb. "Now that I have you, I'm never going to let anyone hurt you."

He moved my hand to rest on his chest, and slid his fingers around my neck, tangling them in my hair. Tate kissed me like I'd never been kissed before, and I knew he would do anything to protect me.

The Collector still lurked in the shadows of Havenwood Falls, but I wouldn't have to face the danger alone.

WE HOPE you enjoyed this collection of stories in the Havenwood Falls series featuring a variety of supernatural creatures. Keep going for an excerpt of *Break Me Not* by Kristie Cook. The series is a collaborative effort by multiple authors.

Also try the YA line, Havenwood Falls High; the historical line, Legends of Havenwood Falls; the darker, sexier side of town, Havenwood Falls Sin & Silk; the local supernatural college, Sun & Moon Academy; and the short story holiday anthologies.

Stay up to date at www.HavenwoodFalls.com

ABOUT THE AUTHOR

Writing unique adventures with heart.

Kallie Ross has a passion for writing that has become an adventure in itself. She desires to create unique young adult fiction that incorporates legend, conjecture, fantasy, and conviction.

In addition to loving her life as a writer, Kallie adores being a wife, mother, friend, and teacher. She began her creative journey with books, a blog, a podcast, and lots of caffeine. Ross never imagined her own adventure would be filled with so many wonderful people or words!

KallieRoss.com

@KallieRoss Instagram

ACKNOWLEDGMENTS

Thank you, Kristie Cook, for trusting me with another adventure in Havenwood Falls. I couldn't have finished this story without the support of Jessica Gibson. Everyone needs encouragement and accountability, and I'm thankful for Jessi's ability to be both. Other friends like Morgan Wylie, Gaby Robbins, Melissa Bailey, and Megan Kennedy inspired me to have fun writing Tate's story, and their support is always a blessing.

Thank you, Havenwood Falls readers! Your enthusiasm for this world keeps me dreaming up stories and writing them down.

~ A Havenwood Falls New Adult Novella ~

Havenwood Falls

Break Me Not

Kristie Cook

Break Me Not (A Havenwood Falls Novella) by Kristie Cook

A continuation of *Forget You Not* and *Lose You Not*, this is Addie and Tase's story.

Addie Beaumont loves her hometown of Havenwood Falls and would do anything to protect it. She also loves Tase Roca—even after all the times he's broken her heart. She would do anything to protect him, as well, so when her two loves are on the brink of destroying each other, Addie gets caught in the middle.

A curse is transforming Tase from a mortal vampire into an unstoppable, bloodthirsty monster. He's become a lethal threat to Havenwood Falls, causing the town's leaders to hang a death sentence over his head. It's up to Addie to break the curse before they execute him.

The Eye of Valerian holds the answers, but the dark artifact is protected by black magic that scares the hell out of her. When she finally unlocks its powers, she and Tase are swept into a dangerous plot that could destroy everything they cherish.

Love may be their only hope, but true love means no secrets, and they both keep plenty. One Addie denies even to herself, but embracing its truth has the potential to save her town, her loved ones, and Tase—and the power to break them both.

BREAK ME NOT

AN EXCERPT

Sometimes living in a small town was all quaint and charm, and sometimes it sucked monkey balls. In Havenwood Falls, everybody knew everybody, which meant it was impossible to go anywhere without being stopped for a million conversations. As I crossed town square, glancing at my phone every twenty seconds, hoping for a reply to my many texts, no fewer than eight people hailed me down for "just a moment of your time, Addie." When I saw Irene Beckett, Biddie Half-Moon, and the Carson sisters—the town's blue-haired busybody gossips—in the middle of my current path, though, I made a sharp left, detouring around the gazebo and not caring if I had to add five minutes to my walk to avoid them. They'd surely take twice as much time with all their questions and assumptions. I was always surprised none of them had broken a hip with all the jumping to conclusions those four did. Of course, they'd likely know where the subject of my search was, but it just wasn't worth the risk. By the time I could extract myself from their clutches, he'd be long gone, on to the next place.

Finally, my phone dinged with an answer.

AE: At the baseball fields. Can you come here?

The baseball fields? What the fuck? What was Atanase "Tase" Roca, aka Asshole Extraordinaire, doing at the baseball fields, of all places? He wasn't exactly the jock type, especially if the sport didn't require a board strapped to his feet. And it was early summer—the ballfields were likely full of Little League . . . *Oh*. As I turned once more and headed for the alley between Howe's Herbal Shoppe and Dress Perfect to catch McFeeney Street toward the ball diamonds, the answer hit me, and my stomach sunk like a rock. *Of course.*

My steps slowed as I considered whether I really wanted to trek all the way there only to have my heart pulverized once again or if I should just keep it all business and tell him to meet me at my office. Except he was supposed to already be there so we could talk before the meeting, and I had no guarantee he'd show up even if he said he would —the jerk was full of empty promises like that.

Over it. I. Am. Over. It.

After sweeping my long light brown hair into a messy bun on top of my head, I readjusted my glasses and squared my shoulders, refusing to let him get to me. Then I typed out a message telling him to stay put and continued on to Cook's Corner Park. The early summer sun was already hanging low over Miles Mountain, but it was still warm enough to make me wish I hadn't been wearing dressy jeans for tonight's Court meeting. At least I'd changed into my Converse All-Stars, leaving my other favorite shoes—knee-high boots with a four-inch heel—under my desk before taking off to find Tase.

Ten minutes later, I found him on the far side of the ballfield, his fingers curled around the chain link fence as he watched the group of little kids at T-ball practice. He wore a black T-shirt that clung just right to his muscular frame, black jeans that hugged his perfect ass without being too tight, and black motorcycle boots. His green-gray eyes spared me a piercing glance and his full lips lifted in a small smile as I walked up, making my mouth go dry and my heart tick up, before he returned his focus to the T-ballers. As always, the sight of him set off my traitorous body in all the right and wrong ways.

I joined him at the fence and immediately picked out his son Carter from the crowd of soon-to-be kindergarteners.

"He's amazing," Tase said, and the way he said it—his voice full of awe and wonder and a love most wouldn't think him capable of—that was why I couldn't seem to break myself of him. It was a side he rarely showed, except with a few trusted people, and I was one. "A goofball, but pretty amazing."

I snickered, trying not to choke on my shock. "Did you really just say *goofball*?"

That wasn't exactly normal Tase-speak.

He shrugged. "Well, he is. Look at him. He's a jokester, hamming it up with the other kids. He likes the attention."

"I wonder where he gets that from," I quipped.

Tase sighed. "Well, hopefully, that's the worst he'll get from me."

We watched the kids for a silent moment. "We had an appointment."

"I know. I couldn't pull myself away. This is the only way I get to see him—outside, from a distance."

Tase had only learned last fall that he even had a son, when a short-term fling from years ago had returned to town and regained her memories of the time they'd spent together nine months before her son was born. The wards on our town caused everyone to lose their ability to recall their time here, except for vague and ambiguous ideas of some small town in the Colorado mountains—it happened immediately for visitors and after a lunar cycle for residents. Well, former residents at that point. It was how we protected our town and our supernatural secrets from the outside world. If they somehow found their way back to Havenwood Falls, their memories eventually returned. Once Shelly Martin's had, she could finally identify her son's sperm donor. To say it was a shock to everyone that Tase Roca was a father was an understatement.

What this revelation meant was mind-blowing and heartbreaking, and not just for me.

With a curse that was essentially a death sentence for Tase if we didn't break it soon enough, he couldn't possibly have a relationship with his son. The curse heightened Tase's bloodlust and would eventually drive him to transform from a moroi, a relatively benign mortal vampire, to an immortal, monstrous strigoi—what happens to moroi when they kill too many humans, each soul taken bringing them one step closer to losing their humanity forever. The Court of the Sun and the Moon, the true rulers of our town, wouldn't allow the transformation to complete—they would execute him first.

So not only was Tase a danger to any human, including his son, but it wouldn't have been fair to Carter to introduce him to his father, only to rip him away shortly thereafter. The Court had "strongly encouraged" Tase to stay away from Carter, and he'd obliged, fully understanding their concerns. At first, I didn't think Tase would even care that Carter didn't know him. He wasn't exactly the fatherly type. Or responsible, for that matter. But this hadn't been the first time Tase had watched his son from a distance, and it didn't take long to realize this kid might be his true salvation. Carter gave Tase something real to live for.

And that had been a bittersweet pill for me to swallow. I was glad he had a reason to continue fighting for his life, but part of me couldn't help but wish that *I* had been his reason.

I should have known better. We'd never been more than really good friends who hooked up every once in a while.

"Have you ever thought about having a family?" Tase asked, startling me.

Closing my eyes for a moment, I inhaled slowly, steeling myself. "We've talked about that before."

"Yeah, when we were younger and stupider."

"We talked about it less than a year ago." Not too long after the curse on him had been revealed. When we found out what he did to my best friend Michaela's family—nearly obliterated all of the Petrans —and to his own family—would have obliterated them, too, if we hadn't stopped it.

Because he'd triggered Michaela's moroi vampire gene against her will, the centuries-old curse on her bloodline—the result of a massacre in their old country—jumped to the Roca family. My coven, the Lunas, contained the dark magic to Tase himself, protecting his siblings, but putting the full burden of the curse on him. When I'd heard the word execution, something in me had snapped. Believing there had to be another way, I volunteered to take on the mission of controlling the curse's effects on Tase while trying to figure out how to break it.

That was over a year ago. My containment spells were holding so far, but who knew how much longer before they cracked?

Tase chuckled. "I was a little younger and a lot stupider a year ago."

I couldn't argue with that. "Well, nothing's changed for me. I still don't know if that's my thing. I just can't see myself as a soccer mom."

I didn't add the obvious fact that it takes two to tango, and I would likely always be one. Because my stupid heart couldn't break its addiction to the man standing next to me and possibly never would. No matter how many times I told myself I was over him.

"You'd be a great mother, Bean," Tase said quietly, using the nickname he'd given me years ago. I'd once made him turn the ski lifts back on after I'd lost my favorite beanie hat on the last run of the night. Michaela and I were still in school then, and Tase hadn't bought the ski resort yet. He'd only been an employee and had risked his job to do that favor for me. He'd called me Beanie for months after, then it just became Bean and stuck. Not even Michaela knew I still had that hat, tucked away in a special box.

"What in Goddess's name would make you say that?" I asked, snorting.

He turned his head to look at me over his arm, his green-gray eyes glinting in the afternoon sun, the lightness of them a stark contrast against his tanned olive skin and dark hair. "You're one of the most responsible people I know. You're definitely the most persistent and determined. And you'll do whatever you have to do to take care of others. You care. About everyone, about this town, even about people you claim to hate. Like me."

"I don't hate you."

He gave me his signature smirk, the one that set every nerve in my body on fire. "You've never said, 'I hate that motherfucking Tase Roca?'"

I smiled. "Well, maybe a time or two."

But thing was, I could never truly hate "that motherfucking Tase Roca." Because I loved him too much. I just couldn't tell him that.

"And yet you still care. At least enough to come down here and drag my ass back downtown to ensure I make my meeting with the Court. I don't think my own mother ever cared that much about any of us. You're already a step ahead."

Yeah, well, Isabelle Roca wasn't exactly known for her motherly ways, so that wasn't saying much. Maybe if she had been, the whole Roca family would have turned out differently. Something else I couldn't tell him, out of respect for the dead.

"Speaking of . . ." I trailed off, knowing he understood.

Turning to face me, he stuck his hands in his front pockets, cocked his head, and smirked. Good Goddess. Why did he have to be so damn sexy?

When he spoke, his voice was low and sultry. "Do we have to go to the Court? Can't we just go to your place and do it there?"

I lifted an eyebrow. He lifted his hand—likely to do something like brush the hair off my face or tweak my chin or some other thing that would surely make me cave, so I jerked back, out of his reach.

"No," I said flatly.

He dropped his chin, now looking at me through his thick, dark lashes. "Please? I miss you. I miss hanging out with you."

Fuck. *Over it. I'm over it. Stay strong, Adelaide Beaumont. Stay. Fucking. Strong.*

His hand darted out, slipping around my waist before I even knew what he was doing, and he pulled me up against him. Grabbing my hand, he placed it against his heart.

"You can do your magic without them. You can report back to them whatever you find. I just don't want to deal with the damn Court right now, Bean. I just want to be with you."

His heart beat steadily against my palm. Mine raced against my rib cage.

With a deep breath, I pushed on his chest and ducked out of his hold.

"I said no," I reiterated.

"Why? I thought you—"

"Whatever you think you know about me, you're wrong. Old news, Tase. Keep up with the times."

His brows rose. "You keep saying things have changed."

"They have."

"Like what?"

"Like . . . there are all kinds of new complications." I gestured toward the ball diamond, where the practice appeared to be breaking up. Carter was running over to his mother in the stands.

Tase snorted. "You're not jealous of Shelly, are you? Talk about old news."

I rolled my eyes. "How the hell can you accuse *me* of being jealous? I've always known exactly what you and I are to each other." I paused, then quickly corrected myself. "Were. What we *were* to each other. I always knew where we stood." Whether I liked it or not was a different story—although sometimes I did like our arrangement of killer sex with no strings attached, which was why I let it go on for so long. "But it has nothing to do with jealousy. I meant complications like Carter. Your curse. What that means not only for your future, but his, too."

"What if it was *our* future? Yours, too?" He almost sounded serious.

My heart seemed to stop for just a moment. That was one thing we'd *never* discussed out loud—a future that was *ours*. Something we couldn't discuss now. I shook my head.

"I'm not going there, Tase." I'd gone there in my mind way too many times, and it wasn't healthy for me. "Let's just make sure you *have* a future. Which means getting your ass to the Court meeting."

Turning, I walked off, hoping he would follow me. Well, first hoping he was watching my ass and regretting everything he'd done to me that brought us to this point, but then that he would follow me. He did. Of course, I was headed for his Camaro, so he was bound to.

His car was parked on Second Street, along the side of the ball fields. Just as we were reaching it, the hair on the back of my neck suddenly stood on end. *Danger.* I looked around. Some parents and their kids were about to cross Second. There were no cars moving on the street, but I somehow *knew* something was about to happen.

"Watch out!" I yelled.

And suddenly, I was standing in front of them, my arms out to stop them all from crossing the road. At that moment, a car squealed around the corner and flew down the street.

"Laroc," I muttered under my breath, recognizing the luxury vehicle. He would have plowed over half the group if I hadn't stopped them.

"Where did you come from?" a woman asked.

"Are you like the Flash?" a boy questioned with awe.

"Did you just apparate like Harry Potter?" an older girl squealed.

I blinked and looked up at the group of parents and kids staring at me wide-eyed. My own gaze found Tase standing by his car, his eyes narrowed, studying me—a good thirty yards away. *Oh shit.* Murmuring a quick memory spell, I flicked my fingers unnoticeably by my side. The group looked around and then continued on their way, completely oblivious to the last sixty seconds.

I might have to account for this with the Luna Coven later, but it was moments like these we were trained for and instructed to act on— when accidents happened and needed to be covered. And crossing a thirty-yard distance in a heartbeat had certainly been an accident. I didn't even know how I did it.

"That wasn't your normal magic," Tase said once we were seated in his car.

"No, it wasn't."

"Not a portal or anything like that."

I shook my head.

"Addie, you moved like we can. Like a vampire. You blurred over there."

A lump formed in my throat, and I tried to swallow it down as I nodded.

"How?" he asked.

I didn't answer.

"Bean?"

"I don't want to talk about it," I bit out. I didn't even want to think about it. The need to protect that had suddenly washed over me. The inhuman speed. *Nope. Not thinking about it.*

He finally turned over the engine. "You will eventually, though, right? You know you can talk to me about anything."

Yeah, except about you. And this. I nodded again. "Yeah, sure. But right now, we have bigger things to worry about than how I ran so fast."

We spent the next three minutes in silence as Tase drove toward town square and pulled around the back of City Hall. Not until he put the Camaro in park did either of us speak.

"We really have to do this?" he asked as we both stared out the windshield.

"You know we do."

"But I'm fine. The containment spell is working."

"At least that is . . . for now," I muttered, opening the door. "They'll be questioning me just as much as you. My report won't be so positive."

By the time I slid out of the car and shut the door, Tase was by my side.

"You're doing everything you can, right?" he asked as we crossed the street, headed for the metal door at the back of City Hall that led to the Court's rooms in the basement. "They can't expect more."

"They do. They expect me to figure out the Eye of Valerian and break the curse. I expect that myself. Nothing short of that is good enough."

We entered the building and jogged down the stairs to the basement level. Only the sound of our steps in the empty hallway could be heard—his boots and my Converse barely more than soft thuds—even as we reached the small waiting area just outside the double doors leading into the Court's main meeting room. We paused, waiting until the doors opened on their own accord, the Court's signal for us to enter.

They were assembled and waiting, so I didn't have time to slip over to my desk and change my shoes. My grandmother gave me a pointed look from her perch on the dais. Court to her was like church to most grandmas, and she expected me to dress appropriately.

Tase and I took seats in the front row of chairs facing the dais where the Court members were perched behind a table, looking down on us. I'd sat in on many of their meetings and trials, but usually from my desk in the corner, taking notes, researching discussion points, and performing whatever other tasks they needed from their business manager, aka me. Lately, their biggest concern was someone known as the Collector, who seemed to have a growing interest in our little town —and not in a good way—but we knew nothing about him or her. There were the occasional trials, too, and although we weren't on trial tonight, the tension felt similar. Even Michaela, my best friend, and Saundra Beaumont, my grandmother, seemed to be judging me and finding me lacking, and we hadn't even begun.

Perhaps I was projecting my own self-dissatisfaction onto them.

As expected, the Court drilled me on everything I'd done since our last meeting in my attempts to solve the riddle that was the Eye of Valerian. According to Mihail and Irina Petran, former prominent members of Havenwood Falls and now trapped in the Infernum, the Eye held the solution to break Tase's curse and free them from the special part of Hell reserved for the worst of the supernatural. The Petrans disclosed this several months ago through my friend Harper Sinclair, a psychic scribe with the unusual ability to reach through the darkness of the Infernum and communicate with its inhabitants, as well as with dark spirits and other fun entities. I'd been with her when she'd first communicated with the Petrans. The Eye of Valerian then became my primary focus. When I wasn't working for the Court, I was working on discovering the dark artifact's secrets.

While many of the Court members had served as resources throughout my research, trials, and experiments, this was my monthly official accounting of what had been done so far. I told them about the many spells I'd tried by myself as well as with my coven—spells of revelation, illumination, opening and unlocking, reversal, etc. Each one performed at various points in the moon's cycle, during the different sun signs, at various times of day and night, by the side of the falls, at the apex of Mt. Alexa, deep in a mine, and next to a fire, testing the various elements. I'd even tried bleeding on it, since dark magic liked the taste of pain, self-sacrifice, and blood.

"Except not on the symbols I don't know," I clarified as I spoke about this to the Court.

The Eye of Valerian, at first glance, looked like an old-fashioned pocket watch, but it was much more than that. Besides a normal twelve-hour analog clock face, there was a layer for the astrological calendar with the symbols of the zodiac, and other layers with more runes and symbols. Some I recognized as Celtic, Egyptian, and from pagan religions and lore. Others I'd never seen before—and some of those actually scared me. When I touched them, I could feel the black magic crackling through them. But I hadn't found a resource yet that could name them, let alone define them, not even in the Court's restricted library kept at Sun and Moon Academy.

"It seems obvious you cannot avoid those any longer," said Mayor Barbie Stuart, the only human on the Court. Although, there were rumors she wasn't entirely human, considering she didn't seem to age properly—she still wore her blond hair in a bouffant reminiscent of the sixties, although she appeared to be only in her forties—along with her tall stature, which made some speculate she had giant blood.

"I haven't been avoiding them," I said, trying to keep my tone even against the accusation. "I've researched every grimoire and book of shadows we have, as well as every piece of historical information in our records, including Madame Tahini's *Art of the Black Covens*. We've discussed it at our coven meetings, but nobody has seen anything like these symbols."

I looked at my grandmother, Saundra Beaumont, who held our family's seat on the Court, then at Roman Bishop and Mathilde Augustine. The three of them were the leaders of the Luna Coven. Saundra and Mathilde nodded in affirmation. Roman only responded with a small twitch of his lips.

"We know the Eye of Valerian was created by the first moroi vampire, who was a sorcerer of black magic," Saundra said, and the rest of the Court members all made gestures of agreement, because that wasn't news to anyone. "It is quite possible Valerian himself created his own sigils for his personal brand of magic. This is not uncommon, especially among the more powerful mages of the time. He could possibly be the only one who knows what those symbols mean."

"And we all know, including Adelaide, the dangers of experimenting with unknown magic, especially of the dark kind," Mathilde added. "However, I don't see how it can be delayed any longer."

"Particularly with evidence of Atanase's worsening condition," said Elsmed Fairchild, a fae with long blond hair, frosty silver eyes, and a long, flat nose.

Tase and I exchanged a sideways glance and straightened at this comment.

"I agree," Roman Bishop said. "Miss Beaumont, you must be more aggressive in your efforts." He paused as he gave me a pointed look. "That is, assuming you want to save Mr. Roca. And the Petrans, of course."

I narrowed my eyes, biting back a few choice curses. Michaela, my best friend who now held her father Mihail's seat, rolled her eyes. She knew how committed I was to this.

"I'd be happy to arrange a consult with Ms. Daryn," Roman continued with a smirk. He bored of the Court's meetings quickly and bringing up Ada Daryn, leader of the Green Coven, was his way of riling everyone up, especially with Tase present. Court members would never admit outside this room that they knew about the Green Coven's tendencies to practice dark magic—it was against the Court's own rules. But they needed the Green Coven to execute those decisions they couldn't sully the Lunas to do. Not that we would anyway. But sometimes, people did some fucked up shit and needed to be dealt with accordingly. The Greens obliged in exchange for being able to stay in Havenwood Falls, and Roman was the liaison with Ada to make those things happen.

But again, nobody was supposed to know that. They only let me in on the secret because of my position and the fact that they were grooming me to take over the Beaumont seat at some point in the future.

"I don't know why meeting with the Daryn woman would help Adelaide," my grandmother quickly interjected as a cover-up, giving Roman a look of warning.

"Especially since you probably know something about dark magic yourself, don't you, Roman?" Michaela asked, backing up Saundra and helping my personal quest to knock the jerk off his high horse. We gave each other a silent high-five in the form of small smiles. "I mean, if we're going to make decisions based on *rumors*, which I'm assuming your comment about Ada was, the rumors I've heard about the Bish—"

"The Bishop family is happy to help Mr. Roca," Roman snapped, cutting her off. He then changed the subject. "Moving on to this business about evidence of Tase's 'worsening condition.' What evidence are you referring to, Elsmed?" He spat the elder fae's name as though it tasted bad in his mouth. The two weren't exactly BFFs.

Elsmed ignored him, training his icy gaze on Sheriff Ric Kasun and nodding his head. Ric fiddled with his phone while whispering something to Mathilde next to him. She flicked her fingers, and the video playing on the sheriff's phone projected onto the wall—a young woman, her head thrown back and her large bare breasts rising and falling with her breaths, muscular arms holding her, a dark head at her neck as her eyes slipped closed, a look of ecstasy on her face.

And then Tase's face lifting from her throat, fangs out, blood covering his mouth and dripping down his chin as he looked at the camera and grinned, his eyes glowing a dull green.

Purchase *Break Me Not* where books are sold.